A Lady of Means

CARLY KAYE

First Edition

First Printing, September 2025

This is a work of fiction. Names, characters, places, and incidents are either the product of the author's imagination or are used fictitiously, and any resemblance to persons living or dead, business establishments, events, or locales, is coincidental.

Library of Congress Cataloging-in-Publication Data

Kaye, Carly

A Lady of Means/Carly Kaye—First Edition

Summary: A steamy historical romance novel and Mean Girls x Persuasion retelling.

ISBN - 979-8-9993274-0-6

EISBN - 979-8-9993274-1-3

Printed in the United States of America

For the girls who've got a list of names and some are in red underlined, your broody-yet-tender-hearted man awaits to help you turn over a new page.

A Lady of Means

CARLY KAYE

BLACK CAT BOOKS

$$Chapter\ One$$

APRIL 1841

The Burn Book: Property of Lady M

Lord Adderton: 30, Essex. Received a significant bailout from the Earl of Drysdale, owes at least ten thousand pounds to a developer from Southampton and another twenty to the auctioneers at Christy's. The total sum happens to be the market value of the property mother left to me in Hampshire. An indebted nobleman, how dreadfully predictable.

"But Moria, I need you."

Moria shrank back, removing the vacuous nobleman's clammy grasp from her cream stitched, pink satin glove. The desperate words of the man before her converged with the sounds of a party: music, laughter, and enjoyment.

Moria *had* been enjoying herself for a few moments earlier in the salon, surrounded by friends, family, French pastries, and the whining strings of the sisters Montmorency at their musicale. She'd been performing as well; unaffected debutante again, the staid routine she knew as well as any piece of music.

"It's Lady Moria, and you don't need me. You need three wishes."

Her voice came out harsher than she meant it to, and for a moment she feared how Lord Adderton, the suitor still on his knees, might react to the sting of her rejection.

Perhaps this man before her was right, he did need something from her. Although Marcus had never found what she could offer quite tempting enough to make her his wife despite giving him her girlhood, her heart, every promise she could make. Bloody Marcus, why was she suddenly thinking of him again *now*? He wasn't the man she wanted either.

"There isn't another woman for me." Lord Adderton shook his head for emphasis.

"How can you know? Have you met them all?"

Before he could mutter a reply, the sound of impending footfalls reached them, and Moria fought the clamor of rising panic in her chest. If it were the duke who had courted her briefly and then buried himself in his parliamentary crusades, or one of the ladies who called her a friend...would she have no choice but to accept the proposal, however unappealing it might be?

But it was Moria's sister and brother-in-law who joined them on the terrace. Moria's suitor found his bearings and rose to his feet. Moria wanted to collapse against her sister Noelle's taller form in relief; but instead, looked over her shoulder at the event inside, hoping no one else had followed them outside.

Before Moria could speak, Fitzwilliam Pomfrey, Viscount Ludlowe cut through the tension. "Lord Adderton," her brother-in-law gave the other man a grave nod. "I presume you were attempting to propose?" The tall, blonde-headed viscount looked between the two of them.

"I suppose this has nothing to do with an article about Moria in the gossip sheets last week," Noelle spoke, pushing her spectacles up further on her nose as she peered up at the man. "Resulting in an insurgence of bets at White's on a forthcoming proposal from the Earl of Drysdale."

At the mention of Drysdale, Moria felt a shard of guilt. He'd clearly been trying to gain her attention with his performance earlier on the flute, he'd even tried to get her to play his sister's pianoforte, but thoughts of him hadn't stuck around. She'd been thinking of a man who was outside of her reach, or *she* outside of *his*.

Noelle cleared her throat, waiting for Moria to pick up the thread and continue. Moria was struck by how her sister could look both sagacious and stunningly beautiful in the same moment, but she would never have given voice to the thought, and instead crossed her arms, turning to Lord Adderton to tap her chin with a finger. "I heard it on decent authority you owed Drysdale a good deal of money."

The suitor made a step toward her, reaching again placatingly for her gloved hand. "My lady, it's presumptuous to bring up such matters of honor between men-"

Moria had heard enough, so she cut him off. "Is it also too 'presumptuous' to suppose that you meant to steal Drysdale's pick for a wife?"

"And then use your dowry and his winnings from the betting at White's to settle his debts," Noelle finished with a scoff, shaking her head. Moria made a mental note; this information was definitely going in her little book of observations, a catalogue she kept on all the scandalous misdeeds of high society.

Lord Adderton raised a finger in Noelle's direction. "You know not of what you speak, my lady. Maybe you should hold your-"

Fitz took a step toward Moria's would-be suitor, speaking in a lowered tone. "If you tell *my wife* to hold her tongue, someone will need to hold mine. As well as my fists."

With a huff, Lord Adderton bent to retrieve his hat, tipped it in

Moria's direction, and strode toward the row of hedges concealing the mews on the other side of the garden.

The society matrons from the musicale chose that as the moment to disperse themselves and the lingering crowd onto the terrace. In the throng of old guard and new alike, she spotted her usual companions eager to be seen with her, as well as The Duke of Andover, with his mother, the dowager, on his arm.

Dukes weren't supposed to look like him, or be nearly as tall. He commanded even more attention than she did when he entered a room. Perhaps that's why there was so much speculation that they'd make a match. He turned curious and expectant eyes on her that made her feel a little warm. Had he seen her exchange with Lord Adderton or her earlier attentions from the Earl of Drysdale?

Just in case, it was to be a performance, then. That's what they all wanted from her. Moria usually knew what people wanted from her, they often told you if you paid close enough attention.

"It's nearly impossible to keep up with your growing menagerie of men, sister," Noelle added in a whisper. Moria didn't respond. Instead, she painted on a smile that was almost indistinguishable from falsehood.

"Ladies, Lords, I'm so glad you've joined us. We were just partaking in the view of the artists on the lawn." Moria gestured to said painters with easels set up creating still lifes of Lady Bertram's flower garden and peacocks, then continued her charade. "But I'd like to issue a challenge."

She felt fickle partygoers' eyes train on her as she trailed down the terrace stairs to the great lawn, many curious pairs of well-heeled feet traipsing behind her. Moria turned to face them, removing a bow from an urn and knocking it with a fresh arrow. The leather of the string and the wood of the bow felt *right* against her gloved hands. Ladies weren't expected to be adept at manly pursuits, but Moria had found pride and purpose in such rote and repetitive tasks while she'd been in mourning. Why not use them as an advantage now?

She widened her shoulders and spread her feet apart.

"All that music has me in the mood for some competition. A chance to stretch my limbs. The partygoer who can successfully hit more bullseyes than my own, I'll personally purchase the painting of your choice."

Moria pulled back the string, hitting a practiced, near perfect bulls-eye several yards ahead in front of a row of hedges. She turned over her shoulder to gauge the reaction of the assembled crowd. Her friends Lady Gretchen and Carina were clapping appreciatively, the Earl of Drysdale was smirking as if he knew she was up to some scheme. He didn't know the half of it.

Moria picked up another flecked arrow, knocked it, let it lose. It whistled its way to a perfect bulls-eye. That wasn't good enough. Moria stepped to another target, another bulls-eye. The murmuring continued, four bulls-eyes in rapid succession by a lady in finery wasn't the kind of accomplishment they'd been expecting. The ladies looked envious or fearful, while simpering and complimenting her; half the men looked as if they'd like to take her to bed. And with that, Moria's distraction had once more kept the fashionable crowd from looking too close.

Chapter Two

MARRIAGE MART-YR MORIA

"A rejected proposal by Lady M a rite of passage for the elite men of London. Perhaps Lady M collects them for sport, aiming for the loftiest title like some sort of big game trophy."

- Scandalous Lives of London, April 1841

"WHAT UTTER ROT."

The sound of a scandal rag hitting the ottoman in front of Moria called her to look up from her embroidery hoop. Her mouth quirked to the side in amusement. She'd already seen this particular headline earlier that day when her friends Lady Gretchen Von Mien and Miss Carina Smythe had come to call, acting as though she had committed some boast-worthy accomplishment. All she'd done was to answer a question in the negative.

"I should find this writer and rip out their innards," Moria's older brother Jasper, The Earl of Westmoreland added, raking a hand through his tousled bronze hair.

Moria's other brother Lawrence followed Jasper in the room on his heels. "I think you might find this particular one lacking in guts entirely, mocking a lady behind anonymity. It's cowardly."

Jasper handed Lawrence a tumbler of amber liquid, the latter perching on the arm of Moria's chair.

"Perhaps the article is right, though. Maybe I am hunting for a lofty title." Moria said, not looking up from her sewing.

"You were right to refuse Lord Adderton, for what it's worth. He didn't deserve you," Lawrence returned, colliding his shoulder with hers the way that brothers often do.

There was a tug at the hoop of embroidery where Moria was ripping out stitches to restart part of the design in a different color thread. Jasper's twin sister Kathleen seated beside her chose this moment to interject, turning on her most matriarchal of tones to her younger sister.

"You can't cut people out as easily as you can your needlepoint. I'm not sure your reputation will survive if you keep turning down proposals, dear," she counseled.

If you give up pieces of yourself, remember your worth. Those that need reminding, my dear, you make them pay. Dearly.

Their mother's words came back to Moria, words meant only for her, something she'd hoarded to herself along with memories that weren't ready for the light of day just yet.

The Pembrooke women were more than ladies, just *more*, their mother included, God rest her fiery soul. Moria had spent the last year since her return to society showing just how much *more* she was than what she'd been boxed up and labeled as when they'd put her on the shelf. Well, she'd taken herself off that damn shelf and no one was putting her back there without her permission.

Moria set down her embroidery, taking her squirming nephew from Kathleen. She settled the infant and a linen cloth on the shoulder of her butter yellow dress. "The Pembrooke ladies are too strong to worry about things like reputations. Don't worry about me, sister."

Moria stood to rock the infant with swaying motions, turning so that Kathleen could check whether his eyes were yet closed. Kathleen nodded, lowering her voice so as not to wake the colicky infant after Moria had successfully gotten him to sleep. "It's Olivia I worry about. Did you have to cause such a scandal right before her debut?"

"Me? I didn't cause the scandal," Moria whisper-shouted over her nephew's head. The infant stirred, Moria bounced him to keep him settled. "*He* didn't have to run and sell the story to the papers! *He* was only after my hand because Drysdale showed interest, *that* and my dowry. I could *never* be married to such a fickle character."

"You *will* have to marry before Olivia can," Kathleen whispered. "It's your third season, Moria."

Jasper chose that moment to aid his twin sister's point. "I think what Kathleen is trying to say is that...the more scandals you find yourself in the center of, the harder it will be for our younger sister to make an appropriate match."

Kathleen placed a hand on Moria's forearm, both sisterly and motherly at once, before she asked, "That is what you want, isn't it, sister? To make a match of your own as well?"

Moria stared at the top of the infant's dark, downy head pressed against the crook of her neck. Three of her siblings stared back at her, awaiting her answer. A lump formed in the back of Moria's throat. Moria wasn't really sure *what* she wanted, only the *who*.

THE HIGH CEILINGS AND WINDOWS OF THE PEMBROOKE London summerhouse and smell of fresh flowers made for a welcome retreat, and Moria needed a reprieve from her siblings. All their good-intentioned worrying and arguing had made it hard for her to hear her own thoughts. She threw herself into a mindless task: embroidering a swath of silk and linen for a gown for her nephew's christening.

She didn't hear her companion, Miss Bridget Kelley, part servant and part friend, as she entered the summerhouse and sat beside her. Moria didn't look up. A piece of ironed white paper with achingly familiar penmanship entered her field of vision. Moria stilled. Willed herself not to show her hand.

"Does *this* have anything to do with your refusal of the lord and his...fickleness of character?"

Miss Kelley narrowed her eyes. Moria pasted on a bored smile. So Miss Kelley had been at the piano attempting to teach Moria's nephew and her own ward to play the scales, but she had been eavesdropping on Moria's conversation with her sister.

"What do you know?"

The other woman toyed with the envelope and seemed to choose her words. Moria wanted to snap the envelope from her hands, eager to hear his words. Even in the few times they'd met in secret, his voice was still so clear and deep in her mind.

Wherever I go, I fear you'll follow me. In my thoughts, at least, my lady.

He hadn't been telling the truth, had he? He was the one following her wherever she went, thoughts of him appearing without being conjured, like some phantom.

Miss Kelley clearing her throat brought Moria back to the present. "I suspect you've been carrying on a courtship with the sender of these letters," she asserted, holding up the offending parchment.

"And if you're wrong?" Moria hedged, only briefly looking up from her needlework.

Her every impulse screamed to hide, except for one. One strong, loud voice inside her that said, *but why do you have to hide* him?

"But I'm *right*," Miss Kelley said with a feline grin.

"What makes you so certain?" Moria threw down her needle-work on the seat beside her.

"Call it...a woman's intuition."

Moria leaned around the other woman to call into the doorway, "Not now, Finn, she's busy!" Miss Kelley, brow furrowed, turned toward the direction to find a doorway devoid of her five year old ward.

Moria capitalized on her distraction to slip the letter from the woman's hands. When Miss Kelley turned around, Moria grinned, fanning herself with the envelope. "If you'll excuse me, I'm going to my desk to answer this correspondence."

Moria made to leave, but the other woman grabbed her skirt.

"Unhand me! You forget yourself, Miss Kelley. You would be wise to remember your place."

"Snobbery doesn't suit you, Moria," she stepped closer to her charge, "I think you will need someone on your side to get what you want. You would be courting him out in the open if you were able to."

The overwhelming urge to tell someone, the soft understanding in Miss Kelley's eyes softened her resolve. The letter pressed against her chest, Moria sat back down. The other woman closed the door and then sat opposite her on a settee.

"He's a captain in Her Majesty's Army. We met at the coaching inn on the way to London for Noelle's first season."

The other woman's eyes widened. "You've hidden this for an entire year?"

Moria nodded. Miss Kelley looked stunned, She shook her head. "That must have been...lonely. Not to be able to share any of what you were thinking or feeling with the rest of your family or your friends. Why didn't you share this with them?" the other woman asked, gentleness in her voice the key to Moria's vault.

Moria looked at the envelope in her hands, his sloping, neat hand as familiar as his face in her mind. "It was all mine for a moment. After over a year in mourning and a whole lifetime of sharing everything with them. After I returned from mourning in the country, and it seemed like society had just...moved on. And then Noelle was engaged. And I was being courted by a Duke, and the Earl of Drysdale. Everyone was singing my praises again...." She blew some air out of her mouth, "It never seemed like the right time."

"But you care for him...or else you'd have broken it off. Are you aiming to keep your relationship a secret and wed someone else... The Earl of Drysdale, or the Duke of Andover, perhaps?" Moria's companion picked some blooms out of a basket on the nearby table, arranging them in her hands and discarding some as she talked.

While it was done by ladies of means, marriages for alliance's sake and then affairs conducted later in secret...Moria had known that kind of love before. Or she'd thought that's what it was. But she saw the unconditional affection that both her sisters had achieved with their partners. She wanted love returned and shared in the open, in the light. Not the kind of adoration of being the darling of the ton, but a love that withstood her every flaw and had room for her failings.

I hear you, even when you're saying nothing at all.

Maybe the man who'd written to her could be such a man. Moria pocketed the letter.

"That's not what I want. I want *Devyn*. I want to share him with my family...but I..." A single tear fell as Moria shook her head as if to bat away any further tears. "What if I can't give up all the ground I've conquered? What if they all think I'm throwing my future away?"

Miss Kelley was beside her in a moment. Comforting hands traced patterns down her back. Moria saw a swath of red hair, a sparkle of green eyes and almost envisioned her mother she'd lost to the unfairness of disease. "When your brother and sister took me into their employ, there was no mention of steering you toward a match with a noble. Your brother's words were: 'men who love my sisters and would treat them with respect.'"

"A union with an army captain that I've been having a clandestine affair with?"

Miss Kelley nudged her good naturedly in the ribs, "If it helps, considering how terrible your lady's maid is at lying and keeping your secrets, I'm not terribly surprised."

Moria gave a watery laugh, taking the blooms from her companion and adding them to a vase. "I'm not sure how, but oddly it does."

"Tell me how I can help."

The woman in front of her looked determined, like she was willing to do battle for Moria: hands on her hips, her chin tilted at a defiant angle. Moria had never been particularly kind to the woman, in fact she and her younger sister had pulled their fair share of pranks on Miss Kelley since she'd arrived the previous season when she'd championed Lady Noelle. Miraculously, the red-headed Irishwoman had handled them all with grace.

Moria picked a few blooms to add to the others. "Aren't you worried about jeopardizing your position?"

Miss Kelley didn't hesitate. "Do you mean to tell me that *you're* worried for my position, Lady Moria?" she questioned, handing Moria her pruning scissors.

Okay, she deserved that. "I do happen to find you somewhat hard to have to replace, Bridget," she said, trimming the stalks of the blooms she was preparing for a bouquet that was to be anonymously delivered to the charity hospital.

It was the first time she'd ever called the woman, not quite a servant, not quite a friend, by her given name and the first time she'd complimented her (audibly at least).

"Then we will just have to be discreet about our plans then if we are to make your epistolary and secret courtship more palatable. If you are willing to accept my help, that is."

Moria removed the tulips and added several hydrangea blossoms in their place, and then met her eyes. "You think you could do that?"

"I might. But you'll have to tell me everything first."

Moria gave a nod of approval to the floral arrangement and sat on the bench on the opposite wall. She'd picked this tale apart herself and knew exactly where to begin.

Chapter Three

FEBRUARY 1840, ONE YEAR PRIOR

> *Lady Margaret,*
> *Our meeting, like some kind of fever dream, feels like an occurrence that only happens once, to those very fortunate. I have never counted myself among their number, until now. I'll always consider myself damned lucky to be the man that got to know your name underneath a willow tree. Please write back to me and tell me when and where I can be so lucky again.*
>
> *DW*

~

SHE HADN'T BEEN LOOKING FOR A MAN LIKE HIM; BUT IN A moment of solitude and weariness, there he'd appeared like a conjured fantasy.

For the length of the entire carriage ride from her family's country estate to London for the opening of the first season out of mourning, Moria had been uncharacteristically silent unless required to speak.

There was much talk about London, and places her family members were excited to revisit, familiar faces to pay calls to after spending the last two social seasons in mourning after the loss of both their parents. It all felt so much like a repeat of her earlier season, only now, her younger sisters were the hopeful ones, and Moria was... *jaded*.

She'd been the incomparable of the season when she'd debuted almost two years before, she'd caught the attention of the man she'd wanted...but it had all ended like a Greek tragedy. More than the ton or her close family members even knew, most of which she kept all to herself wrapped under layers of haughtiness and pink silk.

If she just armed herself with enough, she could hide how much every thought of ballrooms and paying calls reminded her of Marcus. Of her parents who she wished were still here with them. Of what she had lost.

When her younger sisters asked why she was so reserved, she merely said that the carriage ride made her sleepy. The truth was entirely more than she was willing to share just yet. If she could just hold tight to the reins of her composure, she could make something good come of so much bad. For her sisters' sakes, if not for her own.

She sucked in a sigh of relief as the carriage rolled to a halt at a coaching inn to rest for the evening. From the carriage drive, she spotted a quaint little tree-lined stream a short walk from the coaching inn, covered with a stone bridge and ducks swimming across. It was mid-afternoon, and the way the sunlight poured out its droplets of light across the water was like something conjured from a dream.

It reminded her of a painting that had hung in their shared nursery when she and her sisters were small.

She tied on her bonnet before exiting the carriage, and as soon as the footman

had taken her gloved hand to help her down, she broke her hours-long silence.

"I think I'll go for a stroll by that picturesque little pond just over there."

"Would you like some company, my lady? Perhaps Finn and I will take some of the leftover bread from our picnic to feed the ducks," Miss Kelley called to her, her small red headed ward clutching her hand.

Moria fought the urge to blurt out, *"Dear god, no!"* and mustered enough restraint to simply call over her shoulder, "Enjoy the ducks without me. I'll be inside in time to wash up for dinner, I promise!" She noted the bemused and mystified looks on the faces of all five of her siblings, one brother-in-law, and her companion. She had guarded her tongue for an entire afternoon; they could grant her a few minutes of solitude.

When she moved closer to the small pond, a large and inviting willow tree beckoned. She pulled back the long hanging limbs of the willow and the leaning emerald fronds to reveal a carved rock leaning against the tree, large enough to sit upon. It was the perfect place to sit peacefully without hope of discovery. Was it someone's favorite spot she was stealing?

Moria smoothed her skirts as she sat atop the rock, drawing her knees up to her chest. She could sit here with only her own thoughts for company and not have to dodge her well-meaning family members and their worried glances.

The sensations around her now made her feel like a loosed coil. Her bonnet lolled back between her shoulder blades, the wind wrapped around her and blew loose tendrils of her blonde hair about her face. She leaned her head back against the willow, listening to the sounds of ducks and the mill pond, the scent of jasmine filling her every breath.

A deep voice with a Scottish burr interrupted the stillness around her like something heavy crashing through an icy lake. "That's tha thing, I didna want to herrt her."

"Well, you jilted her. You should have known that would cause her some distress." The other voice seemed to be the voice of reason, but its husky timbre wrapped around her like a ribbon of smoke.

"Selah does na care for me, she cares for me Scottish burr and shiny red coat, Captain."

The smallest hint of a laugh escaped her, and she covered her mouth belatedly.

"Who's there?" the husky voice called again.

Moria moved closer against the tree, clapping her hand over her mouth. It didn't take long for a large, beautifully masculine hand to pull back the willow branches and find her there atop the rock beneath.

"I'd expect a young lady to know it's improper to eavesdrop, Miss."

The face that accompanied the voice was carved masterfully from marble; with fringes of inky black lashes surrounding eyes the color of a deep and star-smattered sky, matching black stubble swarthing his jawline. He looked like a pirate in a red coat. A lump stuck in her throat, she should look away, but it was beyond her ability.

Moria had only ever read about such large, dangerously attractive men in novels that she chastised her sisters for reading, but then read herself when they weren't looking.

"It's "*my lady*," and I wasn't eavesdropping, sir."

He let out a low chuckle, taking one tentative step toward her.

She was fearful of him; startlingly aware of his physicality.

"My apologies, then, *my lady*. Might I ask why you were hiding?"

Moria cleared her throat, shifting prettily on her seat atop the rock. "I wasn't....hiding. *Per se*."

The man raised his eyebrows.

"Fine, sir, *yes,* I might have been. But I assure you, I had a good reason."

"And that is?"

It was Moria's turn to laugh. "I can only see your face, and we haven't even been

introduced. I don't go around sharing my secrets with every handsome stranger I meet under willow trees."

The way his smile reached all the way to his eyes sparked something, it lit her from within. He motioned to the seat next to her. "May I join you, then?"

"What about your friend?"

The man looked over his shoulder. "Seems he's deserted me. He probably thinks I'm a loon, talking to a fairy under a willow tree."

His dark eyes teased, challenged, implored.

Moria moved a few inches to the left and looked at the space she had vacated and then to the man. When he moved beneath the branches and made to sit next to her, letting the willow fronds lapse behind him, she realized that she had underestimated him. The rock was barely large enough to accommodate them both.

The man...he was so large that in the small space underneath the willow, he crowded her. He crowded her mind, he crowded her thoughts with his body, until she felt like in all the world, it was only the two of them there, at this moment.

"Tell me your name. *My Lady.*" The last two words grabbed hold of something inside her, so possessive and hopeful. His knee grazed hers, his body so improperly close to hers that there was very little space between their two bodies not touching.

"How about a friendly wager?"

He raised a brow in answer.

"Try to guess my name in three guesses. I bet you'll never guess it."

He laughed a laugh that warmed her from her scalp to her

toenails. "And if I succeed, do I get all the gold in the kingdom... or to keep my first born, *Rumpelstiltskin*?"

She giggled. She actually *giggled*. *Who was she?* "I can't promise that. Is there something you'd like instead?"

His hand grazed hers, and though it caused a jolt of awareness to prickle across her skin, she didn't pull back. His fingers played with hers, wrapping around each in turn. She noticed that a few of his fingers bore tattoos, another one peeking out from his sleeve at his wrist. Where were his gloves? Actually? Never mind, hiding such hands would be criminal. They were the kind of hands that painted seductive images in her mind.

"I'd like to know what your lips taste like."

Her eyebrows shot up. For all her *ennui* with being courted and desired, this was unexpected. But now that he had said the words aloud, she realized she wanted that too. Right here in this enveloping sheet of green that blocked out the sun.

"You want to kiss me? *Here*?"

"There are no better places that spring to mind, *Lady Elizabeth*."

Of this they were in agreement, but she didn't convey as much. She laughed. "You used up your first guess... on *Elizabeth*?"

"It was worth a try, I suppose." The pad of his thumb traced her cheek. "You have the most beautiful skin. It's like silk."

The feel of his scarred and inked fingers upon her skin caused a riot of emotion stampeding within her, but Moria never let her mask slip if she could help it. She pulled her cloak about her tighter and adhered to what she knew: iciness.

"You have two guesses left."

"You *could* help me out a little...perhaps you could give me the first letter?" His finger traced her lower lip. She briefly closed her eyes at the soft ferocity of his touch and fought to find her bearings.

"That would be far too simple, don't you think?"

"What do you mean, my lady?"

"What is a victory without effort?" She eyed his red coat, "Would you not agree, captain?"

"It's Charity."

"What?"

"Your name, my lady. Weren't you speaking in riddles?"

She stared into those dark eyes that stared right back, into her, through her. He was someone she wasn't scared to let know her.

"Well played. But I'm afraid not." She shook her head, underscoring her point.

"Hang on. How am I to know you'll tell me if I do get it right and you won't just tell me I have gotten it wrong even if I haven't?"

She looked at him defiantly. "I am a lady of quality, and honor bound to tell the truth."

He let out a small laugh. "But on the other hand, are you not also honor bound to protect your reputation?"

She wanted to throw caution straight into the wind, into the fire if need be, and say *damn her reputation*. The sound of his laugh incited a very visceral reaction from her more intimate and neglected places, including her heart.

But she merely touched his arm playfully and said: "While that may be true...I would be lying if I said that I didn't want you to kiss me."

He looked down at her lips, so fiercely and tenderly that when he looked away after several heartbeats, she almost believed he had actually kissed her. His fingers traced the edge of her collar, gently tugging at her cloak, and the pad of his finger caught the pendant from where it had lain against the floral muslin neckline of her dress, covering her heart like a promise.

"Your pendant is emblazoned with the letter 'M,' perhaps your name starts with the same letter? Or you're wearing it for an old flame?"

"Can a lady not do both?"

He stared at her assessingly. "To be sure, but you could also be tricking me. And now I'm so intensely curious about this former flame. I must confess, I'm also rather...envious."

He said the last word like he was casting a spell, and she felt like he already had, the moment she'd locked eyes with his dark ones.

"Make your guess, captain."

"But there are no less than a hundred names that start with the letter M. You'd have to have chosen the one letter I could easily have gotten wrong." He said with a provoking dimple.

She shrugged, "I did warn you. But I didn't choose my name. My siblings and I are all alphabetical, starting with J."

"Margaret," he whispered.

Instantly, she let out a "Yes."

At the same time, her maid called out: "Lady Moria, are you out here?"

She squinted and closed her eyes.

"Moria," the man said her name against her lips like an incantation, like he conjured her up and brought her to life- or maybe, back to life?

"I'm Captain Devyn Winter. Now, go on before you're missed."

When the lady before him didn't stir, didn't move her lips farther away, his words were a tempestuous breath near her neck. "I wouldn't dare leave without collecting my victory kiss."

Moments later, Moria materialized from beneath the enveloping willow tree, her maid gasping from where she stood several paces away.

"My lady, you're here. I was sent to fetch you for dinner, I was starting to worry."

"I'm sorry, Ella."

She wasn't.

"It's alright. I understand, my lady."

"You...understand?"

"Sure. You were avoiding the others. Wanted a moment for yourself. Can't say I blame ye, milady." Ella gave her a conspiratorial smile.

"Ahh. Yes. You've found me out, Ella. Clever girl," Lady Moria turned her full smile on Ella.

Ella stammered out: "Don't worry, your secret is safe with me, my lady."

"Then I am in your debt," Moria said, giving the other girl's arm an affectionate squeeze.

Before making her way inside, Moria looked over her shoulder, to see the pirate captain now talking to a group of soldiers. He looked up as though her gaze had compelled him. It took all the steely resolve and composure she had left within her to go inside.

WHEN MORIA WAS SMALL, HER MOTHER WAS THE FIRST TO rise. Moria would climb into her mother's bed, or find her in the sun room with a large shawl that she would drape around Moria and pull her close inside the covering. The two of them would watch as the sun rose over their Surrey estate.

"Isn't it a gift? We take for granted that every day starts just as glorious as the last, some even more than the one before. All while most of us are still abed."

And then she would kiss the top of Moria's head.

Now, when the sun rose, Moria rose anyway, but closed the curtains on the sunrise. She didn't need more reminders of all that she had lost.

But something about this particular morning seemed different. After her meeting with the officer that had felt like something out of a folktale, this place seemed to have a charm all its own. When she'd closed her eyes that night, all she'd pictured was the color green in a kaleidoscope of shades, enveloping and lush willow fronds cradling her like comforting arms.

Her eyes had opened at the sound of birds chirping outside on the balcony of her shared room with Olivia, lulled by whispers of a soft breeze. She felt she'd awoken in the garden of Eden.

She hadn't. Just a humble coaching inn somewhere along the Great North Road.

Moria discreetly dressed and laced her boots, tying her blonde hair into a top knot and draping a woven shawl about her shoulders. Gingerly, she tiptoed down the stairs, careful to avoid the one stair at the bottom that had sounded like a startled goat the evening before.

She made her way out of doors to the picturesque little pond, the rising sun dappling her face akin to the feeling of a well brewed cup of tea that warmed a body from the inside out. Through the fog, she found her way past a small kitchen garden, past the mews, to the willow tree. She sat on a thick tree trunk close to the water for several moments in silence when she heard her name.

"Lady Moria," said like a revelation, a benediction, a new discovery.

She looked at him from his feet upward. From gleaming Hessians, to breeches molded to muscled thighs, red coat that concealed shoulders surely Adonis himself would envy, hair pulled into a knot at the nape of his neck, eyes that pierced and blazed with fierce curiosity.

"You," she breathed, turning toward him but not making to stand.

They were far enough removed from the inn that they couldn't be overseen from a window, and it was early; but she lived in a den of spies. She had years of practice that taught her to be ever vigilant. Even yesterday, when she'd entered the inn, her childhood friend Fitz had noticed her dishevelment and rosy cheeks, though he hadn't given her away.

The captain sat beside her. She fought a surge of prickling awareness as his knee touched hers. His long fingers rested on his knees; they were close enough that she could take his hand again, but no.

"You're a rather shy creature, aren't you?"

No one had ever accused Lady Moria Pembrooke of being shy.

"What makes you say that?" She studied the deep black pools of his eyes, wanting to see through him, to know what he saw when he looked through her.

"Both times I've met you, you have been in solitary repose." He didn't say it like it was a reproach, his voice held a teasing note.

She smiled down at her hands. "I'm not sure I'm ready to be what I'm supposed to be again. A socialite. A rather reluctant, jaded one. But I rather like this lake," she fiddled with the petals of a wildflower in her hands in her lap, "Here, I feel like very little is expected of me, and silence is appreciated rather than sneered at. 'Beautiful girls are supposed to smile and make lively yet proper conversation.' Anyway, it must all sound very silly." She shook her head.

He turned to her, the wind blew a strand of hair from her topknot across her face and he swept it behind her ear with startling tenderness. "I don't see anything silly about you. We all have people we are and people we are supposed to be; but I like this version of you, Lady Moria. Don't lose this one," he gave her an encouraging smile that she pocketed the way the lake in front of her hoarded sunlight. "Were that I had the freedom to stay and find out your many enchanting features," he looked at her like he could perhaps puzzle them all out if he looked at her hard enough, "but I was preparing my horse, thinking of you, and then I saw you make your way here. I must depart with my company, but I wanted to say goodbye first."

She waged battle with the fear and disappointment that rose to the surface at his words. He couldn't leave now that she'd just found that such a man as this even existed, that such a man returned her interest and didn't find her silly or frivolous, but enticing.

"When?"

"As soon as we break our fast."

She nodded, pushing back the growing lump forming in the back of her throat. She would not reveal what a crushing disappointment such news was.

"May I write to you?"

She looked up at him in surprise. Not merely at his words, but at the unease in them.

"You want to write to me?"

He nodded emphatically. "If that isn't too presumptuous."

"You didn't find it too presumptuous to say that you wanted to kiss me."

He laughed a laugh that was so genuine, so warm, it stirred and heated icy, forgotten parts of her. It unlocked doors long sealed off and aired out abandoned, cobwebbed rooms of her heart.

"I don't know why I ever thought you shy. I take it back. We'll go with...refreshingly honest."

"Do you have something to write with, and a piece of parchment?"

He dug inside of his coat and produced a small pencil and a pocket notebook. He handed them both to her, and she wrote down her name and London address, then returned them to him. His weathered fingers lingered over hers for several seemingly eternal moments before replacing the items where they had been moments before.

She told herself she wouldn't, shouldn't think about those hands, long and slender and capable; they were hands capable of ruin and destruction, but clearly capable of great tenderness as well. The picture of them was etched behind her eyelids. She'd forget her own name before she shook off the image of those finely inked hands brushing hers. One inked with a horseshoe swept an errant strand of hair behind her ear.

She swallowed. "Where are you headed, captain?"

"I'm afraid I can't say; but wherever I go, I fear you'll follow me. In my thoughts, at least, my lady."

She looked away and exhaled, trying to conceal her feelings. More than anything, she wanted-

"May I kiss you, my lady?"

Why did it feel as if he'd stolen her thoughts?

"If you don't, we'll both wish that you had."

One hand lightly caressed his. He leaned in closer, pulling her close enough to hold her soft cheek, her jaw within the palm of one of his large hands. His lips were so close, so indelibly close that the stubble coating his cheek collided with her own, she could claim his air for her own if she leaned just a little closer. But she didn't.

He didn't pull away as he said, "I'll claim my kiss, when the time is right. Until we meet again, my lady." He took her hand in his, leaving behind a soft, gentle kiss as though he hadn't been mere moments from taking possession of her mouth right there next to the lake. And as they parted company, lingering glances exchanged like promises, she knew she'd see him again.

Chapter Four

My presumptuous Captain,

I agree to your request. Before your next deployment, you may find me at the Kingsley archery range near Bond Street of any Wednesday afternoon. However, I have only this to request in return: please don't go and fall in love with me. It would be terribly ungentlemanly of you and very inconvenient for me. I also have impeccable aim, so I hope you come prepared.

Lady Margaret

~

My devious Lady,

I never professed to be a gentleman and I would love nothing more than to be extremely inconvenient for you; nevertheless, consider your challenge accepted.

Just don't go and be entirely too loveable. This challenge sounds even more improbable by the moment and I fear I've already lost.

Yours,

D

∽

"You can't send flowers or call on a lady you haven't been publicly introduced to, you dolt. Have you remembered nothing from the etiquette lessons we were drilled on as children or has all of it been replaced by battle briefs?"

Peregrine Winter had at least waited until his younger brother Devyn returned from active duty to call him out. Devyn gave a low chuckle, scrubbing his freshly shaved jaw with an inked hand. "Looking back, I should have known that I was walking into a waiting ambush. That's on me for not coming here better prepared."

Devyn took an empty seat across from Perry, where the two sat in (mostly) companionable silence in one of the solariums at the family house in Mayfair. Peregrine had been the only one who had listened during the aforementioned etiquette lessons he and Devyn had been on the receiving end of. In fact, Perry would have been the perfect match for a woman like Lady Moria, having the right training and smooth manners- as well as the earldom he'd inherited from their uncle.

Devyn had been back in London for only five days. Four of them had been spent on drills with his company, and he'd spent an entire day debating about how he'd call on the woman he'd seen every time he closed his eyes. Right there behind his eyelids like a ballerina in a music box, except far less innocent with that wicked mouth of hers and the teasing in her eyes, the curves of her body that could lead him to ruin. He'd written to tell her that he had returned from Belgium, the same day he'd bought a scandal sheet just to see if her name was inside.

It had been over twelve months since he met Lady Moria Pembrooke underneath a willow tree at a coaching inn. She'd replied to his letters; she'd returned his gifts via her ladies' maid. He'd called upon her family residence, but the butler had said she wasn't at home. He'd been, as promised, bested by her on an archery pitch. He'd met with her in person twice since their meeting before he'd been sent to Belgium for eight months.

The solarium around him fell away as Devyn remembered one such outing: a boat ride on the River Cherwell in Oxford, one of the days he'd turned over and over in his memory while he'd been playing the part of warrior.

That day, she was all golden haired and gold-and-pink cheeked in a heart-stopping dress the color of a perfect British summer sky while he'd rowed them down the river. His focus had been torn between the steady movement of the oars, and the view his perch offered of the glorious tops of her breasts fighting against the tyranny of the neckline of her dress. She was perched on the opposite end of the boat, holding an obnoxious little matching parasol just above her head like she hadn't a care in the world that he could tip their boat over in only a few movements.

"You don't seem like the type of lass who'd agree to step foot in a water vessel with a gentleman of this size."

"Are we talking of the size of the boat...or the size of you?"

Devyn hated to admit the way his skin had burned beneath her appreciative gaze as her eyes traveled the bulk of his form. "And...do I not? I like to think I seem rather...intrepid."

She'd been leaning back on her forearms letting the sun dance over her stupidly perfect face with her eyes closed and her little straw and beribboned bonnet dangling between her pointed shoulder blades. The laugh floating out of him was natural and light in an unconscious way he wasn't sure a woman had ever made him laugh. In the bleakest winter in his memory, the image of the sun kissing her like he wanted to, the feeling of the laugh she brought out of him reverberating in his chest came to his mind unbidden. Not only unbidden; bloody unwelcome, but persistent.

"Well, when you put it like that, I suppose, both? Either? And for a woman who is remarkably fit," he looked down her body, and she must have felt his eyes scorch her as much as the July sun as she'd turned to look at him with a knowing smirk. "No, you do not seem *intrepid* at all to the untrained observer."

"And are you... an untrained observer?" She was sitting toe-to-toe with him in a small wooden boat, looking away and trying to hide that she was watching the tight repetitive movements of his shoulders and arms as he'd rowed them downriver.

"A man doesn't rise to an officer in Her Majesty's Army without being disciplined and detail oriented, my lady. But of you?" He shook his head like he was being silly, but knew what was on his mind was what she wanted from him.

"I notice everything. You fancy yourself well-versed in subtlety and hiding your true emotions and intentions, but I study it all. The pinch between your brows and the rigid way you hold your shoulders...the way your eyelashes flutter or when you're holding your hands in your lap just a little too tightly. I hear you, even when you're saying nothing at all. I do that too... learned to hide my thoughts so the men I lead don't hear them. We aren't that unalike you and I."

She looked at him, at his lips more specifically, another one of her subtle tells. She cleared her throat and looked down at her hands, which were tightly and primly folded in her lap, and then back at him. They barely made it out of sight of her red-haired chaperone before she'd tossed back her bonnet and taken his face in both of her small hands and he'd let her.

He'd held her lithe, tight body in his grateful hands. He'd fantasized about kissing her lips, taking the stunning bow of them with his own and drinking in every sound she made like they were the water sustaining him. But if he did, he'd be just like the scores that wanted to claim her, to have her, but that wasn't what *this* was. There couldn't be a woman this artfully crafted by God in Christendom, and she was there, with him, on a rowboat on a summer day, delicately closing her eyes at the feel of his hands pulling her to lean against his chest, legs tangling with his.

When he closed his eyes at night, he saw her looking back at him when she stepped back onto the shore, admiration in her perfect eyes and one side of her sinful mouth curving into a smile.

He'd have given up his army commission simply to kiss her, but he was afraid to let her know it. There was talk that she'd been courted by a Duke, and then there had been her sister's wedding and her returning to the country at the end of the season, and his being shipped off with his company to Belgium for nearly eight long months.

And so, when the biting winds of winter came, he had sustained himself on the bonfire of a woman tucked away in his consciousness and yes, a woman or two who didn't look a thing like her just to prove to himself that she didn't mean anything and didn't have her tentacles and hooks sunk into and through him, but of course she did. He was lying to himself and a fool to boot. He'd given way more of the corners of his heart (*fine,* more than the corners, it was the prime real estate too) to a woman who seemed to not know what in hell she wanted or did indeed know and didn't want the inconvenience of wanting it.

"I see you haven't given up this...attraction...to Lady Macbeth," Peregrine observed, taking the scandal sheet from Devyn's hands and looking it over. "I'll say this for the girl, she always looks fierce, and she always wins; but she hasn't been easy to woo. In your absence, the Earl of Essex allegedly proposed to her five times and each proposal was increasingly more elaborate. She reportedly told the poor sod that she was "undeserving" of his attention and suggested he find someone more "worthy." A hallmark maneuver of a true diplomat to be sure, or a duchess."

"The Duke of Andover's still courting her then?" Devyn said, casually draping an arm over the boot kicked up atop his knee as if all his hopes weren't riding on the answer. He felt there was some great tragedy, something in her past that drove her to occupy thoughts of a Duke, of an illustrious title, while still writing to Devyn, a mere soldier.

Peregrine took his time answering, seemingly only to torment him. "Well, you missed all the most interesting bits of that whole drama," Devyn raised a brow for his brother to continue. "His Grace announced in Parliament that he'd overthrow the opposition's bill before taking a wife."

Devyn popped a grape in his mouth. "Level-headed, I see. Not theatrical at all."

"The papers loved that one. 'She's either saving herself for a Prince, or-"

"A man who knows the way to win her isn't through self-interested gestures only for show?" Devyn ventured, his brows kissing in the middle.

"And pray tell what 'gestures' have you gone to the effort to do for her?"

Another man would see this as a jibe, but this tenor of conversation gulfed the 9 years between them. They were two sides to the same coin; where Peregrine had been an apprentice octogenarian his entire life, Devyn thrived on joking and carousing when he wasn't warrioring.

Devyn clutched his chest dramatically, miming as though Peregrine had wounded him in the heart. He relied on humor as a general rule; people found him more amenable and palatable that way with his large size, but damn if his brother didn't have a point. Devyn could turn said point around on his brother and ask what ladies a titled gentleman of more than marriageable age had made gestures for, but Devyn never pried. If Peregrine wanted him to know, he'd have told him. Perry suffered no such compunction.

Devyn glanced at the portrait to his left of two dark haired brothers, the older one tall and sleek and more serious looking than any boy of 14 ought to be, a curly headed miniature nearly a decade younger clutching his hand, to remind himself of all the things he usually liked about his brother.

Peregrine lifted a solicitous, persistent brow as if awaiting an answer.

Devyn knew the answer.

I have written to her every day for over a year. I've taken her rowing. I watched her shoot arrows through not just a target but my own heart on an archery pitch. I took her to a tavern one night when she slipped out of her house in a hooded cloak and said, "I want to see where you spend your time. Not the things that you're supposed to do, but where do you go when you aren't a warrior?" We spent an evening drinking, eating tavern food. I had the most unencumbered and open conversation I had ever had in my life. She'd said, "I think we can make room for another one of your men at our table," when Belcher had shown up late, and she'd hooked an arm around my neck and pulled herself into my lap to raucous cheers from 16 of my men and the entire tavern. Her hand rested on my thigh for a moment, she whispered in my ear, "I'd never thought a man of your size could blush," and when she pulled back and laughed, her hand covered her mouth the way my body wanted to. And I took that hand and kissed her small finger, the finger where significant rings go, and I told her, "They all think I belong to you. Tell me one day I will." "You don't already?" she shot back. I gave her the most raucous laugh, Calum and Blaise started laughing too. And when her blue-gold eyes didn't leave my face, her fingers playing over mine, I gave her what was left that she hadn't already stolen right out from under me.

Devyn didn't say that. He hid his inner workings behind a well-timed sip of tea from one of the much-too-small teacups at his brother's table.

He wasn't sure it meant anything to anyone but him. A man who made much of little as a general rule.

"She's worth every effort and every length I could go to. I'm simply afraid that, in the end-"

"You won't be enough?" Peregrine cut right to the heart of the matter. Devyn saw earnest understanding, a brotherhood that left room for failings and misgivings, and was given the courage to try again.

"You could make this easier on your only living relation and arrange a formal meeting yourself," Devyn parried, devouring one of the miniscule tea sandwiches on a silver tray in a single bite.

Peregrine pinched the bridge of his nose between his thumb and forefinger. "Devyn, remind me why I haven't cut off your allowance already. Or better yet, forced you to come home and claim the title that belongs to you."

Peregrine had only been their father's legitimate heir until Devyn had been born years later to a second wife. By rights, the inheritance and the family estate should have gone to Devyn, but Devyn felt as ill-fitted to a title and its myriad obligations as he did to the formal tea table he was sitting at. He wasn't cut out for this, not the way that Peregrine was.

Devyn set down the scone that was in his hand, wiping his hand on the napkin draped over his buckskin-clad thigh. "Peregrine, you are father's heir. I am the spare. I am a warrior, that has always been the case-"

"But what about your lady? Does it make you want to change the status quo now that you could have her if she knew that a title was within your grasp?"

Devyn shook his head. "A title is *not* within my grasp. I'm your heir until you see reason and find a wife. Besides, do you want me to enter into a union with a wife who suddenly accepts my suit once she hears of our... history?"

Peregrine's brow furrowed and he set down his teacup and saucer. "I think you discredit the young lady, brother. How do I even begin to explain Lady Moria? Were you to spend more time in society you would see quite clearly that she cannot afford to marry a captain of her majesty's army set to ship out in a short amount of time. Especially not whilst her younger sister is unwed. Such a match would greatly diminish the...fanfare and revelry that she receives everywhere her ladyship goes. She's not just *any* lady, Devyn, she's *the* lady."

Devyn shook his head and looked off into the distance. He was well aware of why she hadn't accepted his suit. He didn't need Peregrine to point it out. He knew he had little to offer her.

"I'm not willing to take from you in order to win her."

Peregrine's blue eyes softened. "It would only be taking from me if I hadn't already offered it, Devyn," he gestured around him, "All of this is, by rights, yours, brother."

Devyn tilted his head to the side, weighing his words. "By birth, yes. Not by rights. Is the commitment and dedication to justice for those who cannot fight for themselves that you've brought to your role not 'right' enough, Peregrine?"

Peregrine was silent, then after a long moment as both brothers watched the fire in the grate nearby dwindle, the older of the two broke the silence. "You honor me, brother. I only want you to admit that one day the mantle of warrior will grow heavy, and you will want to place it down, and when you do, if my...stepping aside...would ease your way, I'll not protest. I'll do it gladly."

And at that, Peregrine set down on the table an invitation to a ball. Devyn knew what it was. It was an offer to help, a gauntlet being thrown. Devyn could attend as his guest, he could receive an introduction to Lady Moria with Peregrine's help. If he wanted her, he had to play the game.

Devyn reached out a hand to squeeze his older brother's shoulder, noting the graying at his temples and the laugh lines at his eyes. He'd never have the ease Peregrine had with words and with others, hell Devyn intimidated people just by skulking into a room. But if Devyn did take his brother up on his offer, he had only to follow his brother's example.

~

"His lairdship bust yer balls, then?"

Calum Sterling called to Devyn when the latter returned to the townhouse they shared a few streets off the fashionable part of London. Calum was Scottish and had been part of Devyn's regiment for the last 6 years, and as he was from a working-class family, Devyn had suggested he stay with him when they were stationed in town rather than springing for his own lodgings.

There was plenty of room, and someone had to keep Calum from trouble when he was too deep in his cups. There were some in their regiment who erroneously blamed his mischief on Calum's being a Scot; but Devyn knew that Calum, while having an honorable nature, simply couldn't say no to a revel, or a dare, or a challenge. It made for a bold soldier and a reckless civilian, but a good man to have at one's back.

Devyn didn't answer Calum's question, opting instead to remove his boots and rummage through the larder. "Peregrine? No," Devyn set the ingredients on the counter and started making a sandwich. "My brother always means well. He just serves food meant for half pints and not for grown men."

"I fig'red he found out about yer...epistolary courtship...and wanted to talk some much needed sense into ye."

Devyn talked around a mouthful of sandwich, "The opposite in fact."

Calum set down a glass of wine in front of him. "Reverse psychology, then?"

Devyn shook his head. "An invitation to a ball."

Callum grimaced. "Big barrel-chested bastard like yerself at a ball? Sounds like a duel waitin' to happen if ye ask me."

"Good thing I'll have you as my second."

Callum sighed, taking the glass of wine from Devyn and draining it. "God help me, Cap'n."

Chapter Five

THE BURN BOOK: PROPERTY OF LADY MARGARET

Tristan Valentine: If I were a more honest woman, I'd list the trove of information I know about Lord Valentine. However, if he ever found out he'd made an entry in such a book as this and that someone had thought to record his litany of indiscretions, society would never recover from an ego of such inflated proportions.

∽

MORIA MIGHT BE SECRETLY PINING AFTER A MAN SHE ~~definitely~~ maybe could not have, but that didn't mean she was idle. She had learned in her first season that it wasn't the substance of a lady that mattered to the *ton*; it was what she was seen to be, and who she was *seen* to be with. Or *not* seen with.

By outward appearances, Moria had two best friends, Lady Gretchen von Mien and Miss Carina Smythe. In truth, she had many companions, none she held in closer esteem than her sisters.

Lady Gretchen was married to an Austrian diplomat who wasn't particularly well-versed in English and seemed to have a strong affinity for strudel and little else. Carina was accomplished, rich, and beautiful. Her greatest accomplishment, in Moria's opinion, was to be society's most fashionable widow at the age of six and twenty.

On this particular day, they were at a lending library.

"I thought we'd be working on preparations for the debut ball for the remainder of the afternoon, why did you bring us to a library?" Gretchen probed, running a hand over a leather tome and grimacing at the dust that coated her glove.

Moria huffed. "Lady Althea suggested that I be seen at a library or somewhere that paints me in a more favorable light after that scandal sheet insinuated I hunt titled men for sport."

Carina folded her arms. "Well, if you can find me anything in this library as interesting as the things we've put in our little book," Moria shushed Carina who was far too loud for her liking with such scandalous information. "I'll happily put it on my account," Carina finished in a whisper, avoiding the perceptive gaze of their chaperone, Fitz's grandmother, Lady Althea. Moria had one story of her own she could share that was rather riveting, a story of the season Moria met a Captain who'd stolen her heart, and a Duke who'd stolen a dance.

Lady Althea, from two rows ahead, lifted her graying head and narrowed her eyes, so Moria and her companions lowered their voices.

"We could put out the burn book under an alias," Gretchen said flippantly, though Moria knew she hadn't come up with an idea like that on a moment's notice.

Moria closed in their little circle. "Everything we have written down, all the secrets we uncovered between the three of us, that's our security. For the way I had to fight to regain society's good graces when I came out of mourning. For the proposal I had to escape the other night," Moria added with an eye roll. "And Gretchen, you know everything about everyone, which has proved fruitful for your husband's contacts and your parents' business," she said this to Lady Gretchen who nodded. "And now you're out of mourning, it's elevated your station, Carina. This is about the three of us, *for* the three of us. We agreed no one else sees the book without all of us approving. Or we burn it."

Carina sighed. "No need to be dramatic. You are right, as usual. Perhaps that's why of the three of us, you'll be the duchess."

The reminder of her courtship with the Duke made Moria's stomach drop. He'd courted her in front of all of polite society, and then he'd gone and made that pronouncement about delaying finding a wife until his bill was accepted in Parliament, and she hadn't minded being given time. She was still trying to work out whether or not she'd used the time she'd been given to figure out what the hell she wanted for good or ill, while Gretchen held up a book for them to peruse. Carina shook her head.

"Lady Noelle suggested that one, but I thought it wasn't half as interesting as *Adelaide*," Carina said, putting the book back on the wrong shelf. "Perhaps Moria could ask her if she knows when her husband's printing press will be launching a sequel."

But Moria was only half listening because on the other side of the book shelf, Moria heard the sound of half-concealed voices in the throes of an argument. Moria had been told before that she had keen observation skills. Fine, her brothers had told her she was a terrible snoop and she had heard what she wanted to hear.

She found herself one aisle over, speaking with lethal calm to the man now standing before her, far too close to the young woman Moria could barely make out on his other side.

"Mr. Bowlby, I believe I heard the young woman raise objections to you following her throughout the library without her chaperone present. Perhaps I'm wrong, I barely heard her over how loud your ensemble is today," she said, eyeing his arsenic green jacket and aubergine waistcoat.

The man stuttered, picked up his cane and stack of books, exiting with a cutting glance at the red-haired young woman.

"What a brute. He has a singular talent for cornering women

with his unwanted interest." The young woman punctuated her words by straightening the collar of her dark green walking jacket, clearing her throat. Moria's first impression was that if the girl were allowed to let her auburn curls have their own way rather than the hatch job someone had made of taming them, and traded in the somber colors that made her look as white as paper, she'd have been rather pretty. The nervous hunch to her shoulders and the way she bit her lip and avoided Moria's eyes spoke of a woman who didn't want to be seen, or worse to be seen and found wanting.

Was there anything worse?

Probably.

Alright, there definitely was, but Moria's failings had all started with that.

It didn't speak well of Moria's compatriots, however, that Lady Gretchen and Miss Carina looked unbothered.

"I'm Lady Moria Pembrooke. Why don't I know you?"

"Looking for a new protege to bolster your image, are we?" Lord Tristan Valentine called from the other end of the aisle, coming to stand next to the redhead. Moria let out a long-suffering sigh. Tristan was an insatiable gossip and despite being from one of the oldest families in England and a friend to her brother and brother-in-law, Moria thought he often acted like a boor. But he'd given her an idea.

"Ignore him," Moria said, turning to the girl. She caught the command in her voice and gentled her tone. "I didn't catch your name."

"Kate," the redhead introduced herself, "Miss Kate Herring."

"You're...like...really pretty," Gretchen said, always the conversationalist. Miss Herring's face flushed, momentarily speechless.

"So you agree, you think you're really pretty?" Carina pushed, narrowing her eyes.

Moria ignored her friends, leaning toward the newcomer to gesture vaguely in the direction of the golden man standing between them, "*Miss* Herring, I'm curious how you came to be in the presence of two louts in one library. Is he bothering you?"

Valentine gave only a small harumph.

Kate adjusted her spectacles with a gloved finger. "Lord Valentine's mother and mine have become acquaintances. They're no doubt lurking in a corner with your grandmother-in-law to find us in a compromising position so they can call the banns."

Moria turned to her brother's friend, raising a single brow in his direction.

Tristan picked up the tale where Miss Herring left off. "I avoid her vexatious countenance for five minutes and Lord Bowlby conjures himself from the shadows as if he can sense an unchaperoned young lady with a reasonable dowry within a five block radius."

"I am grateful you came to my aid, my lady," Kate added, her eyes finding Moria's.

Moria touched Miss Herring's sleeve reassuringly, noticing a beaded bracelet at her wrist. "This is so pretty. Did you make this?"

The other woman looked down at the simple, rustic piece of jewelry at odds with the fine brocade of her sleeve. "It's from a village near the Congo. A priestess gave it to my mother on our last trip with one of my father's religious excursions."

Moria's eyes met Carina's and then Lady Gretchen's. A young lady on the marriage mart good enough to attract Lady Valentine's notice with parents traversing to the Congo? *There* was a story for their shared, secret book.

Moria looped her arm through Kate's and led her several steps ahead. The others followed in her wake; their stacks of books seemingly forgotten.

Moria leaned toward her new companion conspiratorially. "I can see you are new to society. Would you like some advice?"

Kate raised both her brows in answer. If she had any reservations about the sudden interest of one of London society's most sought after and discussed diamonds, she didn't show it.

"One's acquaintances are of the most importance. Maybe you should come with us," Moria gestured toward the two ladies behind her who, bless them, pasted on the most comically large smiles Moria had ever seen. "We can help you avoid the wrong people."

"Does that mean I'm invited too?" Valentine called from behind her, Lady Carina giggling with one hand over her mouth, Gretchen looking at him like he had sprouted horns and a tail.

When they exited the library several paces behind Lady Althea, Kate gave Moria a bald smile and a curtsy, retreating to find her chaperones as Lady Gretchen and Carina entered Moria's carriage. Moria found herself calling over her shoulder at their new acquaintance, "Get in, bluestocking, we're going shopping."

The red-headed girl looked from Moria to her companions inside the carriage. Moria suppressed a smile at the sight of the nosey older woman leaning out the window, aiming to get a better look at Miss Herring through a quizzing glass.

"I'd love to, Lady Moria."

And Lady Moria left the lending library for the shops on Bond Street one companion greater, a companion she might come to regret making.

~

"Just the lady I was looking for! My favorite sister!"

Moria's youngest sister sprang out to hug her as soon as she opened the front door to their residence. A liveried footman followed Moria inside the door of her family home, carrying her packages and bundle of books.

"I thought Kathleen was your favorite sister?" Moria questioned, taking off her gloves and hat and handing them to the housekeeper.

"I said she was the nicest, I never said she was my favorite."

Moria observed her sister's pink cheeks framed by a few red gold hairs trailing from her braid and an open smile. "Were you...waiting for me to return?"

Olivia tilted her head and looked off to the side. "Perhaps I had a particular reason."

There was the usual mischievous light in Olivia's green eyes and color in her cheeks. Moria might have been known for her eye for fashion and garments, but Olivia needed little adornment. Where Noelle and Kathleen were tall and lithe, Moria was average height, and Olivia was shorter and curvier, still the prettiest girl Moria had ever seen. Especially when her passion for something glowed within her eyes.

"Don't leave me in suspense, you little scamp."

Olivia grasped Moria's hand and towed her into the summer-house. In her wake, Ella, her lady's maid, slipped a folded envelope in Moria's other palm. For a second, Moria worried that her sister had caught the exchange; but Olivia was too far ahead and in too excited a state to notice. Finally, Olivia stopped and looked pointedly outside to their brother, who was talking with a suitor. For a moment, her heart had started to race, then slowed when she saw it wasn't the man Moria so badly wanted it to be.

Moria didn't take her eyes off the two men as she sat on the window seat that afforded the best view, her sister curling beside her. "How long has the Earl of Drysdale been here?"

Olivia tapped her chin. "I'm not sure, I think he was waiting for you."

"What do you think they're discussing?"

"I'm sure a sheltered debutante like myself couldn't hazard a guess."

Moria looked at her dubiously.

Olivia continued. "When I debut, I'm sure the gentlemen of means will be entirely unaffected. I've enough quirks to keep them from taking a keen interest."

Moria draped her other arm around her sister's waist. "When you debut tomorrow night, the right man will notice your quirks only add to your limitless beauty."

"What nonsense," Olivia giggled, "Is that how your debut went?"

"Close. I have no quirks."

Moria looked away from the view of Drysdale saying something that had Jasper tossing back his head and laughing. Lawrence was nowhere to be seen as usual. He'd been spending a lot of time at a rented townhouse after meeting a cyprian from Asia he'd decided to take into his keeping.

So Moria could share with Olivia the truth. "My debut...was an illusion I hadn't known was false until I'd already sealed my fate. But you?" Moria squeezed her sister's hand. "You deserve the debut of your dreams. And you *will* get it."

Moria gave her a smile she hoped was reassuring as Olivia blinked back tears.

Olivia was beautiful and charming and most of all, Moria would make sure her debut was unforgettable.

Wasn't such the way of older sisters? To get all of the angst and sorrow out of the way to protect the ones who came after? Perhaps she'd committed too soundly to the role, but no one had ever accused Moria of doing anything by half measures- fucking up included.

While Moria had known no limit to tragedy, her debut had been one starkly shining moment before it all went to hell. Admittedly, she'd played a solid hand in her own downfall; but she was only a girl after all, and she wasn't strong enough to withstand the temptation she'd endured that night.

No, it was decidedly not her fault.

Not when the sound of her name on Marcus' lips sounded different than it had every other time he'd said it in the past. As though, somehow, that night on the ballroom floor, he could infuse the word with feeling he couldn't have before. As though watching her debut, he finally saw the *more* of her that he'd neglected in all the years they'd been casual acquaintances and neighbors.

Marcus Huntingdon, recently titled Marquess of Thorne, took his position on the parquet dance floor in front of her. His hands and eyes heated every part of her they came in contact with. She had looked up at him with stuttering lashes and stuttering pulse, because by god, was he gorgeous, all golden and wreathed in candlelight.

"Have you always been this earth shattering?" he asked, his voice a sultry timbre against her ear a heartbeat before he pulled back to a respectable distance. His eyes were alight with something. Admiration? Pride? Lust? Some toxic combination of the three?

Moria placed on a practiced mask. "You're just now noticing?" she shot back with a raised brow.

To which, he tilted his head back in a laugh that made the others around them turn to look their way. No one was looking at them with scorn over such flirtatious familiarity, they were looking on with envy. The elite *ton* of London were hard-pressed to find a couple as... earth shattering...as the Marquess of Thorne and its newly crowned incomparable, Lady Moria Pembrooke.

She felt every eye on her in her whole body, but most of all, his. She felt them everywhere, even the places he wasn't looking that she wanted him to.

"Damn me to hell for it, but yes. And I can't look away, Lady Moria."

For the rest of the dance, he held her like water that might escape his grasp if he clung too hard, and then immediately requested a second dance as soon as it was over. Moria had only dreamed the night of her debut could be spectacular enough that she'd finally garner the attention of her neighbor Marcus, or that all heads would swivel in her direction upon her every move.

Moria had learned, after that night, that for even or maybe especially the women of her station, there were only so many moments one got that sparkled before the glitter turned to rust.

~

Her memories were interrupted as The Letter was pulled from her grasp by her interfering younger sister. Moria tightened her hold on the envelope, glancing back at the two men outside to ascertain they were still deep in conversation.

"Who's the sender of this letter you're hiding, Moria?" Olivia was looking at her in such a way that Moria could see every cog and gear in her mind turning.

Moria pocketed the letter for later. The words in his letters weren't made for sharing like so much of her life had always been. They were only for her, *he* was only for her. She was hoarding all of his goodness to herself, and it was selfish, she'd admit, but god, could she not be selfish one time?

"I don't have to inform you of every acquaintance I write to."

"This acquaintance still writes to you even though you are terrible at corresponding back?"

She was, admittedly, quite terrible at correspondence with everyone else. Somehow her comings and goings had come to revolve around *his* letters, somehow she was able to pour so much she kept locked inside a vault most of the time for others into the pages she sent to him. Olivia would no doubt make a meal of this.

Moria felt the back of her neck itch and felt her fingers twitch to scratch at it. She could bluff her way in ballrooms and masquerades and places she had no business being, but her little sister made her itch uncomfortably under her stare. Unbelievable.

"I'm only terrible at corresponding with people who have nothing interesting to say. It isn't my fault that most of the correspondents of our acquaintance fall into such a category."

She picked up a pitcher on a sideboard nearby and poured herself a glass of water, suddenly unaccountably thirsty. Olivia looked at her like she could read the words through the concealing pocket of her dress.

"And what makes this particular...correspondent...so titillating?"

Moria spat the contents of her water goblet across the table. Olivia threw back her head in a raucous and unladylike laugh. Of course, Jasper chose that moment to enter with the Earl of Drysdale following on his heels.

"I'm afraid to even ask what the two of you are talking about," The latter said, eyeing Moria like a piece of forbidden fruit, hands shoved in his pockets, hair perfectly unkempt. He wasn't forever. She wasn't sure she had yet to find a man who was, only one she was willing to wager could be. Drysdale was enjoyable to look at, easy to be around. The contents of him weren't half as deep as the man in her letters and sometimes it was a good, diverting thing; and sometimes she could feel her own heart cleave down the middle for missing a man with tattooed hands and a gentle soul.

Jasper nodded his acquiescence as he took a biscuit on a saucer from Olivia and sat down next to her at the tea table by a large wall of windows. Drysdale remained standing.

"Drysdale? Staying for tea?" Jasper said, motioning to the table.

"The view must be better over there," Olivia said in a stage whisper.

Drysdale covered his laugh with a hand and Jasper shot the youngest Pembrooke a censorious glare. "You are, as ever, one of the most astute Pembrookes, Lady Olivia."

Olivia beamed. "It isn't a close race."

Both Moria and Jasper collapsed into laughter, Moria giving her brother's arm a firm squeeze to brace herself through her laughter. Drysdale met her eyes as he came to sit next to her, smiling at her, at the easy way her family joked with each other.

All she could think was that while he was the perfect teatime adornment—handsome and good natured and warm— her heart was calling another man's name.

Chapter Six

The launch of another beautiful Pembrooke lady and a betrothal on the same night? This year's debut ball at Lady Gretchen Von Mien's did not disappoint the gossips.
- Scandalous Lives of London, April 1841

The very next evening, Lady Moria was prepared to capitalize on every acquaintance and piece of gossip at her disposal to ensure her younger sister's debut ball was a success. When she entered the ball hosted by Lady Gretchen on the Earl of Drysdale's arm, she'd registered every half-concealed half-truth the guests, both male and female alike, were whispering about her.

"Don't be fooled by her pretty smiles-"
"Evil takes a human form in that one."
"Your typical spoiled, selfish-"
"She's a back-stabbing-"
"She looks flawless this evening."
"Oh, she's fabulous, if a little bit mean."

"Luckily for us all, her younger sister seems rather sweet."

Caleb Howley, the Earl of Drysdale ushered her onto the dance-floor. "You alright, my lady?"

Moria gave him a wide smile, letting him guide her even though she was a far superior dancer, because that's what proper ladies did. And she had to be *the* proper lady if she was going to be a Duchess. Or if she was going to make sure Olivia got the launch she deserved. And she had to *appear* to at least be in pursuit of a nobleman's hand - not a Captain's- if she was going to achieve that goal. If all her past troublemaking and scheming maligned her sister, then what had it all been for?

Lady Moria stood on her tip toes and spoke her next words close to his ear. "You ever walk into a room and know instantly that everyone is talking about you?"

Caleb tilted his mouth to one side, thinking. "Only when I'm with you," he said, spinning her in front of him with one hand over their heads.

"And that doesn't ever bother you?" She asked. "You don't want a girl who's...sweet?"

Caleb tilted his head back on a laugh. "Who says you're not sweet, Lady Moria?"

That wasn't an answer to her question. Moria knew a sly deflection when she heard one.

When they exited the dance floor, Moria watched as her sister Noelle's bookish friend Margot fumbled over her words, asking some inane question about Drysdale's performance on the flute at the same musicale where Moria had turned down Lord Adderton's proposal.

Moria raised a brow, Lady Althea tapped her with her cane once, muttering what sounded like:

"Put on your mask, my dear." Moria noticed the eyes that fell on her, waiting for any misstep. She noticed the Dowager Duchess of Andover, the Duke's mother among them, but not the Duke.

Moria schooled her features back into submission and stood straighter. Too much was riding on her tight hold on her emotions.

It seemed her sister's shorter, curly haired friend was...flirting with Drysdale? One would presume extensive novel consumption ought to teach a wallflower better powers of flirtation.

Drysdale gave a good natured laugh. "Do you also play an instrument by any chance?"

Moria probably could have interjected at some point. Moria did in fact also play an instrument, impressively some would say, but she just tilted her head to the side, reading the signs.

Margot talking with her hands, Drysdale dipping his head at something she said and then smiling at her. Margot was talking about the composition she was practicing, Drysdale's eyes flew to Margot's full lips.

Lady Althea pressed a hand on Moria's arm, a gentle perusal of her feelings because there was barely a secret that woman couldn't divine, but Moria gave her a small smile in return. Oddly enough, Moria didn't feel jealous.

Moria had kissed Drysdale, and yet...and yet the thought of Margot kissing him didn't do anything to her. She felt...indignant. But Devyn?

I want to push someone down a flight of stairs or toss a piano out of a window at the thought of someone else's mouth on him. What does that say about me?

She didn't puzzle over it for long, for the next song began. Moria let Drysdale take her in his arms and lead her onto the dance floor. She wondered for a split second how it would feel to be dancing with a different man's arms around her, but batted the thought away when Drysdale's small finger caressed her lower back. Only, she saw that more than twice, his eyes found Miss Wimbley again and his cheeks went a little pink when he realized she'd noticed.

Moria didn't dawdle. Moria was a woman of swift action.

"Aaah!" She gasped, misstepping and grabbing onto him to keep from toppling over.

She winced, leaning down to grasp her ankle through her layers of skirts.

He stopped dancing, tightening his grasp. "Dear god. My lady, are you alright?"

"I miscounted the music is all, I think I…" she winced as he draped an arm around her and led her to an upholstered bench off to the side of the dance floor, "I think I may have turned my ankle wrong."

Several onlookers had started to gather. Drysdale stood before her to block their view.

"Then I shall see to getting you home," Drysdale insisted.

Moria patted his arm. "You're so attentive, but my sisters will see to my welfare. I'm sure Miss Wimbley wouldn't mind taking my place." She looked around him to wave a hand at the young woman in the small circle of onlookers. To her credit, the softening of her eyes showed concern for Moria, or perhaps concern for being the object of her attention.

It was a test, if he was into Margot like she'd suspected, he'd take the out. If he wasn't he wouldn't—

"Miss Wimbley?"

Moria had once thought Margot Wimbley plain, it turned out she'd just never seen the girl blush. When she smiled and blushed and held out her hand, she was radiant. Drysdale's eyes seemed to reflect it. Crinkles at the corners held up by a smile of his own gave him away.

In seconds, Moria's three sisters and companion materialized out of nowhere. All five women had to scrunch their skirts together to fit onto the upholstered bench on the outskirts of the dancefloor, but Moria relished their momentary closeness. At an event like this, she was often holding court, currying favors, collecting secrets, all while being trailed by Carina and Lady Gretchen, Drysdale, or other suitors. There was an uncommon reprieve being next to the people who knew her without wanting something from her.

"Mo, can I be of assistance?" Noelle had been the first one to her side. Fitz stood behind Noelle, staring down anyone who cast glances their way or whispered behind a fan.

Miss Kate Herring from the lending library approached. Moria barely knew the girl, didn't like that smirk on her lips like she saw through Moria. So Moria made a show of wincing and pointing toward her ankle.

"I'll be fine in a moment. Just turned my ankle wrong dancing is all."

Olivia was immediately skeptical. "You've never misstepped dancing in your life."

Trust Olivia to risk outing Moria's ruse. But Miss Herring didn't pick up the thread. "Perhaps it was a waltz? I've always found those rather tricky," Kate offered.

Moria huffed and crossed her arms. "A *waltz*? I'm not an amateur. Please. It was a jig. Which you would know if any suitors had asked you."

Noelle discreetly stepped on Moria's foot in silent reproach. Moria stared a hole through Kate as she said, "You can't sit with us." Sensing this was a conversation she wasn't privy to, Miss Herring made a curtsy and stepped into a crowd.

Kathleen turned her attention from the young woman's swift departure to study Moria's face. "First you give Margot your dance with Drysdale, and then you give that poor young lady such a cut direct. Sometimes I don't know what to make of you."

"Because you're like our mother," Olivia said, tone laced with incredulity.

"But I'm not a regular mother, I'm your sister, like a more calm, understanding mother."

"Please stop talking," Moria said, cringing, then continued. "Miss Herring's acquaintance does make me appear more benevolent in light of how the scandal sheets like to misconstrue my intentions, despite wearing the ugliest effing skirt I've ever seen," she shuddered as if in distaste, then straightened her posture. "But she hasn't earned a place among my confidantes yet," Moria said with a shrug. "As for Miss Wimbley, I witnessed their interaction. It was...*sweet*. I merely got out of the way."

"Why? Isn't Drysdale worth considering as a partner?" Noelle asked softly, pushing her spectacles back up on her nose. Moria shrugged evasively and pulled her glove higher up her arm. She couldn't reveal her cards, the increasingly complex dance between securing the hand of a Duke or giving into her deepening pull to an Army Captain.

"He is quite decent," Fitz added.

"He isn't a Duke, though," Lady Althea said in a stage whisper.

Moria looked toward the dancefloor wistfully. She felt the others' eyes on her, waiting for her to answer. "Margot's never been anything but loyal to you," Moria said to Noelle, with a soft smile, remembering Noelle's previous season when her sister had debuted after nearly eighteen months in mourning and had few prospects, yet Miss Wimbley had remained her steadfast friend.

Moria didn't usually do nice things for people she wasn't related to...unless they deserved it. Moria wished that she could be like her mother, like Olivia, and Noelle, who simply saw the right course, who saw people and their needs. Moria felt like she was always judging people against some harsher standard and held grievances long past the date to relinquish them.

"I'll always like Drysdale but I'll never love him." She shrugged, "I think *she* could."

The lady in question drifted toward them.

"Enjoy your dance? Or...my dance?" Moria asked, raising her chin.

Margot broke eye contact and looked down at her hands. "Tremendously. How's your ankle, Lady Moria?"

Moria groaned. "Oh, it's worse for wear, I'm afraid. I'll need to prevail on your good nature a little longer. My brother is sending for the carriage to take me home."

Drysdale appeared, followed quickly by Jasper. "Are you all right, Lady Moria? I'll be sad to see you go." So she was back to Lady Moria, no longer just *Moria*.

Moria turned a bright smile on. "I will be, Cal. But you should stay."

He shook his head, but she took one of his hands. "I want you to enjoy yourself."

He squeezed her hand, and she used it to pull herself up. She put an arm at his waist and one at his shoulder as she planted a soft kiss at his cheek. He brought her gloved hand to his lips and left a kiss. It didn't rattle her soul, but it was genuine.

"Thank you for that. For everything. Goodbye, Lady Moria." She heard the unspoken meaning in his words. Maybe he was letting her go because he could see her heart had someone else taking up space as well.

Kathleen interrupted her thoughts with a gentle hand at her elbow, proffering a dance card for Moria's perusal. "What do you make of this? Several of the suitors on Olivia's dance card...are former and current beaux of yours."

Lady Althea leaned over Moria's shoulder and harrumphed.

As if summoned, the Duke of Andover appeared in their line of vision, all six-foot-something looking sinfully elegant. Moria let her eyes linger on long limbs and strapping shoulders in formal wear, complimentary green eyes offset by the deep bronze of his skin and dark hair. He had caught her eye the previous season; so she'd made herself hard enough to look away from that he'd been the one to seek an introduction.

"Ladies, I hope I'm not interrupting."

Kathleen turned to Moria. "We'll finish our discussion later, you two go have your dance."

The Duke stifled a grin. "Actually, Lady Thorne, I've already promised Lady Olivia this one."

Kathleen looked at Moria like a victor. Before Kathleen could start in on her tirade, her husband Henry appeared out of nowhere to take her by the arms and waist. They whirled away on a tide of dancing feet and formal wear and laughter.

The Duke of Andover spoke, "I'm relieved to see Henry so happy. He was a few years ahead of me at Oxford...but then he left before the end of his year. Of course, he wasn't a Marquess then. It was that wretched cousin of his."

When he brought up the topic of the previous Marquess, she wanted to tell him about her past. But not here, not with so many watching eyes and listening ears on all sides. Not now. She and the Duke didn't yet have their own history that gave her the security to share secrets. Was he even the type of man who had space or understanding for a woman's secrets?

She settled for: "It isn't fair to speak ill of the dead, Your Grace."

He looked down at her, a keenness in his eyes like he saw more of her hand than she'd meant to reveal. He softened his features with a small smile. "You are right, my lady. I hope you'll forgive my error. I only meant—"

Before he could say what it was that he had meant, it was Olivia who spoke next, materializing on the Duke's other side as if from thin air. "Are you ready for that dance you promised me?"

When Olivia stepped on to the dancefloor of Lady Gretchen von Mien's very full ballroom, Moria felt the atmosphere change. For all her beauty and accomplishments, Olivia hadn't made much of a lingering impression on the ton's fickle palate; but on the arm of a Duke, they had to take notice of her now. Her work for the evening complete, Moria placed her reticule under her arm to depart. She made sure to limp slightly and wince occasionally in order to further sell her injury.

And then, a swath of night-colored hair and a red coat danced in her periphery.

Chapter Seven

MORIA PAUSED, COLLECTING HERSELF BEFORE TURNING IN the direction of a familiar set of wide shoulders in a red coat and dark hair. A lump formed in her throat. She'd seen Devyn only four times in person and they'd exchanged numerous letters, she'd conjured him in her dreams and when she was restless in bed alone, but nothing compared to seeing him in the flesh. Here. At a ball.

He began walking towards her too, people in his path clearing out of his way, his hulking strength parting dancing waters.

No.

He wouldn't.

Wouldn't he?

"Lady Moria," Miss Kelley said, looping her arm through Moria's, "Your brother's carriage is waiting."

Moria met the woman's green eyes and gave her a demure smile. "Of course. I'll just go and retrieve my shawl."

Miss Kelley looked down pointedly at the shawl that Moria was already wearing. She leaned in as though to place a friendly kiss at Moria's cheek and whispered, "You wanted to bring him out of the shadows for over a year, this is your opening. I'll buy you some time;

but if you're not in the carriage in five minutes, I'm sending your brother inside to retrieve you."

Moria wasn't sure what the woman expected her to do in a mere five minutes or how she was going to approach Devyn, here, what she'd even say. Behind her, she heard one of her friends calling for her, but she was borne on an undeniable wind toward Captain Devyn Winter. She had to reach half the length of the ballroom to get to him, praying all the while he was there for her. Only her. Marcus had played her false. A second time would be the death of her pride.

She extracted the folded-up letter from her reticule and ripped out the only part she needed to convey her message, so that it would fit in her fist. She busied herself with pretending to be looking for someone in the crowd, not looking where she was going until her dress collided with a heavy boot.

Moria let out a little squeak.

At the movement and the noise, she saw several heads turn to look in her direction. She gave a demure smile and gathered her dress as though startled. Another woman might have found so many unplanned dramatic performances in one evening tiring; but Moria's heart was racing with excitement.

Words and air whooshed from her as he stood before her, her wrist caught in his grasp.

"My lady, please accept my apologies for my very clumsy friend."

The red-headed Scot from the inn, Devyn's usual accomplice, gave her a sheepish and apologetic grin. "If it 'elps, it were the prettiest dress in the room, my lady. I'm so sorry if I-"

Moria shook her head. She wasn't looking at the Scot, her eyes were on the man next to him. The man who'd written her letters and haunted her dreams. She hadn't dreamed the way his lips twitched to hold back a smile or the way his black eyes weren't black, they were like the sea at night, flecked with starlight. She knew that if she pulled at the queue at his nape, the shoulder length strands of his hair would feel like soft temptation in her hands.

"Do the two of you make a habit of ruining ladies' gowns? Seems a rather expensive way of meeting young ladies."

His lips sprang into a smile. She couldn't help tracking the movement of those lips she'd come so close to kissing a few times. "There's only one woman I wanted to get close to."

"And did it work for you?" She asked, tilting her head to the side.

"You tell me, my lady," he answered, motioning to the dancing couples in their periphery. "On the dancefloor."

It was a moment, and it was her choice.

Something by Elgar was playing, one of the songs she knew by heart on her pianoforte. She surely wouldn't forget that song now.

She could spread the seeds of something that wanted to break through to the surface, something that wanted to grow beyond the reaches of the confines she'd put it in. She could water his hopes, or she could drown them with a word, a gesture. If they were seen together, here on the edges of the ballroom much longer, people would start to talk. Was she prepared to give them more to discuss on the night of her sister's debut?

"I must offer my sincerest apologies, Captain. My brother is waiting for me in the carriage."

His face didn't fall like another man's might. He took a step closer. "That so, my lady?"

"My lady, are you quite alright?" It was the Duke, coming to stand next to her. His chest brushed against the wing of one of her bare shoulder blades. She closed her eyes and mumbled a curse.

"I was just leaving," she said, addressing all three men.

"I'll escort you, then," the Duke said, very Ducal of him; and although Devyn raised a brow, he didn't move or object. His eyes fell back to Moria. It was still her choice.

Moria placed her hand in Devyn's. Warm, capable gloved fingers she knew held tattoos and scars. Fingers that could hold her and her heart in his hands and not drop them. She squeezed them, willing him to feel the tension inside her slip through her fingers and pass into his. There was a knowing spark in his eyes, even more stars coming to life in those black depths, as he gripped the note in her hand.

"A pleasure, Captain," she murmured, then curtsied.

"All mine," he said in return, those fathomless eyes and large hands engulfing hers until they let her go. For now. She wanted to stand right there, engulfed until she was in flames. She felt the Duke's impatience as he waited to walk her to Kathleen. She cleared her throat and looped her arm through the Duke's. When she made her exit and retreated home, it was those words that echoed in her head where he'd planted them.

All mine. That's what she wanted to be. All his.

Moria had to find a way to let him win her, without losing it all.

Chapter Eight

London's second most fashionable ball tonight boasts a guest list not ordered by pedigree. The price of entry? Payment of something dear. What are you willing to sacrifice to avoid the fear of missing out?

    - Scandalous Lives of London scandal sheet

After the ball, was…another ball. Of a different sort. This one was exclusive in the way that gaming hell membership was exclusive, and not in the way that balls were.

Each invitee to the ball had to complete a singular task outlined in their invitation and offer proof of completing said task as their entry to the ball. The whole process made it so that getting there was almost as fun as the revelry itself… *almost.*

Moria's favorite part was that each attendant was required to hide their identity behind a mask. This allowed for the semblance of anonymity, as much as a paltry strip of beaded cloth could allow.

The rich and powerful mixed with the ennobled impoverished in a grand swirl of limitless activity in the black and white ballroom of Pomfrey House. Ladies were allowed to attend unchaperoned amongst gentlemen, and this made for a more illicit tableau than the party Moria had escaped earlier that evening. Moria had had to sneak out over her own balcony in a hoop skirt, she hoped this night proved to be worth her many gambles.

"Are you sure we won't get into some kind of trouble for being here? What about our reputations?" Kate asked, coming to stand at Moria's side at the top of the staircase that looked out over a packed ballroom.

"That's why Lady Moria's hair is so big, it's full of secrets," Carina said, with a wink.

"It's not nearly as big as your ego," Moria shot back, sticking out her tongue as the line to make it down the stairs moved.

"Carina is right. We're your friends, why would we get you into any trouble?" Lady Gretchen asked, squeezing Kate's hand for reassurance.

"I'm in no position to pass up friends," Kate answered, following the line in front of them.

"Why did your parents want you to debut this season?" Carina inquired, smoothing a curl back into Kate's coiffure.

"They wanted me to get socialized," Kate said, adjusting her mask.

"And you'll get socialized alright," Lady Gretchen said, pulling a flask from the sleeve of her gown.

Kate's eyes flew to the other two ladies. "What do you mean?"

"You're a regulation beauty. Own it." Moria paid her new friend a compliment before she linked arms with the three women, making their way down the grand staircase in dramatic fashion that drew some attention. Their entrance drew some attention, but it was Lord Tristan Valentine who was the first to recognize Moria behind her fox mask.

"It had to be you."

From Moria's side, Miss Herring rolled her eyes at Valentine's approach. Moria didn't heed her, pulling her glove higher up her arm so she had something to do to steady her hands. "I thought you were impervious to my charms, Valentine?"

Tristan Valentine lifted back his domino mask and gave her a smile. "Impervious, but not blind."

Moria couldn't help herself. "Beauty only gets you so far." There was a knife's edge to her voice that she hadn't been able to restrain. Kate's face fell, looking at her curiously.

Valentine offered his arm for Moria to take. "Careful, my lady, or someone will mistake you for sounding bored."

"Is my sister-in-law sounding bored already? What a pity." Crooned the voice of their host, Moria's brother-in-law, Fitzwilliam Pomfrey, Viscount Ludlowe.

Moria could hear the familiar thread of sarcasm in her childhood friend's voice. Even in the crush of people who turned their attention her way, her sister Noelle was nowhere to be seen.

"Good evening, my lord. Will Adelaide be attending this evening?" Miss Herring asked.

"There will be a literary salon this evening to discuss works of fiction with interested parties where she *might* be in attendance." There was a twinkle in Fitz's eye, pride and mischief intermingled.

Moria had attended them before, riveted that her bookish, quiet sister could transform into this different person altogether who conversed about art with great minds and was held in high esteem by other artists. Moria couldn't fend off the pang of jealousy that Noelle had all this, including the love of her life, when everything Moria had touched turned to an empty, fleeting gold before it died.

She could never voice such feelings; instead she yawned behind her hand and Carina and Lady Gretchen laughed. Moria felt a little sick making her friends laugh at her sister's expense, but the thought of vulnerability was worse.

Fitz was addressing the group, but Moria followed a head of dark hair towering over the others in her periphery. As he came into view, again, the tension in his jaw, the breadth of his shoulders, the raven's wing depth of his dark eyes were familiar. He wasn't wearing his red coat, or a mask, but a tailored set of fine evening clothes. The effect let her see all his unabashed beauty on display. Her gamble in coming tonight had not been in vain. She was itching to know how he'd gained entry.

Moria noticed other women notice him, eyes darting his way behind their masks and disguises. Kate grasped her hand to point in his direction. Moria didn't hear what the other woman or any of her companions said as she'd already left them behind.

The very lines and shape of him was erotic.

Not that he seemed aware of any of that. There was a singular purpose in his movements as he searched the ballroom.

A woman stepped in his path, he moved out of her way.

All mine. Her heart seemed to echo his words at another very different ball earlier that evening.

Moria's breath caught and her heart outran the pace of the music when he finally caught her eyes, held them. His tell was his eyes. The room descended into a level of heat and noise and madness, but it could have burned down and he'd not have taken his eyes from her face.

"Lady Fox," he said, bending his frame to lean to her height, to her ear.

"Soldier," she greeted.

"Yours to command," he answered her greeting with a playful salute.

"You got my message, then?"

"You owed me a dance."

"But how did you..." Her voice trailed off, but he picked up the thread.

"The dark-haired woman at the door," he answered. "I gave her your note."

Her sister. Dressed as Adelaide. Had she recognized Moria's handwriting?

"Did you come for me earlier too? At the other ball?"

He took her in his arms, pulling her with him onto the dance floor. She eyed the dancers around them caught up in complicated patterns to a music that seemed to have no end, drunk on champagne that saw no limit.

"As I said," His fingers twined with hers, his other hand wrapping at her waist. "You owed me a dance."

"Are we not already? Dancing around one another?" she asked. He gifted her one questioning brow and a smile that tugged at the corner of his delicious lips.

Moria leaned into him, letting him guide her. She'd been afraid that a man so large and imposing would drag her around the dance floor clumsily stepping on her feet and tripping to the time of the music. But beyond a long and muscled form, he had an innate and instinctive grace she hadn't anticipated. Questions tripped through her mind, she almost stumbled but he adjusted his pace and kept her on her feet.

"Something you want to say, Lady Fox?" he asked, that damn smile tugging at his lips again. Moria had never once had to resort to counting the time of the music in her head before, but she was doing it now. Dance had always been a performance, but with him it was something else entirely she couldn't name.

"Where did you learn to dance, Captain?"

His gloved hands were so large and so warm. "I told you my father was the heir to an earldom, and my brother after him. Believe it or not, I attended lessons in deportment and elocution, and yes, dancing. I think it's aided in my swordsmanship as well."

The candelabra above his head shed iridescent light on his night-colored hair.

"You never fail to surprise."

He let out a low laugh. "Not nearly as much as you, I should think."

Moria was vaguely aware of people staring in their direction. She changed partners briefly and then was returned to Devyn.

She had to stifle the urge to close her eyes as their hands made contact again. Her mind conjured images of those hands on her skin, the places he could touch with those hands, with other parts of his body as well. Drat her corset, she couldn't breathe. She'd gone from debauched and jaded debutante to wanting to *be* debauched in a matter of moments.

"Me? What about an army captain seeking out an elusive debutante at two very different balls in one evening? Now there's a tale."

He said his next words low enough that only she could hear them. "I think, my lady, the more interesting tale I have to tell starts with finally getting to hold you in my arms after thinking about it for an entire year."

Her eyes closed briefly, savoring his words and his nearness. She was vaguely aware of the music ending, of dancers applauding. They were likely too intoxicated to notice she didn't clap; she was intoxicated on something else entirely. *Someone.*

Not just someone. *Devyn.* Moria had lauded herself for being sensible, she'd lost her head to a boy before who clouded all objectivity and reason until the clouds parted and revealed how very solidly he'd deceived her. But Devyn was a man.

There was only raw honesty painted on his face when he looked back at her, only genuine affection when his voice caressed her ear to ask, "Would you like to dance again or would you like to talk?"

Her gloved fingers touched the side of his neck near her mouth as she whispered in his ear, "I would love to talk. Just give me a few minutes."

"Moria."

She heard her name at her back and knew who it was.

"Fitzwilliam Pomfrey," she said through gritted teeth, turning toward her brother-in-law. Fitz had always been one of the tallest men she knew, but he was still more than a head shorter and much less broad than the captain. The two men made quite a stark contrast as they stared at one another. Devyn was the first to introduce himself, Fitz followed suit but the keen amusement and curiosity on his face was telling.

"Captain Winter and I were—"

"Already acquainted before this evening, I gather?" Fitz said, a dimple pulling at his cheek. His ocean-blue eyes were rife with amusement. She was sure her sister would be hearing about this. Somehow the thought was...comforting?

Before she could speak, Fitz held up a hand. "Save your lies, Moria, I won't tell a soul. Just stay out of trouble and don't force my hand, alright?" but there was a soft note to his voice. He was her friend, there was a goodness in the young, blonde viscount that understood the weight of secrets and pride in a way that not every man of his station did.

He turned to Devyn, sticking out a hand. "Captain," he said with a firm shake, "I'm better with a sword or a pistol than I look, so no compromising my sister-in-law on my wife's rather delicate furniture, I'd hate to call you out." And with a dramatic flourish he was gone.

A laugh bubbled up from Devyn's chest. "That was your infamous brother-in-law? This ball's host?"

Moria put a hand over her mouth to stifle a laugh. "I'm afraid that is indeed the Viscount Ludlowe."

"Rather disappointed in him for leaving you alone with a scoundrel like me," he said, taking a step closer to her. They were not alone, they were still in a crowded ballroom in one of Mayfair's most coveted parties.

"We aren't nearly alone enough," Moria said, immediately biting her lip and squeezing her eyes shut at how forward she sounded. But somehow, he could find her in a crowded room and she'd watch it all burn down just to have him all to herself.

Chapter Nine

D,

I've never seen you at a ball, and you've never seen me at a ball. Maybe a time or two, I envision the hand at my waist is yours. Maybe I envision the eyes looking down at me are like a starry night, like yours. If you don't know, fortunes and reputations are made on a single dance. And no one dances better than me.

Lady M

~

My Lady of the willow tree,

Naturally. No one dances better than a goddess. But to whose tune are you dancing?

D

~

D–

I've danced to them all. I think I might like to try yours. At least once.

M

~

SHE COULD ONLY BE TESTING HIM. TEASING HIM AND THEN darting off to find her female companions, leaving him to navigate the large and overly dressed crush of revelers in the noisy ballroom in search of the billiards room. He was to meet her there. Sounded easy enough, but this party and her brother-in-law's house were gargantuan.

Suddenly, Devyn felt the strength of what could only be a masculine hand at his shoulder.

"Captain," the man said, and when Devyn turned, he found the blonde viscount, Moria's brother-in-law, smirking up at him. Devyn was taller than most men, but Ludlowe wasn't much shorter. He didn't have a warrior's build, but he looked fit, for a nobleman. Devyn registered the dandy beside the viscount wearing an aubergine coat and a domino mask, he believed the man had been talking to Moria when he'd arrived.

"Thought you might stoop to join us gentleman for a brandy in my study," Ludlowe ventured.

"He keeps the good stuff locked up at fetes like this," explained the man who introduced himself as Valentine.

Devyn eyed the other man through his mask. "And how are you acquainted with Lady Moria?"

Valentine laughed. "She punched me in the face once."

Ludlowe pinched the bridge of his nose. "I can't vouch for the truth of virtually anything Valentine says, except for the high-quality liquor."

"Lead the way," Devyn acquiesced.

When they were seated in what Devyn could only call a tastefully hedonistic gathering space, complete with not one but two billiards tables, Devyn complimented his host on his fine taste in vintage.

"Only to loosen your tongue while we interrogate you, Captain," Viscount Ludlowe drawled.

Devyn choked on his drink. He was a soldier, and a damned good one, he should have seen through the ruse. Valentine slapped him on the back, "I say, Captain, you are built like a tree. I can see why you've captured Moria's interest."

"That is what it is, isn't it?" The Viscount swirled the contents of his glass. "Interest?"

Devyn shook his head. "I don't take your meaning, my lord."

One blond brow quirked. "Surely you see it from my perspective? A lady who could have her pick of titled suitors, and a Captain in Her Majesty's Army? You two aren't planning a torrid affair? An elopement perhaps?"

This time Devyn was prepared and did not choke on his drink. "I have nothing but honorable intentions where she is concerned."

Valentine tilted his head to the side and asked with a jovial expression. "And does she have honorable intentions where you are concerned?"

Devyn couldn't help it, he choked on his drink again.

Both men laughed raucously. He should have expected this, should have prepared better. But he led soldiers, men trained in battlefield arts, not politics and social etiquette. Peregrine would know how to navigate conversations with men of their social standing. What would Peregrine say?

Both men were looking at him intently. "Lady Moria is a lady, I am sure such insinuations are beneath her character, my lord."

"Lady Moria is THE lady, but any ruinous insinuations are neither beneath her character or—" Valentine scoffed.

"Valentine..." Ludlowe growled. "She is my sister and my oldest friend."

"She is your *wife's* sister, and you yourself thought about getting a look under her skirts before—"

Devyn was shocked at how quickly the lithe young lord had launched from his chair to grab his friend by his ruffled collar. "And she is *your* friend, Valentine. Her brother is one of your oldest friends too. You absolute *twat*. Dare you forget I have secrets of yours to keep next time you open your mouth to spout such inane slander about my family, I shall remind you that I can ruin you with a whisper." And with a forceful shove, Ludlowe released Valentine, who calmly sat back down, brushing off his lapels.

Devyn met Ludlowe's eyes; the Viscount was looking at him as if he expected him to say something. Devyn merely raised his glass at the viscount and drank. Devyn knew how to bodily threaten a man but such a flaying rhetorical set down? Anything he himself could say or do to the...twat Valentine, would be redundant.

"There were many who thought that Moria would have made a better match for a viscount than her younger sister, still do, in fact. But those people," Ludlowe looked at Valentine and then back to Devyn, "Don't know Noelle. They saw past her, but I'm so glad that I didn't."

Valentine was looking at Ludlowe apologetically, then he turned to Devyn. "Lady Moria is the other face of her coin. She is impossible to look past. The man who can see *through* her, will deserve her."

Devyn knew Valentine was right. From her letters, he saw so much more to the woman than she wanted people to believe. She was a bright blinding light trying to eclipse the darkness she hid inside, he knew it, he'd lived it himself.

The two men turned to him, seeming to have made their amends as quickly as they had broken them. "I have a feeling you might be such a man, Captain—" Ludlowe began.

"But if you are not, there are plenty waiting in the wings to take your place," Valentine interrupted.

"Was that absolutely necessary, Valentine?" The Viscount asked.

"Was what absolutely necessary?"

Devyn whipped around at the sound of Moria's voice, having found their little assembly at last.

He drank her in like a dying man, stunned in the heart and vocal cords for a third time that same night at the sight of her. She'd freshened her appearance and her blonde coiffure while she'd been gone, as if she'd needed it. Did *he* make her that nervous? Perhaps it was the fact that everyone was always looking at her, half to drink her in as he was doing, the other half to find fault.

Standing beside his chair, he brushed her fingers with his own. Her fingers singed his in return. He felt his cheeks heat like a schoolboy at the precise and intimate contact. If anyone noticed, they gave no indication.

Finally, he found his gift of speech. "Lord Ludlowe and Lord Valentine were just singing your praises."

"You lie beautifully, Captain. I'd never believe such untruths of these two knaves. How many ways did they threaten you?" She turned her gaze to the other two men who were looking at her and the Captain with the avid fascination of two scheming mamas.

Casually, Moria popped a sweet into her mouth, and Devyn swallowed at the movement of her painted lips.

"I'd never dream of threatening a man of his brute strength," Fitz chimed in.

"That might be the first time common sense prevailed for you," said a feminine voice over Moria's shoulder. She was joined by a woman with black hair in a dress so dark purple it was almost black. Devyn recognized her from the door, she'd been the one who'd accepted his note as collateral for entry. He couldn't help but notice the way Ludlowe's eyes lit with mischief as he roved the length of her body in a way that was entirely beneath a happily married man.

"Should have known you'd turn up at the first opportunity to make a jest at my expense." Ludlowe parleyed. Devyn met Moria's eyes, she was stifling a laugh behind her hand.

"May I join you?" the woman said, motioning to the open seat next to the Viscount. Devyn felt protective of the virtue of that burgundy damask settee.

"I'm afraid I was saving this seat for my wife," Ludlowe answered with a debonair smile that Devyn had attempted on women before but never perfected to this degree. It was punctuated with a casual draping of his long arm on that innocent settee.

"Shall I go and find her?" the dark-haired woman answered astutely with a toss of her tousled dark curls.

Valentine groaned. "I can't witness any more of this foreplay, I'm going to get another drink."

Devyn met Moria's eyes in confusion, surely her brother-in-law wasn't flirting with another woman in front of her? Moria touched Devyn's arm and whispered into his ear, "That's Noelle, she's in character." He barely registered her words at the sight of her cleavage so close and her breath warm and sweet against his neck.

Devyn answered, "For the masquerade?"

He barely had three brain cells left with which to ponder her words; they'd all fled south to his groin.

Moria chomped on the sweet she was holding in her mouth and shook her head. "No, it's a ruse. She's a writer, that's her character, Fitz is her publisher. Apparently, this is something they both…enjoy." She said the last word with a toss of her champagne flute.

Devyn used this opening to his advantage. "And do you also… enjoy other personas?"

Devyn enjoyed that Moria was the one this time to choke on her champagne.

"Perhaps I do."

And at her lowered tone, her unblinking gaze, he finally saw beneath her mask. All the Moria's she inhabited. A dutiful sister. A sought-after debutante. A pretender holding on to all her masks. And most simply, A Woman asking to be cared for by A Man.

As Moria's sister sat atop her brother-in-law's knee, Devyn took Moria's hand and led her out of the billiards room. When they rounded the top of a set of marble stairs, Moria pulled on his hand in the direction of an empty sitting room. The room behind a solid oak door was dark.

As soon as she shut the door behind him, she was on him like a scent in a matter of moments. Her gloved hand clutched greedily at the front of his shirt, her face indelibly close. His own hands removed her mask and then stole to her waist, one of them curling a fist around the fullness of her skirts.

"Did you come to claim your kiss?" Moria spoke the words so close to his mouth he could taste the lingering notes of champagne and sugar on her breath. Her fingers curled into his hair; he fought the urge to close his eyes as her nails scratched against his scalp. *Christ.* No woman had ever captivated him so fully with so little.

Just kiss her already, his body screamed.

On the other side of the door, there were voices. Moria let out a curse and hung her head at his shoulder. He tore his gaze away from the rapid rise and fall of her breasts against her dress, surely her nipples were hard from the way her dress must be scraping against her tender flesh.

She pulled away and turned to step around him. He stopped her, a hand at her wrist. "Stay."

He tightened his hold on her hand, feeling her pulse leap under his touch. Her teeth were clinched but there was a flicker, then a glimmer of longing in her eyes, but she withstood it.

"I can't."

Why was she walking to the door?

"I should not have come. The girl who meets men in secret and accepts only a half-life, I should have left her in the past."

He was beside her in a moment, thanking God for his long,

powerful strides. He closed the door just as she had opened it and put his back to it.

Her nostrils flared in challenge just as her body pressed into his. "What do you want from me?"

"My letters for the last 13 months weren't clear enough? My asking you to dance at more than one ball in the same night wasn't clear enough?"

"Not necessarily, no. How is this supposed to work?" she gestured between them. "You and me. A captain in Her Majesty's army and the season's incomparable? Are we having tea and discussing military strategy?" A small smile played up at the corner of her bow-shaped lips before she turned her head to the side.

"I'm sure you could hold council on waging war with the best military strategists in Britain."

He came from a long line of men who had served The Crown, he and his brother had played at strategy with tin army men and practiced swordsmanship and marksmanship farther back than he could remember. But her kind of battle tested even his own tactical skills.

The wood panels of the door cut into his back. His hands found her waist. The way that her waist dipped down to her hips was made perfectly for his hands.

She was of average height or a little taller, but he was not. He towered over her. Her chest was flush with his abdomen, her arms around his torso.

She tilted her head back as his lips lilted over her skin, up her jaw, a breath of temptation against her earlobe. "Tell me one truth, General Moria, and I'll tell you one of mine."

Moria swallowed, her eyelids stuttering, then went to smooth her skirts. He stilled her hand and brought her hand to his lips. Her eyes rose to his.

She must have found something to trust in his eyes, as she nodded and said, "I'm not a nice person."

Devyn shook his head, but she continued.

"I've done some things that I.... that I regret. Someone hurt me, a long time ago," she pulled away and started to pace but she kept talking. "He took everything I had to give and left me to carry the weight of it all alone, and I can't hurt him back, because..." she took a deep inhale. "He's gone now. And it feels so wrong, all the conflicting feelings of love and hate and joy and disappointment that are tied up with *this*," she gestured around them, to the well-appointed but luxurious sitting room they inhabited and to the party just beyond the mahogany door. "This institution, these people...and so sometimes it's easier to *hurt*, than to be hurt."

He hadn't interrupted, just felt the serrated age of every one of her words like knives against his heart, wanting to ask for more; but unwilling to risk her pulling away again.

"You're a soldier, I suppose that's what I am too. They wanted a mercenary, someone who could be bought for a price for their own purposes, but no cost they offered was worth the price of my pride, my revenge."

"And how have you had your revenge, Lady Moria?" He asked, one hand grasping hers to pull her into him.

"By being gloriously unattainable and exacting. They wanted perfection, I gave it. They wanted courtship, I gave it. They proposed, I refused. They asked for a dance, I gave them only one and left them wanting more. They wanted conversation, I listened. I used what I learned to my advantage, whispering their secrets here and there," she exhaled, he didn't miss the way she straightened her shoulders before she continued. "They wanted my good opinion, I tested them to see what they would do to receive it. They wanted invitations to a ball. I told them it was a masquerade when it wasn't and they came dressed in costume and I had a laugh. I was never not a weapon, never anything but a vixen looking for her next victim to poison."

He saw what she was trying to do. She was taking a gamble, testing him to see if he was afraid or aghast at anything she'd said.

Worse, if he pitied the choices she'd been forced to make. But he'd been a weapon too, not just in battle. His father had honed him into one long before that. He wanted her to feel that they shared similarities more than they did differences.

"And am I...your next victim?" he said the words against the shell of her ear and when her eyelids fluttered for a moment, he was almost undone.

"That's the problem," she said, and this time her heart was in her eyes. "I thought you could be; but I'm afraid that while I've ingested small doses of poison here and there," she placed his hands at her hips, "this time, it might be a lethal dose."

"Lethal? Or addictive?"

"Aren't they the same thing?" her lips were a prayer's distance from his own. It wouldn't take more than a flinch to bring her bottom lip close enough to devour until she sighed his name and forgot it all.

She was faster, interrupting his thoughts with, "Now tell me your truth."

One hand came up to hold her jaw. He swallowed before answering. "I am leaving in a month, again, to Halalabad this time. I'm supposed to be preparing to leave, but I lie awake at night, and I hear your voice and I see your face. Even though I know I shouldn't, I still see you in front of me and all I can think of is how I can keep you this close and never let go of you."

"Even after everything I've just said?" she asked, eyes catching on his lips where he wanted them, wanted the rest of her to be.

He pushed a strand of hair that had fallen back into its pin.

"I want all that you are willing to give me, Moria." He said her name against her lips, her own brushed against his in answer. Her thieving hands stole him into her, her mouth closing in any distance between them. Her tongue slid across them and into his mouth, her leg drew over his.

He was grateful in that moment, that he hadn't kissed her that first meeting, or any since. This wasn't merely a kiss, they hadn't yet invented words for what this was. She tasted like summer days by a lake, a million little promises leaping off her tongue and finding purchase in his mouth. God, the girl knew how to snog him within an inch of his own demise, but he wanted her to know it wasn't just slowly fading lust between them.

His heart nearly outpaced his thoughts until he saw her affection for what it was. He pulled back.

"I know what you're doing. It might work but I'll keep asking for the same thing until I get it."

"Which is?" she asked, her lips feather light and so tempting against the curve of his neck, the suggestive press of her body so delicious against him that he grew painfully hard.

She was no innocent, blushing debutante. She was playing games with him when he'd asked for more of her, that was fine. But he was a soldier by trade, and an exceptional chess player, and he could play her games better.

In one swift motion, he turned her. He had her pressed against the wall, holding both of her hands in one of his above her. His groin pressed into the small of her back where it curved to her ripe little arse jutting into his breeches.

The silk of her skin and her dress against him was...*holy hell*. Her back heaved heatedly against his chest, her breasts where they pressed against the wall made his entire body envious of plaster and wallpaper. He didn't have to remove her dress to know that she had gorgeous breasts. The exposed skin made him want to see them as much as he wanted to fucking taste them.

He let the slight stubble he'd accumulated since shaving earlier scratch softly against the sensitive skin of her neck as he dragged his mouth up to her ear. His voice was a silken, seductive purr against her as he said, "Everything I want. I'm not playing to win a trophy, Moria," He licked at the tip of her earlobe and delighted in her shudder and the way she pressed her backside against him. He tightened his hold on her hands.

"Because you are no trophy. You're the game, you're the strategy, you're the victor, the game maker. You're *all* of it," he said against the shell of her ear.

She undulated against him. *Fuck.* He wanted more. He took his free hand from where it rested at her side and trailed it toward her breast, grazing his thumb over where her nipples would be hiding in that dress. He languidly dragged that hand down to her entrance. His fingers cupped her through her dress. Her little fucking whimper of pleasure scalded his self-control, and one finger circled her entrance.

The scrape of fabric against her skin and another soft moan from her were the only sounds in the room, until he pulled his hand away from where he toyed with her to add, "I'm playing for keeps."

His entire body shrieked in protest, *"you bloody asshole,"* as he pulled away from the apex of her and with a sensual drag of his hand down the backs of her arms, he released her and turned her back around to face him.

She had nothing to say, which gave him almost as much satisfaction as having her pressed against his groin. Her arms curled around his neck, and singed him with a searing, elevating kiss. Her teeth nipped at his lips, her fingers scraped through his hair.

The feel of her breasts pushed against his chest and the single undulation of her hips against his own, and his heartbeat was a single repeated syllable: more. More. More.

"Moria," he panted, tilting his head back against the wallpapered wall as she nipped at the flesh of his neck. He felt the bite everywhere. What was it about this woman that did this to him?

"You want me?" she questioned.

He took her hand and placed it against the hard evidence of his unflagging want. She cupped him so hard through his breeches he had to bite his tongue to keep from crying out. She was toying with him too.

"You have competition, Captain. And I have to go back to the country in a few days. I hope you're willing to do what it takes to 'keep' me."

And with that, the dratted woman spun on her heels and turned to leave him there panting after her in a dark room at a ball he'd come to solely for her. He was faster, he had her hand in his in a moment.

He tugged her to him, and his mouth found hers like the stars guided a sailors' course home. She kissed him back with such ferocity, with what felt like her whole body. He groaned into her mouth.

She pulled away again.

This time he let her. He wanted to ask so many more questions and learn all of her until there were no secrets left between them. For now, he had to let her have the upper hand or she'd never fold all her cards.

He pulled her close enough to straighten her dress, to shake and smooth out her skirts, to repin the fallen pieces of her hair, to retie her mask, to pull up her gloves. Every touch was bliss, every touch was misery. He savored each intake of breath or waver of her eyelids like a man headed for the gallows who might never know such contact again.

He planted a chaste kiss on her gloved hand and offered her his arm. He led her outside the darkened room into an empty hallway, where she squeezed his hand once before taking several steps and slipping into the room beyond with calculated grace.

Once, she looked back to him, a triumphant curve of a smile appearing before she turned back to the open doorway and joined arms with two women inside as though she hadn't just been compromised in her sister's library.

Chapter Ten

IF YOU WEREN'T AT THE SECOND MOST EXCLUSIVE BALL IN London last night, I'll tell you: it was not one but two ladies in a fox mask that stole all hearts on offer. Perhaps...even a Duke's?
-Scandalous Lives of London scandal sheet

WHEN MORIA REJOINED THE MASQUERADE, IT WAS CARINA in a matching fox mask, similar dress, with brown hair instead of Moria's blonde, that brought her back down to earth. The gratification of feeling Devyn's lips against her own after so long pining in secret, had almost carried her away. She'd been moments away from letting Devyn take her in her sister's library. She'd been so close to telling him about Marcus, about his tragic death that had been the loss of a dream and the start of a new one. And about the loss that came after.

She hoped her friend only saw the masks she'd used to cover over it all.

"Dear god, there's two of you." Valentine interrupted her

thoughts, placing Moria's hand through the crook of his arm. He straightened her mask and adjusted the cuff of her sleeve without a word, but she read something in his eyes. She didn't think he had seen her disappear (or reappear) with Devyn, but Valentine was observant. And apparently discreet.

"And somehow you aren't lucky enough to secure the affections of either of us," Carina parried.

It sounded so much like something Moria would have said, while looking so much like her. Why did Carina want to imitate her? Why would anyone? Was she easy to imitate, and therefore easy to replace?

"What about me? Am I lucky enough?"

Carina, on Moria's other side, turned toward the voice, pulling Moria with her.

It was some friend of Valentine's that Moria would once have been enthralled by, wanting to know his name and particulars, but now that she'd come so close to a man like Devyn, this one seemed... wanting. She'd leave him to Carina; a widow could do practically anything she pleased. And Carina seemed very pleased with the sight of this one.

Valentine's companion gestured toward the open doorway of the lavish game room Pomfrey House boasted, several heads and pairs of eyes turning when the two ladies entered.

"Billiards, ladies?"

Moria pasted on her usual smile and said, "Of course, I'm sure you're looking for a redemption round since I trounced you last time. Wouldn't count on it though."

Moria sank a ball into the pocket, surrounded by men of high status and rank. They were all looking at her like they were on a hunt, and she was the prey. Rather the reverse was true, less so now than ever as her heart was thumping over her...overtures...in another room with a man she'd shared her secrets with. She supposed he had reversed their roles by seeking her out, asking to court her, turning up at not one but two balls on the same night to seek her out in public. Even without all of those things, he was....

"Your shot," Carina interrupted her thoughts with her words and a soft nudge of her hips. Moria expended little effort sending Carina's next lover's ball into a pocket a second time.

"Marry me," one lordling with an artfully mussed head of bronze hair spoke.

Moria laughed, taking a step away to retrieve the pool chalk from Valentine. "You'd never be faithful to me, Weller."

"You're after fidelity, then?" a friend of Moria's brother Lawrence called. Moria had more than enough on her mind to worry over one of her five siblings, when he was just as capable of getting himself out of any trouble as he was getting into it.

"Of course," Moria said, absently dusting her pool stick with chalk.

"Romance, then?" This from Valentine. She noticed the raised brow and smirk he gave her. He was definitely remembering Devyn from earlier.

"I'd like to not be made a fool of," Moria made another shot that sent Valentine's askew. She noticed their eyes all drift to her cleavage when she leaned over the table for her turn.

"I'd never make a fool of you, my lady." Valentine's handsome friend parried as he attempted to recover from the sound beating she was delivering him and Valentine on the billiards table.

"No, you excel at making a fool of yourself," the dark-haired man standing next to Valentine added.

"What else, my lady?" she'd lost track of who was speaking this time. Did it matter? None of them were going to marry or ruin her anyway.

"Someone who makes me laugh."

Carina gave a little "ha" and said, "Lord Bowlby is quite a joke, my lady. And rich."

Moria made a show of grimacing in a way that was still attractive. "Too old. And I've no need for money anyway with my dowry."

"What else?" Valentine pushed, as he often did.

"Someone strong." Moria said it with a casual shoulder shrug, but she was remembering the effortless way Devyn had handled her earlier. These dandies before her didn't have the bulk or size of a warrior. It hadn't been so noticeable before, but it was hard to ignore now.

Carina raised a champagne glass Moria assumed one of the men seeking her attention must have retrieved for her. "If you find a man like that, I'd like a crack at him myself. He sounds keen."

"He have to be titled, then?" The Duke of Andover called from the doorway, hands folded over his sculpted chest. He was masked too, but not hard to identify. He was a duke, what did he have to hide?

Moria glanced at Carina's open-mouthed stare and the group of gentlemen around the billiards table that had stopped their movements. The irony of his words made Moria purse her lips and look off to the side, mock pensive.

Moria was thinking of Devyn when she said, "I suppose it depends on the title, or the man."

His Grace nodded, taking the pool stick from Valentine. Belatedly, she noticed his wavy hair was artfully mussed, and Moria saw what looked like a bruise on his neck. Given what she'd been doing with Devyn, she didn't have a right to be as curious about who had put that mark on him, who had mussed his hair.

"In that case, consider your game over, Lady Fox," His Grace said as he lined up his shot, sinking two of her balls in one pocket. When he locked eyes with Moria, her mouth went a little dry, she tightened her hold on her pool stick. She didn't like this feeling, like wishing she could stand in two places at once, not one bit.

She merely smiled at the Duke and the other men before her.

"It's over when I say it's over, Your Grace," she said, making another successful shot. When she looked up, Valentine gave her a knowing wink.

Chapter Eleven

The Burn Book of Lady M

His Grace, The Duke of Andover, George Worthington: I would never be so bold as to record scurrilous sentiments about a man of such elevated station, if I only could think of such sentiments to write regarding his character.

"For once, the flowers arriving on our doorstep are for someone other than you," Moria's brother Lawrence chided. Turning to their younger sister Olivia, Lawrence added, "Moria is living proof that the more people are afraid of you, the more flowers you get."

Moria stifled the urge to kick him in the shins underneath the breakfast table. Ladies did not resort to such behavior. "Don't you have somewhere else to sleep now?"

"Lawrence, stop baiting our sister," Jasper called from behind his newspaper. "Moria's maneuvers at last night's inaugural ball, it seems, especially Olivia's dancing with an eligible Duke, have been successful. I don't even recall seeing you in attendance," Jasper lowered his newspaper to eye their brother skeptically. Moria preened, smug at the praise, at Jasper sticking up for her. Lawrence let out a huff and rolled his eyes, and when he left the table, tugged on the end of Moria's braid.

Slamming her teacup hastily into its saucer, Moria chased after her brother, like they were still in short clothes. She nearly tripped over one of her nephew's toys in the hall, but when she rounded the corner, the sight before her made Moria stop short, clutching her chest to catch her breath.

The London Pembrooke drawing room, foyer, and dining room looked like the contents of London's florists had been ignominiously deposited. Flowers of every shade and variety addressed to both Lady Moria, and on the card Lawrence handed her, her newly debuted and equally lovely younger sister, Lady Olivia.

Olivia entered the sitting room behind her, holding a calico kitten. The butler and housekeeper had already started sorting through the flowers and cards, but Moria wanted to know if any were from Devyn. He'd sent them before, it had given her a reason to return them, to prolong their...whatever they were. Now he was back from Belgium and happening upon her at a ball for the first time, declaring his intent, and she had to, in the light of day, plan her next move.

She felt Olivia's hand at her elbow. "Moria," she said, handing her a card, "these are from the Duke. He sent flowers to both of us, but I thought you should read this card."

"I heard that you have an affinity for orchids. But you, my lady, are no hothouse flower. I've arranged a selection for you from my mother and sister's terrace garden. They persist without constant sunlight and through repeated downpours. A much better arrangement for a lady of all seasons.

George Worthington, Duke of Andover

～

WHEN THE DUKE CAME TO CALL AN HOUR LATER, SHE WAS still thinking of the thoughtfulness behind the flowers. She sat nervously anticipating him bringing up the Captain, or even Drysdale, readying a plausibly evasive response in her head.

But he didn't. He only asked after her dancing injury. Told her he admired her taking pity on Miss Herring. She wasn't sure what to make of that. Perhaps it said something of her relationship or potential for one with the duke that she had known him for nearly 14 months and still found him hard to read. She asked after his family, expecting a cursory answer.

"May I speak plainly?"

Moria had been wanting him to do so for the 14 months she'd known the man. "I adore speaking plainly," she said, taking a bite of the biscuit on her plate and keeping her eyes on him.

Miss Kelley cleared her throat from her seat to Moria's left.

"I am not sure that you have had the pleasure of meeting the dowager duchess yet, but she is rather keen for me to marry," he said, fidgeting with his hands. *That wasn't exactly speaking plainly.*

"I can't imagine why. The longer you are on the market, the longer she curries favors from eager families wanting your..." she looked down at his fingers, "hand."

"You make me sound like some maidenly debutante."

"Are our positions all that different?"

This garnered a smile from him, and good god, how did he go anywhere with teeth so blindingly white? He was dazzling. Wasn't he?

"I concede your point," he said.

"Can't imagine a duke utters those words often. I'll make a note of the date and commit it to memory."

He laughed. It wasn't the kind of laugh that incited riots of longing or affection, but she could grow to find it one if she were a patient woman. Wasn't she?

"I daresay a woman of your conversational powers, with your heart for charity, could make an even better duchess than the dowager."

"A conceding of the point, a compliment, and flowers on the same day. Why, your grace, if I were a sentimental woman, I might think you were declaring some intent."

"My intent," he leaned forward, the napkin resting on his thigh for his teacup and saucer fell between them.

"Allow me, Your Grace." Moria made a great show of leaning to pick up the linen, replacing it on his thigh where her hands shouldn't go even if it was the briefest and most testing of touches. His eyes fell to her breasts, then he cleared his throat and met her eyes. His green eyes held her for just a breath, she felt warmer than she had a moment before.

"My intent, now that my campaign in Parliament has been successful, is to find a wife this season."

"A wife."

"Not just a wife. An impressive match. Someone who proves those who judged me for my mother's heritage, to be wrong. Someone worth making mine."

Another man's words entered her mind at the very same time:

This challenge sounds even more improbable by the moment, and I fear I've already lost.

WITH THE DUKE HAVING DECLARED HIS LOOMING INTENT and made his goodbyes, Moria was left in the drawing room with only her embroidery hoop and her flowers for company.

But as is the way of large families and sought-after debutantes, this was short-lived.

"Sister," Jasper entered, followed by a familiar young man. "You have a visitor. Were you expecting the reverend?"

Moria looked around him, her friend Llewyn Fortney gave her a conspiratorial smile from his vantage point across the room.

"The vicar has come to inquire about my salvation," she said, taking his proffered flowers, noting the unusual inclusion of Jasmine that almost made her eyes go cloudy. "Flirtatious and vacuous debutantes such as myself require extensive effort to convert from our path of destruction."

"Godspeed," Jasper said to the man in his sitting room, and exited, twin hounds at his heels.

Moria crossed the room, placing the flowers in a vase over the mantle. "Is it just me, or are your eyes bluer than the last time I saw you?"

Brookevale's fledgling vicar, a gentle, tender friend who had kept her secrets and sat vigil with all of them, Llewyn Fortney shook his head at her.

"And this beard of yours..." she narrowed her eyes. "Llewyn, you must be beating off the young women of Brookevale with your Bible."

The man tilted his head back and laughed. "I've missed you, you madwoman."

She swatted at his arm playfully. "Don't go getting sentimental on me, vicar."

She took a seat at the tea table and he followed suit. He motioned at the flowers in the sitting room that seemed to be multiplying. "It's like Vauxhall Gardens in here."

Moria refrained from asking what a country vicar knew about the infamous pleasure gardens and looked from him to the dozens of artfully arranged flowers, some large arrays of roses, some more exotic flowers, as the men of the ton had heard that she had a penchant for the more unique assortments.

"Oh yes, that," she shrugged. "It's just a normal Wednesday around here."

Llewyn looked at her with knowing eyes. "I remember your partiality to Wednesdays."

~

AND SUDDENLY MORIA WAS FALLING THROUGH TIME, INTO a sea of remembrances to one blustery day two winters past. Lady Moria had been nearly insensible with fever. In her delirium, she'd felt the calendar mocking her and her aversion to Tuesdays, as the worst events of her life had all happened on a Tuesday. Her father shipping off for what was supposed to be a mere nine months, the night that Marcus had died, the night she'd woken with her sheets slick with her own blood. But Wednesday? Wednesday appeared like a changing of the guard, unaware of what Tuesday had brought.

When she woke to see the date on the calendar, her heart rate had accelerated until she clutched her chest for air. She usually brought flowers to the mausoleum behind the parish church, not just for Marcus, but for the life they'd created and lost, for the life they'd never even started. It seemed such an inane and small thing to still consume her when her mother was also ill abed, but there it was.

Somehow, flowers were already waiting there at the mausoleum for the boy she'd loved, the child she'd lost.

She let out a small gasp that sounded more like a sob when she saw it. The small posy in her hand that she'd dug from the dregs of the garden paled in comparison to this display. It was vibrant and stark against the snow-covered ground, standing out just as Marcus always had. Tears burned at her eyelids, she wiped at them with her kid glove, kneeling next to the towering piece of marble. She grit her teeth as her knees hit the ground, the bitter snow cold against her limbs even through her many layers.

Lady Moria looked around to see who might have seen her before closing her eyes as more tears scorched a path down her icy cheeks.

"My lady, I hope you don't mind my placing the flowers in your stead." It was a masculine voice behind her, but it was gentle.

Lady Moria turned to see the young vicar, uncomfortably rubbing the back of his neck. She recalled the Sunday morning when her younger sisters had seen this man for the first time and how silly she'd told them they were for gawking. They didn't feel so silly to her now. He was tall and wiry, with blonde hair and the kind of eyes that you just knew held a deep soul within.

Of all the men Moria would come to know, Llewyn had the kindest eyes.

She wiped her own eyes awkwardly. "Thank you," she breathed. "But how did you...?"

"I saw you here before, my lady. Then I kept seeing fresh flowers left here. I'm something of a botanist myself, but I was impressed. Jasmine in winter? I figured it would be the charitable thing to do to leave something in your stead while you were...missing for a few days." He paused for her reaction, there was no censure or judgment in his words, or in his tone.

As Moria was still trying to control her tears, he kept talking.

"I paid a call to your mother while you were ill. I looked in on you as well, but you were resting." He offered her his hand to assist her with rising to her feet, she took it gratefully.

"It seems you have a habit of coming to my aid, then," Lady Moria said as she smacked her hands together to shake off the snow on her gloves. She wiped the remaining snow from her dress and smoothed her hair where her cloak had mussed it.

Lady Moria had always been beautiful, that had never been a secret. When Llewyn Fortney looked at her, she felt that he saw more than just a pretty face. He saw *her*. Grieving and half healed and somewhat lost, but not broken.

He swallowed uncomfortably, looking away. "Yes, well. That is rather the calling of a man of God, my lady. And also, to tell you, that pain may last for the night, but joy comes in the morning."

She leaned, picking a spare tendril of Jasmine from the posy at her former lover's grave, and placed it in the buttonhole of the Vicar's thick wool jacket. When he offered to show her the hothouse next to the church where he grew his flowers before walking her home, she felt that she had been given a rare gift: a true friend.

A CLOCK TOLLED IN THE STUDY. MORIA SHOOK HER HEAD to clear it of her reverie. She took a seat across from the vicar in her London drawing room. He'd aged some since, new laugh lines adorned his face, stubble coated his jaw, and he seemed more comfortable in his role. But the gentle demeanor of a fledgling vicar who placed flowers on a young man's grave for a girl who mourned in secret, remained.

"London feels too...tarnished and worldly for a saint like you." She offered him her best smile.

"Don't know where you get such notions of my sainthood, Lady Moria."

"That is the only explanation for your being such a long-suffering friend of someone like me."

"Long-suffering," he scoffed. "That's more the word I'd use for whatever poor fellow finds himself saddled with you for a wife."

Moria sighed, deflecting. "Why does everyone keep talking of my marriage? Perhaps I'm too interesting for matrimony."

Llewyn laughed again, a sound that was all him, light and ebullient. "Nice try; but you sent me a missive that you had a matter you needed to discuss, and here I am, my lady, all ears."

Llewyn took the cup of tea she offered him, prepared with two sugars as he preferred. The butler entered, announcing a visitor who was close on his heels and entered the room in a huff. "I tried to tell her you were entertaining company, my lady."

Llewyn stood at the sight of the woman who entered, ever the gentleman. Was Moria imagining it or was Llewyn studying Letitia's upswept dark hair, the chocolate shades of her eyes, the heart shape of her bronze face as though he found something to admire?

Moria went over to the young woman, kissing her on both cheeks. "Letitia? Is everything alright?"

The Vicar looked between the two women expectantly, so Moria made introductions.

"Reverend Llewyn Fortney, this is my friend, as well as my brother-in-law Viscount Ludlowe's private secretary, Miss Letitia Blackshear."

Moria thought that Llewyn took a little longer than propriety allowed bowing over her friend's hand. Maybe Lllewyn would be impressed by her story, or her beauty; he seemed to find ladies in distress an array of some expertise.

Moria motioned for her friends to sit, picking up her teacup and saucer as Letitia poured her own cup.

"It was your missive that brought me here, my lady. I received a note that you had a matter that required urgent attention."

Moria choked on her tea.

"Is that so?" Llewyn asked her, but looking at Moria. Moria saw how this looked, but she wasn't the one who had sent either of them missives. Before she could reply, Letitia produced the note from the ample bosom of her topaz gown, a blush spreading up Llewyn's neck and seeping over his cheeks as he averted his gaze.

Moria glanced down at the note. She knew that handwriting. *Her companion.*

"It is to be a confessional then," she said with a resigned sigh.

Llewyn sat back in his chair, his arms folded at his chest, waiting.

Letitia piled a plate with teatime treats. "Start talking, lass."

Moria cleared her throat, fussing with her skirts. "There's a man."

Llewyn and Letitia looked at each other, then both burst into laughter.

"You've been seen with many a man, and with a face like yours I would do a lot worse," Letitia said, her south bank manners taking over.

And then in a rush, Moria gave them an abridged version of her history with Captain Devyn Winter, and his presence at not one but two balls the night before. She conveniently left out the interlude in the sitting room with a man of God present. Still, it felt like she'd been holding in one long breath for over a year and had finally exhaled letting her friends in on her secret courtship.

"If he wants to court you, and you're enamored with him enough that he hasn't been on the receiving end of your unparalleled cold shoulder," Letitia inquired, "What do you need the two of us here for?" she motioned between herself and the Vicar.

Moria toyed with the wrapper on a sweet she held in her lap. "A soldier's wife isn't exactly the...position in life that I had sought after. Marcus was a-"

"A prig. A toff. A jackass. In every sense of the word. Yes, we *know*." Llewyn said, nodding.

"Why is it that when I use language like that, I get a chastising like "'*Be careful, my lady, God hears all. He is in the very air around us*'," she had committed to her bit, assuming a dignified air. "But it's excusable for you?"

"That's different," he shrugged. "I've devoted my life to His calling, I have a little more shall we say...*cache*...with the creator than a heartbreaking debutante."

Moria let out a laugh that pulled one out of Llewyn as well.

"I think this time it's your heart on the line, though, right, my lady?" Letitia asked, bringing them back to the topic.

Letitia took Moria's silence for an answer and reached for her hand. "Then we shall have to arrange a meeting with the rest of your siblings first, and one that will seem like the stars have aligned to bring a Captain and the diamond of the season together in the least salacious tableau. Perhaps back at Brookevale when you return for the christening?" she questioned, looking to Llewyn.

"That could work," he said, nodding. "And the seclusion of the country would offer the two of you time to better understand one another apart from," he gestured to the drawing room and its protrusion of blooms and calling cards, "all this."

Before Moria could answer or puzzle on it further, the butler entered again. This time, he escorted two young ladies both wearing startlingly pink frocks.

"Lady Gretchen von Mien, and Miss Carina Smythe."

Llewyn stood with her to greet them, but Moria did notice that he didn't linger on the sight of them the way he did with Letitia. Moria made the introductions, Letitia doing her best to hide her amusement with a shared glance of camaraderie with Llewyn that Moria would definitely be bringing up later when they were alone.

Lady Gretchen greeted Moria with an air kiss at each cheek. "We waited for you at Lady Sinclair's luncheon for nearly an hour before we gave up and came here to tell you ourselves what we witnessed."

Carina took a seat at the tea table. "Your new little friend from Africa was all too happy to keep the Duke company in your absence, I'm afraid."

Moria raised a brow, but Lady Gretchen pulled back to give Moria a glance over. "And what on earth are you wearing? Yellow? You know it's Wednesday, correct?"

Before Moria could return to the subject of the Duke and Miss Herring, Letitia leaned her head in her hand where her arm was resting on the linen covered tea table and asked, "What's Wednesday?"

The inhabitants of her drawing room from all quadrants of her life were all looking at her awaiting her answer on the significance of

Wednesday's and this wasn't how or who or when or where she explained that particular credo aloud for the very first time.

Then who?

Soft, dark eyes, and lips that spread into a bracing smile flashed in her mind.

I want all that you are willing to give me, Moria.

Moria pasted on a smile, trying to make it look genuine. "On Wednesday's," she said, looking to Lady Gretchen and Carina. "We wear pink."

Across from her, Llewyn caught her eye, a spark of curiosity in them even though he kept quiet.

"That's it, then? Just the pink-" Letitia cut in.

"And we promenade! But it's always in pink," Carina supplied.

"And our dear Moria is in this washed-out shade of yellow," Lady Gretchen added.

Llewyn's countenance was soft and understanding, like he could see through Moria. He looked to the jasmine on the mantelpiece and then back to his hands folded in his lap.

"Is the priest here to deliver your last rites or something?" Lady Gretchen said, looking at Llewyn suspiciously, but addressing Moria.

"Wouldn't mind that being the last face I see," Carina said in a conspiratorial whisper linking an arm with Moria's.

Moria sniffed a laugh. "Reverend, I'm afraid you'll have to forgive my friends."

"There's nothing to forgive, my lady," he replied, but Moria could see the apples of his cheeks starting to redden as he brought a teacup to his lips.

"I'm sure the Lord requires Lady Moria's supplication on other fronts, perhaps," Letitia said, with an obsequious smile that Moria knew meant she had some explaining to do later.

"That is one of my favorite subjects to discuss: the grace of our Lord for every sinner, regardless of origin or sex," as the Vicar sipped his tea, Moria could see the edges of Letitia's fine-boned face soften like that had been exactly what she needed to hear.

"He'd be the only *Lord* who did, it isn't a common experience for a woman to be on the receiving end of any grace at all," it was Lady Gretchen, surprisingly, who made such a profound pronouncement. When Moria looked at her, she saw another layer to a friend she might have misjudged as somewhat shallow.

"Hear, hear," said Letitia, holding her teacup in mock salute in a moment of unlikely camaraderie.

"'She is clothed with strength and dignity, and she laughs without fear of the future.' Proverbs 31: 25. That's God's blessing for women who count him as a friend," Llewyn offered, looking at each of the women at the table.

"Why, you've almost described our dear Lady Moria perfectly," Carina said, placing an arm on Moria's shoulder.

Moria sucked in a breath. "That's very kind of you, Carina. It wasn't always the case, I assure you."

"Regardless of our pasts," Llewyn said, holding Moria's eyes. "We needn't fear what's ahead."

Chapter Twelve

~

"You came."

Devyn had almost expected she wouldn't show. It had been her invitation, the first contact with her since the ball a few evenings prior: a torn piece of paper slipped into his hand by her lady's maid as he'd left his brother's house.

But now she looked good enough to devour in a purple dress and he was glad that he'd rearranged his schedule at her behest. He counted himself among a number of men who weren't quite sure what they wouldn't do for her, but somehow he was the one she'd crossed a full ballroom to get to and trusted with her carefully guarded secrets.

"I invited you," she replied.

There was a biting edge to her voice. Icy blue flecks and golden embers floating in her eyes contrasted with the delectable sweetness of her curves poured into that purple dress. He liked her in purple. Wasn't purple the color of queens?

The taut set of her shoulders and the tilt of her jaw made him want to take her into his arms and show her all the ways he could melt away the ice in her veins.

He took her hand and led her into the meeting room. There were trays of food spread before them on a table, a fire in the hearth. He took in her hooded cloak, the fact that she was unaccompanied. He could hear the proprietary voice of his father, a general, inside his head telling him he was a damn fool and a reckless one at that.

"You came without a chaperone," he said, trailing a finger down one arm of her cloak.

She gave a small laugh that almost made him forget his own name. "I'm good at diversion."

He was well versed in that fact. Every thought he'd had since meeting her outside a coaching inn had been diverted in her direction. "You don't have to be."

Moria sat on the settee, he sat next to her. He took her hand and placed small kisses on the back of her hand. Her eyes tipped up to his in challenge. "So, you're in the market for a wife then?"

She was bold, direct. It was one thing he found attractive about her. One of the many things.

He tightened his hold on her hand, looking into her eyes in challenge. "I'm in the market for *you*."

She placed one hand on the side of his face. "And after the month is up? You'll go to Jalalabad? There's no seducing you into staying in England?"

There was a teasing note to her voice, but he saw the sincerity in her eyes. He owed her the truth.

He kissed her hand, then placed it in his hair. He scattered more kisses on her jaw, trailing down her neck. "You have fought your battles to get to where you are, my lady, I've fought mine. And just like you, I have my pride," he inhaled the sugar scent of her skin, willing to tell her anything so long as she kept curling her fingers in the hair at his nape. "Giving up my leadership of my men, even for a perfect woman, doesn't feel like the honorable course."

He met her eyes. "I'll share the plans I called you here to discuss. But first, I'd prefer it if you kiss me while you still have the chance, soldier."

His lips took over, crashing into hers, drinking in her little whimper of surprise when his tongue circled hers. Her hands ran down his shoulders. He could feel every inch of her that pressed against him. The heated rise and fall of her chest against his had her pulling back.

"It's this blasted corset, it's too hot in here."

He spun her around. Slowly, he peeled off the delicately embroidered gloves and each sleeve of her bodice and set them gently on a table. She was just in the 14 other remaining layers of clothes she'd put on today.

"This is absurd. Were these clothes designed to make women suffer?" he said, pulling back her chemise so that he could unlace the strings of her corset.

"If they'd been designed by men, perhaps."

"No, there'd be a lot less of them in that case, my lady."

When he untied them and placed a finger in the panel to release some of the tension, she sucked in a large breath and leaned her back against his front, her hand still at her abdomen. She hadn't need of a corset so blasted tight, his hands already fit around her waist. She was perfect, just like this, with her hips, even in her skirts, jutting into his manhood. He bit down a groan. He needed his hands on her.

He spun her to face him. "Better?"

She nodded, her eyes never leaving his face. His hands tightened on her hips, his mouth drew swirls and licks against her breast until she sighed audibly. That sound embedded itself underneath his skin. She arched underneath his touch.

He was startled back to alertness by the rattle of the locked door handle. There were always interruptions with her, always intrusions and demands on her time. But if it were like this just being with her for a few minutes, what must it be like for her?

Her eyes darted to his. "What do we do?"

There was the sound of voices on the other side of the door, Moria must have recognized them because she muttered, "Drysdale."

"You know him?" His jaw and fists fought the urge to clench in jealousy.

She winced. "We were almost engaged a couple of times. He's not a threat."

As Devyn held his tongue over her nipple, and the back of her corset in his hand, he arched a brow at her. A low growl escaped before he could rein it in. "*Moria.*"

"My dress requires...resettling...I'll hide in that adjacent chamber over there and you buy us time. Just make conversation about...military strategy," she instructed.

Before he could protest, she'd disappeared, and he was left with a young dandy in the now open doorway.

"Oh, hello, there." The man Moria had called Drysdale said as he entered. He was a blond-haired fop in finely fitted tailoring. Devyn couldn't help noticing the farcical contrast between himself and the other man.

Devyn gave him a noncommittal nod as he looked up from his papers he'd had the sense to remove from his bag in the nick of time. The toff looked at him askance, then tried to peek at the papers Devyn was reading.

"Sorry to be a bother...only...I'm damn curious why the door was locked."

Devyn arched a brow. "Important military documents," he said, holding up the parchment in his hand. He felt like an idiot as the other man eyed him skeptically. His eyes settled on an intricately embroidered glove beneath a seat cushion, then turned to Devyn.

"Moria Pembrooke, I know you're here," the other man said, leaning back in his chair and folding his arms. He was the picture of smug arrogance. Not *Lady* Moria Pembrooke, just *Moria*. He'd known her by her glove? Had she been here before, with him? Hate was too watered down a word for how Devyn felt about it.

Moria appeared from an antechamber somehow immaculately dressed and coiffured. Drysdale smiled and kicked a leg up on his other knee like he'd won some sort of contest.

"Lovely to see you, darling," he said, taking in her appearance, his eyes falling on the lack of a glove on one arm before taking a sip of his drink. Devyn wondered if he could simply knock the toff out cold and shove him in the antechamber and leave with Moria.

Her voice was like honeyed steel. "I hear felicitations are in order on your impending nuptials. Glad you wasted no time with Miss Wimbley."

Drysdale inclined his head and raised his glass at her. "I'm just glad I've finally found the right woman to tolerate me. Although," he paused to sip from his crystal tumbler, "I can see why you never did, Moria. This man is ghastly hard to look at without feeling inferior."

"Isn't he just?" Moria added, then turned to Devyn, whose cheeks were surely pink. "I'm sorry have we met?"

Drysdale chuckled. "Don't you *dare* try that one on me. I saw your glove beneath a cushion." He grabbed said glove and handed it to her.

Moria closed her eyes and grimaced. "You're an ass, Drysdale. Anyone ever tell you that?"

Drysdale ignored her jab and turned to Devyn with an outstretched hand. "Caleb Howley, Earl of Drysdale, I don't believe I've made your acquaintance."

"Captain Devyn Winter, Her Majesty's Army." Devyn shook the

other man's hand harder than he likely ought, the other man retrieved his hand, shaking it as though in pain.

"Message received, Captain. I never saw either of you here." He looked to Moria. "Not that I'd ever be a snitch."

"I rescind my previous statement; you're not entirely an ass, my lord," she said, with a winning smile.

"I won't take offense. I'm sure you're acquainted with my finer qualities."

Moria shook her head at Devyn in caution. Was his ire was written on his face? He'd been told in the past that his nose was too large, his eyes were too black, and his body was too large to be anything but a brute. He'd only be proving everyone right if he gave into a violent impulse right now.

"Is that any way to speak to a lady, sir?"

Moria's eyes widened in alarm as Drysdale spoke. "Oh, unclench your fits, Captain, it was only a jest. Lady Moria has made far more colorful jokes at others' expense in the past."

While he didn't doubt that was true, Devyn didn't back down. He let his full stature tower over the other man.

"Devyn," Moria whispered, her bare fingers warm and soft against his arm. An entire language passed between them when he looked into her eyes.

"I'll play chaperone and help you two evacuate the club without being seen."

Devyn looked at him, brows raised, fists still clenched.

"Your fists are the size of cannons, I know better than to cross a man of your size," the Earl bowed over Moria's hand briefly before letting it go. "He'd level a peer of the realm for you without batting an eye. You are worth fighting for, dear girl. Just because I was never willing to, doesn't mean you don't deserve it."

Moria's eyes went a bit cloudy at that, but she wasn't looking at her former beau, but her current one. Made Devyn feel like less of a chump and more of one at the same time.

"That was...oddly touching, my lord."

"I don't know what came over me. Please let's never speak of it again."

Moria chuckled. "If you're still willing to help, I'll agree to that."

"Did you...have an escape plan when you snuck in here?"

Devyn said, "Servant's entrance," at the same time Moria held up her reticule and said, "Spider."

The Earl of Drysdale shook his head. "I should have guessed one of your sister's animals would factor into this."

Chapter Thirteen

THE BURN BOOK OF LADY M

The Dowager Marchioness of Thorne: With Marcus gone, there was no one to corroborate the growing secret he left behind, that it wasn't some trick designed to trap him. One day, Your Grace, you will answer for the way you shamed and blamed a young girl for falling victim to the monster you created.

⌒

WHEN THEY MADE IT INSIDE DEVYN'S FOYER, DEVYN kissed her like a dying man seeing the shore after months at sea. They were kisses Moria wished she'd saved just for this man. But then again, it took a counterfeit to help a person to spot the real thing.

When she looked back now, she saw the differences. Pity she hadn't seen them before the differences had ruined her. But ruination wasn't her greatest offense or highest pain. Only two mothers, hers and Marcus', had known about that, and her mother had taken the secret to the grave.

Moria could still picture the burning bronze of her mother's determined eyes, every time she was asked of her time, her good opinion, her company, her hand, in the years hence.

But now, when the Captain took her coat and hat, a worn callous on his thumb brushed over her skin, and her insides clenched at the subtle but heated contact. There wasn't a tawdriness or a secret possessiveness in that touch, but an open affection. He'd waited for her. He had all but begged to love her in public, and she'd been the one holding back. Until now.

She brushed her fingers over his arm. He led her in the direction of the dining room and let her enter first.

"Och! You're home early, Winter! I'll grab a plate for ye, then." Called a shirtless figure from the kitchen with his back turned. She recognized the same brogue and red hair from the man at the inn, he'd also been at the ball.

Devyn called back, "Grab two, and put on a shirt, you brute."

When the other man turned around, he almost dropped the serving spoon he was holding.

"Ye might 'ave given a mate some warnin'" he said, and if a man as tall and broad as he could blush, Moria was sure he came as close as he possibly could.

He handed Devyn what looked to be a crocheted potholder and excused himself.

Within a few moments, Moria was party to the weirdest and most enjoyable meal of her life.

She was seated at a scarred table in the most comfortable chair, across from a man who looked at her like he was contemplating making her his next course, and his roommate who had a filthy mouth and a quick sense of humor, eating the most delicious and comforting fare. Devyn's company was something quickly becoming more familiar and earnest than she wanted to admit and she didn't want to leave.

When he stood from the table and took her hand, his friend said,

"As your chaperone, I'd prefer the two of you stay to the common rooms," in his most serious of tones.

Devyn shot him a look. And then Calum's boots retreated from the room while she was still standing, staring at Devyn. He gestured toward a divan for her to sit, but she couldn't move. The breadth of his shoulders and his height made a perfectly adequate-sized sitting room feel smaller. She swallowed a lump in her throat. She needed something to do with her hands, they wanted to touch him so desperately. Or was it simply that he had the kind of body, like some kind of lovingly hewn sculpture, that demanded appraisal and appreciation?

When she didn't take his invitation to sit, he stepped closer. Calloused fingers brushed her own. They felt so small in his grasp.

"Come here," he said, taking her hand, leading her to a wooden bench in front of a pianoforte in a corner. He sat down, pulled her beside him. She liked being the one who told others what to do, where to go, where to sit, what to wear, but she found that following him and letting him lead didn't cost her anything, and gave her reassurance in return.

The bench groaned under his weight, he had to place one leg off the edge to make room for her. He was so close, she felt the scrape of his clothes and his body everywhere. A solid shoulder was close enough that she could lean her head on it. He had the kind of strength she could lean into, and he'd hold her upright.

But he was taking a small pair of glasses from a shirt pocket, unfolding them, wiping them on his shirt, and placing them on his face. A piece of music appeared in front of them.

He turned to look at her when a small laugh flew out of her.

"Is there...something wrong?" he asked, lips twitching, one brow elevated.

"A man as large and lovely as you...in a pair of spectacles. How do you continue to get more adorable? And how am I supposed to sit here and fumble through the notes with you so close?"

There was only affection in his laugh, so much affection, his laugh felt like a caress. If his affection was in his laugh, hers must surely be in her eyes.

"God, woman, the things you say," he said, punctuated with a capable hand wrapped around her jaw.

"And if I said that I'd like you to come to the country to meet my family?"

A finger caressed the soft skin of her cheek. "I think you already know the answer to that."

She raised her brows, she needed to hear him say it, she couldn't handle subtleties and half answers, not after Marcus.

"Your vicar friend visited me yesterday. We've worked out a plan."

For a moment, Moria didn't have words for what this answer did to her, she just kissed the palm of his hand. "I look forward to you getting to know the ones that make me who I am, in the place where I am most my genuine self, rather than a...facade, a rehearsed performance of what I'm expected to be."

"No more solo performances, not with me," he shook his head and Moria felt like she was tumbling, floating suspended in the celestial pull of those eyes of his.

"Do you know this song?" he gestured with his head in the direction of the sheet music on the piano. She had memorized a repertoire of songs to perform in company, to impress the other sex, they all evaporated from her head the moment his thumb skated over her bottom lip. There was silence, but no need to fill it.

Finally, he spoke. "I'll play the right hand, you can play the left."

Moria's mouth fell open. "How did you know I was left-handed?"

"I'm a trained observer, remember?" the words came so close to her mouth, her eyelids flitted closed, a tear escaped. He brushed it away, kissing the corners of her eyes. A soft tendril of his hair had fallen in his eyes and brushed against her skin.

It was all too much. He was too much, she worried she wasn't enough. She had never been.

"How long have you played the piano?" she asked, tilting her head to one side to look up at him. She wanted more of him, the inner workings of a man as solid as an oak tree, as gentle as the wind in its branches.

"Since I was about seven. My brother, Peregrine, was taking lessons and I wanted to be just like him. My mother thought that I was too large and jittery to sit at the piano with the discipline Peregrine did; so naturally, I took to it and worked hard to play the same songs my older brother was learning just to spite her."

Moria let the laugh bubble out of her, unrestrained and unladylike. "I started for a very similar reason."

"Something about older brothers, they're quite smug, aren't they?"

"Jasper was once..." she looked away pensively. "But then we lost our parents within six months of each other, he had so much responsibility on his shoulders at the age of twenty-seven. He's carried the weight of an entire family, siblings who needed him as more parent than brother, an estate needing his care, and he's done it with grace."

She looked down at her hands fidgeting in her lap. Devyn brushed a stray curl from her face and held her hands to stop them from pulling at a hangnail.

"But there are things he can't let go of. For example, there's no piano at our house here in London. I'm not even sure what happened to it, it's just.... gone. I think it had something to do with the musicales and my mother always playing for guests. She was a great proficient. And now that remaining connection to her, it's missing."

He tipped up her chin with his thumb and forefinger, so her eyes were level with his. "I get wanting to hold on to things that bring us comfort or connection, I feel the same about my own mother even though her passing was so long ago. My father was a hard man for the loss of her. So, trust me, you don't need that piano to keep her close. She didn't leave you," he shook his head. "How could she? Look at you. Who could let something like death keep them away from a face like yours?"

How did he do it? Peer into her soul like the clearest window and pull out the words she needed to hear? Moria didn't say anything, she just ran her fingers over the keys, her left-hand caressing middle C, an old friend.

"On my count," he spoke. She nodded. He knew music would distract from anything she felt. Maybe he knew because he'd done the same.

The numbers rattled off, and his fingers were moving. She followed, playing the lower keys. There were times he leaned an arm around her to reach the keys, to have an excuse to touch her. His legs tensed and brushed hers as he played the pedals. The sound of an A minor quintet filled the room, only a few notes missed or false.

No one had ever played with her, no one had ever offered, and no one had ever tried to keep up. They admired her and lauded her performance, but that's what it had always been, and she had always been alone. Felt sad now that she thought about it, but the music didn't let her stay there. When the notes carried her higher, she felt pulled along with them, when the notes were lower, she didn't fall with them. When the music sped up, it only matched the rhythm of her heartbeat, the rhythm of two bodies creating the music of one.

And when the final chord was played, they crashed into each other.

Chapter Fourteen

DEVYN FELT THE SCRAPE OF HER FINGERNAILS DIGGING into his shoulders as she kissed him, in his whole body. Her mouth collided with his and her tongue scraped the back of his teeth. He let out a hiss, leaning closer to her onslaught.

One hand gripped her small waist, fingers clasping to hold onto her. The other traced down her decolletage to the strap at her shoulder. He pulled it down gently, his mouth following the exposed skin down to her breast. Her skin was so gloriously soft and glowing under the glow of a candle on the piano. He felt her head tip back at the contact.

His tongue brushed a circle around her nipple, and the fucking whimper that came from her throat made him swear.

"Don't forget the other one," she demanded.

"Yes of course, my lady," he murmured, moving his mouth to the other nipple in a slow stripe.

"You're teasing me. Take them in your mouth. And be quick about it."

She needed to be taught a lesson, his lady. His fingers in her coiffure tilted the back of her head so that he could speak his next words into her eyes.

"You don't set the pace, my lady. I do. And I want to take my time," he palmed one of her breasts tightly in his grasp, and she let out a gasp. "I didn't imagine you could have tits this perfect and expect me not to give them the attention they deserve."

He felt her pulling him up her body, her arms caging him closer, her legs wrapping around him. Her mouth wrapping around his and stealing his air. He didn't need air, he could sustain himself on drinking the sighs and sounds she made. The tight space between her legs notched with his arousal, he felt his erection pulse against her.

"You want me?" she pulled back from his kiss to ask.

Why did she need to ask? He'd spent his concentrated efforts making sure she knew it and could feel the level of his want.

"I'm going mad with wanting you," he breathed.

The exquisite contact of her hand snaking beneath his shirt pulled a groan from him. He arced into her touch, her hand traveling the taut planes of his torso, her body writhing against his own.

He swore. He leaned to take one of her breasts into his mouth. The attention his mouth gave to her breast and nipple in a rhythm with the strokes she gave him through his breeches. Her tight fingers making him sigh around the orb in his mouth. He could feel her spasm around him as he worked her other breast, his teeth lightly grazing over the bud like some sort of wild berry.

He was the instrument of her unmooring. Oh, but she was his too. Working him so artfully and deftly he could feel how close he was to release. And then there was the sight of her. Her pupils blown wide, her back arched, her bottom lip between her teeth. She'd given up part of her power over to him, but he'd given up all of his.

But slowly, he found it again. He licked his way up her neck and pulled her mouth into his possession. While she was distracted, he pulled up her bodice, tightened the strap on her shoulder, and brought her hand to his hair.

She pulled back to look at him. "I told you, Moria. I want you, but not like this."

"You are…a terrible tease." She gave the thick tendrils of his dark hair and affectionate tug he felt echo through his whole body, but mostly his cock.

"Me?" he laughed, pointing a finger at his chest. "Your hand was…"

"Occupied with something quite large and hard?"

He kissed her, his laugh echoing into her mouth, small, staccato kisses punctuated by roaming hands and sighs.

"When I make you come," he said, grasping her face to whisper the words into her ear. "You will come with my ring on your finger."

She pulled back to look at him, the words he wanted that she couldn't say, wouldn't say, reflected in her eyes. There was an awe in the way she looked at him, in her fingers trailing over the lines and planes of his face.

"We shall see about that, won't we?"

Devyn leaned to kiss the small, feminine hand at his jaw. "It's a promise."

When Devyn walked her home, all he could think about was how necessary she had become while there were six blocks and a whole world between them.

Chapter Fifteen

THE MOST SURPRISING BETROTHAL THIS SEASON: A HASTY love match between the Earl of D and a mousy, flutist spinster. Maggie? Maisie? Assuredly, the widows and opera singers are mourning their loss.

- Scandalous Lives of London scandal sheet

~

THE FOLLOWING MORNING MORIA LANGUIDLY LAID IN BED past the ninth hour and missed breakfast altogether until Miss Kelley and Olivia entered with a tray.

"For me?" Moria said, sitting up in surprise. Her plait fell down her back and the blankets fell around her.

Olivia set the tray down on a table by the window, then dove onto the bed next to Moria and pulled her into an embrace. Moria tucked Olivia around her the way her mother used to when they were young. How she'd give anything to lie in her mother's bed once again with all three of her sisters and dream about the *one days* and *maybe some days* and *not yets*. She'd redo the days in between in a way her mother might be prouder of, that she herself might be prouder of.

Olivia's blonde head was on her shoulder and her arms tightened about Moria. Moria thought suddenly of the daughter she'd almost had, but how could she ever tell Olivia that? So, she planted a kiss atop her head, and pulled back, under the pretense of stretching and getting ready to dress. Olivia tugged on Moria's long braid.

"Not like you to have a lie-in past seven am. Anything you want to tell me?"

Moria only sighed and took the hot tea with a slice of lemon that Miss Kelley offered on a saucer.

"Being so popular is tiring."

"Well, you must make haste, calling hours start soon and His Grace's sister told me he intended to call today to see you off before you leave for the country."

Moria's eyes widened and she set down her teacup and saucer and ran to the mirror. Did she look like a woman who'd come close to being ravished by a different man the night before? Olivia came to stand behind her. Miss Kelley, who had already gone to the wardrobe, laid a dress out on the bed for Moria to change into. It was the two colors of an orchid. Like the flowers he'd sent.

Moria ran her fingers over the lines beneath her eyes. "I think I'll need to borrow some of your...cosmetics today, Libby."

Olivia smiled and disappeared.

By the time calling hours came around, Olivia and Miss Kelley had Moria more than presentable and all were seated seemingly unbothered and peacefully reading or sewing in the sitting room when the Duke was announced. Moria barely heard any of the words or pleasantries that were exchanged between any of them, including (especially) Jasper, until the tea tray was brought around, and the piquant smell of cinnamon spice buns broke her from her torpor. They smelled like the back of Devyn's neck. She sunk her teeth into one, imagining it tasted the same as Devyn must.

"So you lived in the Congo…for nearly a decade?" Olivia was asking Kate Herring, whom Moria had forgotten she had invited.

"My mother met my father in the Cape Colony," the Duke joined the conversation. "They were married in a tribal ceremony, and then in our parish church when my father brought her to England."

Moria knew this already, but she liked hearing him talk about his origins. She wanted to hear more of the man and not just the Duke, but he was like a steel vault. A pretty one, but uncrackable.

"Have you ever visited?" Kate asked.

The Duke looked away from her and at his folded hands. "No, I haven't. As my father's sole heir, I haven't traveled extensively. He was in ill health for a long time, and I didn't want to leave him."

"Such a dutiful son," Kate said.

It was an unlikely scenario, Moria hadn't thought that the two of them would have much to talk about, but she'd been wrong. The Duke seemed to find her stories about growing up in the African bushlands with her missionary father and botanist mother riveting, Moria felt that some of the details of her story seemed far-fetched. If anyone were to spot an imitation, would it not be her? A career false diamond? Everyone had secrets, secrets that might be useful to her purposes.

The topic of conversation moved to the Dowager Duchess and the culture she'd shared with her son.

"So, you're the product of a love match? That must be how you got such lovely bone structure," Moria said, eyeing him flirtatiously. The Duke's eyes fell down to Moria's lips. She had him on the ropes now. It wasn't Kate that Moria was wrestling with exactly, it was Moria's own pride she was battling. How could she let this Duke fall from her grasp, literally, when her every step the last few years had been for this very moment?

"And your hair," she turned to the redhead watching with reddened cheeks, "Kate, doesn't His Grace's hair look *sinful* pushed back like this?" she said, leaning to push a stray strand of The Duke's dark hair out of his face. Was she dangling him in front of Kate? Maybe a little, just to see what she or The Duke of Andover would say.

Kate didn't move or speak, but radiated discomfort from her seat. His Grace cleared his throat, took Moria's hand, and kissed her fingers. Her bare fingers.

Two dimples, one in either cheek, had her own cheeks flushing. Behind them, Moria heard the sound of clattering teacups and saucers. Olivia was calling for a maid, Miss Herring was apologizing for dropping her tea saucer. The Duke asked if Kate was alright, noting her wringing her hands and downcast eyes.

In front of Moria was her beau of over a year who was still somewhat an enigma, a woman who wanted his attention, and a cinnamon bun that smelled like the man she'd kissed the night before. She chose the cinnamon bun.

"Are you going to eat that?" She broke through the melee to point at the last treat untouched on the Duke's plate.

He gave a small laugh. "If you want it, it's yours."

"You might have put up a bit more of a fight, your grace," Olivia said in a conspiratorial whisper shout. That made him laugh, like really laugh, and something about the sound had Moria laughing too, even as she stole the cinnamon bun and put it on her own plate.

"But then Lady Moria wouldn't get something she wanted, and then where would we be?"

Moria heard the bitter note in Kate's rhetorical question, it took Moria back to every whisper and every cold shoulder when she'd come out of mourning. There was her pride racing ahead of her good sense. She paused her sensual onslaught of the cinnamon spice bun to ask the enigma of a man before her: "Would you like to take a ride on Rotten Row this afternoon, your Grace? Chaperoned, of course."

Moria paused to lick a jot of cream from a finger. She watched as the Duke's Adam's Apple bobbed. She caught Miss Kelley's eyes, frowning at Moria at the piano. Moria set down her now empty saucer.

He gave her a rare and genuine smile. "That would be sublime, the weather is perfect."

THE WEATHER WAS NOT PERFECT.

Three and a half hours later, Moria, her dark blue riding habit, her horse, her groom, and her suitor were all nearly drenched before they could make it back to Pembrooke House.

"That downpour came out of nowhere," Moria cried, huddling closer to the duke on her horse as he held his great coat over them both where they had pulled their horses under an outcropping of trees. The edge of the path wasn't perfect cover, but it was better than being exposed entirely to the elements, and worse, to the gossips.

"I can't be terribly upset about it, my lady," he said, a few drops of water running down the heavily-tanned skin of his neck and falling on the collar of her dress. "It's been fourteen months since I stole a dance to learn your name. I haven't been this close to you, this alone with you before. Though I've wanted to be."

It had been his own badly timed and overly dramatic words on the floor of Parliament that had kept him from pursuing a match, but Moria didn't point that out.

"Am I close enough now?" she asked. She wanted him to kiss her, so she could do a full analysis of his kiss versus Devyn's. Did soldiers kiss better than noblemen? But not all noblemen had the same lips as the Duke. The full-bodied muscularity of Devyn led her to believe so, but she needed...harder evidence...to reach a full conclusion first. Perhaps she was terrible, in the face of how much she was starting to, okay had already come to care for Devyn, but the cautious voice in the back of her mind wouldn't be quieted.

"Too close for society standards. Not close enough for mine."

There was no denying that the teasing note in his voice might have tantalized a version of Moria from the past. The current one felt like a stranger watching the scene play out from above as she dipped her head and blushed what she hoped was prettily. "Your Grace, I'm sure I'm quite flattered you still hold such designs considering how utterly soaked and unpleasing a countenance I assuredly present at the moment."

A man who laughed so openly in response, so charmingly, couldn't be a terrible husband. The Duke met Moria's eyes, a smile playing at his lips. He leaned in, keeping his voice low. "You are quite the actress, my lady. I can see why the men of London are so besotted with you."

"I'm not sure I take your meaning," she said, stealing a glance at the bunched fabric as it stretched over the muscles of his arms as he held his coat over them. Dukes didn't have such muscular arms, but this one did.

"You've turned down no less than eight marriage proposals, if the books at White's are to be believed. All of which, had me feeling like such a cad for being...relieved."

"Well, three of them were from the Earl of Essex who was rather persistent so it's really more like...five. If one is being singularly technical about it."

"He must have done a properly bad job of it then. I think I'd need only the one were I to take it in my head to propose to the lady of my choice."

Moria's eyebrows hit her hairline. "Quite the boast for a man who's never made a proposal of his own. Who knew the Duke of Andover had such a cheeky wit."

He did that thing where his lips flinched like he wanted to laugh but reined it in.

The rain let up finally, and the clouds opened up. Her groom called to her, "Your ladyship! You still alright?"

"I'm fine, Houndsley!" she answered, removing herself from her all-too-friendly vicinity to the Duke. She wiped away the hair plastered to her face and replaced her hat to conceal her mussed hair.

"Race you back to Pembrooke House!" she called to the Duke, spurring her horse on. With a muttered curse from him and a "you cheeky little she-devil!" from Houndsley, both men clamored after her. Regina was all speed and agility, a mount fit for a queen.

She turned her head to see the Duke trotting after her, laughing. She had the lead on him, but she was in side-saddle. (Or was she?)

Faster than wind, was Regina. Moria tossed her head back to the sky and let out a whoop. Finally, he came close enough to catch up to her and she slowed her horse with her reins. Houndsley was still lecturing her as she handed him the reins; but as usual, she wasn't listening.

Andover came up beside her and said, "There's no way you're really riding side saddle or am I thoroughly embarrassed, my lady."

Moria let out a girlish laugh as he helped her from her horse and into his waiting carriage. When he placed his hand at her elbow, the other at her back to assist her with the stepping block, she felt... warm. Wildfire didn't race through her veins and her breath didn't hitch. But there was a kind of amiability, a companionship between them that perhaps she could grow accustomed to.

Chapter Sixteen

Precious furs, peacocks, pearls, and now a pianoforte. One must have deep pockets to woo London's favorite debutante, and even then, all bets are off.
- Scandalous Lives of London, scandal sheet

Moria turned up on her own doorstep to a very disgruntled Jasper who greeted her with a towel to wrap

around her shoulders. Really, it was very cute the way he took her hand and towed her inside chastising her like she was a child of seven, slamming the door in the Duke's face.

"You are absolutely soaked to the bone, my girl. Go upstairs and change. I'll see to the Duke."

"You slammed the door. He's still outside on the stoop."

"Oh dear god," Jasper's hazel eyes widened in mortification, "I slammed my front door on a Duke!" He pointed at her with an accusatory finger, "And you let me, Moria!"

"I couldn't get a word in edgewise, Jas."

Jasper leaned in and kissed the top of her head. "I'd hug you, but you're—"

"I know, I'll go upstairs and change."

"I'll go make obsequious apologies to the Duke."

Moria paused at the bottom of the stairs, still dripping. "Probably just pour him a brandy."

"I'll do that."

Moria took three steps up the stairs but something just inside the open door of the sitting room caught her eyes.

"Jas? Where did the piano come from?" she cried out at the same time the Duke entered with an affronted: "I'm not going to keep running after you, my lady."

"Fine. Then walk," she said, stepping past him with cool unaffectedness to the sitting room. She didn't pause to gauge the Duke's reaction, pausing only to run a hand over the fine piano.

On the oak music desk, there were painted flowers. The bench was upholstered in a soft blue velvet cushion close to the shade of her eyes.

"Do you know who sent it? It must have cost a fortune!" Olivia called.

"I don't think you're helping, actually," the Duke leaned to whisper to her with a playful grimace.

"There was a note," Jasper said, clearing his throat uncomfortably, holding up a mostly chewed, handwritten note.

"Bad Fitzy!" Moria called to the hound at Jasper's heels.

"You have a dog...named after your brother-in-law?" The Duke questioned, looking between the three siblings.

"If you'd endured their whole saga last season you'd understand," Olivia said, patting the Duke's arm.

The Duke of Andover ran a gloved hand through his hair and then replaced his hat. "I'll be back to fetch you for the ball at Lady Lansdowne's at seven, Lady Moria."

∼

So this was it. Tonight would either be the ball that everyone saw her on the arm of a Duke or discussed the overly large gift that had been delivered to her by a secret admirer. It was up to her what she gave them to talk about. One of the few things that was ever up to her. She only had to give interested parties something new, something different to take apart and poke holes in like a wheel of cheese.

When they were alone, Bridget helped Moria prepare for the ball.

"It was from him, wasn't it?"

"I couldn't possibly know which *him* you are referring to," Moria shot back, dabbing perfume between her breasts.

"Your captain. Who I helped you sneak out to meet with in secret yesterday," Bridget pushed.

Moria sighed, setting down the perfume on her dressing table. "He had a piano in his rooms. He knew I played with my left hand, somehow. Maybe I told him, and he remembered, though I can't recall mentioning it. Maybe it's a soldier's skills of observation. I played with the left, he played the right."

"Well...then I hope the Duke is prepared for you to turn down another proposal. Your captain's ruined you for the others."

Moria said, "Devyn hasn't ruined me, perhaps that's the problem."

Her companion, bless her, sighed and seemed to quell the urge to roll her eyes; though Moria had been goading her.

"No, that isn't what I mean. You can't give your hand away, even to a duke, when your heart already belongs to someone else."

"Perhaps I'm waiting for the duke," Moria said, splashing cold water on her face.

"Perhaps that's what you want us all to believe," the other woman tossed over her shoulder before making her exit.

Chapter Seventeen

D.

If only I could be where I wanted tonight. I'd be thanking you for that piano that I know you sent. I thought I could play many tunes, but yours is the one that's stuck in my head.

M

~

"ALL YOUR MANEUVERING ON HER BEHALF, AND THAT'S who she chooses to dance with?"

Moria followed Lady Gretchen's line of sight, where Kate Herring was dancing with a mere mister, a professor from Oxford. He was rather ordinary at first glance; but as they passed, Moria heard him asking Kate some question or another about exponents that she could not begin to comprehend. She saw the way Kate animatedly set off on an explanation.

"Math is the same in every language!" The candlelight set rays on her red hair and as she was animatedly speaking, she was almost....beautiful. Guilt and pride warred inside of Moria over her actions in her drawing room earlier.

"All I did was...give her some life advice and some better clothes," Moria answered.

Carina continued Lady Gretchen's argument. "Well, with your... efforts, and your connections, rather, she could do better than a professor."

Tristan Valentine placed a hand on Moria's arm. "Maybe we spoke too soon."

Moria followed their line of vision, to the edge of the ballroom. Kate exited the dancefloor, only to take the Duke of Andover's hand and follow him onto the floor for a waltz.

Moria swallowed a growing lump in her throat. She felt the turning of so many pairs of eyes in her direction. Bracing for something scandalous to salivate over, to save for later to discuss over tea.

Moria was not surprised given the rapport between Kate and His Grace in Pembrooke House's sitting room. Her shoulders tensed. Surely he was merely being kind, the way he'd danced with her sister Olivia.

There were at least three lords walking in Moria's direction, she could let one of them take her hand and claim the dance, or any open on her dance card. Well, she'd given this one to Fitz, who was conspicuously absent, probably somewhere with Noelle.

Moria chose instead to make a trip to the ladies' retiring room.

When she returned, she joined Lady Gretchen and Carina having a conversation with Kate.

"He offered to introduce you to the Dowager Duchess? But that's *Moria's* beau. They've courted for like a year."

"Beaux are off-limits to friends-" Gretchen backed up Carina's argument.

"And former beaux too!" Carina added.

Kate crossed her arms. "Well, unlike Lady Moria, no one is sending pianos to me. We don't all have the same choices."

"But, it's like against the rules of-" Gretchen was interrupted by Kate.

"The rules of what?" Kate interjected, her tone bored and borderline defensive.

"I don't know, it's just a rule," Gretchen said, gesturing vaguely with her gloved hands.

"Well, I was having a nice time with Professor Carlisle, maybe I'll —" Kate made for the dancefloor, but Moria was faster.

"Oh no, you can't," Moria tugged at the bow at the back of Kate's gown, a shade of blue more complimentary to her complexion and eye color. "A second dance...that's social suicide." She shook her head, handing the lemonade she'd spiked with the contents of her flask in the retiring room to Gretchen.

"Kate, you are so lucky you have us to guide you. Here," Moria bit down the large sigh that sprang from her lungs as she looked down at her dance card. "Take mine. I'm going home."

"Lady Moria," she heard the Duke's voice over her shoulder, but she didn't stop walking. His fingers grazed her forearm.

She slipped on a practiced mask as she turned to face him.

"I must prevail upon you to endure my absence," she smiled up at him. "My brother's carriage to Brookevale Park departs early in the morning with or without me, Your Grace."

She was tired. She didn't really want to play this game anymore. Of all the men in this ballroom, none of them had eyes like a starry night, a warrior's heart, and knew she favored her left hand.

Chapter Eighteen

M,

In the three days since your departure, the Duke of Andover was seen calling at the Herring residence. The little redhead doesn't have much by way of slander (other than her clothes, which, despite your efforts are still tragic to say the least) that I could find, but that father of hers is a different story. Write back to me and tell me if we should ruin her and her whole family.

Kiss,

G

~

G (and C, I know you're reading this over her shoulder),

Write it in the book. We will decide what to do with it if we must.
    Kiss,
    M

❧

WHEN MORIA AWOKE WITH THE HOUSE IN THE COUNTRY rather than in town, decisions were still weighing her down like a heavy coat. She carried the added weight of how little time there was left before Devyn had to leave on another military campaign. She could set down that weight here, bask in an early summer sun and feel grass beneath her feet and clean air in her lungs.

"The inhabitants of the country, human and animal alike, care not for things like *reputations*," that's what her father had said a few years back, and Moria couldn't really hear his voice anymore, but she heard it clearer in the country.

Her siblings assumed she was quiet because she missed being back in London, because she was bored. Because she missed her friends or didn't want to lose her chance at being a duchess. It was simply that Moria didn't have to say anything. There was no audience to entertain but her memories and her foolish dreams.

Even so, Moria had selected a white dress sprigged with green leaves for luck for her nephew's christening. She'd chosen a matching hat with white flowers and green grosgrain ribbon to match the sash of her dress. Noelle and Fitz were to be christened as new godparents, and she'd dressed them as well. She figured maybe Noelle had asked for her "wardrobe expertise" to distract from the fact that Moria was the elder, she should be the godmother, but she wasn't the one with a husband.

They were always worrying about the wrong things with her. Moria could have corrected them, could have pasted on a broad smile and a cheery demeanor, but anytime she heard the cry of an infant, something protective inside of her tensed and shivered. She did at times feel like there was only so much happiness in the world, and it had been snatched from her and given to the ones she loved instead. It didn't pain her anymore, they were more deserving of happy endings and forevers and sunny spring Baptisms of adored little babies anyway.

Anyone witnessing Moria on this given spring Sunday in the village chapel would have assumed she'd been rapt by the vicar's sermon.

She lifted her blonde head when rustling in front of her occurred.

He was here, a welcome reprieve, the most welcome of reprieves she could have conjured, from looking at her sister, baptizing her nephew in the church where she would have baptized her and Marcus' baby.

Her soldier only turned to look at her once. Feigning strangers, they smiled cordially at one another. But there in that brief mutual gaze, an entire conversation passed.

You. A lifted brow.

Me. A tug of his lips.

You're here. Two blinks.

I'm here. But you don't know me, remember? A barely there nod.

As if I could ever not know you. Her eyes resting on those lips.

And when he turned back around, she was reminded why she hadn't been able to forget him, not in the last week, not in the last year. Maybe not ever. He was gloriously made. The slope of his hulking shoulders beneath red wool, the curl of his dark hair at the nape of his tanned neck were almost too delectable to be real.

"Do you know that man?" Olivia stage whispered as she placed a hand on Moria's muslin sleeve.

"Do I know what man?" Moria met Fitz's eyes as he gave her a knowing smirk.

Olivia scoffed and rolled her eyes. "Is there a man alive who isn't taken with her?" Olivia groaned her disappointment to Miss Kelley on her other side.

Moria willed him, or the back of his head, to turn back around. *Look at me again. So I know you're really here for me.*

He didn't.

For the rest of the sermon, she was silent. Anyone would have thought it was the vicar's words that had brought about this change in her; the rigid, pious posture and the emotion in her eyes.

At the conclusion of the sermon, Devyn appeared to be absorbed in rebuttoning his coat. He walked right into her the way she'd walked into him at Olivia's debut ball. She dropped her hymnal and they both leaned to pick it up. Her body raised all the bells at his nearness, bracing for the slightest, torturous touch from this man.

"Follow my lead," he whispered as his hand touched hers for an infinitesimal second, the red wool of his coat grazing, no singeing, her skin through her kid glove. She fought the growing lump in her throat. They'd done this dance before. She hadn't acquiesced then, but he hadn't given up.

"I'm so sorry my lady, I'm an oaf," He said in a stage whisper that had others craning to overhear as they milled about the exit of the church. The sound of his voice, rugged and beautiful, unlocked something in her.

She gave a small flirtatious laugh that surely God wouldn't smite her for in His house. He listened to her many prayers; He knew her heart.

"I'm afraid the fault is mine, sir. I was so in thought over the vicar's words I wasn't looking where I was going."

Others around them stopped. She was no stranger to being noticed, it was merely encouragement for her performance. She feigned shyness, all blushes as the captain bowed and made an introduction.

"I'm afraid I'll intrude upon your good manners further…I'm

Captain Winter, my lady," he said with a smile, as if the name wasn't already dear to her as air, as if she hadn't traced her fingers over it written on parchment for over a year. She saw her sister Noelle open her mouth to speak, brow furrowed, but Fitz was ushering her in the opposite direction, heads conferring together.

Devyn, with the aid of her loyal friends, was gifting her a proper introduction. One they could repeat years later at dinner parties. *They...we...*a shared possessive similar to the dark gleam in his all-too-familiar eyes.

Moria turned to the Vicar behind her, only to see the young man of God grinning in Miss Kelley's direction. Both shepherd and wolf simultaneously. Bridget winked back at Moria.

Be brave, said Bridget Kelley's green eyes.

"Lady Moria Pembrooke, sir." She gave the captain her name, watching his eyes caught on her full lips. Moria didn't blush, at least she thought she didn't, she was used to controlling her blushes instead of the other way around.

"A beautiful name," the way the words escaped him with that cheeky half tug of a smile, she knew he was thinking of the willow tree, of their game, of their informal introduction that felt like another life ago.

And then, her entire family descended upon them with the full force of all their well-meaning wholesomeness, all of them talking to her at once.

Jasper glanced at the other man; eyebrow raised. The captain extended a hand cordially.

And before Moria knew what had happened, the Captain had won every one of them over with his artfully polite words, his manners, some distant connection he'd likely stolen from her letters or concocted from thin air, and his good-natured laugh. When he complimented her nephew, Moria saw the approval in Kathleen's eyes.

She heard her eldest sister inviting him for the christening meal along with the other celebrants invited to partake, and Moria heard him give his assent. She was just looking at him. *Looking* was such a simple, innocuous word; but the sight of him made the word a religious act.

She looked over her shoulder for the Vicar, who gave her a sheepish smile.

"You lead the way, my lady," the captain was planting a kiss on her gloved hand, placing it in the crook of his massive arm. Those lips had kissed other parts of her as well. Here she stood lying before her family and her village and God and the image of Mary and John the Baptist and Apostle Paul in the stained-glass windows, lying to all of them that this new suitor was a stranger until this day.

He grinned, a smile that reached his eyes, reached her very soul.

He was worth it.

Chapter Nineteen

Moria, either a beautiful liar or just out-of-touch, had described her family's country estate as "modest." He was no stranger to country estates, having grown up the rightful heir to Wintersea Manor, but Brookevale Park's sixteen bedrooms and the lake behind it made him seem like the "modest" one.

"Your house is...nice." he'd said, walking three paces behind the rest of her family, arm in arm, on the way from the church when a Jacobean manor came into view.

"I know, right?"

Perhaps she hadn't wanted to intimidate him. He was intimidated anyway. How was he to compete with an orangery and a boat house and an armory and a stable with twenty-three of England's finest horses? Her younger sister was running a veritable undomesticated animal halfway house. And he shared a townhouse off Belgravia with Calum. Moria's fingers flexed around his arm, pulling him back to the present. Back to her, and the fresh dotting of freckles on the bridge of her nose from a couple days in the country.

"I wouldn't want to be anywhere else," he said.

Jasper eyed him over the luncheon table in a breakfast room in which the windows had been opened to let in a breeze and they'd had to pull up extra chairs to accommodate everyone. It was more than nice.

"You look terribly familiar, Captain. Have we met before?"

To Moria's left, her sister, the bespectacled viscountess from the masquerade, made a soft choking noise, her husband giving her small attentive pats on her back. Devyn found it ironic the inhabitant of a guise like hers found such difficulty with a ruse when someone else was playing it.

"Perhaps you are acquainted with my brother, the Earl of Clairville?" Devyn answered the Earl.

"I believe he was a few years ahead of me at Harrow. Before he inherited from your uncle, and before I inherited, we both attended a house party with some legendary shooting at the late Duke of Andover's place in Somerset."

Devyn was born to a title, but he didn't know how the other man managed such a broad slate of affairs, with two unmarried sisters to boot. Moria had been distracting Devyn enough from his duties that a couple of his men had commented on it. He had only a short furlough before he'd be shipping overseas, and he didn't care what anyone thought of how he spent them.

As usual, his defense was self-deprecating humor when he had to talk, and quiet stoicism when he didn't. His seat at the tea table offered him the perfect view of the woman he'd crawl on glass to make his. She was wearing a dress that was white, set off by a shade of green that deepened the gold rings inside of her blue eyes. The slope of her shoulders and the curve of her breasts were edged in a lace he wondered matched what she was wearing underneath. *Had the sun kissed the skin beneath those undergarments too?*

Mother of god, she had him noticing her clothes and thinking about her undergarments. He was beyond hope.

Belatedly, he registered that he'd been seated between her younger sister Olivia and their chaperone, and no one had spoken in a full four minutes. Five? He should probably stop eye-ravishing Moria and say something.

Her youngest sister Olivia took him in like he was under a microscope. "He is quite the specimen."

Moria gave her sister an exasperated look from across the table. He loved the way she looked when she was exasperated. "Specimen? Really?" she tipped her teacup to her lips. His whole foolish body felt envy for that teacup.

Olivia nodded and then said to Moria in a stage whisper, "He should be studied for science. I didn't know they existed in his... variation."

Their companion groaned, before resuming her occupation of feeding the newly christened baby atop her lap. How did these people keep up with all the inhabitants at one table? It had always been him and Perry, Perry had never let him want for joviality when he was around, but how lonely must it have been for Perry before he'd come along? Perry was the type of aristo that could sit at a bedecked table such as this, brimming with circumstance, yes, but also wit and conviviality.

Devyn winked at Olivia. A chuckle escaped from him when a blush crept up Moria's neck.

"Nothing I haven't heard before, my lady, but I'm nothing special, just a warrior."

Olivia tilted her head to the side. "Tell me, what does your diet consist of? And your exercise regime? I'm assuming...weights, running, maybe drilling, boxing, and some swordplay?"

Moria rubbed the bridge of her nose. Her sister and brother-in-law looked on with appreciative eyes.

"Of course, my lady. A captain must be a master of many...skills."

"I've always thought Moria would have made an excellent soldier."

"Olivia, that's—" the Earl of Westmoreland tried to cut the youngest of the Pembrookes off but she was unflappable.

"She is the most accurate shot of my siblings and an excellent horsewoman. She's always been good at games of strategy as well."

The open affection with which Lady Olivia beamed at Moria cracked him open a little bit. Moria gave a soft smile and looked away uncomfortably, shaking her head. Why was she uncomfortable with hearing such genuine praise?

Her words from the library came back to him. *They wanted a mercenary, someone who could be bought for a price for their own purposes, but no cost they offered was worth the price of my pride, my revenge.*

"Not a mere foot soldier, then; more like the goddess of war."

Olivia gave an appreciative tilt of her head. "Are you sure you've only just met her?"

Moria set her fork down on her plate with a loud *thwap*. She was staring at him, teasing her bottom, perfect lip between her teeth. The other occupants of the table had fallen still, awaiting his answer like they'd sensed the familiarity too.

His eyes were trained on hers; he said the words like a caress between them. "I met her in another life, perhaps."

"How fortuitous that you found her again, then." Said Lady Noelle, raising her water goblet to him in a small salute before taking a sip.

He wasn't expecting it when Moria chimed in with, "You know that I've always made my own luck, sister," and popped a morsel of bread in her mouth.

God help him, he had scant days left until he left for foreign enemies, but his world had narrowed down to claiming one little huntress and her perfect mouth.

Chapter Twenty

THE BURN BOOK OF LADY M

General Waddingham: Your Christian name proved harder to find than a list of your many transgressions and abuses of power, and there were many voices willing to talk about how you've accepted a laundry list of bribes for favors.

"STUBBORN AS AN OX, THAT'S WHAT YE ARE." CALLUM shook his head. "If ye'd only used yer brother's connection, ye could have stayed under her roof instead of with the handsome vicar friend. You could ha' stayed there, instead of waitin' here for her to return. But no, what do I ken? Jest a dunderhead from the highlands wi' nae connections t'call upon meself."

"First," Devyn pointed with the roll of linen he was using to tape Calum's hands for a scheduled boxing match against a fellow officer. "That's not really how any of this works, not for a baptism. It made more sense at the time to say that I was a visiting friend of the vicar's. That's the scheme her companion and her vicar friend decided upon.

Second, I'm discovering that my battle strategy does not seem to carry over to drawing rooms."

Devyn was taping Calum's hands for a fight when Calum pulled a startled face, clutching his bare chest dramatically. "Ye don't ken."

Devyn rolled his eyes. "Peregrine never saw fit to inform me that he was acquainted with the Earl, in any event."

To boost morale for a looming deployment, Devyn's regiment occasionally held public boxing matches. The preparations kept the men in shape, and the betting and competition were good for morale. But just now, the assembled crowd of men in uniform and out of it had gotten quiet, too quiet. Devyn looked over his Lieutenant's shoulder to see a circle gathered, a swathe of yellow skirts visible from where he was standing. He heard a laugh. The hair on the back of his arms stood nearly on end at the sound of that laugh.

"Shit," he swore.

Calum turned to look. "What?"

And then two soldiers were walking Lady Moria Pembrooke to a spot at the end of the wooden grandstand next to the ring outside the Royal Military Academy like she was some porcelain doll that might spontaneously shatter into a million shards. Booker, one of the youngest recruits from the Southbank, was asking if he could fetch her a cup of water. Her maid was standing behind her. Devyn saw his friend's eyes fall over her, and he swallowed a lump in his throat.

Devyn rolled the tension from his shoulders. She shouldn't be here. It wasn't fit for a lady like her. He wasn't fit. God, but the sight of her here, on his own turf...

Devyn blew out a large breath. "She's a fucking menace, that girl."

Calum chuckled. "Tho' that was wha' ye liked abo' *'er ladyship*?"

Now Devyn was the one swallowing a lump in his throat as her hungry eyes fell down his body. She fanned herself like she was too warm. Her maid handed her a fan, Lady Moria held it over her face, still holding his eyes. Devyn was a fool, so besotted that he didn't foresee what came next.

"Looks like the little deb fancies a bit of rough," said the voice of Calum's opponent as he stepped up to the little stairs leading into the ring.

"Captain," Calum called, but Devyn could hear nothing but the sneer in Sergeant Fox's voice, the blood roaring in his own ears.

"Care to say that again, you bastard?" Devyn was pulling on the other man's shoulder to face him. Another man might be intimidated by the size of Fox, but Devyn was taller, broader. He stared down the other man, daring him to recant his words.

"I said," Fox gave him the stupidest fucking grin, sizing him up. "The pretty woman over there," he jutted his chin in Moria's direction, Devyn watched her face fall out of the corner of his eye that she registered they were talking about her, "Seems like she likes a bit of rough, like yourself. Maybe I'll give her a crack next. Would hate to leave the little minx unsatisfied."

Devyn wasn't sure that in the span of his life, he'd thrown a punch faster than he had right then. He heard the crack of the man's jaw and the splash of blood and possibly a tooth hit the floor of the boxing ring. Fox swung, but Devyn ducked, hitting him with another one-two punch to his ribs. The other man doubled over, holding himself. Bastard still swung at Devyn with his other hand anyway.

Devyn grabbed the other man's fist, turning back his fingers till he heard the sound of a cracking knuckle or two. It wasn't enough. He could shatter him bone by bone, and he wouldn't stop.

Several soldiers rushed the ring at once, Calum was wrapping arms around Devyn, pulling him back. Devyn didn't register that he was hurting his best friend trying to get to Fox, until Calum cursed. Devyn was looking over all their heads, around them all for her. He made out her maid, rushing her to a carriage, pulling Lady Moria inside after her.

Devyn swore again; but Calum had such a hold on him that when he shoved Devyn to a bench, he sat.

"Yer an idiot, ye know thon?" Calum said, losing a breath as he plopped beside him.

"A prize idiot, yes, I know," Devyn ground out, grimacing at the tightness in his shoulders.

"Well," his comrade let out a long sigh, folding his hands underneath his arms, "I reckon if you're knee deep in shit, then we both got muddy boots, lad."

Devyn wanted to say thank you, something, anything, but he heard the sound of his own name first.

"Captain Winter!" A commanding voice called. Devyn and the others turned to see their superior officer, a large and unyielding man with an impressive mustache, standing in front of his tent.

Both men stood at attention, saluting their commanding officer.

"Yes sir," Devyn answered.

General Waddingham motioned for him to step inside his tent. Devyn had to bend his frame to enter, biting down a likely-deserved wince at the strain the movement caused his muscles. He wasn't sure what to expect, but being called into his superior's chambers after a fight like that one, spelled disaster.

And still, he'd do what he'd done, bloodying a man for speaking ill of the lady he- never mind- point being, he'd been willing to bloody a man for her. Hell, he'd probably have bloodied Fox for sport for speaking ill of a woman the way he had, but the level of his anger, his fury, that was reserved for *her*. He tried to box up thoughts of her and what little he wouldn't do for her when he was asked to account for his actions.

"WHAT THE HELL HAPPENED TO YOU?"

Moria said, barging into the townhouse Devyn and Calum

shared on a wave of chiffon, smelling like lemons and looking like pure sunshine but with perfect breasts and hips to die for, without so much as a greeting. Devyn turned to traitorous Calum, who followed only a pace behind her, Moria's petite lady's maid on his arm acting as chaperone.

"Really, Calum?"

Calum sighed, running a hand through his ruddy hair. "I walked all the way to the wrong side of town for a bloke like me and got nearly turned away by her prissy butler-"

"Hey, don't call him that-"

Calum rolled his eyes at Moria's interruption. "All to bring her back here, so jest bloody tell her, mate!"

"Tell me what?" Moria looked between the two men. Devyn felt torn between wanting to tell her that he'd fought for her and wanting to protect her from what had been said.

"That man was defending your honor, my lady."

"Might you give a lad a moment, Lieutenant?"

Calum held up both hands in surrender, and took three steps back, taking Miss Dempsey with him, and turned to face the opposite direction with his hands clasped behind him.

"I promised you a ring on your finger. I said a lot of things, and you know what, I damn well made my intentions clear where you are concerned. So, you can believe that no man, no woman for that matter, is going to say anything that I find deplorable in my earshot about you and walk away."

She took a step toward him, until they were toe to toe, and reached a hand up to his split brow. He tried to read the emotion in her eyes before she was too close to him to see.

Her lips curled near his ear. "I wish I'd found you a long time ago."

Devyn pulled back in surprise, and her little fists capitalized on his surprise, hauling him against her for a kiss. His hands, catching on quickly, found her hips and held her. His lips, catching on just as fast, gave her back every bit of the drugging intensity she poured into the kiss.

"This could be ruinous for my career. You aren't angry with me?" he asked, chest heaving, when she'd released him to come up for air.

"Do you...*want* me to be?" She said, closing the inch of space between them. Her fingers dug into his scalp, her hips pressed so tight against his own.

"Do you care that I'm right here? And, och, not in front of the tea and scones, please," Calum said, looking at them aghast with a teapot in hand. Both Devyn and Moria looked back at each other, an easy laugh coming out of both of them at the image. Even Miss Dempsey, cheeks crimson, covered her mouth to stifle a laugh.

Their conversation was interrupted by a clamor outside, what sounded like a riot of men. Calum shoved open the kitchen window to peer outside, pulling Miss Dempsey, Moria's chaperone with him.

"Wha' are ye fool hearted louts doing on the street outside me rooms?"

"We took care of it."

"Evenin', Sergeant. Took care o' wha'?" Calum asked.

"Captain Winter's disciplinary hearing. It's been handled."

Letting go of Moria with a playful squeeze of her hip, Devyn pushed Calum aside to make room to lean his head out the window. "Hang on, I don't think I heard you correctly because there's about three dozen of you standing outside my window like a bunch of gits," there was a rumble of laughter from the street. "I thought I heard you say you handled my disciplinary hearing."

"No, right, Cap, that's definitely what McFee said."

"Do you mind?" Devyn's elderly neighbor was leaning out her window, all five-foot nothing wrinkled and frowning. "Some of us don't care to be privy to your conversation."

Devyn and Calum were both hanging their heads and elbows out the window, but Moria jutted her hip against Devyn's saying, "I've got this," and leaned her head out the window, one arm around Devyn.

"Gentlemen, I apologize for the...lukewarm reception," she gave Devyn a wink. His heart nearly fell right into her pocket as she held onto him leaning toward the window, the men below rapt at her words. "Since you came all this way, and have gone to some trouble to organize yourselves on the Captain's behalf, why don't you gentlemen bring yourselves upstairs and deliver your message in person?"

The wind blew a stray piece of hair from where her blonde tresses were intricately pulled back, the cool air was pebbling the skin just above the neckline of her gown, her cheeks were flushed when she smiled up at him so big her blue and gold eyes were a little squinty. Yep, he was all fucking hers.

"Wha are ye doin'? There's abou' thirty-seven lads in th' street, they cannae' all come up 'ere." Devyn cleared his throat, Calum added with an eye roll, "my lady."

"You heard the lady, come on up, lads!" Devyn leaned further out the window, giving them an encouraging wave. Miss Dempsey groaned, but then Calum gave her a wink. *Bloody Scots.*

There was a chorus of "Thank You, Captains" and the shuffling of boots as the group reassembled themselves inside.

There was a comically large group of men dwarfing the sitting room and entry of Devyn's town house. Several of them shoved for precedence or seating. Calum was doing a headcount of them all like some sort of house mother in a dormitory. Moria was offering them tea which Miss Dempsey set to work preparing in Devyn's kitchen, they were all just staring at her or stumbling over themselves like a bunch of infatuated schoolboys rather than highly trained warriors, cavalrymen, and sharpshooters. Christ, the effect she had on men.

She had that effect on you, too, still does.

"Out with it then," Devyn said, nodding to the young Welshman who seemed to have elected himself the spokesman of their haphazardly organized group.

"We told General Waddingham that you were defending the honor of a lady, and Fox said some things that don't bear repeating."

"And?"

Belcher nodded, continuing his explanation. "If you are sacked, he'd be your replacement, so we all told General Waddingham that if he replaces you with Fox, he'd have to replace us too."

The others nodded in agreement.

"Oh, Christ," Calum said, pushing two underlings out of his way and sitting down on a settee, running a hand over his mouth.

Moria's fingers found Devyn's. Like she'd sensed exactly what he needed from her. Her fingers squeezed his, and suddenly he could hear anything, bear anything, they had to say.

"He's not the kind of man I'd follow into battle, Captain, but you are."

Devyn's hand flew to his temple. "Belcher, you *didn't*."

Moria and Calum's heads swiveled back and forth from Devyn to the men in the sitting room.

"Oh, no, *I* didn't, we *all* did." Belcher.

"And what did Waddingham say to that?" Devyn.

There was a taut beat of silence that stretched on. Devyn ran a hand through the lengths of his dark hair, tied it back at the nape of his neck. He felt Moria's eyes on him the whole time. Several men shifted uncomfortably, fidgeted, or propped themselves against furniture or a nearby wall. Still no one spoke.

"Oh, you lot are worse than a bunch of debutantes! Enough of the dramatics, don't leave us hanging, gentlemen," Moria said, crossing her arms.

"He said he was moved by our loyalty...." McFee began.

"So you won't be forced to sit through a disciplinary hearing," Booker continued for him.

Moria squeezed Devyn's hand so hard he couldn't tell if she was delighted or disappointed his captaincy wasn't on the line. She hadn't come out and said as much, but he knew his going away was hard for her, that she didn't want him to go. But he had to see this through, see these merry, brave men through this conflict, and then he'd be home to her. They were putting their trust in him to do right by them.

His men who were now clapping him on the back, shaking his hand, cheering, and laughing. Somehow Peregrine had entered with Tristan Valentine in tow for some god forsaken reason, taking stock of the general melee in Devyn's townhouse.

"I came when I received your note about Waddingham's little tirade," Peregrine said, clapping a hand on Devyn's shoulder. "Didn't even need any input from me to save your hide, you never do."

At the same time, Devyn noted Tristan handing Moria a flask and whispering something in her ear that had her laughing raucously and slapping his arm.

"Where did you pick up the stray?" Devyn asked.

Peregrine sighed. "He has a sixth sense for celebrations, does Valentine. Always seems to find his way in wherever there's a good time to be had and good cognac to be drunk."

Devyn raised a brow. He felt like there was a story there but before he could inquire further, liveried footmen entered through the front door delivering case after case of ale and good liquor. The men were uncorking it and passing it around.

"You didn't," Devyn said to his brother, groaning.

"Oh, this was definitely not Lord Bird's doing, he'd have gone with the cheap stuff," Tristan cut in. Moria nudged him in the ribs, he gestured helplessly. Peregrine looked at Tristan with an amused expression, who said, "You only have the one brother," with a shrug, taking a proffered bottle in hand. Tristan offered the bottle to Moria, the only lady, first, which actually suited Devyn down to the ground that the man did have manners.

"Might as well celebrate his accomplishments while he's still on English soil."

Devyn noted Moria's discomfiture at that last statement, tossing back her drink in one go with her body so close to his but not close enough.

Devyn answered Tristan's pronouncement. "I fail to see what I've accomplished worthy of celebration. I let my fists do the talking for me instead of—"

"You gave him a moment to recant his words, he didn't back down, Captain," a private interjected.

"I'd have done the same in your shoes if he'd talked about my girl. You taught him a lesson," another added on, throwing an arm around their Captain's neck. At Devyn's grimace, he removed it.

"Devyn, you stood up for me," Moria said, pulling his head down so they were closer to eye level. "You risked your title...for me."

At the word title, his heart almost gave a little somersault, thinking she knew of the other title that was just as much his. But there was so much admiration swimming in her eyes, so he answered, "I'd risk my last breath for you," into her ear and stole her lips into a fierce kiss with raucous, drunk cheers and her heartbeat filling his ears.

Chapter Twenty-One

"THE COURTSHIP OF YOUR DREAMS," HE'D SAID, STANDING on her doorstep after walking her home from his apartments in time for dinner. "Before I have to ship out. What do you say?"

Standing from a step above him and still not quite eye level, Moria placed her hands on his lapels.

"A ball and a masquerade, a piano, a formal introduction to my family in my ancestral home, and now risking your neck for me," she tugged on his lapels, and his heart. "I'd say the courtship of any girl's dreams *fails* in comparison to the courtship we've already started."

"A proper one, the kind we won't have to lie about when our grandchildren ask. Isn't that what you want?"

I want you.

"To be worth the trouble."

One large hand wrapped around hers and removed it from his jacket, bringing it close enough to kiss. "Get yourself inside before I show you *just* the amount of trouble I think you're worth," he whispered, his lips gallantly hovering over her hand in full view of London's elite.

The door to her London house was pulled open, to both Olivia and Miss Kelley's curious faces.

"Captain," both of them fell over themselves to greet him at once. Moria nearly rolled her eyes but caught herself at the last moment.

"Keep better eyes on this one," Devyn said, tipping his hat as he let go of Moria and turned to leave.

"You don't want to stay for dinner?" Olivia asked as Moria turned castigating eyes on her.

"I'm not dressed," Devyn answered.

"See, he's not dressed," Moria said with a helpless shrug.

He lifted a brow up at her from the sidewalk. "I will be. Tomorrow," he called. "Clear your busy social calendar, I'm taking you to the opera."

"The opera?" she said, a laugh in her voice.

"My brother has a box," he pointed to her chaperone and her sister, "You can come with her."

"I already have plans, but this sounds highly entertaining, so on second thought, maybe I'll cancel," Olivia said animatedly.

"No," Moria ground out, then sighed. "Pick me up, tomorrow then, soldier," and lifted her skirts as she stepped inside and closed the door behind her.

AS ALL THE WOMEN IN HER HOUSEHOLD SURROUNDED HER, Moria thought it should be noted that she'd been courted by a Duke for over a year and hadn't garnered near this much fanfare. She could point out that they all just wanted a look at the Captain, and she'd probably be right. There was something *more* than attractiveness to Devyn. He was the kind of man you noticed, and you didn't just move along.

"So...The opera?" Gretchen asked.

"His brother is the Earl of Clairville, he has a box apparently," Noelle supplied.

"For a soldier in Her Majesty's Army, he is extremely well connected," Lady Carina said, tying one of the straps of Moria's gown.

"I agree. Not a duke though," Gretchen added, fluffing the dark blue skirt of Moria's dress. It was so dark blue it was nearly black, embroidered with stars and crescents and Moria thought it was almost as captivating as Devyn's eyes.

"Will His Grace be in attendance tonight?" Olivia said, that tell-tale storm of mischief in her eyes.

"Heard on good authority he's taking your little bluestocking protege," Gretchen added.

"I'm not the Duke's keeper," Moria said as Olivia applied rouge to her cheeks.

Moria kept the Captain waiting longer than necessary at the bottom of the stairs at her family's London mansion. Over a quarter an hour since Bridget had heard from a servant that he was in the foyer. Moria was ready, but she'd changed her jewelry and stockings, drunk a glass of champagne and eaten a tray of cheese and fruit just to keep him waiting and gauge his reaction.

"Why are you toying with the man? I thought you were looking forward to this evening?" Noelle asked, tilting her head to the side and studying her like some manuscript riddled with hieroglyphics.

Moria dabbed at her lightly painted lips with a linen napkin and set down her empty plate. "Perhaps I enjoy playing with my food before I devour it."

"He does look downright edible, I have to say," Olivia added, peeking her head out the door to look down the stairs at the end of the hall.

"Boo you, whore. Where did you even find such a man?" Gretchen joked.

"Gretchen, we don't call women whores."

Gretchen threw her hands on her hips. "It was a term of endearment!"

Moria and Noelle collapsed into each other's arms in a flood of giggles like adolescents.

"Pretty sure he either heard us or noticed Olivia sneaking glances. You have to put him out of his misery now," Noelle said, giving Moria a playful shove.

Lady Carina and Gretchen refreshed the paint on her lips and helped her put on her gloves. Moria batted them away, letting Ella help her instead.

When Moria appeared at the top of the stairs, his back was turned. No, it wasn't just a back, backs weren't all this broad at the shoulders and tapered at the waist. As she took a step, the sound of her heavy silk skirts announced her arrival, and he turned.

Olivia was right. He *was* downright edible. Dark hair combed out of his eyes, black and white formalwear tailored to display all his masculine glory, a damnable smirk holding up one of his kissable lips. She'd always said men's formalwear was made for a tall man, but god, the shape of him and his long limbs, defied description.

"I think I stopped breathing for a moment there, you made me forget how," Devyn said, echoing her thoughts and taking her hand at the bottom of the stairs. He took a step back to take her in, spinning her around in front of him.

"More than worth the wait," he said with a wink as he tipped her gloved hand up to his mouth for a kiss. Sparks ignited through her at the slight pressure, the sensation of having this man so close, so in her grasp. And he was. She knew by now the tells, an experienced player in the game of courtship.

She didn't know that she had her own tells, written all over her in that moment too. Moria looked over her shoulder with a knowing smile to her sisters, her friends, her lady's maid, and her chaperone. His was the reaction she'd been hoping for.

WHEN MORIA EXITED THE CARRIAGE AT THE THEATER ON the arm of Captain Winter, she was immediately engulfed in stares and whispers. When he placed a hand at the silk at the small of her back, the glares concentrated there. She could feel them all hone in, like bees to honey. She noticed the tension in his jaw and shoulders and grazed his pinky with her own. He tensed his digit around hers, before letting it go. He met her eyes, there was only adoration when he looked at her.

He'd likely insist he was rugged and a brute, but the set of his square jaw and his fathomless dark eyes wreathed by guarded, low brows did things to her. Devyn took a step back to let his brother lead the way into the opera house. He leaned to whisper close to Moria's ear, "Do these people have to look at you like that?"

Moria forced a fake laugh as people started to notice his closeness, then said where only he could hear, "Like what?"

"Like a jewel in a display case."

"Did you just call me a jewel?"

"You are a maddening woman," he said, but there was a smile on his face and in his voice.

The Earl of Clairville stopped a few feet ahead, the chaperone that Moria and Devyn needed for multiple reasons on his arm.

The lobby of the theater was like the inside of a kaleidoscope, full of color and movement and sparkle. From beneath her hand, she could feel the flex of Devyn's arm. There were no less than seven acquaintances of Moria's, all male, who spoke to them as they passed. She looked for the Duke, but didn't see him. If Devyn asked, she would tell him the truth. Male friends were good to have around when she needed a powerful ally, and she had promised herself that she wasn't going to be a girl without well-placed allies again.

When a young couple called to her, she gave Devyn's arm a reassuring squeeze.

"Lady Moria, you look incandescent as always," A brunette Moria knew to be an insatiable gossip stopped to talk to her under the pretense of close friendship.

"And you! Regal as usual, Countess. I should have known the two of you would be in attendance tonight, such charitable patrons of the arts."

The Countess of Markham's smile didn't reach her eyes. "I don't believe I've met your...suitor."

Devyn bowed gallantly as his brother made introductions.

"Oh yes, I forgot you had a younger brother while we were at Harrow, Lord Clairville," The other Earl said. Moria couldn't keep up with all the Earls of her acquaintance, in this conversation even. Throughout the exchange, the Countess was looking at Devyn, at Moria, where her hand rested on his arm. His taut bicep flexed underneath Moria's fingers and her mouth watered.

Music sounded from inside the theater. A call to find their seats. Peregrine placed Miss Kelley's hand in the crook of his arm and made their excuses, ushering the group to their box and leaving the awkward tableau behind. Moria admired the way that Devyn led troops into battle, and Peregrine was astute with the battles of social niceties and politics. They were two shiny, handsome-profiled sides to the same coin.

When they reached their box, Devyn took a drink from his flask. Before he could redon the cap, Moria took it from him and tipped it back herself. He looked at her with his mouth agape and then a laugh bubbled from his barrel chest. Devyn laughing was so rare, like a laugh of his was something he kept in a china cabinet and only set out on rare occasions; but in that moment, she wanted to make his laugh and his looking at her with mirth-filled eyes something fit for daily consumption.

Chapter Twenty-Two

DEVYN WATCHED THE WAY HER LIPS WRAPPED AROUND the flask, the way her throat bobbed, and had to flex his fingers and count his breaths to master his control over his lust.

"I thought you were good at this sort of thing, my lady," Devyn asked, taking the proffered flask from Moria.

"I'm good at providing entertainment, but bores like those two prigs? They require a stiff drink to tolerate."

"I'm glad we agree," he said, replacing the flask in his pocket and ushering her to a seat at the front of the box. When she was in front of him, his eyes fell down her exposed back and the curve of her hips. She looked over her shoulder and smirked when she caught him staring. Devyn coughed and looked away, studying the theater instead of the shape of this woman in a perfectly fitted dress.

The packed theater was enormous, all red and gilt and renaissance paintings on the ceiling like the ones in the ballroom back at Wintersea Manor. Devyn had spent so many hours in that ballroom on dancing lessons, his mother determined her overly large, athletic son not embarrass the family honor by being a terrible dancer until she'd smoothed down all his rough and jerky movements. His mother would have loved Lady Moria, actually. She'd have set her up with Perry, but still.

When Lady Moria sat down in her seat, he felt rather than saw the eyes that trained in their direction. Devyn sat next to her, angling his back in view of the exit, but her chair was so.... far away. She was wearing a dress in shades of blue that looked like moving water at night and he loved her in blue.

She was unreachable in more ways than one. He supposed that theater boxes were designed that way. Propriety and reputations and all that.

As the curtains opened, the music started, her attention was rapt on the stage. She played the piano, loved talking about music, clearly wanted to come tonight not for the theatrics off stage...but the ones onstage. He could see the excitement in her bouncing knee. Her head was held high and her shoulders painfully straight, but she had a tell.

The play began and everyone trained their attention on the stage, until the female character was introduced as a stunning blonde.... named Marina.

She was simpering and flirting with a young lord, the male hero of the play. And the eyes and binoculars trained in her direction. In *their* direction.

Devyn's heart fell down a flight of stairs. Peregrine heard it or sensed his brother's plight—he always had—and touched his arm for the briefest of moments. Their father didn't do simple affection like that—but Peregrine did.

"Well, this is rather...unexpected," Moria said, leaning over to his chair.

Devyn's knuckles pressed tighter against each other.

The sounds of the dialogue, the gasps and laughter of the audience, he barely even heard what was being said on that stage. He was trained on her. He wasn't the only one. Peregrine pointed out the Duke of Andover staring in their direction. The Bloody woman had to also be courted by a Duke.

You could give her a title too, weakling. That dark voice that sounded like his father's, invading his head whenever he least needed it to, irked.

The woman next to him smiled tentatively in his direction, but it didn't reach her eyes. Devyn only cared about her.

So, he did what any possessive and domineering man like himself would do.

He dropped his flimsy program at her feet. Little matching satin slippers just barely there peeked out from her too-many-skirts. He muttered something under his breath. Made a grand show of picking it up from the floor. And he hooked one strong arm around the foot of her chair and dragged it closer to his own. Her chair made a little scraping sound on the carpet that caught others' attention.

The air whooshing out of her lungs was enough to make him smile like an idiot. Then he took her hand in his and kissed her gloved knuckles. Onlookers and Dukes gasping in shock be damned to hell.

THE PLAY THAT NIGHT WAS ABOUT A SOCIETY PRINCESS who breaks many hearts, including that of the main character who says he will never love again. Then, she introduces him to a shy and confident girl who is not after his money, she is a princess in disguise. It was like a backwards *Adelaide*.

Drysdale and Fitz had called on her the day before and explained that Drysdale and his brother were behind it, and that Fitz was publicizing it in the newspaper he'd inherited. She didn't hate the story, it was the kind of thing she was sure would be a massive success.

"Does she have to be called Marina?" she'd asked Drysdale, poking him in the shoulder.

He'd blinked a couple times. "Well, no, actually. It's just already printed on the programs."

"And you didn't run that bit by her first like we discussed?" Fitz had said, crossing his arms. Drysdale had looked at her apologetically. The dolt.

Moria could only do what she had always done. Lean into it.

And so here she sat, on opening night, between the man she was pretty sure she was starting to fall in love with, and her chaperone. So many eager eyes looked in her direction throughout the play to see if she was angry or hurt, whether she knew about it or was as surprised as everyone else.

Somewhere in another box, she saw the Duke of Andover looking as handsome and polished as always and was that...Kate Herring? Good god, perish the thought. Both were looking at her, and when they saw her looking back, trained their eyes and binoculars back on the stage.

So, naturally, Moria's face had to take on an amused expression, her demeanor had to reflect that she wasn't hating it, or they'd all rejoice in her turmoil. She couldn't appear to be loving the attention either, even if she was, because they'd call her all manner of things that may or may not be true.

And then...Devyn. He'd done the chair move and she'd almost collapsed on the spot.

A Duke wouldn't have done that. Some inner, primal voice riled her.

He grinned at her, the devil. He took her hand and kissed it.

There was a dryness to her throat and a clamminess to her hands that felt out of the natural order of things. When she'd dreamed about courting this man in public, she hadn't dreamed of this. When he'd escorted her tonight, she had hoped *maybe he won't find the level of attention directed at me humiliating,* but she hadn't foreseen this.

His hand, holding hers, resting against the armrest of her chair.

All the binoculars looking would catch that.

He didn't seem to care.

And his brother was saying something to him on his other side, leaning toward him. He was large enough that he could do so without letting go of her hand. Could he do everything without ever letting go of her hand? If she asked him to, he'd find a way.

He only let go when it was time to clap, and he didn't try to hold her hand again.

Likely, Peregrine had said something like *we don't hold hands of women we aren't married to at the theater.*

The thought made her smile, and Miss Kelley met her eyes. "Try not to look quite like you're having the night of your life, my dear."

Moria giggled into her ear, maybe it was the contents of Devyn's flask. "And if I am?"

Miss Kelley tamped down her own smile. "Because of the play, or the Captain?"

Moria pretended to keep her eyes on the stage. "Definitely the latter. Did you see the chair?"

"*Impossible* to miss. That was kind of the point, I suppose."

She'd been playing a dangerous game tonight, stepping out with the captain the same night as the play's launch; but even when she caught the Duke staring again, she could barely tear her thoughts from the man who had so publicly declared his intent.

Chapter Twenty-Three

Devyn Winter, Captain, His Majesty's Army: I think I might like to keep this one, actually.

At the after party at Drysdale's estate, she'd excused herself to her chaperone and said she was going to the ladies' retiring room. Miss Kelley made no argument or offer to go with her, likely she knew Moria's intent. Moria looked past all the eyes turned in her direction and made eye contact with Devyn, who was in conversation with his brother. And in a few minutes, he'd found her on the terrace outside.

"Did you know? About the play, I mean?" he asked, coming to sit beside her on a stone bench.

"It's just a story," she shrugged. A play meant both as a jab at a girl who collected hearts like insects in jars and praise of her at the same time?

"I've lived through much worse," she offered, bunching up her skirts so that she could sit with her knees underneath her, leaning her elbow on the back of the bench and her chin on her hand so she could face the beautiful man next to her. Difficult in a dress this form-fitting, but not impossible. She could breathe better like this, curled up next to him, than in a ballroom. When had that happened?

He arched his brow. "A story highly dramatized for audience appeal, I'm sure. Thought I'd have to fight my way out of that theater the way that Duke and so many of those so-called gentlemen were looking at you—"

"You aren't the first man to want me, Devyn," she interrupted.

"Maybe you've been wanted, but not by men." His throat bobbed as he looked down at her, shaking his head. "Only so-called men who saw you as a pretty, dutiful lady... a bauble. Men who don't admire your honesty or your wit."

She felt the callous of a fingertip as he pushed a strand of hair from her face. She closed her eyes against the sharp wave of longing that sprang forth with his caress, his body so indelibly close. She willed him to continue, to continue talking or to continue touching her; but she *wanted*. Her mind and her body wanted so much more of him. All of him that there was to receive and to *take*. She wrapped an arm about his nape, her fingers exploring the downy tendrils of dark hair and spurring him to speak.

"Such men would run at the first sign of your having opinions or use you and push you away. Those "men" couldn't find their spine if they were kicked in it," His voice, low and guttural and possessive, did things to her that she felt in her core. "Those men, they aren't me."

Hell no, they weren't.

She hadn't thought a man like Devyn real until she'd found him. She didn't intend to let him go.

But that wasn't what she said.

"What would a man like you do with a woman like me?"

Could he read all of the insinuations in her eyes, roaming over the width of his shoulders and down the rest of his body everywhere her hands wanted to?

He smiled, the effect beautifully sinful on those lips of his. "Guess you'll have to marry me to find out."

She rested a hand against one of his sharp cheekbones, the warmth and stubble of his skin radiating through the gloves she wore.

"I think you should know that if you wanted me, you and your misplaced sense of honor don't have to propose matrimony...because you wouldn't be...ruining me...Devyn."

He reached for her again, pulling her closer to him, eyes intent and dark. "Christ, woman. Are you listening? It doesn't matter what or who is in your past, I want you to be my future."

She didn't let him finish. She couldn't wait to hear the rest of his words, she'd heard enough.

Her lips searched his, taking them both in their possession all at once. The press of his tongue into hers had her pressing more of her into his grasp. One hand slipped beneath his jacket, hitching up his shirt to better access the smooth expanse of his abdomen. The warmth and tautness of his skin ratched the pace of her heart. She felt him suck in a breath, chasing it back into her own mouth.

Moria wasn't good at declarations. She wasn't good at baring her soul. This? This she could do. Displays of affection that both shared what was on her heart through her greedy hands and sated her lust all at once.

IT WAS DEVYN WHO PULLED BACK.

"That's not an answer, Moria."

Why did she do this?

Just when he shared himself with her, she distracted him with lustful hands and lips thinking he wouldn't notice she didn't match his sentiments. He knew she felt the same. He'd witnessed enough of her mollifying and terrifying the weak men who didn't deserve her to know he'd have been cast aside long before if she didn't want him back.

"Wasn't it?" she said, her voice a sultry brush against his mouth.

He pulled back to look down into the blue-gold foundries of her eyes. There was a lusty haze there, but he saw the love too. It made him brave.

"Not for me."

"You want to hear me say it?"

With a calloused finger, he tipped up her chin. "I want to hear you say it."

He watched her throat bob and her eyes lock onto his. "Very well," she lifted her head proud like a queen, "but you didn't get on your knees to ask the question."

This woman.

"Woman, I've been on my knees for you since that willow tree and you know it."

He didn't know what he was expecting, another heated rejoinder or witty setback, her usual avoidance maybe; but it wasn't tears. The watery laugh through tear-studded eyes sounded so much like joy it almost sent him to his knees. He'd made that smile crack through her surfaces, he'd made her eyes glint like that, and he'd made that sound come out of her that he instantly wished he could bottle, not just for his own ears, but for hers, so she could hear it later. It was something solid, something real, something he could say he gave to her.

Moria was crying, he hated that he was making her cry, even as he removed her glove to place the ring on her finger. He didn't wait for her answer, he took her hand and placed a kiss on her palm. She held up the ring to study it in a stray beam of moonlight.

"It's beautiful," she whispered, "Like you."

He chuckled. "I'm not sure it or I are worthy of you, but—"

She shut him up with her mouth again. She was leaning toward him and kissing him fiercely, stealing all of his air in a kiss that poured all of her affection into him and scrunched up his nose. Her breasts pushed against his chest. He snaked a hand around her waist and one around her jaw. His entire body responded to her, mirroring everything she put into that kiss.

"I think a display of your ...skills...would accomplish that. You told me you intend to make me come with your ring on my finger."

The brute in him thrilled at the way her pupils dilated and her cheeks blazed. She was biting at her lip as he dropped to both of his knees in front of her.

"Here?" she squeaked, "Now?"

The shriek to her voice thrilled him even more. He was already moving underneath her skirts, working to move her drawers out of the way.

"Can you wait? Because I can't. I'm hungry."

To punctuate his words, he kissed his way up her leg, the silk of her stockings tickling the stubble on his face. He'd shaved earlier, but his beard grew back fast. He planted a kiss to the underside of her knee, feeling her toned legs shake, then parted her knees. He felt her writhe under his attention, the way she grabbed his hair and pushed him forward, rocking her cunt into him.

Both hands wrapped underneath the perfect globes of her tight arse, bringing her to his mouth. Above him, he heard her whimper. He was going to have her dripping for him. The fact that they were at a party where they could be discovered by revelers inside the ballroom only added to the thrill.

Still, he took his time. He lathed, sucked, nipped, and licked at her like his last meal.

"God that's so...so good, Devyn."

He could feel how close she was in the way her thighs squeezed tighter around his neck. In response, he cupped a hand around the globe of her arse and gave a gentle squeeze.

He gave her slow, small flicks of the flat of his tongue, and then varied them with faster, broader strokes as she rode his face. At the sound of her desperate groan, he used the friction of his beard against her to bring her even closer to release.

She was so sweet, so damn sweet, and so soft against him. He'd known she would be, but watching, feeling, her melt above him, being the cause for it, was a shot right to his groin.

She arched her back and he felt her legs quiver beneath him in response. With an indulgent swipe of his tongue, he licked her and then slipped one of his fingers inside her to aid the concentrated efforts of his mouth. The tight feel of her seizing around him drew a moan out of them both at the same time.

The stone pavers dug little needly pin pricks into his knees. The pain a counter point for the pleasure they both sought. He sped up, using both fingers and tongue, her holding onto his hair frantically through her skirts.

He added a second finger, stretching her, as she gasped, "Devyn, don't stop. I'm going to-"

And then he felt her shatter around him. He was there, under her, taking all of her wetness into his mouth. He suckled her, still letting her ride his fingers as she came again on his hand. God, she tasted so briny and sweet he had to adjust the hardness in his breeches. He reached in his pocket for a handkerchief to clean her up.

"Devyn," her name was urgent and frantic on his lips. "Some-one's coming."

"I know, *you*. You just came on my-"

"*No*, I mean, someone found me out here alone."

And then he heard her name on someone else's lips. She was straightening her skirts to cover him. Dear god, how had she moved in skirts large enough to cover a grown man of his size?

"Darling," she cooed, "Have you been looking for me?"

A young woman answered. "Everyone has been looking for you after that...performance."

The voice was in front of her. Devyn tried to place it but it was unfamiliar.

"Just out here...taking some...fresh air." Moria improvised, her voice sounded hoarse and flushed. Devyn fought the urge to shift his weight.

"Maybe you've had too much fresh air, you look...flushed."

Devyn coughed before he could stifle it. Moria was fast. "Pardon me. I've got something in my throat, I believe."

"Should I fetch your escort?"

He felt Moria reach out for the other woman's arm, the cage her skirts made around him swaying in her direction.

"No!" she sounded frantic then gentled her voice, "I mean," she said in a conspiratorial tone, "I think I might have...misplaced him?"

The young woman scoffed. "I don't see how. He seemed rather besotted. How you get both the dandy and pretty ones and the big and burly ones on their knees for you I wish I could figure out for myself. Even after the play...he didn't look fit to cower or run from such a show. And the thing with *the chair*."

Devyn felt naive for previously having no inkling that debutantes talked this way.

"I'm so glad he isn't here to hear you say as much. I'm sure his ego would never recover," one of her legs nudged against him as she crossed her legs, a subtle but teasing graze of his cheek.

The other woman giggled. "If you find another, send him my way this time, please?"

Devyn planted a furtive kiss to the inside of Moria's calf.

"Who says I'm looking for another?"

"Isn't that why you're out here alone?"

"You never asked, Gretchen, but he went inside to fetch me a refreshment, I believe."

There was an awkward silence.

"Is he missing a boot, then?" the other woman asked in a whisper.

Devyn heard Moria gasp and look down. Belatedly, he realized the toe of his boot was sticking out from under her dress.

Fuck, fuck, fuck.

"Ladies, I've been looking for you!" called a masculine voice.

Devyn willed his body to be still. It sounded familiar, but not quite close enough for Devyn to make out.

"Lord Clairville, I see you've met my friend, Lady Gretchen."

Devyn covered his mouth with a hand to stifle a breath of surprise.

"I have. We set off in search of you and my brother and we got separated. I see she's found at least *one* of you."

Devyn was trying his damnedest to be so very still, but it was almost impossible at his size and even more so when his older brother made quips like that. He felt her move her legs, the silk and linen underside of her dress scratching against his face. An itch was hurtling through him. He brought a hand up to still it. Before he knew it or could stop it, a sneeze sprang out of him.

"Achoo!" Moria covered, he hoped successfully. He felt the stupidest idiot in existence for proposing to this woman, making her come apart on a terrace, and hiding underneath her wide skirts.

"I don't think she's feeling herself this evening after the performance, my lord. Perhaps we should find your carriage?"

Devyn knew his brother. He heard the held back laughter and recrimination in the other man's voice as he said, "If you'll come with me, my lady, we shall find Miss Kelley and see to getting her out of her... *misery.*"

When they were both gone and Moria had ascertained that they were alone, she pulled Devyn up from his perch by his lapels, kissing him breathless. She was laughing against his mouth, and his arms were around her waist.

He kissed the top of her head. "My ring's on your finger now," he spoke between them, "and the taste of you lingers on my tongue." He looked down, falling inside the cool, blue lakes of her eyes, "No going back, my tempest."

Her arms squeezed his midsection. "Stay right here for a moment, just like this."

He nodded, wrapping her in both arms; losing himself in the staccato of her heartbeat against him, the cool night air and the smell of flowers on a breeze, the sound of music and revelry just a few feet inside.

Chapter Twenty-Four

Could it be that our Lady Marina is taking some time to lick her wounds after the play written about her (or wasn't it)? Or... has someone turned her head?
- Scandalous Lives of London: August 1841

Not one of their family members had been altogether surprised to hear that Moria and Devyn had gotten engaged the night of the play. They'd not been able to hold it in the moment they'd entered Clairville's carriage. When Devyn had taken her home and spoken to her elder brother with her in the room, Jasper was a little put out that Devyn hadn't spoken to him first; but he'd conceded that Moria was four and twenty, and her own woman. Moria had wanted to kiss Devyn for not sending her out of the room for the conversation.

And then her whole family was rushing in, Olivia just returned from a ball in a flowery dress yelling: "My sister's going to be a bride! Finally!" making everyone laugh.

Every congratulations, every hug, each champagne toast to the couple's happiness from all the loved ones who truly cared, in her family home, felt like everything she had waited for.

But even with all their support, she'd found sleep hard to greet that night.

Be happy, her inner voice berated as she tossed and turned.

Why does it feel like being happy is only delaying the inevitable? That in my happy delirium, I won't feel the other shoe getting ready to drop?

Devyn was expected back at her family home in London at any moment, committed to spending all the time he could with Moria until he deployed. Moria left the breakfast table intent on taking her correspondence upstairs to her desk, contemplating how she'd spill the news that she was engaged, and not to The Duke.

But as soon as she turned the corner, her feet nearly collapsed from beneath her the moment the calendar on her desk caught her attention. She might have forgotten to take the page off a few too many days in a row, she had to rip a few pages to find the correct date. The bother was, she'd been so happy, her darkest days hadn't been on her mind.

"Ella?" she called, trying and failing to hide the strain in her voice.

Ella returned with a bundle of fabric over her arm. "Yes, my lady?"

"What day is it?"

"Friday? The 6th, I believe."

Moria's stomach dropped, her heart fell down a flight of stairs. How could she have forgotten? Her own daughter's birthday was tomorrow and she'd celebrated in Brookevale the last two years, but somehow she was here. In London.

"Pack a bag, we're going to Brookevale," she said, walking toward her closet.

"My lady? Is everything alright?" Ella asked, placing a hand on her arm.

Moria wanted her to leave. She felt a sob tearing its way through her chest, trying to escape through her mouth. Her eyes burned with tears pushing to break free. Her throat burned as she choked down a sob.

"Perfectly fine," she said, wiping at her eyes.

She wasn't perfectly fine. Rose was *there, alone,* in a graveyard, with no one to celebrate that she'd existed.

Moria felt the cold wood floor meet her as she slid down her door. The hem of her lavender morning dress tore as her foot collided with it. Her hair fell from her coiffure as she buried her head in her arms. The glint of her ring, Devyn's mother's ring on her finger, caught her gaze. The tears fell harder.

"My lady," Ella cooed.

Moria's throat was starting to feel raw and her head was starting to hurt. Moria didn't care, she let arms pull her into an embrace, resting her arm on a shoulder.

"There, love. It's going to be alright. I'm here."

But it wasn't Ella's voice. It was a masculine voice. She opened her eyes and pulled back. She had been so distraught, she hadn't heard him enter.

"Devyn, you're here," she tried to coax her voice into an even tone as the words came out, but they sounded choked and pained even to her own ears.

"Yes, love. What can I do for you?" His hands were so gentle and warm as he pushed her tear-soaked hair from her face and traced her cheek.

"I need. To pack. A trunk." She could feel how swollen her eyes were as she forced them to meet his.

"Where are we going?" he asked with the most steadying voice she'd ever heard. She didn't miss the 'we' in his voice. Her ears caught it, nestled it into her conscience, counted her heartbeats in its cadence.

"The church."

He nodded, never taking his eyes off hers. "Where is this church?"

"Brookevale," she said, biting her lip to stop it from trembling.

"And it will make you feel better if we get to this church?"

"I have to," she hated how the conviction and determination she felt in that moment didn't register in her voice. She followed his eyes as he noted the way her fist was curled around the lapel of his jacket.

"Is it alright if I leave you for just a moment to have the carriage sent for?"

Relief washed over every muscle and sinew. She sagged against the door and sucked in the first full, cleansing breath in minutes. She could only nod. She sat, curled up against the back of the door to her antechamber, unable to speak until he returned.

"Ella has your trunk packed. Mrs. Brierley packed us a picnic basket for the drive. They've all agreed to cover for you for 48 hours. The carriage is out front. Can you walk or shall I carry you, my lady?"

He'd arranged all of this in the span of a few minutes after seeing her in tears and asking only a few questions. She wanted to say all the things that this did to her, but she could only show him. She held out a hand and let him help her to her feet.

And then, she buried her head in his chest, both arms clenching his waist like a buoy in changing tides. When she'd felt like she was drowning in her own tears and grief, he'd been solid and steady. When he curled his spine to place his head atop hers, she took in another large breath.

"I can walk," she said against his chest.

"I figured you'd say that," She tucked the hint of a smile in his voice into the pocket of her being for later remembrance. "But if you change your mind, I am only a step behind."

I love you.

Three words standing on the edge of her tongue.

Three words she didn't have the courage to say.

Yet.

"Thank you," she said, leaning back to speak them into his eyes, into the small cracks between their bodies.

And he did as promised. He was one step behind her, a stalwart soldier sworn to protect her against all her own demons and pain and pride, as they walked down the stairs and into the mews. He handed her into the carriage and then sat across from her.

"Are you comfortable?" he asked once the carriage turned onto another street.

"If I said I'd be more comfortable next to you?"

"I'd happen to agree."

When he pulled a small laugh out of her, a few stray tears made it out in its wake. She didn't know why those four words affected her, but having someone understand, reciprocate even, to want to hold her as much as she wanted to be held was a luxury she hadn't always been afforded.

His strong, gentle arms pulled her across the seat. They tucked her into his side. They curled around her shoulder and her waist. She placed a hand atop his, tracing a vein from the back of his hand to his forearm. He briefly closed his eyes at the contact, settling them both deeper into the carriage seat.

Surely, he wants to know what sent me into a crying fit?

"Why don't you rest your eyes and I'll let you know if we make any stops."

She looked up at him, into the starry night of his eyes. "What about you?"

"I'm holding you. Don't you think I'm perfectly content right now?"

Then he must have read her mind, either that or he saw the way her eyes fell to the full, pouty pillow of his bottom lip. He placed her chin between his thumb and forefinger and tipped her face up to his. The light in his eyes became darkness, taking in the bow of her lips seconds before he set his mouth to hers. The press of his lips against hers, one lip circling another, one lip succumbing to the invitation of another. She could taste the mint of his breath and the salt of her own tears. Her hands grasped the back of his head, twining in his dark locks.

A torturously pleasurable groan escaped from him, she chased it into her own mouth. She wanted to taste his sounds. It blocked out the taste of her tears. He blocked out everything else, holding her against him as he said, "You should rest for a while. I'll be here."

∾

When Moria closed her eyes, she saw the same dream she'd seen before countless times.

Her brothers supported Marcus' weight on either side in the kitchens of Brookevale, his arms slung over their shoulders.

"Moria," Marcus called, reaching for her with a bloody hand. The sound of her name on his lips sounded differently than it had any other time in the past. Moria placed a palm against the nearby doorway to steady herself at the sight of him, a trail of blood in his wake.

"Sister, we need you, go and get your sewing kit," Lawrence called over a shoulder as their eldest sibling, Jasper, the heir, laid Marcus on the emptied table in the kitchen.

Moria choked on a sob. "My...sewing kit?" she asked, swallowing the lump in her throat.

"The Marquess was shot," Jasper explained without meeting her eyes. "We've sent for a doctor, but he's losing so much blood he'll never make it if we wait. I'll do my best to remove the bullet, but you've the steadier hand with a needle."

Marcus' turquoise eyes darted back and forth between the two of them. It was evident her brothers still didn't know about her and Marcus. That hadn't been her doing, Marcus had been the one who insisted they wait before telling anyone, which she hadn't understood before was wrong; but now she did.

She wanted to run to him, to take his hand in hers, to run her fingers through his gold hair...

"Moria!" Lawrence snapped.

When Moria returned with her sewing basket, she was ever so careful not to jostle the table underneath Marcus with her movements. She was more careful with him in that moment than he'd ever been with her, or her heart.

Lawrence supported Marcus' head as he poured a hip flask of liquor down his throat and then laid him back down on the table. Marcus reached for her hand and pulled her close with the hand of his uninjured side even though it seemed to use all his remaining strength.

"My girl...I'm...sorry," he breathed, clutching her hand like a tether to life. He'd grabbed her like this before, but she'd been so swept away by his attention solely focused on her, she hadn't listened to the alarm bells in her head. When both of her brothers looked at Moria in shock, she felt it then. The secret possession he'd made of her, it felt wrong when she saw the way it must look through their eyes.

"Don't...go," Marcus bit out, his face paling under the light of the fire in the kitchen hearth. She kissed the white skin of his knuckles just before his eyelids fluttered and he lost consciousness.

She counted the rising and falling of Marcus' chest and felt his fingers occasionally tighten around hers, his head occasionally lolling to one side. For a few moments, none of the occupants of the room spoke.

"Don't think we won't be discussing this later," Lawrence said as Jasper's capable and slender fingers dug with instruments procured from God knows where to remove a bullet lodged in the abdomen of their neighbor, Moria's secret beau.

A small gasp tore through Marcus's pale, parted lips as though he were regaining consciousness when Jasper held up a bullet.

"He'll need sewing up now, Moria."

Was she supposed to sew up the father of her unborn child with the same needle she'd just begun stitching a little linen bonnet?

She couldn't get enough air. She couldn't breathe—

HANDS SHOOK HER. SOMEONE WAS CALLING HER NAME.

When Moria opened her eyes, she saw who it was. She read the pain and confusion in his face.

"It was only a dream," Her Captain said, reassuring them both.

"I need to tell you something," the words leapt out before she could hold them back.

He held up a hand between them. "Wait. Whatever it is, love, it's yours to keep till you're ready to share it. And whatever it is, you're not carrying it alone. Not anymore."

Moria's hand toying with the hair at the nape of his neck fell back like she'd been burned.

"You wouldn't say that," she shook her head, avoiding his eyes to look out the carriage window. "Not if you knew the truth."

Devyn ducked his head, searching for her eyes, a large finger tipping up her chin.

"None of that, my girl. I want all of you, for a lifetime. You try me and see if I run. You ought to know by now that I won't. Whatever you throw at me, I'll catch it," he said, dark eyes somehow so gentle and trustworthy, or maybe Moria had made friends with the dark.

Moria didn't meet his eyes for a moment, couldn't. She'd been so tempted by this man and the thrill of him, but the innate gentleness and affection of his words, his touch, had deepened whatever was between them. The word for what it was danced on the tip of her tongue, she knew what it was. It meant that she had to give him all the facts.

"What if I told you someone had left a hole inside I was unsure if anyone could fill? Until you."

His eyes went to the chain she usually wore around her neck. His fingers skated along her collarbone. "It was him," he said with real-ization.

But when he went to reach for the pendant that she wore, it was different. It looked similar, only this time, when he turned over the pendant instead of an M, there was a D carved there. When he saw it, he pulled back, and she caught him by one of his thick wrists. He took her hand to his lips and kissed it.

"As good and honorable as you are, you need to know. And if you still want me—"

He crushed her to him, his lips overtaking hers, showing her without telling her just how much he wanted her. As the carriage wheels rolled, they were pushed even closer together. She slid her tongue into his mouth, slipping it around his and drinking in the little sounds of pleasure she drew out of him. It was sweeter and headier than any wine.

He pulled back, then granted her one more chaste kiss at the tip of her nose that made her feel cared for, both sturdy and a little wobbly at the same time.

"You and your body and your words have my undivided atten-tion, my lady," Devyn said, making a show of crossing his arms and sitting up straighter on the carriage seat.

Moria wasn't sure where to begin this tale, so she started at the beginning. "Marcus lured me with false declarations and promises and a hundred other things, but I didn't realize until afterward how false it all was. The only thing that was real was that I meant and I believed everything I said, and I gave him my full heart."

She swallowed, then nodded. "Marcus took, that's all he knew how to do. He took everything that I willingly gave, without proposing to me. There was always some test of my love for him, some reason keeping him from offering for my hand. I didn't see it for what it was," she let out a long exhale and leaned more of her weight into Devyn.

"Or maybe, I also didn't tell anyone because I didn't want them to tell me what I already knew: it wasn't love. Love doesn't..." She shook her head as a tear escaped. "Love doesn't inflict words harsher than any slap ever could. Love isn't lies and coercion. But in the end, Marcus was shot in a duel over some gambling debts. He was planning to marry me only if his scheme to make money fell through, and he made sure that I was thoroughly ruined so I would have no other choice and wouldn't know until it was too late."

"I'd rip the man to shreds if I wasn't already too late. Why did you wear his initial around your neck?"

Moria paused, her hand on the window curtain, familiar hills rolling into view. Soon, they'd be at her family home, and the realization made it possible for Moria to take in a bracing breath.

"It wasn't the loss of Marcus I mourned as much as the loss of what we had, the loss of our child. She'd have been turning three tomorrow. Had she lived."

When she turned shadowed eyes upon him, she didn't know what reaction she'd expected her words to garner from this gentle brute of a man, but his mouth fell agape. Belatedly, he closed it. Tears swam in his eyes, he reached for her like he wanted to hold her. He wiped at his eyes with the back of a hand, and then linked his fingers with hers. The tactile comfort was more than comfort, it suffused her with bravery, warm fingers covering the cold places inside of her enough to keep talking.

"This is what you were dreaming about?"

"It's a dream, a memory I live over and over. Even when I start to hate him for what he did, I picture the end. The night I stitched him back together after my brother removed the bullet lodged in his side, and he never came to. I was so young and naïve that I laid in bed for over a day thinking I'd caused it myself. And then, at the funeral, no one knew I was mourning a man I'd.... I'd loved in secret. At least, I thought that's what it was."

She couldn't look him and her foolishness in the eye so she avoided both and looked away, shaking her head at her past folly.

"And then my mother found out my courses hadn't come, so she whisked me away to a seaside cottage for "my health," but it turned out that she was the one who was unwell. There she was with her wasting disease while I puked up my guts and whined constantly," she dabbed at her eyes with the back of her wrist. His capable hand held her other one in his as she continued.

"One night I woke up and my sheets were soaked with blood. I thought I'd never stop crying. I was in so much pain. And I thought she was going to say, "maybe it's for the best." But she didn't. She held me, and I held my little girl who never took her first breath in my arms. I wanted her, I wanted to be her mother, to show her such fierce love she'd never know the loss of a father, especially not a cold, hurtful man like Marcus."

She watched the way a tear tracked down his cheek, not of sadness, but the pride in his eyes as he looked at her cracked her open even more.

"And she's at Brookevale now?" he asked, his voice gentle.

"We buried her by the sea. And then my mother made me promise that I'd..." she choked on the words. "That I'd make the match of the century, that I'd spurn everyone who'd hurt me or talked behind my back. 'The only way forward...is through.' That's what she told me, and I hear her voice, telling me that, all the time."

Devyn sat up straighter as the carriage wheels hit a particularly rocky jut in the road. She'd been- what? Nineteen? Twenty?- grieving in secret and carrying the child of a man who'd hurt her and tried to trap her before dying a grisly death.

He reached for her, and she let him hold her against his chest. The sound of her long, slow inhale against his chest unbalanced him. Nearly as much as seeing that pendant she wore replaced with a *D* instead of an *M*.

"Your daughter...her birthday. That's what had you so distraught."

He could feel Moria's throat bob against his collarbone, and then she nodded.

He wrapped his arms tighter around her. "I think you are very brave, Moria."

She pulled back to study him. The setting sun through the window lit her golden hair and golden face, but there was wonder in her eyes directed up at him. "I don't know that anyone has ever called me that before."

She was so strong, had been so strong for so long, had no one ever held her and told her she didn't have to be strong anymore?

"You are," he wrapped a hand around her jaw, slipped it into her hair. "You are the strongest, bravest woman I know that you could take so many losses and build a life for yourself amongst the ruins. My strong, beautiful girl."

"Your girl," she repeated the words like she wanted to savor the taste of them on her own tongue. "Does that mean that you still want me?"

Devyn had no words to answer this question. He took the finger bearing his mother's ring and held it to his lips. He kissed her finger, the words coming to him in a rush.

"I want you every day, in every way that you will have a humble soldier like me. I'm yours, my lady, and I promise to make you know it every day of our lives."

The mid-afternoon sun limning Moria's childhood home, visible through the carriage window, caught their attention. The carriage slowed to a stop in the front drive. Brierley, the butler who didn't leave Brookevale Park, rushed out to meet them flanked by other house staff.

"Ready to scandalize the servants?" she asked, brows dancing.

His laugh was ready and filled his chest. "I'm in for a lifetime of scandals with you aren't I, my lady?"

She didn't say it, but it was in her eyes. Later, he'd question if it was the golden hour; but at that moment, he knew. The radiant spark in her glorious eyes, it was one word, a feeling that started with an "L," and didn't ever end.

Chapter Twenty-Five

When the sun rose on an early autumn day, Moria was already awake. She sat on a window seat and watched every single color painted across the sky, crying when shades of orange turned to pink and then purple and then blue. Pink was always Rose's color. It was a color Moria clung to, even if sometimes in secret, for a girl she never got to know, never got to love.

It was fitting that she greeted the rising of the sun alone. She could almost feel the familiar, soothing presence of her mother watching the sunrise with her like they had in the past, the phantom touch of a hand on her shoulder. But she didn't have to be alone.

Moria rose from her seat at the window, replacing her wrap about her shoulders. She slipped her feet into a pair of misshapen slippers that Olivia had made for her, smiling to herself. Of all the finer things Moria owned, she loved those slippers and the care that had gone into them. Not that she'd ever said as much, for if she did, Olivia and her skill-less needle would make her ten more pairs.

Moria padded down the hall to the room she'd shown Devyn to last night.

They'd arrived together, explaining that Captain Winter was here on business, to see one of the Earl's horses put up for sale. No one had the cheek to question why Lady Moria, of all people, was acting as broker.

She'd shown him to a room, then she'd gone for a walk. Something about carriage rides always made her limbs feel restless. She'd picked flowers for a posy for her daughter's grave on her walk: wildflowers from the edge of the fields and forest, roses, jasmine, and peonies from the hothouse.

He'd found her there, tears in her eyes and blooms in her hands, and said, "There's the flower I was looking for."

It felt so domestic and real and uninterrupted to have him all to herself in her family home, in the place where she'd spent countless hours imagining her bridal bouquet, growing flowers for her family's table and for the arrangements at the village church altar.

He'd stood behind her, draping those powerful arms about her middle. The way he craned his neck to lean down to traipse the sweetest kisses from her cheek down her neck and shoulder had her knees turning to marmalade. She could smell the hint of mint and parchment and sweat as her body pressed against his.

She'd closed her eyes at the exquisite contact, bringing up a hand to touch his jaw. They stayed there like that inside a protective bubble, like time and all the things racing toward them couldn't find them there. His stubble against her exposed skin, her mouth against his, hands touching and bracing, his male heat radiating through the linen of her day dress. They spoke few words, there was a whole language translated between them.

And then the dinner gong. She'd gone to change for dinner, he having brought no other clothes, forced to make do with something that belonged to one of her brothers. He'd showed up at her door, holding his dinner jacket split down the seams at the back.

"I told you it wouldn't work."

She'd been unable to hold in her laughter. "The shape of a man like you wasn't made for dinner jackets, my darling," she said, placing a hand on the fine linen of his shirt. The heat of his skin beneath warmed her hand.

He looked down at the ring on her finger. "What was I made for then?"

Moria looked around the hall to make certain there weren't any servants watching. Slipping a hand inside his shirt, she stood on her tiptoes. She poured all the fierce, bubbling emotions into a kiss. His teeth gathered her bottom lip into his mouth, one hand squeezing her waist. That tender pressure concentrating so close to her core, her veins throbbed with the need for him to take those large, beautiful hands and move them lower.

"You were made for me," she spoke the words against his lips.

A servant rounded the corner then.

"Greta?" the maid turned to her with a curtsy at the sound of her name from her mistress, Devyn pulled apart from her. "Could you tell Brierley that Captain Winter and I will take our dinner on trays in the library?" Moria gave her a saucy wink.

The maids' cheeks reddened. "Yes, my lady," she muttered and tore off down the hallway toward the servants' stairs.

DEVYN SAT ACROSS FROM HER AT A LARGE TABLE IN THE library in only his shirt sleeves and waistcoat. The outline of his muscular thighs in breeches and bespoke boots kept snagging her attention as the footman laid a tray before them.

Without proper warning, they'd had to settle for a dinner of cold meats, sandwiches, cheeses, and fruits. Moria had chosen to supplement her dinner with a liquid one.

He took the bottle from her hands. "I'll have one, just the one."

"So very disciplined, Captain." The way his throat bobbed as he swallowed, keeping his eyes trained on her, made her feel feverish.

"Have to keep my head around you."

She tipped her drink back. "Thought you'd already lost it."

"My head, my heart, my family jewels, my sanity," he laughed, pulling her against his side. She rested her head on his shoulder.

"Do you have to smell so good?" she asked, nuzzling the side of his neck with her nose.

He pulled her tighter to his side. The feel of his arm draped around her, here, alone in her family's house without any regard for what her family would say if they knew, took her back to another life. To a different man she'd never gotten to love in the light of day. Devyn wasn't that man, and she wasn't that girl, but her mind was playing tricks on her.

"Hey," he tipped her chin up with a finger, a very large finger, to meet his eyes. "Where did you go? Come back to me."

The concern in his voice, the smell of him, the sheer size of him, the dark tempest of his eyes. He was so much. There was so much to this man. And she wanted everything with him.

Her hand fisted around the strands of hair at the nape of his neck and brought him to her mouth, hitching up her skirts to straddle him. His lips opened, letting her drag her tongue along the inside, scouring the roof of his mouth. She took in the rumble that emanated from deep in his chest and swallowed it greedily. Her hands were hungry marauders, roaming the wide expanse of his shoulders, down the slopes of his honed pectorals to his abdomen, and inside his shirt looking for purchase.

He pulled back and swore. "Moria," he breathed her name against her hair.

"Mmm," she whispered, teasing her lips across the exposed skin of his neck.

"What is it you want?"

"There's a ring on my finger now..."

He swore, low and guttural and heating her to her core. "You've been drinking though."

"I am in full use of my faculties," Moria covered her eyes. "Ask me about the paintings in this room."

"The one right behind me?"

"A glowering old miser named Frederick. He was married to the once ravishing redhead in the green dress, in the painting over by the decanters."

She could feel Devyn turning to look. "And how about between the two windows along the far wall?"

"That's a picture of my grandfather's eleven most favorite hunting dogs, and his sons."

Devyn let out a singular *ha*. "This family of yours. And the one hanging beside the dart board?"

"It isn't a dart board, it's for throwing knives. Lawrence got it for Noelle after our parents died, she needed something to do other than write letters. And that would be the seventh Earl's fourth wife. Isn't she a beauty? No relation though, but I always loved that purple necklace and was quite sad it got willed to Kathleen."

Devyn peeled her hands from her eyes. "That's a lot of eyes watching us."

"There are no eyes in my bedchamber."

Devyn looked down pointedly at the barely touched plate on the table in front of them. "You also drank, rather than ate your dinner."

"I was hungry for something else," she said, devouring him with her eyes. "Why are you blushing? I'm the debutante, aren't I supposed to blush?"

"Come here, you viper," he said, reaching for her.

There was a note of laughter in his voice that wrapped around her, comforting and warm. God above, she could wear his laugh as her favorite frock and never get tired of it.

He was kissing her, one massive hand pulling at her hair pins. She opened her mouth for him. He rewarded this small act with a swipe of his tongue that possessed her own. Her hand snaked into the collar of his shirt and down his back, aiming to pull it over his head. He nipped her bottom lip into his mouth, sucking on it until it released with a pop.

"Oh my god," she breathed. "You are a fantasy."

He laughed again, wicked and sinful and boyish. "What fantasies am I conjuring..." his devious mouth traveled to her collarbone. He licked up her neck, bit her earlobe. "Right now?"

"The naked kind, definitely," she said, reaching for his trousers.

They'd started this before, in a rowboat, in his club, at a party, but now they were alone. How many more moments would they get like this before he had to answer the call of duty and leave her behind?

"Are you sure?" He stilled her hands.

"These clothes? I need them off you or..." she shook her head, still looking at his perfect form. "I swear I'm going to go mad."

She pulled at his shirt as he lifted his arms for her to haul it off and throw it over the back of the settee. His broad bared chest heaving made her impatient.

"Are you sure you aren't outrunning your feelings?"

"I'm *running toward* a different feeling," she answered, gripping his erection through his breeches, when he let out a groan. "A very hard one."

He let out a curse, nipping her shoulder.

"You are not the only one with a wicked mouth." She kissed his neck, licking her way down his bared chest, stopping to nip at one of his perfect light brown nipples.

"That so?"

"Would you like a demonstration?" she said, undoing his breeches, freeing him. The tantalizing V of his hips led to dark hair surrounding what she'd been searching for.

"Fuck," he ground out. "I should say no, but as usual, I'm powerless when it comes to you."

"You're larger than I thought you'd be," she said, wrapping a hand around his erection. His very large erection.

"That's half mast, sweetheart."

"Jesus Christ," she said, eliciting a laugh from him.

Devyn was wiping tears of laughter from his eyes. Then she was kissing him, holding onto her with his mouth while she moved him up and down in her hands. He pulled away to lick her palm with two broad swipes, then set it back to the length of him she held in her grasp. Her core clinched.

She began moving her hand again, kissing him harder. With every stroke of her hand, he was moving with her, kissing her. One large hand cupped her breast, but she wanted more.

Moria took the sheet of her unbound hair and held it in one hand. She dropped to her knees in front of the settee. Devyn leaned down, lifting up her knees to place a velvet pillow beneath them. He was always looking after her; the smallest, most intimate gestures stealing pieces of her heart as much as that piano.

She licked up the groaning length of him. When she took him inside her mouth, the deep groan that came from his lips made her feel powerful. She moved him up and down, back and forth, using both her mouth and tongue to taste, to suck, to lick. A large hand held her hair in his grasp as she moved up and down, she felt his release move closer at her coaxing.

"Fuck," he ground out, hips moving in the same rhythm as her mouth. "That's right, angel, fuck me with your mouth."

His hip and stomach muscles flexed taut as he moved with her. Fire coiled at the base of her spine at his coarse words. She'd done this before; but it had been furtive, taboo, elicit, done in the dark. Having him spread out on her settee, his ring on her finger, his heart in her back pocket, it was different. *He* was different.

Devyn's member hit the back of her throat, she kept moving, feeling him flex and move inside her.

"Look at me," he whispered, pulling her face toward him. "I want you to look in my eyes when I come down your pretty throat."

She let out a little whimper, taking him deeper still. She kept her eyes on him as she licked him from root to tip. His eyes fluttered closed for a moment as he groaned, fisting her hair a little harder. Her nails dug into the full, muscled ridge of his backside as his hips bucked off the settee, pushing him into her mouth. Her cheeks hollowed. She moved faster up and down, hollowing her cheeks again.

Devyn spilled into her, not holding back or quieting the groan that accompanied his release. She drank down his sounds, his ecstasy, his dark eyes on hers, and his seed down the back of her throat. She wiped her mouth with the back of her hand, keeping her eyes on him like he'd asked.

His hands stole her from her perch, dragging her up his length to perch atop him. She placed both hands on his firm chest. The dark hair on his chest somehow made her feel molten again.

"Christ, woman, I was not expecting that," he said, willing his breath to even out again.

"Which part?" she said, tracing her fingers over his chest.

"The part where you got on your knees for me," a hand pushed her hair over her shoulder, "the part where you sucked me off," that hand trailed down her decolletage, "the part where you did what you were told most of all."

There was teasing laughter in his voice. She hit him playfully in his chest. He pulled her to lay against one of his bare, pectoral muscles.

"I will be promising to love and honor and *obey* soon."

His voice was strained above her head. "Not if you don't want to."

She turned to look up at him and raised a brow.

He clarified, "The obey part."

"Devyn Winter, I could get on my knees for you again hearing you say that."

He answered her with a long, drugging, slow kiss. "Would you like me to get on my knees for *you*?"

She wanted a release, but his arms were around her, his chest was solid and safe and warm. There was a fire before them. He'd pulled a plush blanket around them. Not that it was necessary given how warm his skin was, how warm he made her feel. His calloused hands were drawing tender little patterns on her back. His heartbeat beneath her cheek was steady. She could feel his breath on her temple, in her hair.

This was a brand of intimacy she'd never before been party to... until Devyn.

"I want you to stay just like this." She wrapped her arms around his bare torso, holding onto him tighter, burrowing into his chest further.

"Whatever you want, Moria," he said softly, and he held her, drawing patterns on her back, his hands playing in her hair, until her eyelids drifted closed.

AND SO HERE SHE WAS NOW, LIT BY MORNING SUNLIGHT, in front of Devyn's door, again.

He pulled it open before she could knock.

"Come here," he said, pulling her inside.

He'd obviously been dressing. He was in his breeches and boots, but no shirt. The sight of him was like a strike to her senses.

She wrapped her arms about him, burrowing into his warmth and the smell of *him*. She was home, at Brookevale Park, but he was home to her too.

"I love you," she said, against his pectoral muscle.

"Say it again."

She heard the awed smile in his voice, and felt it against her ear. She held him tighter.

"I love you. Like...in a way that scares me so much, but it fills me up so full that I have to let it out. I have to tell you. Devyn Winter, I am so stupid, mad in love with you. And everything you do for me, everything you are, feels too good and too right for me. I don't know how I'll breathe when you leave me. Because I've tried to be so in control, but somehow, I've completely lost the plot. And yet it doesn't matter that I've lost control of my head or my heart, because you are the best thing in my life."

A tear collided with the top of her head. She craned her neck to look up at him, not slackening her grip on his waist.

"I love you back," he said, pouring the words back into a fiery, desperate kiss.

It tasted like all the things she'd ever wanted and thought she could never deserve, spearmint, and tears. Hers or his, both, she wasn't sure. She lost track of her lips, the rest of her body, the rest of time, in his kiss.

She pushed him backwards until his knees backed up against his large bed.

"We have somewhere to be today. We have plenty of time for that later."

And he threw on his shirt, tucking it into his breeches. Moria let out a gasp, noting the color of his shirt. Tears pricked her eyes. He pulled her hand in his, planting a kiss on her knuckles.

"Lead the way to the church, my lady."

"Your shirt," she choked out, "it's..."

"Pink," he whispered, planting a kiss to the top of her head. "It's Wednesday."

Tears spilled out of her eyes. He wiped them away. He was walking out of his room, pulling her along behind him. She followed him to the stables where Challenger, the horse he was meant to be considering buying as pretense for his visit, was saddled along with her mount, Regina. They rode in mostly companionable silence, hands clasped between their saddles a taut rope holding them together, to the church.

They could have walked. But Moria drew out the short ride, stopping here and there to point things out on her family's property to him, to share little stories and parts of her life with the man she loved. Soon, he'd be gone, and they wouldn't get this. And then the chapel and its graveyard came into view.

Marcus' large, ornate, marble mausoleum stood out above the smaller graves. The large *M* caught her eye first. The rose she'd planted had bloomed into a large, spilling dark pink rose bush that almost blocked the entrance. She knelt to run a hand over the rose quartz stone beside it. Devyn had let her dismount first, then followed after tying his horse to a hitching post. Then he was a wall of sturdy man behind her, his hands at her hips and his mouth close to her hair.

"This isn't where my mother buried her," she said. "She's...somewhere by the sea. Where I lost her. But this is where she should have been. Near her..." she choked out. "Near her father. Something in me felt that they should be together, that some part of her belonged with him, and not all by herself. There was a curl of her hair buried here."

"Hello, Rose," Devyn whispered. "I'll forever feel the loss of knowing you, but that loss is shared by all humanity, I'm sure," he looked up at the mausoleum in front of them. "And Your Lordship, I trust you are taking good care of your daughter. I'm sure the two of you won't mind if I care for her mother for you. I don't need your blessing," he squeezed Moria's fingers. "But I'll love her for the both of you."

His side profile was even more beautiful then in Moria's eyes, the wind whisked a strand of dark hair from his eyes like a caress as he turned to the larger mausoleum where her parents had made their final resting place.

"My Lord and Lady Pembrooke," he inclined his head. "I want

you to know, I'll do my very best," he looked at Moria, and she fell into the starry depths of those dark eyes. "To give her all that she deserves."

Moria didn't collapse like she had the other times at this grave site. She kissed his fingers entwined with hers. She didn't shake or tremble. She held her head high, the love of an extraordinary man who saw all her flaws and cracks making it easier for her to breathe under the weight of it all for the first time.

Chapter Twenty-Six

The Burn Book of Lady M

The Earl of Clairville, The true *Earl of Clairville. You were in front of me this whole time. How did I not see the signs? What a stunning liar you turned out to be.*

~

It was a night she'd cherish forever, all the people she really loved sitting around a table, sharing a meal that she was sure Jasper had spent days poring over a menu for and she'd never fully appreciate. The conversation and the wine had flowed until the late hours, no one making moves to leave.

The ladies and gentlemen had all retired to the same sitting room rather than separate spaces. Kathleen had been adamant that with Devyn's departure in only a couple of days, that they give the betrothed time together, not to force them apart. And so there had been parlor games, music, and drink, and laughter in Pembrooke House of a caliber not seen in decades.

And at the center of all of it, wasn't just her, but the man that she…. loved.

Love wasn't a word that carried the full weight of what she felt for him. It was too watered down, too much for everyday use, not rare enough.

Devyn was not an ornamental man. God, but he was beautiful though.

It had lit her from within with a kind of unfamiliar iridescence to see the people she loved laughing at his jokes, asking him questions about his deployment, smiling at him appreciatively while he gave diplomatic answers with important sounding words, being happy for her. *Being happy.*

And at intervals all too frequent to count, whether anyone had been watching or not, he'd given her pieces of affection that she wasn't sure how she was supposed to go months without. His lips brushing her forehead, his fingers brushing hers, his hand at the small of her back, his knee touching hers. They weren't scripted or to gain her attention, they were as natural as air.

An air supply that was cut off when Peregrine had taken his coat from her at his departure and said, "I'm glad you weren't too angry with him."

She'd thought the other shoe dropping was her daughter's birthday, needing to be there, needing to share it with the man she loved. This, *this* was the other shoe dropping.

"I'm a forgiving woman," she said, not sure exactly what Peregrine was referring to.

"Naturally, I told him he should tell you sooner rather than later."

Thwap, the other shoe hit her in the head. Pain lanced through her heart.

What had Devyn not told her?

You're not the only one who can keep secrets, some inner voice mocked.

When Moria was tongue-tied, unsure how to respond, Peregrine's face fell.

"Oh god, he *didn't* tell you, did he? I've just gone and fucked up the whole damn night with my big mouth after two many glasses of port. Forget I said anything, my lady, I'll see myself out."

The shoe had dropped, she had to know what it was, if it was a shoe she could wear, or a shoe that would rub raw places in her soul.

Moria was fast, seizing a hand around Peregrine's upper arm. "Oh no, you don't. You lit this fire. Put it out or I'll carry a grudge for this for longer than you can imagine."

Peregrine leaned in and did just that.

DEVYN KNEW THE MOMENT THAT SOMETHING HAD GONE amiss.

He could see it in her eyes before the words fell out, she was spoiling for a fight.

Moria didn't say goodbyes to the others as they left, instead telling them all she was tired, until Devyn was the last to come bid her goodnight. He wrapped his arms about her and leaned in to kiss her.

She didn't say anything, she took his hand and pulled him up the stairs to her room. He was as quiet as he could possibly be at six-foot-three and the size of a door. But she was squeezing on his hand, towing him down the carpeted hall while her glowering ancestors looked down on him in portraiture, finding him wanting.

When they made it to her room, the pinkest room he'd ever seen in his goddamned life, she closed the door. She took two steps, pressing him up against it. For a woman of her size, she was surprisingly formidable.

"When were you going to tell me?" she whirled on him.

"When was I going to tell you what, Moria?" He willed his voice to sound gentle.

She let out an angry little huff and crossed her arms over her chest. "That your brother isn't the heir, you are. He's your father's bastard. *He's* the spare, *not* you."

The floor dropped out from beneath him.

He was going to murder Peregrine. He'd wanted to tell the woman he loved all about his family history, he just...actually, there was no excuse, he should have fucking told her already.

When?

He didn't know honestly, but before now. He'd wanted to show her he was better than all the other men she'd known, but maybe he wasn't.

"He told you. Earlier when you walked him out."

"I'm glad someone apprised me of the truth," she said, her jaw set.

He'd gotten so far, knocked down so many of her walls, heard her say *I love you*, and now she was looking at him like an enemy. He fucking hated it.

"It doesn't change anything." He shook his head, letting her step backward.

Her mouth was agog, then she closed it, flaring her nostrils, and opened it again.

"I don't see how!"

She was angry with him. Good, that meant she still cared. Hadn't shut him out completely. Not yet at least.

He took a step closer to her, closer than he'd meant. But he was trying desperately to pull the ground back beneath their feet. God, she was so close he could easily kiss her.

"No. It wouldn't," he could see she was waiting for an answer, so he sat on the edge of her bed, pulling her to stand between his legs. He held her hands in his as she looked down at him, listening to him explain.

"My father raised Peregrine to be the heir, he was the heir for almost a decade before I came along. My father pushed me to take it all away from Peregrine, for us to be in competition for every scrap of paternal pride and affection, every material possession. He dangled them in front of us, asking us to carry out increasingly awful tasks to get them. If I failed, well I bear the scars of that," he gestured to his inked torso covered by his shirt. "Most of them I covered up with tattoos. Some of the blows I took were for Peregrine. Even though I was younger, I was bigger, stronger."

He watched her lip wobble at his admission, taking it between her teeth. Devyn ran a hand through his hair and blew some air out of his mouth to keep talking instead of kissing her.

"But when I became a man, I realized something. I was better suited to soldiering, and Peregrine is tailored for land management and shaking hands in Parliament sessions. A soldier is all I've ever been. That's *all* I know how to do. And I'm damn good at it—"

"You're lying to yourself," she said, a hand coming to rest against his stubbled cheek when he thought maybe he'd better deserved a slap. He leaned into the softness of her hand and closed his eyes.

"You are more than a soldier, Devyn. You," she poked him in the chest with the pointer finger of her other hand for emphasis, "Are not a spare anything. You're honorable, and just, and a man that people look up to. Your men put their careers on the line for you. In any way that counts, you're just as fine a man as your brother is and just as noble."

Devyn's heart swelled with pride at the words. To hear such words from her lips made him hold her tighter. His fingers dug into her waist.

"To hear you say that, that's all I've ever wanted. But Peregrine's whole life is Parliament, his causes. He does more good for the working class than I even know about. The work he does-"

"Is accomplished more easily with his influence but he would still accomplish it with yours."

"You don't want me without a title, is that it?" The words came out harsher than he meant.

Moria grabbed his hands, held them to her heart. Her little fingers were trembling, nails digging in like little cold needles to keep him close.

"Listen to me, you don't have to go. You don't have to fight. Sell your commission. Stay. Take up the role that's yours to take."

"It's not that simple."

Moria was quiet for a moment. "I wish for once it could be."

"Moria, I-"

She held up a hand, he hated the emotion in her eyes. "You listened to me. I told you my deepest, darkest secret. The darkest hours of my life. You promised yourself to me, but you kept this from me?"

"It was never my secret to tell, it's always been Peregrine's."

"I trusted you, but you didn't trust me with something that could make our lives so much different. You didn't tell me because you didn't want me to talk you out of going. You didn't trust me to keep your secret."

"It isn't that I don't trust you, but I can see how it would appear that I didn't." He shook his head to punctuate the words he said next. "I can't lose you over this."

Both of her hands came up to the back of his head. "You and me, we don't need proposals or rings or formal introductions to define what we have."

Her small fingers pressed into his nape as her ocean-colored eyes bore into his.

"You found me when I needed you, you kept finding me. You never let me push you away, and I kept holding on. I'll keep holding on. Keep..." she gripped him tighter, like he might blow away on a breeze, blew some air out of her mouth. "Loving you," she gritted out.

Tears marched down her cheeks like two steady soldiers.

"Because I know you'll come back to me. You told me yourself, remember? *'Who could let something like death keep them from a face like yours?'*"

His eyes were swimming, drowning in tears, in the sight of the woman he loved, the woman who loved him, in front of him maybe for the last time. He was here, in her rooms. A place he'd have given his soul to be invited into in the past.

With a fluid motion, he reversed their positions, so that she was on her bed, and he was above her. She wrapped her legs around his middle. He kissed the inside of her arm.

"You were supposed to see me off tomorrow," he trailed kisses down her arm to her shoulder. "This is how I planned to say goodbye."

Then he was possessing that stupidly perfect mouth of hers, losing himself in a kiss that just kept going. Every flick of her tongue to meet his, every nip, every little whimper, every roll of her hips to meet his bringing him that much closer to ruination. He was done for.

"Please," she begged. "Devyn, you have to give me this, please. Just be mine, this once. I want you to be mine and I want you to possess me, even if it's only the once."

His hands bracketed her cheeks. "You've possessed me for longer than you realize, my love. You'll possess me in body and soul until I'm nothing but dust and bones."

"I want to possess you *right now.*"

"I'm afraid I haven't more to give you than this battle-worn body. I'm not enough for you."

She wanted it all, matrimony, a future with him. He wanted to give her that. He didn't want to leave her like this, without something real to cling to.

He also had honor just like she had hers.

He loved his brother.

He loved his men.

He loved her too.

Agony must surely have been written on his face, for she burrowed into him. Her skirts brushed his thighs, her breasts a mere prayer from his face. She started removing her bodice, her sleeves, and cast them on the floor.

His throat constricted, he swallowed the lump in his throat. She removed her garments and let down her hair until she was standing in front of him in only her chemise and unbound hair.

"Promise me, Devyn," she said, placing his hands about her waist.

"Anything," he vowed against her lips.

Sitting on her bed, she stood finally just a little more than eye level with him, holding his face and his heart in her hands.

"You'll come home from fighting in Her Majesty's Army, and I'll still be yours."

He closed in the space between them. "You will never not be mine, Moria. And I will never be anything but yours. Until I draw my dying breath."

Her greedy hands drew his lips toward hers and she drank him like a starving woman.

He pulled back to whisper, "I don't want to take you like this."

"You can't take what's freely given, Captain," she said, bringing one of his hands up to cup her breasts.

"Fuck it," he groaned.

With both hands, he pulled her in for a kiss that seared away all doubts with every flick of her tongue, every stroke of his hands against her jaw. She pulled his shirt from his breeches, he leaned back to pull it over his head and cast it onto the carpeted floor.

He watched her eyes roam his body, the large expanse of chest and torso, the scars that mapped his pain. He drowned in her gaze, forgetting to breathe until she touched him again.

He ran a hand down her chest, cupping one breast and bringing it to his mouth. The sound of her little breathy moan spurred him on. He blew on it, watching it harden and darken underneath his attention. He gave the same attention to the other side.

Belatedly, he realized she was unfastening his breeches.

He slid a hand to cup her between her thighs, throwing one leg over his shoulder.

"Oh my god," she let out, clutching his shoulder with intent fingers.

He kissed the inside of her thigh. "I'll be your god, I'll be whatever you want me to be."

"Just be the man I love, the man who loves me. That's enough for me."

Devyn sank beneath her, giving her a full demonstration of the range of pleasure he could give her with his mouth. He intended to show her, in the plainest bodily truths, that he was hers.

His mouth was on her sex. His tongue was moving closer to her clitoris. One of his fingers found it, curled around it, making her bite her lip to keep from crying out.

He was giving himself over to her pleasure.

She wanted to give herself back.

They had exactly eighteen hours.

Eighteen hours and then he was leaving for Afghanistan. And Moria couldn't even tell you for what purpose Her Majesty's Army was even there. She didn't want to know, it might make her angrier to be losing him, for months, potentially forever, if she knew the reason. Information was currency, powerful men said, but sometimes it was also just pain.

He found that secret, hidden spot again. Again.

His tongue curled inside of her. Thought evaporated, she was only bliss borne away on the patient strokes of his tongue and fingers.

Her head was tilted back on her counterpane, she clutched at his shoulders to keep from floating into the clouds.

Speech was out of her reach, but he knew what she needed and how badly she needed it.

"Raise your arms, my lady," he said, a whispered appeal in her darkened room.

She did as he requested, he pulled her chemise over her head. He laid it out on a chair with the others, lit two candles on her dressing table, then returned to her. He removed his boots and breeches. He was fully nude now, the candlelight illuminating the muscles carved where she didn't know a man could have muscles. His thigh muscles and stomach muscles flexed as he breathed her in.

She was bared to him in nothing but her stockings. She felt the need to cover herself, to cover the marks at her waist where her skin had stretched to carry her little girl who'd never got to live.

Reminders of a loss she'd tried to hide. But his mouth found them. He left kisses like tributes on those marks.

"Beautiful," he said, meeting her eyes.

Moria trailed a hand down the inked flesh of his abdomen, then down his spine, her hands finding the places he'd inked over his own scars the way she'd covered her own with silk.

"Beautiful," she returned.

He sat on his haunches, taking one of her slender legs in his hands. He slowly peeled away her stocking, placing kisses up her calves and thighs. He peeled the other stocking on her opposite leg, wrapping it around his waist. His fingers found her sex between them.

"You're so wet for me," he ground out, his fingers stretching her.

"I have been since that willow tree," she said, bringing his cock to her entrance. Giving his words back to him that he'd said when he had proposed.

"You're sure you want this?"

She crashed her lips to his, searing him with her kiss. "I want this."

"Say *please*," he pulled on a long strand of blonde hair, pulling her head back from his lips.

"You first," she said, squeezing the tight round globe of his arse.

"I love you," he said, kissing her shoulder.

The moonlight through the window lit the profile of his handsome face as he licked down to her breast. She took his cock and rolled a French letter onto him, and pushed it inside of her. She widened her legs. Her heels squeezed into the muscled divots of his back just above his backside. He pulled out, thrust into her again. She felt her muscles constrict to make room, to seize around him.

"Fuck, you're so tight," he said, ramming into her.

"Again," she whimpered as she dragged her nails down his back.

He slid into her, harder this time. The friction of his body sliding against hers made her skin start to sweat, contrasting with the coolness of her silk sheets beneath them. She dug her heels in deeper, squeezing his ass again.

"You're perfect. Do that again, Moria."

She bit him on the shoulder hard enough to leave a mark. He groaned. He drove deeper this time, rolling his hips and conducting hers.

"Harder," she ground out, panting.

He slammed into her to the hilt. She held onto him, clinging to keep him there. The pressure she had been searching and longing for built at the base of her spine. He cried out, she held on.

She felt his legs quaking above her, he was close too. She wasn't ready to let go. She wasn't ready to let go of him now, not ever. Moria held onto him, kissing him, and then turned him so that he was beneath her. He hadn't let go. He was still inside her.

"Fuck," he said, gripping her hips. "You're unexpected."

He kissed her with drugging sips and flicks of his tongue in her mouth. She slid hers into his, rolling her hips. She liked the look of him beneath her, flushed and glistening and half spent with her sweat on his skin. She tilted her head back, clutching his chest. One of his hands was palming her breast, the other pulling and twining the tips of her long blonde hair in his inked fingers.

"Let go," he said, adding a finger to her folds. "I want to see you come for me."

"Come," she writhed, "with" another buck of her hips, "me." She slammed down at the same time he drove further into her.

She pulled his mouth into her own at the very moment they both cried out. She swallowed his cry into her mouth, giving him her own. He kept moving, riding out her release with his lip tucked between her teeth and his finger still on her bud.

"That's it, take what you need," he panted.

Suddenly she was hot, a white-hot star streaking across a starry sky, taking him with her. Every part of her was filled, molten and sated. Her legs quaked and her shoulders slumped. She fell with a sigh against Devyn's wide, firm chest.

She rolled off him, laying beside him to kick a leg over his hip. He rolled over her, kissing both of her breasts, and then her abdomen.

"Sore?" he asked, looking down at her. He rolled off the French letter and discarded it in the fire in the grate.

She caught her breath. "God, I thought once would be enough; but I don't know if there is an *'enough'* with you."

He sat between her legs, and kissed his way up her thigh, taking his mouth to her again.

"What are you..." then realization dawned. She was glistening with sex and he was licking all of it off her rather than getting a towel to dry her off.

"You're still just a little wet, my lady; but I like you that way."

He was grinning up at her with his chin resting on her abdomen. His dimpled smile caressed her inner thigh.

"I like *you* this way."

"Between your legs?" he kissed the mark on her stomach. "Or in your bed?"

He pulled the covers up partly over them. He pinched the round curve of her backside.

"Devil," she whispered, looking down at him. "Come up here with me."

He did as she asked, landing on a pillow beside her and towing her into his arms and holding her head in the valley between his thick pectoral muscles. There were miles between his shoulders, and she felt so small when he held her like this.

"Admiring the view?" he asked, noticing her staring at his nipples. She tweaked one of them in her fingers.

"A little lower," he whispered in her ear.

She gave a little laugh as he kissed the top of her head.

This was everything it was supposed to be, not what she'd done before. It had never been like this with another man before, during or afterward.

This was truth, what they created together. The way he worshipped her body. The way he knew how to unravel her and put her back together with the same hands and lips.

All the other times, the other acts before, those were all lies. They'd been founded on something real but it had been changeable, inconstant. This was real. Being touched intimately by Devyn felt like being found when she had never known she'd been lost.

"I'll miss this," she whispered against his heartbeat.

"Come back. Stay here. Let's not borrow tomorrow's problems right now. Focus on this," he tipped her face up to say into her eyes. "Focus on how much I love you, my beautiful reckoning."

He cupped her backside, brought her hand to his lips.

"With every part of me," she answered.

Chapter Twenty-Seven

Devyn,

I live my life one envelope at a time. My days, my comings and goings are measured by your words. Obligations and appearances mean little without your words and the images they conjure of you. I know little of war, but I picture you doing the same. Sometimes I try to picture you among your company of men in the far-off places that get to harbor you, and other times I cannot picture you at all for the pain it causes me to think of where you might be that I cannot reach you. Please come home and make this the last adventure you go on without me.

M

~

Goddess of War,

Live your life outside these envelopes. Don't measure your comings and goings by my words. I never wanted to limit you. A different man might, but not this one, however much it fills me with hope to hear how much my words mean to you. There is nowhere, no corner of this earth or the heavens that you cannot reach me. I will come home, as you wish. I'll take you anywhere you want, for however long you want. There are no adventures, not without you. Not while you're walking around carrying my heart in your hands. I love you, desperately.

D

                            ❧

INK AND PARCHMENT WERE A PALTRY SUBSTITUTE FOR THE flesh and bones of a man, especially one like Devyn. He was the man her heart clung to, even if she hadn't told anyone outside of her family the truth.

Still, Moria threw herself into her letters when she wrote them, into reading his letters when they arrived. She swapped the Burn Book she usually she carried in her reticule for his letters, so that his words were always close at hand.

At first, she threw herself back into the life she had built for herself. Without a good-natured, muscled mountain of a man, she still had dancing, sewing dresses secretly with Fitz's seamstress friend, gardening and arranging flowers for hospitals and orphanages, shooting, archery, taking care of her nieces and nephews, and social calls.

But all of this busy-ness was just a cover, so she didn't have to spend any time alone or with her thoughts while *he* was *out there.*

More than all of that, she had her family. Three of them were currently looking at her over the afternoon tea table while Moria gathered her sewing and asked the housekeeper for her cape.

"Where are you going?" Noelle said, moving to grasp her hand.

"It's Wednesday," Moria shrugged.

Noelle and Olivia looked to one another, a whole conversation passed but neither stopped Moria from leaving. If she stopped moving, all the things chasing her down would catch up to her. So, she kept running. And she'd become one hell of a runner. It was being still she didn't have the stamina for.

She found herself, once again, on Bond Street, a footman following close behind with an armful of packages, buying things she couldn't possibly need. It was Kate Herring who had found her in a milliner's shop and offered her something she hadn't been expecting.

"You've been...distant...the last month or so." Kate mused, holding up a green ribbon that Moria grimaced at. It was too putrid.

"I fell in love with the man that would completely obliterate my social situation I've extorted and schemed to maintain and now that I have been loved so thoroughly, this whole scene feels hollow in his absence," is what she *wanted* to say.

Moria settled on, "I don't expect you'd understand, Kate."

Kate took the bolt of bright blue cloth Moria held up. "You could try."

Moria ran her fingers over a piece of lace, eyeing it next to the blue. "Why is it that *you* think I've been distant the last month or so?"

"You look...lovesick," Kate touched Moria's arm. Moria pulled away as if scalded.

"Please, you'll have to do better than that." Moria tried to add a touch of laughter to her voice as though the idea were foreign. It wasn't. She was lovesick, but she wasn't about to tell *this* girl.

"Is it His Grace? You wish him to hurry up and propose?"

Moria thought for a girl so adept at mathematics, Kate hadn't quite come up with the right answer for this particular equation.

"Why? Worried he'll be taken off the market soon?" Moria said with a playful smile, just to gauge the girl's reaction.

"I'm sure that the daughter of a reverend and a bluestocking would never aim so very high."

"If you did, no one would blame you," Moria said, holding up a swath of green silk against the girl's face, then giving her a decisive nod. "This one. A little lower cut this time. He seems to like the color green. And stop slouching."

The other woman stood to her full height; Moria gave her an appreciative nod.

"Another thing, less talking about maths and your trips abroad," Moria said, adding a pair of gloves to Kate's stack of wares. "Men love to talk about themselves, His Grace especially. I hope you like politics and shooting. He's not just looking for a duchess, but a politician's wife as well."

Moria pulled an auburn curl free from the girl's coiffure and placed a necklace from a nearby display about her neck.

Then she turned her to face the mirror,"If you aim high, make sure you arm yourself."

And with a wink and a sashay of pink skirts, Moria exited the shop.

FOUR DAYS LATER, MORIA STILL DIDN'T WANT TO BE around her well-meaning siblings. She didn't want to be around Letitia, who knew her too well, and she didn't want to answer her correspondence to Llewyn, who would see through every line of half-hearted banter she would pour onto a page. That's how she wound up at Gretchen's house, gift in hand, for a friend she hadn't seen in weeks.

"I should have left you standing on the stoop longer just to prove a point."

Moria sat across from her friend, handing her a pink and white hat box bearing a piece of headwear that was overly ostentatious and Gretchen was sure to love.

"Naturally, you saw I was carrying a gift, so you took pity on me."

Gretchen didn't laugh, but one corner of her mouth lost the battle against smiling. "I was just in shock that you still remembered my address."

Moria bit into a scone. "I deserved that."

"When Miss Herring told me that you'd gone shopping together, and selected a dress for her to wear to entice His Grace-"

"She said *what*?"

"Open the gift you brought me first," Gretchen straightened her shoulders and lifted her head proud like a curly-haired queen.

Moria lifted the striped lid off the hat box and held out the confection of millinery for her friend.

"I thought you said my hats were too big." Gretchen said, pulling her lip between her teeth.

"They *are*. You have a small head and beautiful hair. But *you* like them. That's all that matters."

Gretchen's eyes turned a little watery, but she accepted the hat and turned it over gingerly.

"She said that you confided in her. That you thought she was a better friend. That's why you took her shopping and suggested she try and aim for the Duke."

Moria scoffed. "And you believed this bit of farce?"

"The *dress*, Moria. She wore it earlier this morning to a breakfast that you didn't show up to and everyone was talking about how regal she looked. But it was...so unlike her. It was more like *you*."

Moria dusted her hands of the sugar from the sweet treat she'd been eating then reached for Gretchen's. "She isn't a better friend than you. I barely know her. I was shopping. She was shopping. She was just there. And then…" Moria blew out a long breath, "She started prying, I didn't want to tell her about something, so I picked her out a dress and told her she should wear it if she wanted to get His Grace to notice her. I didn't give my blessing on their marital union."

"That little redheaded—"

"There's something else, Gretchen."

Gretchen leaned forward, squeezed Moria's hand. "On Carina's dead husband's grave, I swear I won't tell a soul."

Moria scrunched up her nose. "You couldn't promise on something better?"

"No, because why would I break a promise or tell a lie and risk being haunted by that lecher?"

Moria laughed, truly laughed, for the first time in weeks. "I've missed you."

Gretchen waved for her to keep talking. "Don't change the subject."

Moria bit her lip before continuing. "There is a reason I've been…keeping to myself."

Gretchen squealed, stood from her seat, and then ran to close the door. "I'm going to need to close the door for this, I can feel it."

And when she sat down next to Moria, Moria finally unburdened herself to her friend of all the things she'd kept buried and felt several pounds lighter. If Devyn could love her enough to promise life and death, enough to give her his mother's ring and every oath he could make to come back to her, then she could share all of it with her friend. He would come back, and she would need her friends.

Chapter Twenty-Eight

II WEEKS LATER

The outpost in Bajgah had been ambushed. Captain Devyn Winter and his Lieutenant, Calum Sterling, tried to get everyone out, all of the men, the civilians, and locals that they could. Still, more and more enemy attacks kept coming.

Death was all around him. Death walked at his back and stood at his side and ran towards him. He couldn't tell if it had come for him, or to use him.

"Where's Belcher?" He heard Calum's yell above the artillery fire.

He heard someone to his left swear. He followed the other man's vision. There was one of Devyn's men several yards ahead, being forced into a caravan at gunpoint. Sweat beaded on Devyn's brow, he wiped it, feeling the dark dirt sticking to his skin. His heart pounded so loudly he barely heard another onslaught of folly.

"Go with the others," Devyn was forcing a group of men onto a boat, his voice hoarse from yelling over the intermittent blasts. "I'll get Belcher, I'll find you at the rendezvous point as quick as I can."

"Christ, no, man. I'm comin' wi' ye," Calum said, grabbing Devyn's middle. The movement pulled at the bandage wrapped horizontally to hold Calum's dislocated shoulder in place that was covered in blood.

"No! Stay with them, lead them," Devyn ordered his friend. Devyn was taking off his jacket removing the bundle in his pockets, "Take this for me, in case I don't come back." The ring she'd left behind on her pillow when he'd woken up without her, glinting. It was tied securely in the ribbon he'd bound them all together with.

"*Don't* do this, Captain. Don't ask it of me."

"Don't ask me to leave Belcher behind."

Calum swore again. Ducking at the sound of another blast.

Devyn loaded the remaining men he was responsible for on a boat, taking off to get Belcher back. He was running down the gangplank onto the bank, dirt kicking up around him to catch up to that wagon. He thought his lungs would burst but he pushed, harder, faster. Those men weren't taking away his comrade, if he lost sight of that wagon, he'd never see him again. Belcher's blood would be on his hands.

Blood and sweat and the tangy smoke of cannons and gunpowder assaulted Devyn's senses.

He'd never catch up on foot. He lined up his shot, aiming for the driver of the wagon. But there somewhere in the haze stalked a familiar figure, gorgeous and ethereal and at odds with his surroundings. He didn't pause long enough to look in its direction.

The figure floated closer, closer, and then her familiar voice curled into his ear as his finger hovered over the trigger. "Get down."

But she was too late.

A bullet pierced his hip, shattering tendon and bone. He exploded with agony. As he fell, the battle raged on within him and around him. How many of his men would die today? How many on the boats he'd loaded would make it out? Would he ever see England, see her, see his brother again?

Shadows crept over his consciousness; he could feel them dragging him toward the ether. But there at his ear, he felt her lips caressing him, another caress at his cheek.

She wasn't here, she couldn't be.

He had to get up, had to fight for her, had to protect her.

"Don't move," a voice bellowed, hands staunching the bleeding at his wounded side. "Your shot hit its mark. He lost control, the horses careened. I was able to make use of the distraction and jump out of the caravan. I just wasn't quite fast enough."

"Belcher?" he asked.

"Aye, Captain, I've got you."

Belcher was applying pressure, but the pain was holding fast.

"I'm here," she whispered in his ear again. "I'm waiting for you."

He groaned her name, it was barely audible, carried on the wind and shouts and bullets and horse cries. He was so tired. So bloody tired. He could just give himself over to the pain until it took him prisoner and it would all be over.

He felt her lips at his temple. "Stay. For me. *Stay.*" The voice was insistent.

She wasn't here. She wasn't *really* here in this hellscape, he was only imagining her. Or was she real, and it was the hellscape he was imagining? Surely, even a weary soldier such as he couldn't conjure such a realistic layer of Dante's Inferno.

"There is nowhere, no corner of this earth or the heavens that I cannot reach you." It was her voice again. He recognized those words. The letters. The ring. Had he gotten them to Calum?

Hands lifted him onto a stretcher, the constriction of the movements causing him such tremendous, overwhelming agony. Blackness seeped over his vision.

"*Stay.*" She commanded as he drifted away from her, unable to do exactly as she bid.

He peeled his eyes open with all his remaining strength. An unending sky of stars stared down on him. Haze wrapped around his consciousness, taking the form of a woman. A woman with unbound blonde hair and impossibly gold-green eyes who took his hand and led him away like a spirit guide.

The cool breeze of her phantom touch calmed the pain behind his eyelids, the pain in his hip dulled its roar. He could feel little pain if she was here with him.

The battlefield and all the sounds and sights of death that lay around him fell out of his orbit. They couldn't touch him or hurt him anymore. All he knew as his eyes closed was her as she spirited him away somewhere beyond its reach.

Chapter Twenty-Nine

Devyn,

Come home. Tell me all the ways I'm wrong. Tell me a joke. Tell me to stop being strong. Tell me to just give in. Tell me to stop fighting and that I've held onto all the wrong things. Tell me the truth, tell me lies. Just come home and kiss me. I'll do nothing but let you hold me until we wake up one day and we are ancient with a whole bunch of grandchildren. Just come home.

M

(message received with no reply)

~

THE WRONG MAN WAS HOLDING HER, THE WRONG HANDS were at the small of her back.

The wrong man was courting her openly in front of the entire *ton*.

Moria had been batting the thought away for the last 6 weeks since Devyn's last letter. A different, less jaded woman might have pined, sitting at home, making plans for a beloved soldier's return. Moria didn't know how to be such a woman.

The Duke had called on her, they'd been riding in the park whenever the weather allowed, he'd accompanied her to social events. As it had always been between the two of them, his presence was amiable and gentlemanly. He never pushed her to define what they were or made any kind of affectionate overtures. But every time she was seen out with him, more suitors showed up for Olivia, more invitations arrived, more names filled her dance card. Unjust, given Olivia's many admirable qualities any suitor should be so lucky to find in a match, but such was the way of the ton. They all sought favor, a connection to a Duke. She couldn't fault them, she was doing the same.

None of her siblings mentioned the connection, in Moria's hearing at least. She could feel the worried stares and silence from her siblings, but Moria didn't know how to voice the paralyzing fear of being a woman alone with few options a second time. She couldn't win the battle with the voice in her head that told her being seen on the arm of a Duke held all her critics and their knife-like words and stares at bay, for a time at least.

But the thought returned tonight.

George Worthington, seventh Duke of Andover, twirled her in a glittering ballroom hosted by her younger sister, Viscountess Ludlowe.

The room was exceptionally decorated to celebrate the year that Noelle and Pomfrey had been married, filled with candles and flowers and fabric and formalwear designed to impress, to daze.

And Moria was impressed. She was dazed.

But not by the man before her.

He was beautiful in his own way, all long lines and perfect hair and a smile that weakened most of her defenses. He was a good and honest man, who never pushed her to be more or do more than she wanted. But she wanted to be pushed, she wanted to be brought outside of herself, to be expected to be more than the part that she played. Devyn had done that for her.

She felt the Duke's long, lean trousered leg graze her hip for one minute moment in their dance.

His hands found her waist again.

Her arms met his shoulders. They were solid beneath her touch. He was perfectly made. It would be no inconvenience to let this man have her, taking her body with his own in some massive ancestral bed.

"Have I made you blush, my lady?"

Her eyes shot up to his. She cleared her throat. "Your ... shoulders...made me blush, your grace."

She saw the questions on his face that he was too well-bred to say aloud. Another turn of the dance, and he was dancing with Kate again, who gave Moria a saccharine smile that had Moria speculating over her intentions. Moria partnered with Tristan Valentine, then was returned to the Duke.

"Would you like to retire to the balcony for some air?"

A rush of relief surged from her lungs. *Air.* What a very pleasant invitation indeed.

She looked over her shoulder for Olivia, her usual accomplice in all matters clandestine. But Olivia was conferring with her other siblings, including Fitz, and Miss Kelley, in hushed tones in a dark corner. Moria noted Peregrine speaking and the slump of his shoulders.

What the devil could unite the passel of them all to such a conciliatory huddle in the middle of a ball her sister was supposed to be hosting? She found Lady Althea ahead, playing hostess in her stead.

Lawrence looked in her direction, his eyes did not meet hers, his jaw tensed before looking back to the others. God, they were discussing *her*. They had to be. They'd never dream of quietly excluding her in public unless she were the topic of discussion.

Kathleen handed her husband a folded piece of paper which he stuffed back into a pocket in his jacket. Fitz pulled Noelle closer to his side. Olivia took Jasper's handkerchief. Peregrine looked at his feet, having no one to console him. Moria almost mis-stepped dancing, the Duke's gentle hands led her and her body followed on mostly muscle memory alone.

Lawrence started walking toward her with purposeful strides. Jasper reached for him, but he kept moving in Moria's direction. It had been Lawrence who broke the news to her three years ago, of Marcus' death. She'd tried to save him, the three of them had. She'd fallen asleep clutching Marcus' hand, when she'd woken—

Moria read the signs in the ballroom before her like a fortune on the palm of a stranger. Or, rather, she read her own fortune. Fear and some dark, familiar grief spread over her.

She shook her head as if she could deny what she already knew.

Lawrence's gray-green eyes were hooded from the other side of the dance floor.

I'm sorry, his lips mouthed.

"Is anything amiss, Lady Moria?"

Moria looked to the Duke, his eyes serious and tender.

The music came to a halt, and he did not immediately let her go. He held onto her like a wilted flower with a broken stem that needed support to stay upright. She both admired and hated the protective embrace at once. She identified the feeling as something more akin to self-loathing, she hated that she appeared to need it more than she loathed his willingness to give it, or that he was the man to give it.

She followed his eyes to the terrace, and she nodded. She would not cry, she would not misstep, she would not give the hundreds of pairs of eyes any reason to see anything less than the image she had crafted so artfully over years of hard work. She hadn't crumpled in the past, and she would not now.

Not a mere foot soldier, then; more like the goddess of war. That's what *he'd* called her.

She could get through this night, if it came close to killing her, and she would pick through the pieces tomorrow.

"Go on, I'll meet you in a few moments," the Duke prompted.

She had been about to say the same thing, giving herself time to ask her family just what the hell they were on about; but she couldn't publicly contradict a duke, in case anyone was listening. It was a strong possibility that many around her were.

This is what you wanted; some voice told her.

To be noticed, yes, but watched?

No.

There was a chance she had played her part just a little too well.

SHE WAITED NO MORE THAN FIVE MINUTES ON THE balcony in abject misery when the Duke joined her. He came to sit next to her on a stone bench, shucking his coat and wrapping it around her.

"Thank you, Your Grace."

"George," he corrected, taking her hands in his.

"Are we on first-name terms, then?" she heard the playful words that came from her lips like they'd been spoken by some other woman who didn't feel her world shattering into rubble around her.

He gave a warm, affectionate little laugh, and her heart was seized with so many emotions at once: hope, tenderness, anguish, self-recrimination, the sheer injustice of it all.

"I would like for us to be. Very much."

Even as terror gripped her heart, she play-acted.

She contorted her mouth into a little moue, and said, "How much?" leaning closer to him.

"I'll show you," he whispered, his hands coming around to cup her face, pulling her lips to his. She could feel how badly he wanted her in the way his lips cradled hers, the way his tongue made its way carefully into her mouth- possessive, but not greedy. His hands snaked around the back of her coiffure as he pulled her closer, closer still.

Even as she wrapped her arms around his neck, she fought with herself, a targeted effort to push out all other thoughts but the feel of this man who was with her, here now, kissing her.

He broke the kiss, removing himself from the seat to kneel before her.

He took her hands that had come up to cover her mouth, with his own.

He stayed that way a moment, this golden prince, looking up at her with anticipation, with admiration.

"*Moria*," he punctuated her first name. "I think we both know this moment has been coming toward us for a long time. I've considered what I would say to you, and replayed it in my head many times, always falling short of what you deserve. But the point is, I'd like to spend a lifetime with you, finding all the right words, saying all of the things that you deserve to hear, hoping that you'll return them. Would you do me the honor of becoming my Duchess?"

All the tears that Moria had been holding back behind a dam of steel will, expelled themselves.

She wouldn't have the man that she would die for, who would die for her, but she would not be alone. And she could come to love this man before her.

Couldn't she?

The tears wouldn't stop.

"Moria? Have I shocked you?"

In answer, she pulled him to her, dropping the coat she'd been wearing on the ground next to them. She stood and pulled him up to her, unlocking him with her lips, letting his hands wrap her into him. She felt the length of his body against her own. Wool and linen against the silk of her dress.

At some point he'd removed his gloves, and she felt the soft press of his warm hands against the cool of her back.

"Yes," she said, against his smiling lips. "I'll marry you, George."

He laughed his satisfaction. He had locked eyes on her, but in the darkness he couldn't or wouldn't see the sadness that was surely there. He was fidgeting in the pocket of his waistcoat for the ring.

Touch as light as a breath, he tugged her glove from her hand and slid the betrothal ring on her finger. To Moria, it felt like a shackle. As final as a death knell.

He curled her fingers into a fist and kissed her hand. He held her ringed hand up to the moonlight, the jewel glowed like a smaller moon glistening atop her hand.

"It's perfect," he whispered.

It was perfect. But it wasn't perfection she had wanted.

It had been, once, a lifetime ago.

Perfection was what everyone else had wanted.

"Should we go tell your family?" He made to re-enter the ball-room, but she stalled.

He held onto her hand, not understanding her hesitation.

How often would he misunderstand me? She wondered.

Devyn had always understood her.

"I will never be anything but yours. Until I draw my dying breath."

But now, he was gone, and this man remained. Of all the months he'd waited, why did it have to be tonight?

She couldn't face them inside, not yet at least. "Can we simply... enjoy this moment? The two of us?"

He closed the short paces between them. Her arms came around him, looking up at him to find reasons to cling to him, things that she could hold onto and choose to love. He misread it for true affection. He placed a kiss to her temple. His lips moved to her cheeks, then to her jaw, and finally to her ear.

"I'm sorry. I should have proposed to you ages ago. I made a bold claim on the floor of parliament, years of frustration spurring me on in the moment. And then I got caught up in winning, in seeing a cause through to the end. But I never should have made you wait for me."

That wasn't the part she objected to. It comforted her to know that there was more to him than the cool veneer she so often witnessed, a man who could get heated over injustices and work to wrong them.

He'd courted other women, bedded them, even, likely, somehow it didn't sting. Moria had done more waiting in her lifetime than this man realized.

She'd waited for Marcus.

She'd waited for Devyn.

She hadn't been waiting on this man, but she merely touched his face in answer. The skin beneath her fingers felt foreign.

This man wasn't a villain, and neither was Devyn. Damn Devyn for dying, but surely *she* was the villain here. Becoming a duchess, that had been the aim of a grieving girl who wanted a pedestal high enough she couldn't be brought down ever again. She was someone else now, wasn't she?

The man kissing her was doing a thorough job of showing her affection, and it too felt wrong. The word rattled around inside her skull.

Wrong, wrong, wrong.

But Moria had become comfortable with dissonance inside her head. Had it felt right, she would have felt more confusion. Instead, she stared down those words, and kissed the duke back, even as self-loathing crawled into her skin.

Her hands were in his hair, then, pulling his lips home to meet hers.

And his hands...they were everywhere. Both were consumed by raw need, to find some different but altogether similar comfort and absolution in the other.

A throat cleared behind them.

"Good god, how revolting," Valentine spoke.

The Duke pulled back, his head dropping onto Moria's shoulder.

"Valentine, you're most welcome to return to the ballroom," he turned to the other man, "If you do not like what you see."

"I came to...escort the lady back inside."

"As I've just proposed to the lady and she has accepted, you will do no such thing."

"Your Grace, you've finally done it? Huzzah!" Tristan offered, but when Moria met his eyes, she let him see the disappointment for a moment.

Tristan gathered her in a hug. "I never doubted you for a moment," he said against her cheek. A tear collided with Moria's cheek, and she knew. She'd been right.

"Will you let go of my betrothed, please?" The Duke said, laughter in his voice.

"Sorry," Tristan said, squeezing her shoulder one last time before pulling away. "The emotions of the night got the better of me."

Moria swallowed. She felt so cold. A shiver traveled down her spine. The Duke draped an arm around her. They weren't the right arms, they weren't long enough or sturdy enough and she doubted he bore a bear, the image of a militia battalion, on his left forearm, or a sparrow inked on his hand.

He wouldn't. Those arms belonged to a dead man.

She shivered again.

"Christ, let's get you inside, dear. We should find your family and tell them the good news."

When she re-entered the ball wearing the Duke's jacket and his ring, she was at the center of a single beam of light when all she wanted was to cower in the darkness spreading inside of her.

Chapter Thirty

ALL OF POLITE SOCIETY UTTERED ONE WORD FOLLOWING the announcement of the betrothal of His Grace the Duke of A to Lady M, all for different reasons: Finally.
  - Scandalous Lives of London scandal sheet

ONCE, WHEN MORIA WAS VERY SMALL, SHE'D FOLLOWED her brothers out to the lake to skate on the ice.

Jasper, ever the leader of the family, had tried to caution her about patches of thin ice. She hadn't listened, she'd thought that she knew better. She'd been skating in a circle when the ice had cracked around her. Lawrence had been close enough, fast enough to get to her before she was submerged. But her clothes had been soaked through.

Had she also been skating around thin ice these past few months, ignoring the signs until, tonight, she'd been submerged?

The evening's events were holding her under.

A hammer was striking an anvil in her head that she felt everywhere. Her lips and fingers and extremities trembled. Hands enveloped her, grasped her and carried her up flights of stairs, pushed her hair back from her face. A warm cloth was laid on her temple. Someone was speaking gently and softly to her as they undressed her from her gown and helped her bathe. The same voice was feminine and kind, dismissing the servants.

As she was helped in the tub, even the warm water didn't slow the cold seeping past her bones into her blood. Rosemary and lavender soap filled her nostrils and replaced the smell of fear.

"Here. For your nerves," her sister's voice cut through, wrapping her hand around a wine glass.

Moria drank, letting the bittersweet tang of a cabernet soothe the clamor inside of her. She peaked her toes out of the bubbles, stretching her body against the cold spreading through her. She closed her eyes and leaned back in the tub until she was warm again.

She was helped out of the tub, the softest robe she'd ever felt draped around her and those hands again- wringing the water from her hair. Dressing her. Applying lotion to her skin and chapped lips.

What had happened? Why did she feel this hollow? Would she ever feel warm again?

When she laid in her bed, she turned to lay on her side, curled up in a great ball like a cat. A soft, warm body lay behind her and wrapped an arm around her that smelled like citrus. A strand of red hair fell on her shoulder. This time, it wasn't her mother, it was Kathleen in her place.

Moria had fallen through ice of a different kind than when she was eight.

How did she get here?

"He's gone," her voice broke on the words. Were they statement or question?

You'll possess me in body and soul until I'm nothing but dust and bones.

Her sister's hands drew circles on her back. "I'm afraid so," her voice broke too.

Salt streamed out of Moria's eyes, into her ears, and onto her pillow. For once, she didn't immediately try to wipe them up, they kept flowing. It wasn't just sadness she felt, it wasn't numbness anymore, it was anger.

How was he gone? Why did the ones she love go where she couldn't follow? Why did everyone always leave her? Was loving her some sort of punishment that deserved a death sentence?

How could anyone let something like death keep them away from a face like yours?

When she laid a hand beneath her cheek, she felt the press of her betrothal ring against her skin. She pulled her hand back to look at the Duke's ring, the glint of a diamond bringing back the night's events and the decision she'd made.

There was anger with nowhere to go but heat her bones. She felt the layers of ice inside of her thaw. A cool resignation settled upon her as she drew the counterpane further around her: The man she loved was gone and she was to be a duchess, the wife of another man.

~

"Your friends have been asking after you."

It was Noelle's voice above her, the sounds of morning around it.

"Which friends?" Moria pulled her blankets higher, the plush counterpane blocking out the sunlight. *How many days had passed her in her grief?*

"Lady Carina and Gretchen brought a gift for you."

Moria pulled back the covers to see Noelle holding out a pink box, a miniature pink wedding cake inside decorated with little flowers, one large bite missing. Fitz didn't meet her eyes, shrugging unapologetically under Noelle's glare.

"And the redhead," he added. "Miss Herring called as well. There's something about her that feels a little...off."

He handed her a message from Kate, one that she immediately balled up and threw into the wastebasket under the window without a second thought. She didn't care what Kate thought of her actions. Couldn't.

"And the Duke came to call," her sister laid a gentle hand on her arm. "Henry and Fitz and Jasper told him that you caught a chill from being on the balcony with him at the ball two nights ago."

Moria caught the hint in her sister's words. So it had been two whole days.

"What did George say?" Moria sat up a little against the silken pillows behind her.

"That he'd like to see his fiancé for himself," Fitz answered.

"Jasper told him you were still resting. That when you roused, we would send for him."

Moria curled her legs beneath her. "Thank you. I'm sorry I just can't face him right now."

Fitz plopped down beside her, fully dressed, resting his head on his arm behind him.

"Oh, my dear girl, anyone who wants to survive in this family has to be well-versed in Greek drama."

Moria wanted to cry, and she wanted to laugh at the same time. She burrowed her weight into her brother-in-law, her childhood friend. Fitz kept one hand in Noelle's and wrapped his other arm around Moria before she crumpled. Moria sobbed into the lapels of his jacket. Noelle was on the other side of her now, soothing trails down her back.

Moria pulled away. "I'll ruin your coat."

"It's alright. Your sister hates this coat. She'll be thrilled. You were just saying this morning how hideous it was, right, princess?" He looked to his wife, who nodded as she wiped her eyes.

"I guess I should have seen it coming, you all said I'd be a duchess one day. Suppose it was meant to be this way."

Noelle laid her head on Moria's pillow, still holding her hand. "You don't have to be resigned about it. You're allowed to be upset, disappointed, angry, sad, even."

"What would be the point in that? It isn't going to change anything," Moria said, staring at the pink cherubs in the Rococo style painting on her ceiling.

Noelle tugged on her hand, forcing her to meet her eyes. "It won't. But admitting how you feel, sitting with it, not pushing it away, it keeps the grief from choking the life out of you."

Moria curled her head in her sister's lap and tried not to think of him until she fell asleep again.

Chapter Thirty-One

8 DAYS LATER

Moria had risen from her bed for the first time in days to fetch a book from the library.

She heard voices.

The Duke. Her *betrothed*. "That's too much. Just put it in a trust for her."

"People have a way of finding these things out. I don't want anyone claiming that money factors into this union on either side."

"That's probably better than what they already think." *Lawrence.*

"Why? What are they saying? Have you heard anything untoward?" *Jasper.*

"They don't have to say anything in my earshot, I can fill in the blanks myself."

"They'll all stop once she becomes a duchess."

"I think she kind of enjoys it, honestly," Lawrence added.

"Would you please desist?" There was a note of authority in Jasper's voice despite using "please."

"I'm only pointing out that if she was uncomfortable with

gossip, she'd behave a little differently," Lawrence pushed, voice neutral.

Of course, it would be her brother that sparked the first tinge of anger over something other than the great unjust hands of fate. But it felt good to feel something again nonetheless.

The Duke's voice dropped low and challenging in reply. "Who are you to judge your sister?"

Moria wanted to feel something at the Duke standing up to her brother on her behalf. But he was to be her husband, that's the least of what he was supposed to do, wasn't it? Devyn had stood beside her, he'd stood toe to toe with all her darkness.

"That's a fair fucking point, Your Grace. I can see my error. I'll leave you two to your discussion."

Moria kept walking before she could run into her brother. She pulled the brim of her large hat over her face and walked out the door and onto the sidewalk. Up the street and around the corner, past papers announcing her engagement. Past Carina's house. Past the lending library.

Moria wondered what they would have printed if she'd been announcing her engagement to a different man, a better one but without a showy title. A gilded sign for a modiste came into view, and Moria realized she was walking to Letitia's. Her family hid the papers from her, at least they had tried to, but Letty would be honest.

Letitia opened the door before she could knock, ushering her through a curtain, to a plush divan in her workshop. "Sit, here's some tea and scones."

"What do you put in these? They taste like sunshine and summertime."

Letty handed her a broadsheet, sitting beside her and pouring her a cup of tea.

Moria didn't read the words so much as she absorbed them. They rattled around inside of her in great blasts of wind that made her feel like she was going to topple sideways. But still, none of them knew her secrets. They were still just hers, hers and Devyn's. She felt Letitia's warm, soft hand on her arm.

"Easy, friend."

Did she look like she wanted the earth to just stop so she could get off it?

"This wasn't what I wanted." The words came out in great heaving gulps. Tears splashed onto her dress, and she tried to swipe at them with the back of her gloved hand. That dratted glove. She began trying to tear the glove off with angry hands as the tears just wouldn't let go of her.

"I know," Letitia murmured, closer than she had been a moment ago.

"It wasn't...he wasn't.... we were supposed to...I wanted..." Moria couldn't finish any of the sentences that were clawing their way out of her throat, it felt so painfully dry.

Letitia had her. Scarred hands were smoothing back her hair and making soothing trails on her back and shoulders. Comforting sounds were falling near her ear. Letitia had her, rocking her back and forth.

"My lady, I'm here. I'm here. Let it out. I have you. I have you, Moria."

Eventually, Moria felt she'd reached the bottom of her tears. Letitia still had an arm wrapped around her. "I wish I had something to say," Letitia spoke over Moria's head.

"He'd have known what to say," Moria said, staring at the two dresses Moria had embroidered on mannequins in Letitia's shop. She felt a small surge of pride at that, something she'd created, on display, for someone else to wear, to love. "He was so good at words."

"What would he say?"

"I'll forever feel the loss of you, but that loss is shared by all humanity, I'm sure," Moria smiled dimly.

"When did he say that?"

"To the stone marking someone I loved."

Letitia held up a flask. "To you, Captain Wordsmith with the heavenly thighs." She took a drink, then handed it to Moria. Despite her pain, Moria let out a little laugh at Letitia's words.

"To you, the only man I will ever love," and the whiskey burned, scouring the back of her throat, washing away all of her regrets over the choices she had and had not made. It was just Moria, her friend and her sewing needle for an afternoon. The stragglers of her usual self-admonishment that wouldn't be quiet couldn't reach her in Madame Blackshear's Modiste on Princess Street.

OUTSIDE OF HER CLOSE CIRCLE, THERE WAS NOTHING FOR it. For intervening weeks, Moria put on her best face for callers, for dinners; but when the effortlessly elegant man in front of her sitting room mantle turned to face her upon her entry, the mask fell away.

"Peregrine," she said, more whisper than greeting.

He gave her a ghost of a smile, and before she could protest, he wrapped her in a bracing hug. Although he was nowhere near as tall as his younger brother, she could rest her head on his shoulder.

She could rest her tired facade, and let her grief reveal its true face for a moment in his company. What a silent, lonely luxury to not feel the need to hide not just her secret pain, but her secret love.

For a second time I am the girl mourning in secret. How did I get here so I never wind up here again?

Before words were even exchanged, he was pulling her back to remove a handkerchief from his coat to dab at her eyes. "Christ, what an injustice. Here I am trying to come up with something to say to comfort you, my lady, and become dumbfounded by how your eyes are even more beautiful when you're crying. Usually I'm much better with words, but," he cleared his throat, scrunched his nose like he too was fighting tears, "I find I'm all out of the right ones, or any of them, at the moment."

Moria chuckled through her tears. "He'd have found that some small victory, I'm sure."

"Rendering me speechless? He made a regular sport of it." Peregrine's laugh had the same hint of goodness in his baritone that she'd always loved in Devyn's. She nodded in response. It struck her that while she'd tried to understand Devyn, and wondered what his family had been like, the person responsible for the man she loved had been right in front of her.

Peregrine went to stand at the window, looking out onto the street outside. Moria came to stand beside him, but placed her back to the panes. Watching the finely dressed and liveried traffic beyond move about like so great a loss was only shared by the two occupants of the sitting room and not something to bring her world to its knees was not something she could do. She knew by now the ways that grief had to be constrained to a slow trickle rather than a raging torrent.

"I asked him not to go. I offered him my title to stay. At first, I was angry. I called him stubborn and bull-headed," Moria felt a tightening in her chest upon hearing Peregrine sharing her thoughts. "Eventually, I came to the realization that that was only partly true."

Moria placed a hand at her chest, toying with the high lace neck of her gown.

"The only thing that Devyn was ever given without any strings attached, was his army commission. He used his winnings at cards, money he made from investments, and an inherited property from our grandmother he rented out, to purchase it. Our father offered to purchase it for him, but he had a history of controlling Devyn and manipulating his appreciation or guilt for his own purposes. Devyn wouldn't have wanted anything he didn't earn." He gave a sad smile, the laugh lines at the corners of his eyes felt so oppressive, so hideously unjust as they were something Devyn would never grow to have.

"I think he thought one last heroic stand would make him worthy of being a nobleman, and worthy of you."

Moria shook her head. "He had it all wrong. It was me...who wasn't worthy of him. And all of his goodness."

"And now you're to marry the Duke?"

Moria nodded.

"He asked, and you said yes?"

She swallowed the lump in her throat. "Devyn was gone. I was left," Moria didn't meet Peregrine's eyes, couldn't. "So I chose the very last person that I wanted to commit to- *myself*."

He took one of her hands in his. "You're to become a duchess, as we all predicted. Then, be a good one, my dear, find a way to make something good from all of this," Peregrine said, giving her a firm hug before he departed.

Chapter Thirty-Two

Devyn,

We were a good lie. The sweetest kind of lie all doomed lovers believe, until the bitter truth sinks its teeth in: all lovely things die. It's the uglier things that are harder to kill.

But I can't stop reliving our death. Bitter though it may be, I savor it. The last fleeting hours before the funeral, holding a solo vigil for all we could and should and would have been. How do I bury a love so young and beautiful? All I have is the ashes of us, these letters an urn, my black crepe-shrouded heart your shrine.

I suppose now I am the lie. The smiling, dancing future duchess clutched with silent grief. At least here to you on these pages I can admit, I'll carry every memory preserved like flies in amber, flowers pressed in a page until I die.

But they don't get to know what's in my heart if I can't say it to you one last time.

I love you. It's you that I love. It has always, ever, only been you. Only you could make me keep writing torturous prose in these letters for weeks on end with no reply.

M

~

OVER THREE YEARS AGO, MARCUS HAD MADE THE WHOLE ballroom go silent at a ball his mother was hosting.

"This is it," she'd thought, squeezing her mother's hand. "He's going to announce our betrothal, or he's going to propose."

Instead, he'd toasted a business venture with Viscount Lynwood, Kathleen's first husband, and several other noblemen that would turn out to be false. "To endless returns and smooth seas for *The Thorne's Blade*!"

Moria had yawned, pretending that all the talk of shipping investments and a ship Marcus boasted about but she was pretty sure didn't exist, bored her, giving her mother a pinched smile as she made her way to the ladies retiring room. It was there, that night, that she'd met Gretchen.

Now, she was looking at George Worthington, Duke of Andover, as he clinked a fork against a champagne glass, seeking his guests' attention. Their engagement had already made the rumor mills, the gossip sheets, even *The London Times* had printed a large column about her engagement. She'd thought before that this would be a glittering culmination of all that she'd strived for. Her first public appearance as the fiancé of a Duke was overshadowed by the dark specter of her lost love, her silent grief.

"My ladies and gentleman, I thank you for joining us for a fine evening celebrating what's sure to be one of the best decisions I took far too long to make," the Duke said, standing on the orchestra's circular stage, to general amusement and smiles, a few laughs. Noelle reached for Moria's hand, Moria tipped back her champagne flute. Fitz took Noelle's hand instead to cover the snub. Gretchen, on her other side, met Moria's eyes, remembering their meeting, and stepped closer to her till their skirts brushed.

"Luckily enough, this particular lady is a very patient and forgiving woman, as well as beautiful," the Duke reached his eyes and his hand toward her.

Moria had to cross several groups of people to reach him. He took her gloved hand in his, squeezing it once. Moria tried to tell if his emerald eyes were a little pinched or were they glassy? Shouldn't she know more about his face than the fact that it was handsome? Anyone could know an incontrovertible truth like that simply from looking.

She blushed, ducking her head, like the praise was too much. Humble and dutiful, that was the part they all wanted her to play.

"So, I request your assistance in raising a glass, a toast to my future wife, the incomparable Lady Moria Pembrooke. To Lady Moria!"

Hundreds of glasses raised in unison, her name on their lips. Some contorted into a smile, others a thin line.

Hundreds of pairs of eyes on her, all looking at the diamond they thought they knew, in a bright pink dress, her gloved hand held in a Duke's. None of them were the eyes she wanted to find, because they had closed for the last time, on some distant battlefield.

It felt like she'd come so far and fallen so short all in the same half-second.

George tipped her champagne flute with his, his eyes drinking her in like she was the champagne in his glass. When Moria drained her glass, he took it from her and handed it to a waiter.

"Moria Pembrooke," George said, taking her hand and ushering her to the dancefloor where couples parted around them. "If I didn't know any better, I'd say you look," he angled his head to the side like he needed a better angle to study her, "Like you're either very happy or very nervous with all the praise." He let out a little boyish laugh. "Although, one would not usually associate you with the latter, would they?"

She gave him the small laugh he was aiming for. "For a moment, I wasn't sure what you were about to say. I would have been very cross with you if you had stood up there to announce you bought a new racehorse or something."

He tilted his head back on a laugh as he spun her in a turn of the dance, his legs brushing her skirts through layers of fabric.

"You stole my idea for an engagement gift, now I'll have to resort to jewels then."

"I suppose I shall have to shoulder the burden. I'll put on a very brave face," Moria said, lifting her chin. She was relying on humor in another situation she had been unprepared for.

His ducal hands braced her as she spun into his chest. He steadied her with a hand on her hip, his warm, champagne scented breath at her ear. "You don't have to, not with me. I am beginning to think I like all your faces."

When his other hand grazed her hip, she suddenly felt a jolt, a spark, a flicker of want. But for another man. Another man had conducted her hips in a way that she wasn't sure any other man ever could, even this one who was built like a Greek god, if gods liked fencing and rowing.

When the dance ended, she was greeted by The Duke's mother and sister. Moria bowed deferentially to the two equally beautiful women, the younger with skin the same bronze shade as her brother's, their mother's more the rich color of tea before you put your milk and sugar in. They both shared the Duke's emerald eyes.

"My dear," his mother said, taking Moria's elbow. "You look radiant. George, you've taken her for a dance, let the young lady have a moment to breathe."

Moria's eyes filled with tears, she didn't know why. Something about having a protective, motherly voice and warm, encouraging eyes looking out for her.

"Thank you," she said, suddenly feeling like she wanted to hug this woman and run from her at the same time. "Your Grace."

"Oh, mother," Lady Geneva said, towering over Moria and looking into her tear-flecked eyes, "I think she's a little overcome."

"It's a good thing I'm here, my lady," the Dowager said, a hand at Moria's back. "You've had a very big night, yes?"

Moria nodded, meeting her eyes.

"My son told me that you lost your mother. Are you missing her tonight?"

Moria only gave her an answering smile in return, words felt so hard to form. She was missing so much more than just her mother.

The woman's face betrayed no emotion, but her eyes were kind. "The retiring room, then. Eva?"

"I think I need to cast up my accounts! I must have had a bad shrimp or two," Lady Geneva said in a loud voice, looking between her mother and Moria with a hand covering her mouth. Moria had been on the receiving end of Lady Geneva's cold shoulder in the past, but decided in that moment she liked this girl. Surprisingly, she reminded her of Olivia. Where Olivia was fair-haired and fair-complected, as well as petite, this girl was her mirror opposite, but matched her for spirit. The two of them would be unrivaled co-conspirators.

Moria let Lady Geneva loop her arm through hers, following the Dowager Duchess to the Ladies' retiring room, until she saw it. Red hair, a grim smile. Moria stopped in the hall just outside of the retiring room, pulling Lady Geneva with her.

Aware of precedent, Kate bowed to the Dowager first, then Lady

Geneva, and Moria last with a mockingly short bow. A reminder, lest she forget, there were still others above her.

"Lady Moria, congratulations to you on your splendid match," Kate Herring said, leaning to kiss Moria familiarly on both cheeks. Next to Moria's ear, Kate whispered, "When you aim high, make sure you arm yourself."

When Kate looked back to Moria, Moria realized that the other woman was returning her words from that day they'd run into each other at the modiste a few months prior.

Shit, Moria really had made it seem like she was encouraging the woman to seek a match with the Duke, when Moria had been in love with another man.

Had been? A voice mocked her somewhere in the general vicinity of her conscience.

When Kate departed company, the Dowager asked in a lowered tone, "Should I have left her off the guest list, my dear? My son assured me that the two of you were friends."

Did he, just? Moria pondered.

"A lady of Lady Moria's caliber and means, mama," Lady Geneva supplied, "Must always keep her friends close and her more envious friends on a tight leash."

If only Moria had listened.

<h1 style="text-align:center">Chapter Thirty-Three</h1>

Miss Kate Herring: *Said young lady advertises her family's* ~~*exploits*~~ *adventures in the Congo. Some light digging shows that one Mr. Thaddeus Herring came back a ransom richer. One has only to wonder if the purpose and activities Miss Herring extols, were, in fact, mercenary in nature rather than Godly. How does a man of God afford a manufactory in Manchester and two of the Earl of Westmoreland's prized racehorses?*

~

"WHAT ARE YOU ALL...."

Several days later, Moria entered the breakfast room and immediately her words fell away as soon as she saw the pamphlet the occupants of the drawing room were holding.

The Burn Book.

She snatched one from the nearest hand, it was Lawrence's. He didn't try to take it from her.

"No..." her stomach dropped.

She'd written some unkind things. She'd mostly written truths. But they were salacious, and they were about people that garnered attention and sold headlines.

Someone had stolen her words. Words written by an angry and heartbroken and guarded girl in her own notebook in her room. Lady Gretchen and Carina had also written in the book, but there was no audience intended. At least she and her friends hadn't signed their own names to them. Although their names were conspicuously absent.

"Did you write this?" It was Jasper, walking to stand in front of her, pamphlet in hand.

"There's no proof of that," she shot back, straightening to her full height as he peered down at her.

"Whoever stole this took some of the worst of the worst and the most damning," Noelle put in, standing from her seat at the table.

Moria felt like sights and sounds were happening around her, to her, but she wasn't a part of it.

Who had done this?

As if on cue, Lady Carina and Gretchen entered, Olivia in tow.

Before Moria could ask any questions, her two friends rushed her, pulling her into their arms.

If anyone ever found this, it'd be quite the scandal, Gretchen had said, was it a fortnight ago? Or longer?

You mean people would pay to read some debutante's diaries?

No. She wouldn't. But when she looked into Gretchen's face, she knew she had reached the same conclusion.

Here, Moria had said, putting the book in Kate's hands, *Write something.*

Kate had taken the quill. *What should I say?*

Do your worst. Moria had said.

You let it out, honey. Put it in the book. Gretchen.

And then Kate had inked her quill, she'd written entry after entry. The four of them had passed around a bottle of champagne Carina kept in her carriage. Moria had been so in the throes of grief and drink and the safety of friendship that she hadn't noticed that Kate didn't take the bottle. She hadn't noticed where the book, black and pink and so necessary to her survival, had ended up when she'd returned home hours later.

"It was Kate," Lady Carina explained to Moria's family.

Lawrence and Fitz looked at each other. Jasper swore.

"How many people have read this?" Moria heard herself asking as though from someone else's voice, far underwater or on the other side of a chasm. Perhaps her body was on the other side of a chasm from her heart. It might as well be, it had dropped all the way through the carpeted floor, at least.

Gretchen and Olivia both took a step toward her. The occupants of the breakfast room were rapt as Olivia spoke first. "It was all over the Piccadilly news stand. Lady Carina, Gretchen, and I bought all they had and then went to three more stands and bought those too, but..."

"Then we had to keep an appointment for tea with one of Lady Olivia's suitors and his mother," Gretchen continued.

Moria looked to Olivia, no doubt not the only one of them all noting the red tip of her nose. Jasper's voice dropped low and lethal. "What happened?"

Olivia shook her head, unshed tears in her eyes. "It doesn't matter."

Moria felt the remaining dregs of her willpower strengthening. A fury that tasted like spite fueled her.

Moria and the others all looked to Carina, "We were turned away by the butler. Apparently, Lady Olivia was no longer welcome."

Moria registered Kathleen's defiant scoff and her copper curls moving as she shook her head. It was their Mother's voice Moria heard inside her head:

Head held high. Shoulders back. Smile like you have a secret. Even if they hurt you, don't let them know it. You're not their porcelain doll, you're unbreakable.

"We made sure to convey the message that Lady Moria Pembrooke, future Duchess of Andover, would not be pleased to hear this pronouncement," Gretchen said, an arm about Olivia's shoulders and steely pride in her voice.

"That was very forward thinking of you," Moria said, touching Gretchen softly on the arm.

The others all fell silent, but it was Fitz who cut through the tension first.

"I don't know that I like that look in your eyes," Fitz observed, glancing around his wife who stood next to his seat at the breakfast table.

Moria narrowed her eyes at him. "What look, Fitz Pomfrey?"

Olivia was looking at her not in fear, but in awe. "Like a warrior."

A head of the darkest hair and a pair of eyes darker than any night flashed in her vision. He hadn't shirked his calling or backed down from a fight, and neither would she.

Moria turned from her siblings and friends, and exited the drawing room. In the foyer, she scribbled something on a slip of paper in the escritoire, handed it to the butler who wrapped her coat about her. She turned to the eight souls who'd followed her out into the hall, who'd likely follow her to the ends of the earth if she asked.

"Are you coming?" she asked.

"Lead the way," Her older sister returned, letting her husband wrap her in her coat. No questions, linking her arm with Moria's and following her out onto the street. They followed her into Hyde Park, the place to be seen of an afternoon.

The green park was filled with carriages, with prominent people and their servants following behind, all talking closely with one another. At the sight of Lady Moria, flanked by a battalion of titled relations, their gazes and whispers seemed to find a focal point.

The woman in question continued walking, head held high, on

her brother, the Earl of Westmoreland's arm. The sky was conspicuously cloud free and the foliage of the park more verdant than usual. Who could accuse her of perfidy in a yellow and blue flowered dress, the sun wreathing her countenance, and birds chirping at her back?

"Lady Moria!" A man about thirty with a mustache called to her.

She waved at him, and he caught up with her.

He exchanged pleasantries with her family, then said: "Suppose I'd like a gander in that little book of yours."

Moria harrumphed, crossing her arms. So would she, if she had it in her possession.

"I'll reckon you would, my lord."

"How much would you offer for it?" Lawrence parried.

Moria pulled on his arm and then gave the other man a pleasant smile. "Never let it be said of me that I am ungenerous. But as it happens, I have no written proof of your clandestine tryst with your ward. Though I'm sure if someone did, I could see why you might want to burn that before your wife finds out."

Moria tapped her chin, mocking as though in thought, "On second thought, maybe she's already suspicious given her zealousness to see the girl wed."

The other man was agog. "That's not...That's slander!" His face started to redden. He took a step in her direction. Henry and Jasper pulled him back as he called out, "You will regret-"

"Watch yourself, Garth," a voice interrupted from behind them.

The unmistakable, perfect brown and chiseled face of the Duke of Andover was plainly visible over Jasper's shoulder. "That's my betrothed you're speaking to."

Moria hadn't been sure how quickly he'd receive her missive and find her in the park, but he'd answered her call for his aid. Other park-goers of all stripes had stopped to gawk, to listen.

The other man broke free of Henry's grip on his shoulder and turned in the Duke's direction.

"Fine then, your Grace. Do you know what *your betrothed* has done?"

The Duke stepped around him to stand in front of Moria. Her heart stuttered at the protectiveness of his stance and defiant gleam of his eyes. "My betrothed? She isn't the one who committed the acts, Lord Garth. To my knowledge, she is a young lady who wrote down witnessed events in a personal diary. If any crimes were committed, they were not by my betrothed, but by those who stole the book and aimed to profit by blackmail or extortive means."

She could feel watchful eyes on the Duke's reaction, but George turned eyes on Moria. She could read only acceptance in them, even though some of the people she wrote about had been his friends.

"If it was even your little book. Some of the things in that notebook are quite scathing, but by my reckoning, the people who ought to be concerned here," he turned to peer in Lord Garth's direction, "are the ones who perpetrated them."

My beautiful reckoning. Why was Devyn the man her thoughts ran to at that moment? When this one was here, healthy and hale, coming to her aid?

Tears stung like tiny bee stings, but she fought them off and wrote them off as relief over the Duke's public show of support. She was sure to be adding more fodder for the gossips today with this display. With a Duke at her side, though, who would dare turn her sister away again?

Warm, soft fingers intermingled with hers and offered her the protection of his good name and his body. "Come on, my dear," the Duke urged.

Moria looked down at their hands. Her engagement ring on her finger glinted in the afternoon sunlight. It was bright and shiny and large, but it wasn't as beautiful as the pink stone that Devyn had given her. One of the Duke's hands brushed against her fingers. To his left, Noelle and Fitz were looking at them in obvious fascination.

Olivia's eyes saw through her and held her for a moment, and then Moria looked to Kathleen.

"I hope to deserve you one day, all of you," she said, meaning it with her whole patchworked heart. "The combined force of you all behind me, I felt like I could do anything."

"We've never been able to counsel you when your mind is set on something, so we've just accepted our lot," Lawrence replied. But pride was in his eyes. He'd have hunted down whoever stole from her and released her words; but instead, he'd walked at her side, staring down any and all potential challengers.

"I'd like to have a private chat with His Grace if all of you don't mind, though?"

Jasper huffed out a breath, and then he was hugging her. "I'm proud of you, you know?" he said, his chin on top of her head. He was so sturdy and warm and unexpectedly hugging her, she didn't pull away until he did.

She saw the unshed wateriness in Kathleen's eyes. Henry gave her a small wink. God knew she complained about being part of such a large family, but they showed up for her and stood at her side on her worst occasions. No questions asked. Maybe she could finally tell them the truth. She knew she had to finally tell the Duke, he deserved to know before being shackled to her for life.

Her three sisters and brothers and brothers-in-law all partnered up; Olivia on Fitz's arm this time, as he waved at an old school friend and introduced the young lord and his mother to Olivia.

Miss Kelley followed three paces behind Moria and the Duke with her ward holding her hand.

"I meant what I said, earlier."

Moria turned to face him, clutching his arm. "Oh?"

"You didn't commit any crimes here, Moria. If you were even the one responsible for that book."

"I was, I wasn't the only writer; but I won't deny it. I didn't say anything that wasn't true."

"But why...why did you write the book, Moria? Surely it would have been easier just to burn the pages than to risk it leaking?"

She met his eyes, sensing her opening to give him a version of the truth, for good or ill.

"When I returned from mourning last season, there were all kinds of rumors...when the dancing partners and invitations dwindled, I found it hypocritical. They seemed to have no problem turning a cold shoulder to me over what they'd *heard* when I had witnessed worse. The first time I used such information to recover an invitation to a ball I felt..." She gave him a small smile, "Awful, yet proud of myself at the same time. I only had to use the information a handful of times to get what I felt I deserved, or to get myself out of situations that were not of my choosing; but I told myself information was currency, and I was never going to be a lady without such means again."

"Do you know who has the book?" He lowered his voice, next to her, tipping his hat at some matron as they passed.

Moria looked up at him, nodding. "Thank you for answering my note, for meeting me here. I was afraid—"

He turned his head to face her, slowing his strides. "I chose you. Whatever is said about you or to you, it affects the both of us. We handle this and whatever else comes. Together," he punctuated his words, his finger brushing over hers where she clutched his arm.

Moria leaned her head against his arm, resolving to tell him everything he didn't know. Olivia's reputation and future were secure, seemingly, for another day. She let herself feel contented for the first time in a long time walking companionably with him in Hyde Park, listening to him recount his latest parliament campaign, and watching all those they came in contact with either vying for his attention or sporting a knowing smirk.

Chapter Thirty-Four

D–

Where are you? Where have you gone? The report I read said that we may never know where you made your flight, or found eternal rest.

I know this: you will be safe in my memory until there is nothing left of me. It isn't the same as the kind of heralding infamy promised a warrior, but it's all I have. You used to say that you didn't have much to give me and I wish you'd seen how much the reverse of that was true. I was never much of an offering for your hand, but a devoted one.

Your silent soldier,

M

~

Chapter Thirty-Five

All roads lead back to you. The footpaths and the highways too. The sea lanes. All of them. You are the journey and the destination. There is nowhere else but you.

My lady.

-Captain Devyn Winter

(MESSAGE FOUND AMONG UNCOVERED PERSONAL EFFECTS)

~

"OUT OF THE WAY!" A VOICE CALLED THAT SOUNDED LIKE someone's father and brother at once.

Was it Devyn's father or Devyn's brother?

His eyelids felt too heavy to hazard a glance. At least two Army orderlies carried a stretcher up what felt like a lifetime of stairs. The canvas at his back had started to chafe against the sweat of his linen-wrapped skin.

The labored rise and fall of his chest took so much of his concentration. If he was back home in England, where was *she*? Was there a pair of ocean-colored eyes and a golden head of hair waiting for him at the end of all those stairs?

The familiar smell of expensive brandy hit him, with it so many memories.

Peregrine. His brother. The man who gave him his first brandy when he'd had to have stitches when he was nine for fighting another boy who made a crude comment about the same older brother who'd rocked Devyn to sleep, who'd taught him how to climb a tree, how to take all their father's jibes and threats and lay them down. Peregrine had been born serious and Devyn had been born careless, and together, they'd survived all the shit that shit parents do to children they didn't really want but were supposed to have.

The man who had placed a hand on Devyn's temple, who was ordering the servants to move his things to his own room, who had tears in his voice, was all the father that Devyn had ever known, without having ever had much of one himself.

"Lord Clairville," that would be the doctor, following behind.

"Tell me," the rasped voice said, one that sounded scratchy from excessive drink, lack of sleep, and hope that felt more like fear.

"Bullet to the hip, he's made it through the worst," the doctor explained.

Devyn had been barely conscious for so long that his brother's house felt like another world, another life away.

She was still another world away too, probably.

"An Army postillion roused me from sleep in the early hours for transport. He was liberated at Bamiyan and General Dennie had him sent back to England to recover, given his rank, as their surgery was spread too thin. He's been given enough laudanum to fell a tree to get him here due to the pain. He isn't able to walk at the moment; but with assistance, he will get there in time."

Peregrine ran his hands over Devyn's face, pushing back the too long hair in his eyes.

"I knew you'd never leave for good," Peregrine said.

Devyn clutched his brother's hand. Devyn was weak, a feeling he'd never been familiar with even as his father had tried to tell him that he was.

Moria's name sang through him on a tide of longing, he wanted to go to her.

God, I'm always missing her. Was she missing me too? Does she know where I am?

Devyn wasn't even sure he knew where he was until he heard Peregrine giving directions.

"Take him to my rooms. I'll move to a smaller one down the hall. He'll need the one at the top of the stairs. It's got a servant's entrance at the ante chamber as well. Corbett!" Peregrine's authoritative voice called for the housekeeper, "Have my things moved to a smaller room. And get the doctor whatever he needs."

"I kept... my promise," Devyn spoke, eyes barely adjusting to the light, strained and searching for something familiar in a world of foreign blurs.

"I never doubted you," Peregrine returned, squeezing his brother's hand as he was carried to his rooms.

Devyn was poked and prodded, and then given something else; it was probably something to help him sleep again. It was a too-welcome relief when his eyelids drifted shut again, dreaming about a blonde with eyes like twin oceans, staring at him across a church, tracing her eyes over his body underneath a willow tree, wearing a gown dusted with celestial shapes like she was wrapped in a starry sky.

"He's alive," Perry's voice broke to someone as the door snicked closed behind them.

"I gathered. You were right not to give up hope."

Had anyone ever comforted my brother before in all his years of comforting everyone who needed him?

"He can't walk. He was shot in the hip."

Devyn's body knew that, felt the marks and the aches; his mind, however, registered this belatedly.

How am I to get to her if I can't walk? How am I to stand in front of a church like I promised her? I'd made it this far, I would crawl if that's what it took.

"You are linked by blood, and more than blood, that's what you told me, remember? He will be alright, because you will make it so. There isn't anyone in the commonwealth who can stop you when your mind's made up."

Peregrine ran a hand over Devyn's shoulder.

The other masculine voice spoke again. "I never knew he had so many tattoos. His chest, his torso, his arms..."

Peregrine sniffled. "I was older, he was bigger. Father put more marks and scars on him than he did to me. I suppose he found a way to cover over them."

"Christ, what a monster. I'm glad that you had each other. I'm glad you didn't lose him."

"So am I." Devyn heard Peregrine echo his thoughts.

"I'll stay."

"You'll...stay?"

"You'll need a hand. He's quite heavy. And your cook's rather decent. Your cognac's better than mine, too."

"Tristan, you are far from impoverished."

There was a long pause, in which Devyn slowly felt some of the energy start to re-enter his body, in which he felt the weight of his family curse that had kept him from staying in England with the woman he loved, kept his brother from something close to happiness with the person he seemed to care for.

"I want you to stay," Peregrine said, finally.

Devyn barely heard it, felt awful for hearing their confessions, and wondered if his big, weighted body was actually still asleep.

"Then I'll stay, however long you'll have me," and the words Tristan Valentine whispered, the words Devyn should have said to the woman he loved, echoed on repeat in the dark valley of Devyn's laudanum filled dreams.

~

PEREGRINE SAT BY HIS BROTHER'S SIDE FOR NEARLY FOUR days until he was fully conscious. Tristan never left. He brought Peregrine meals which he ate after helping Devyn to eat no matter how Devyn insisted his brother eat first. Tristan even shaved Devyn a time or two, rather skillfully, in fact.

"God, I guess I never realized that you must have shaved every day, that's how burly you are."

The Devyn before would have laughed at that, this one wasn't sure he remembered how.

"Did I choose the wrong brother?" Tristan said, cleaning the razor in a bowl of warm water, eyes lighting on Peregrine with this affection that Devyn was beginning to understand, but felt was something rare.

Peregrine made an effort to involve Devyn in games of cards, reading to Devyn, getting him to drink water, checking his bandage to make sure it didn't get infected. Through all of it, Devyn had been biding his time, waiting for the moment someone would escort her into a room, or answer his questions.

Finally, Tristan brought up the one thing they'd all been dancing around: the woman Devyn loved. Clearly his brother and Peregrine didn't think he could hear them through the open door or thought that he was asleep, but it was the first real answers he'd been given.

"What about...*her*?" Tristan urged.

"What about her?" Peregrine retorted. Devyn didn't like the defensiveness in his voice.

"Shouldn't someone tell her he didn't bleeding die?"

"What business is it of hers? She's marrying a duke."

Devyn pressed the heels of his hands into his eye sockets. He pulled at the ends of his hair as his heart fought its way out of his chest. A strangled sob escaped him. The words ran him through worse than a dull lance.

How could she? But then, how could she not *consent to marrying a duke, a prince, a king even, because that's what she deserved.*

Devyn rubbed a hand over the ache in his chest. He'd never been enough for her. He'd been fighting like hell the last seven months to get back to her, and to recover the last week to get her back, but what did he have to recover for now?

"Once my brother makes it through his next hurdle of fighting the infection of his gunshot wound, and then standing on his own, I'll let him tell her himself."

Devyn heard his brother's words like they were at the surface, and he was falling head first under waves of relentless ocean water.

Tristan returned in a low voice. "What if he doesn't tell her?"

"Don't see how that's my problem."

"She's gutted," Tristan pushed.

Images of her in pain, the heartbreaking shade of blue her eyes went when she cried, tears hanging from her lashes, the heavy pout of her fuller lower lip, the way she must hate him for doing this to her and then not being able to comfort her, all drowned him further in his grief.

"I would hope so, she did claim to love him."

"Just be the man I love, the man who loves me. That's enough for me."

Had she said that to me? Had all of it even been real? God, I'm not clear-headed enough to sort this shit out.

Tristan's voice sounded a bit pleading. "And she doesn't *want* to marry the duke."

How did he know? Had he seen her and not shared any details to avoid setting back Devyn and his recovery?

Peregrine's voice was neutral. "No one's forcing her."

"Aren't they?"

Fire frenzied along his veins. Devyn couldn't take it anymore. Using one leg to stand, bracing himself on a chair, he leaned over to the nearby table and swiped its contents onto the floor. A loud groan and a crash accompanied a parade of glass shards before him where there once had been bottles of laudanum.

Peregrine stood in the doorway, assessing Devyn's shirtless form and cocked up hair and red-rimmed eyes, the mess he'd made.

"Oh, Devyn. What about the pain? Your last dose-"

"Was my last dose," Devyn interjected. "I need to move without it."

He needed to *think* without it, he couldn't stand the way it heightened everything and then left him dull and hollowed out. He had started to count the minutes down to his scheduled dose and he knew if he followed where that would lead. He was definitely no use to her a slave to the contents of a bottle.

"But your injury-"

Devyn rotated his shoulders, stretched his arms almost above his head, winced, then brought them back down.

"I've felt worse," he groaned.

A maid entered with a broom and a dustpan. He felt like an ass, so he took the instruments from her small hands and told her to step back, biting back a grimace as he did so.

"You're as stubborn as father," Peregrine said, shaking his head.

"If I were less stubborn, I'd probably be dead," Devyn said, cleaning up the large shards of glass first and putting them in the dust pan with a handkerchief.

"If you were less stubborn, you'd have given up your commission when you were asked."

Devyn could feel his face falling, and Peregrine's regret was written in his eyes.

How much sleep has my brother lost over me? Why was I always taking from the people I cared for? What had she *seen in me anyway?*

A tremor shot from his hip through other parts of him and Devyn braced the side of the bed for support.

"You're probably right," Devyn said, his head falling backward onto the bed as he sat on the rug stretching out his legs, the fight leaving him.

"Holy shit," Peregrine replied. "You're worse than I thought. You hate admitting when I'm right."

For the first time, Devyn gave him a half smile and watched Peregrine inhale a deep breath.

"I might have come to that conclusion myself, sometime between entering a shoot-out and being hit with a bullet."

"I'm glad you're stubborn, I'm glad you're here. Devyn, I was sick with worry."

"I know you would hate to live without your reckless brother causing you constant worry."

"I would hate to live without my brother. That is all."

Devyn's dark eyes met his, lingered over the grey at his temples, the laugh lines at the corners of his eyes, his frown lines. "Even though I've cocked it all up?"

Peregrine took up the broom and finished sweeping the bits of glass, then sat beside Devyn.

"You didn't. A man is alive because of you. I'm so proud of the man that you are, the leader that you are," he placed a hand on Devyn's shoulder. "You made a choice, it cost you. You didn't take the easy route, you never have. There's honor in that."

"Honor," Devyn said the word almost like a scoff, "Doesn't help me walk."

He crossed his arms and avoided Peregrine's eyes. He was working to keep all of himself together, and letting Peregrine see might undo his efforts.

"Then it's a good thing you have me. You're stubborn, and I'm stubborn, we just won't give up then."

"And... Moria?" the word scraped out of his mouth. It hurt him to speak her name, yet he closed his eyes, savoring the sound.

"What about her?" Peregrine asked tentatively.

"She's marrying him, isn't she? The duke?"

Devyn looked at him now, unsure if he wanted the truth or if he desperately wanted him to lie.

"She is."

"Then I'll have to get back on my feet to spite her."

The set of his jaw and the pain in his eyes, could Peregrine read the love there? Love and pain and loss and anger all stirred into one toxic brew that needed somewhere to go.

Peregrine stood, wrapping an arm around Devyn who, though his injury had taken a considerable amount of his bulk, was still so much larger than him. It took all his strength, but Peregrine pulled him to the edge of the bed and bore his weight to help his younger brother to stand. And he didn't stop, didn't let go, day in and day out, pushing his brother to move, pulling him up, and refusing to let Devyn fall.

Chapter Thirty-Six

Raise your hand if you've ever been personally victimized by Lady M.

Did you find your name among those in the pages of her fiery book found bound and printed for mere pennies at every rag seller in Mayfair, or, like the Duke of A and many others, were you spared?

- Scandalous Lives of London scandal sheet

THE DUKE HAD HAD A SHINING MOMENT TO EXIT, AND he'd chosen instead to stay by her side.

Moria didn't know what to make of that.

She should be happy with her choice, but she was angry that she had to make such a choice, though who she was angry at, she couldn't say.

Devyn was good, he was honorable, leaving her had not been a choice. Neither had staying. Neither were choices he could make.

The choice that she could make was to keep on loving him even as it ripped her soul to rags.

The Duke appeared in the doorway of her sitting room the day following the scandal of the Burn Book, standing over Moria to admire the embroidery hoop in her hand.

"It looks like... willow fronds," he said in awe.

Moria looked at the white-on-white garment in her hand. "Do you like it?" she whispered, not meeting his eyes.

It had been the design she'd started stitching for her wedding to Devyn. She'd tried to take a pair of scissors, a seam ripper, a knife, a match to it, but she couldn't.

"I think it's lovely," he said jovially. "I think you're lovely. You're so..." He paused. "Creative. It's different from what I pictured you'd choose, but I'm sure you will look divine." He placed a kiss on her forehead, walking over to the other side of the room to take a scone from a tea tray just as her chaperone entered.

Miss Kelley gave Moria a reassuring smile. Moria hated seeing her, or any of her loved ones, walking on eggshells around her like one misstep might send her reeling.

"My lady," he spoke, interrupting her thoughts. "My mother sent me to ask if you'd mind playing something tonight before guests arrive for the dinner she's hosting?"

Moria followed his gaze to the piano in the corner of the room, to his right. She quickly looked away.

She knew what she'd see if her eyes hesitated too long. Devyn's body crowding hers, playing the right hand while she played the left, him loving her so fully on a piano bench. A pianoforte with hand painted flowers on the music desk showing up at her family's London house after she told him she didn't have a piano to play in town.

She shut the memories in a drawer quickly.

"I don't...I don't play anymore."

His face fell. "You don't....play anymore? Is something wrong? You have a gift."

Moria felt the tears pushing behind her eyes. She shook her head. She could tell him the truth; but then where would she be?

"Your Grace," Miss Kelley began.

"Could you give us just a moment?" He interrupted, crossing the room to reach Moria.

His eyes were so kind. That was Moria's first thought. The green of them was a hue that could only belay kindness, and maybe want.

He touched her cheek. She closed her eyes at the contact because it had been so long since she'd been touched so softly, so intimately, not because it heated her throughout.

"I won't pressure you. The Burn Book yesterday, and your feelings about the piano...I just want to understand."

As words go, that was the right thing to say just then. She felt grateful to him for it. She hated him at the same time for not being conspicuously terrible so she didn't have to care for him. But some part of her knew that in time, she would trust him with more than just the surface of her heart, and his tender touches and those green eyes would work their way deeper.

And then how could she hold allegiance to more than just one man without being a traitor and every other name her mind called her at night? She looked down at the embroidery in her hand that she'd begun for a union with another man.

"Playing music is something...tied to parts of my past...I'd rather not hold fast to. If I let go of music, I let go of that too." She swallowed the lump in her throat.

His eyes were confused, but he nodded, more out of a desire to understand than genuine understanding. "And not playing the pianoforte, does that for you?"

He was on his knees before her. His hands rested on his thighs, she set down the embroidery and took them in her hands, turning them over. They were lined, but smooth. A warm shade of brown. Long and lean. Nails neatly trimmed.

"You have beautiful hands," she said, tracing the edges between his fingers. If she could focus on something before her, not all the things behind her and ahead of her and inside her head, she could push through.

"The only way out is through." The memory of her mother's gentle voice pushed.

"I will only ever use them to be gentle to you. I will never use them to hurt you, Moria. I swear to you." One hand pushed a stray strand of golden hair behind her ear.

She was no adversary for such tenderness. "No," she swallowed her tears. "No, I know. I know, Your Grace."

"I wish you would call me by my given name. Call me George."

He had to know, she had to tell him the truth and risk losing him. Moria looked down at their joined hands, and nodded.

"If we are to call each other by our given names, then I feel that you and I should have an honest conversation. And if, at the end of what I have to tell you, you want to call me something other than *Moria*; I won't fault you for your choice of words. Only I should give you the truth. It wasn't always given to me."

"Is it about the Marquess? I was a few years ahead of him at school," he sighed. "Ours was a strained friendship, but I had a vague notion there was something between the two of you."

She nodded, tracing a finger of one of his hands intertwined with hers and spoke in a subdued voice. "I am not a virgin, Your Grace." She felt as though her teeth had ground the words out, her lips being forced to form the syllables whilst groaning in protest, but they were necessary.

"If you think that you've shocked me, you haven't, Moria."

Her eyes shot up to his, searching for purchase while she fell into altering waves of confusion, regret, and guilt. "What do you mean?"

"You were engaged to Marcus, were you not?"

Moria took a steeling breath as though she'd been holding her breath before for his reaction, and now her lungs could fully expand.

"What I was... was a stupid girl of eighteen. I'd been infatuated with Marcus for years. His family's estate was not far from ours growing up. When I look back now, he didn't even formally court me the same as.... well, the way he ought to have. I suppose I took for granted that he would. He gave me lots of pretty words and promises and ideas when I pleased him, and much worse when I didn't. He showed me the vault where the family jewels were kept, and he said that one day they'd all be mine. It wasn't technically a proposal, but I'm sure he wanted me to think of it as such."

"Moria," he shook his head. "You can't blame yourself. You were very young... he was several years older than you. He took advantage of you. He hurt you. God, if he weren't dead, I'd kill him myself."

The Duke ran a hand through his hair, as a thought struck him. "Wait, did your brother...."

"No," she said, her eyes wide. "Marcus was killed in a duel by a gang lord he owed money to. He was planning to marry me to obtain the funds to pay him back, but wasn't quick enough about ruining me or making profits on his business venture, I suppose. Jasper didn't find out about our relationship or his debts until Marcus was already dead."

"Moria, this doesn't change anything," he pulled her closer to him, draping an arm around her.

She swallowed, looking at him with sorrowful eyes.

"There's more, isn't there?" he asked, rubbing the back of his neck with one hand.

"I was with child." The words came out of her little more than a whisper, but he heard them.

"You and the marquess...had a child?" The words were a breath of air, soft and awed.

She shook her head, dabbing at her tears with her sleeve. "I lost the child. A little girl with blonde hair and blonde eyelashes. She was so small, but she already had my hair. Or Marcus's hair."

He pulled her to him, his strong hands painting comforting

patterns along her arms and her spine. Tears were gone, she'd already used them all up before now.

She pulled back to make sure that he could hear her next words clearly. "George...the doctor that attended me...he said that I mightn't have any more children."

"Stop," he forced her to look up at him, "Moria, I wish that I could undo all of this history for you. If I could bloody Marcus from the grave, I'd do it. But you need to understand, none of this means that you and I can't wed."

Moria felt hollow. Was she so hollow that she had misheard him?

"What are you talking about? Please speak plain, Your Grace."

His Adam's Apple bobbed as he swallowed, seeming to pause to think through his words.

"I am a Duke, I have no end of resources at my disposal. I must marry, and it needs to be soon, and it needs to be, I feel crass to say, someone of the highest pedigree. There are those who look down on me for my mother's heritage, I need a match with someone enviable. Add to all of that, I am quite fond of you. I would even go so far as to say that I feel some affection for you. I think that I am the partner that will give you everything that you desire. But if we don't suit," he drummed his fingers on his leg, "physically, I mean...we wouldn't be the first nobles in history to...seek elsewhere to continue the lineage."

Was he proposing that he would sleep with some other woman to carry his baby if she couldn't?

"Oh my god," she breathed, standing to put some distance between them. "Are you telling me that you're—"

He closed the distance between them, taking her hands in his.

"Moria, I want to be faithful to you, and I want your fidelity," he held her eyes and she saw no malice, no judgment which felt like a gift. "But I'm not your jailer, I'm not your keeper, nor are you mine."

Moria couldn't help thinking of Kate just then and how she'd been included on the Dowager's guest list at her ball a few weeks prior at His Grace's assurance the two ladies were friends.

He continued. "I don't see why two people can't set out with the best of intentions, and still refuse to be victims of circumstance. Neither you nor I are the type of people who just accept our lot," he gave a little huff of laughter, shaking his head at her as if in awe. "My god, you were ruined."

"Okay, no need to harp on about it," she interjected.

"No, you're not listening," he shook his head, pulling her tighter in his embrace as she gave a little breathy laugh of surprise. "You were ruined, just a girl with very little knowledge of the world—"

"Me? Very little knowledge of the world? Really, George, if you're getting to the part where you impart some praise or some positive message, I'd really appreciate it if you'd get to it. I do have a fragile ego, if you weren't aware."

He was laughing, shaking his head at her. "The breadth of your worldly knowledge notwithstanding, you turned a very bad hand into..." He searched her eyes like he'd find the words written there. "A legacy. You are the kind of lady that people don't forget. You made sure they didn't forget you. Hell, you made sure *I* couldn't forget you."

"Seemed like you did for a bit, though," she said, unable to hold back her criticism. However, his time spent on campaign had given her time to decide what she wanted, time with Devyn that now she couldn't get back. His name introduced tears, like they'd been waiting in the wings to present themselves on a tide of longing. She wiped at her eyes with her hand.

"I won't make you cry anymore." He held her against him, speaking the words next to her ear, "I'll try not to, at least. I'll consider your feelings. You are an incredibly unforgettable woman, for all that you have accomplished, and I will make you a duchess. You will have all that you want, the envy of those who likely scorned you or any of your family members added to it. You'll have no one's loyalty more than my own. And you and I will...we will consider one another, above all things, but we won't get in each other's way."

It was different from the words full of love and tenderness and heat that Devyn had given her. God, he'd built for her castles out of his words, hadn't he? What he hadn't had to offer her, he'd made for her, he'd promised to make for her, with his own hands and heart.

And the words she'd had from Marcus, they'd been the barely there romantics of a boy who wouldn't get the chance to be a man, the verbal blows of a boy who'd had everything and would never appreciate her.

And the Duke, George, could have promised her all sorts of things, god knows he had them to offer, but he'd been honest. Probably not entirely, he was a man and a Duke after all, but he hadn't lied, and he hadn't offered more than he had or was willing to give.

"We...won't get in each other's way? I kind of wanted someone to want to get in my way. I'm not just a subject pledging fealty to a noble. I'd be a partner to you, wouldn't I?"

"A partner," he said the words, sparks of appreciation lighting the dark olive skin of his face and his warm green eyes. "I'd like that very much, Moria."

"Good. I think you should kiss me now."

He tipped her face up to his, his eyes taking on a darker hue to match his voice. "The lady wants to be kissed, then?"

Moria nodded once, lied into his eyes. "She does."

His lips teased her own. "By whom?"

Moria bit her lip, mock pensive, but really it wasn't a mockery, she really didn't know if she could ever want any lips but Devyn's on hers; but the alternative was never being kissed again, and she hated how it sounded, but that was an awful prospect. God had not put her on this earth for dowdy and contemplative spinsterhood.

"By a man who knows how," she said, moving her lips closer to his. This time she told the truth.

"Christ," he swore. "I hope I'm up for the challenge," he said, a hand at her hips pulling her closer.

"From what I hear, you've had lots of practice."

His lips captured hers, tentative and lingering at first. When she moved her body closer to his, he pulled her lips in with his, exploring her mouth with his own.

He wasn't a bad kisser, he was just the wrong man. She should not be kissing him. But his hand was at the small of her back, and she was marrying him instead of choosing a life of tragic loneliness. His lips were large and soft, he tasted like peppermints, but he didn't have a thick end of the day stubble scratching her face. He didn't kiss her with his whole body, he kissed her like you might expect a duke to kiss...a little more than perfunctory, but not like his life depended on her air.

Chapter Thirty-Seven

M. Honnimers to launch sequel to follow up *Adelaide* at publisher's mansion. A long-awaited book making its debut at a masquerade? The fictional events had certainly better rival the fanfare in store at another one of Ludlowe's lavish parties.
- *Scandalous Lives of London*

Noelle had offered to postpone the launch of her second book after Moria's wedding. Moria wouldn't hear of it, arguing that any drama detracting from her own personal one and able to quell the attention she received, was more than welcome. And if it happened to be a masquerade to rival that of Noelle's first book launch? That just meant Moria didn't have to sit at home.

Moria had an idea in mind for a costume, which Olivia immediately loved; but Noelle said it was macabre, even for her. She'd gone through the remnants of dresses left behind at Letitia's seamstress shop and had found two dresses that they'd worked to sew the two halves together into one dress. When Letitia had questioned literally all of these sartorial choices, Moria had shrugged. "It's all about the symbolism here, Letty."

The origin of one half was a white wedding gown, in the fashion of Queen Victoria's; and the other half was a mourning gown. Both had bodices made of lace and high necked, one had long sleeves, the other had puffy ones. There was even a white veil and a black one sewn in two layers on top of the other. Underneath, she wore her hair in an elegant coiffure, and a black and white mask.

When she stepped back from the mirror, she admired her handiwork.

"Only you would devise something this...devastating...for a party," Noelle said from over her shoulder.

Moria quipped, "I'm always devastating at every party. That's the point."

Noelle took her hands in her own, looking down at her from their height difference. "The point of this particular party, I will remind you, is enjoyment."

She was in her usual costume as Adelaide, her trim figure highlighted by an emerald-green dress, a departure from her signature red for this new book's themes about greed and envy. But with her breasts pushed up, and her hips accentuated, she looked devastatingly good.

"Forget being devastating for a moment and enjoy a night with the ones who love you, free flowing champagne, and your freedom."

Moria gave her sister's hands a firm squeeze. She didn't tell her sister about the agreement that she and the Duke had come to, or that while being the center of scandals had cost her, Moria wasn't sure who she was without it.

As Moria walked down the stairs of Pomfrey House's ballroom flanked by Letitia and Bridget and Kathleen, Moria shrouded in white and black, her friends turned out for a party in increasingly more scandalous costumes, the feeling was like...being back in the house she grew up in.

Many felt nervous in a ballroom, in a crowd of this magnitude, but the closely dancing bodies and reverberating music and lively aura gave her clarity. Moria's shoulders were straight, her head held high, as she descended the stairs. She was immediately met at the bottom of the stairs by a suitor requesting a dance.

"The Lady isn't dancing tonight," Letitia answered for her in her best imitation of a posh accent.

The suitor eyed Moria's attire, bowed, and departed.

"Only you could attract suitors in a costume like that," Noelle said, eyeing her as she took a flute of champagne from a tray held by a masked footman dressed as a highwayman.

"Maybe it will deter them long enough for us all to dance...not with suitors, but together."

Moria linked arms with the women around her. They had held her when she cried, they'd dried her tears, they'd listened. They were here with her tonight, to celebrate Noelle and her work.

It was Kathleen who led Moria onto the dance floor. When the strings of the violin started, Henry slipped out of the shadows and slipped an arm around Kathleen's waist, the others moved to accommodate him. Kathleen tipped her head back on a laugh, it was so full of surprise and joy and adoration it made Moria's eyes sting.

I'll never know such open affection from a spouse like my sisters, will I?

But the music was playing, and the masked, costumed dancers were moving, so Moria turned on her most devastating charm. She pivoted and locked arms with Letitia, who spun her into Noelle.

Gretchen and Carina linked arms with her on either side. Moria looked at Carina's costume.

"Your costume, Carina, what on earth are you?"

Carina pointed to the felt ears attached to her coiffure, "I'm a mouse, obviously."

Moria laughed, looking at Letitia who made a face while she danced side to side with Bridget as though she were looking down at her cleavage, ever in character. Moria tipped her head back as the sounds of joy escaped her for the first time in a while. Her mask slipped down on her face, and Noelle righted it for her. She changed partners and swayed elegantly with Kathleen until it was time to change partners again, and this time it was Bridget.

Her companion said in a lowered tone: "Don't look now but there's a man staring at you."

Moria only gave a little laugh, the champagne going to her head as she said, "There usually is."

They kept moving to the music, and just before Moria changed partners with Letitia, Bridget whispered, "This one looks... familiar."

The music warred with Moria's heart beating in her chest. The champagne had made her vision feel a little fuzzy around the edges, but she glanced over her shoulder in the direction Bridget had indicated. The man was too far away to make out more than an austere black shape.

He made his way a little closer in the crowd, and she noticed a scar on his face interrupted by his mask. Bridget had been right, even with shorter hair the man did look familiar, as familiar as her name and the breath in her lungs; but it couldn't be him.

Her throat constricted, her knees felt a little wobbly. It wasn't beyond her to conjure figures in crowds; she'd done the same thing when she'd lost Marcus, seeing him everywhere until she'd faced the earth-upending reality that he really was gone.

She was interrupted by the music ending abruptly, the sound of a gong chiming from the top of the same stairs she'd entered on half an hour earlier. At the top of the stairs was Fitz, a radiant dark-haired woman beside him wearing a green dress and beaming up at him beneath her mask. Fitz waved a hand, and the footmen interspersed within the crowd, delivering more French champagne for a toast. Moria's companions linked arms with her on either side.

"Friends, foes, we are gathered here to celebrate the next adventure of our dear Adelaide. I won't keep you all from your enjoyment of the festivities, but my companion has some words she'd like to share."

The man caught her attention again. Moria felt a chill titter up her spine. His profile and the bulk of his shoulders were so similar to Devyn's. Was there a way to ask him to remove his gloves so she could see his tattoos? How would *he* recognize her?

Moria kissed her companion's cheek. "I have to go."

Bridget followed her vision and muttered something that sounded like "Good luck, you'll need it if she finds out you missed her moment."

Moria intended to bump into the man, causing him to spill his drink like she'd done to gentlemen countless other times for some end or another; but when she bumped into the man, he grabbed her wrist.

Searing hot awareness broke out all over her body.

The way his shoulders bunched beneath his coat, his purposeful strides, the way his dark hair curled at his nape. Those gorgeous lips. If it weren't him then she needed spectacles like Noelle's.

He turned, leading her by the wrist, and escorted her to the edge of the room. If it really were Devyn, she'd follow him anywhere. Wouldn't she? But what if it wasn't?

Finally, they reached an alcove, she pulled her hand free of his and untied the gold cord draped over the alcove until it fell into a curtain. He held it back with one hand and ushered her inside.

Pushing back his mask, he said, "Willow trees, and now curtained alcoves, we have got to stop meeting like this."

Moria gave a little whimper, bottom lip catching between her teeth and her vision going wobbly with tears. She threw back her veil and launched her body into his arms as he wrapped them around her.

"Devyn, thank god!" she cried into his shoulder as he leaned down to hold her.

She'd almost forgotten how incredibly tall he was. One of his hands almost wrapped around her waist. His body was so solid and familiar and warm like the trunk of a willow tree that offered the consolation and safety she'd been searching for. The feeling of his calloused finger pads wiping at her tears was a very real sensation, not a fever dream at all.

For what felt like an eternity and not nearly long enough, the two of them stared at each other in disbelief. Due to the small alcove opening and their need for each other, there was very little of their bodies that wasn't touching.

And still, she needed him closer.

She took him in next with her hands, roving his scarred face, his shorter hair, his nape, down to his chest and arms, like she was looking for the places he'd been put back together. She could find the places he *hadn't* been put back together and do the job herself.

She landed on the cane in his right hand and then met his eyes. A profound ache, like he was her phantom limb, throbbed through her.

"I was hit in a skirmish outside Bajgah and taken prisoner for six weeks until General Dennie liberated us."

He must have been in so much pain, he must have had to survive such unimaginable suffering, and here he was. And here she'd been, attending balls and getting betrothed. But he wasn't looking at her like she was guilty of anything reprehensible, anything at all, there was love in his eyes.

Chest heaving, she said, "But you're alive."

His throat bobbed. "It killed me to be apart from you."

Her hands found his lapels. "We died the same death. Come here. Let me bring you back to life."

She drew him in with her mouth, his lips crashing over hers possessively. She wanted to possess him. She wanted to *be* possessed, by him, by this moment, by madness; she didn't care, just not possessed anymore by grief and the unforgiving hands of fate.

She pulled at her skirts, one of her legs wrapping around his. She pressed her body closer, he let out a little groan that she could taste inside her own mouth, mingled with the taste of champagne. This was where he'd belonged, she'd been saying it since before he left, and him trying to save the world and her trying to save her image had only caused suffering and heart ache.

No longer.

"I love you," she cried into his mouth.

He was holding her, he was kissing her back like she was the one who was a phantom, he was touching her. She wondered if he'd dreamed about holding her like she'd dreamed about being held.

"Still?" he pulled back to ask.

She ran a gentle hand over the scar on his face. "Is this why you didn't immediately come to me and tell me that you were alive?"

He didn't say anything.

She wrapped a hand around his jaw and brought his eyes to hers. "Answer me," her voice was part plea, part protest.

"I've gone through months of rehabilitation to stand, to walk. Don't know if I ever will fight, or ride, or hold a sword properly. I would have crawled to you, if I thought you'd still have me."

She pulled back as though he'd slapped her. But she would never compare her pain to his; she knew her engagement to another man, a Duke no less, had only been a liberal sprinkling of salt in a festering wound.

"That isn't fair," she injected steel into her voice, enunciating her words. "I wish you'd told me. I wish I knew that you'd—"

"Would it have stopped you from becoming engaged to the world's most perfect man?" His voice was laced with anger.

"Is that what you came here to ask me?"

He muttered profanity under his breath. Shook his head.

"I'm sorry. I don't know if I ever did deserve you, but how could I ever claim to now? I'd just go on without you and let you have the perfect life you always wanted," he swallowed, tracing a rogue tear that fell out of her eye. "Only I just can't stop loving you. From afar doesn't seem like enough. But I had to tell you, figured you'd find out anyway, in case there was a chance you weren't disgusted by me."

No tears came. No words came. What could she say?

She poured all the words that were locked away, buried under years of neglect and dust and trauma, into his mouth. Her lips formed the words tangled breathlessly with his like she could scourge the pain away with a kiss.

"I need you." She groaned the words into his mouth.

He shook his head. She pulled his hair, pulling him closer, till their noses touched. If he couldn't see a world behind or beyond this alcove, this time-stopping box they were in, he couldn't say no.

"You need me," She said.

He could go to war, he could nearly die and let her believe that he did even after he'd been back, she'd not even asked how long he'd been back, but she *did* know him.

"Show me where the pain is, or where you can't feel my touch anymore."

She traced a gloved finger softly over the bisecting scar from his hairline down to the hollow at the base of his throat.

He closed his eyes. "Nowhere. I feel you everywhere, Moria. The hollowed-out parts of me that feel nothing can still feel you."

She placed his hand at her waist. She raised her eyebrows at him, his throat bobbed again.

"Not here." He shook his head, but his hand at her waist drew her tighter into him.

"When we went to the opera," she breathed next to his ear, "Did you think about having me behind the curtain?"

He took her hand, placing it against his erection, the hard proof of how badly he wanted her. "There are hardly any ways left I haven't thought about having you," he said into her ear.

"Did you think you'd have me tonight?" she said against his lips, undoing him.

She wasn't sure what her plan was, with him, with George. She wasn't sure she had one.

He closed his eyes, breathing her in.

"You did, didn't you?" she said in his ear, nipping at his earlobe and then licking down his neck. She kissed his scar like he'd kissed hers that single night they'd had together. He groaned against her, swore her name like she was the god he was taking in vain.

"What are you doing?" he asked. "You break off your engagement, then? That why you're dressed..." he eyed her like he was looking at her costume for the first time. "Like some kind of ghost bride?"

Moria couldn't help it. It wasn't the champagne. Watery laughter bubbled out of her like so much joy that had been locked behind a cupboard. He started laughing with her too. They were here, together, behind a curtain at her sister's book launch masquerade where she'd come with her sister and friends, and they were laughing, and his hand was still on her waist.

She wiped at the tears in her eyes. Were they from pain or grief or joy or some intertwined concoction?

"It's part wedding gown and part mourning dress."

His face fell. "God, that's...." he shook his head. "Devastating."

"It's a visual depiction of my heart at the moment."

"I know I don't understand women's fashion; but your heart is tragically unchic, I'm sorry to say."

She laughed again. She'd always laughed easily with him. It was everything else that was difficult.

"I missed you," she said, the words just ushered themselves out like visitors who'd stayed too long.

"We're always missing each other," he said in a solemn voice.

"We don't have to."

"You still want me?" he said, looking into her eyes with intense focus, her answer critical to their survival.

A choking sob came out of her. She gave him back his words.

"The hollowed out parts of me that can feel nothing can still feel you too."

He kissed her. More accurately, his mouth crashed into hers like something had been unleashed in him. He lifted her so that she was up against the wall, and then it was quick work from there. Hands grasping, mouths licking and teeth nipping. Her leg slung over his, his legs pushed between hers. His mouth at the pulse point of her neck.

"Fuck this thing," he said, removing her veil unceremoniously for good. And then he pushed up her skirts.

"Does that mean I'm next?" she questioned, and he chuckled against her exposed breasts before taking them in his mouth. His fingers found her entrance amidst all the black and white fabric, he swallowed her moans into his mouth to silence her as he undid her at last.

And then she stilled his hand. "I want you. I need...I need you." her voice was strangled with need.

"Say it," he said. "Tell me what you need."

"I need your cock shoved deep inside of me so I know you're real."

He blinked a couple times like her response was more than he expected. "Whatever you want, use me."

And it was her hand that unfastened his breeches, guided him to her entrance, both of them gasping at the fit of it as he made his way inside. And they were moving with urgency again, fast and needy and desperate.

"Take what you need," he said, eyes locked onto hers.

He was notched inside, then pulling back, in, out, rhythmed like breaths that were coming faster and faster. The fabric covering of the bookcase she was perched on created friction against the bare skin of her back, but she didn't care. She wanted to be close to him forever, to feel all of him and not feel everything that was waiting behind the curtain.

Her fingers dug into him for purchase, he moved one of her hands to his hair. Moria pulled at his dark strands, missing the long locks he'd had before; but his shorter hair was devastating with that scar.

He tilted his head back, ramming deeper into her. Moria let out a low moan.

"That's it, I want to hear all your sounds."

He held her backside in both hands. One finger slid from behind to stroke her center as he slammed into her. She looked from his fingers, meeting his eyes, the wicked satisfaction had her taking his mouth in her possession again. He thrust deeper this time, finding a place inside of her that made her back arch off the bookcase.

Then she was clutching him, screaming his name into his mouth, spasming around him. She felt like she was floating somewhere above this scene for a moment, lost in another time where they weren't lost to one another, until he convulsed and groaned against her. He quickly pulled out and came into a handkerchief with one hand, holding her with the other.

His lips kissed her neck, and then he was kneeling in front of her. His lips disappeared for a moment, between her legs. She closed her eyes at the exquisite lathe of his tongue, at the memory of how he'd care for her like this before, afterward. And then he placed a kiss at her inner thigh. His hand adjusted her stockings and replaced the layers of her skirt, retied her slippers, and shook her skirts out around her. He took her hand and kissed it, still breathless.

How was she meant to walk away from that?

"That was..." she breathed.

"I know," but she barely heard him.

His voice was low and far away as he stared at her. She now wished they had done this somewhere else, somewhere they had privacy and time and space. She'd had Devyn back if only for a moment, and her relief had taken hold of her before she'd thought about the aftermath.

"I can't lose you again." His voice sounded even farther away, like she was already losing him.

"You never lost me," she said in an urgent voice. She wrapped a hand around his stubbled cheek.

"Moria," he started to say something that would damn whatever they still had left to hell and she couldn't hear it. She kissed him again, longer and slower this time. And then he pulled away.

Her pride was the only soldier she had left now, and so she let him let her go, and made him watch as the curtain fell behind her for the last time.

Chapter Thirty-Eight

Devyn was sure now that he hadn't fallen in love with a mere woman, but a goddess.

Only, before because she was beautiful, more than beautiful. Visually perfect in a way that made artists believe in God, and turned doubting heretics into believers. The kind of noticeable gorgeousness that men fought wars over.

And she had been his.

He had told himself while he thought he was rotting away that he'd do the noble thing and give her up, let her be happy, let her get all that she wanted that he couldn't give her. He'd have sold his own soul to give it to her, but not his brother's, and that was the cost.

But tonight, now that he'd had her again, he didn't know that he could do it again.

Because she wasn't just a woman, she was a goddess.

In that ethereal way in which you're cursed, you meet a goddess in the woods, or in Devyn's case, beneath a willow tree, and it fucks you up forevermore. There is no going backwards or forwards, because you're in her grasp. And no matter how many mortar shells she throws in your life, no matter how bad you think maybe you'd like to hurt her back, you're under her spell.

When she'd closed the curtain behind her and slowly let go of his hand digit by digit, Devyn knew that the spell was still cast all over him, and there was no cure.

"Whose perfume ye wearin'?" Calum asked, eyeing Devyn as he took a seat across from him in Peregrine's club.

Devyn leaned back in his chair, propping his cane beside him, his brows going all cross and defensive. He pointed with one finger in his friend's direction. "You're taking the piss, man, I don't—"

"Oh my god," Peregrine threw his head in his hands. "You didn't."

"He definitely did," Calum argued, shit-eating grin on his swarthy face.

Devyn avoided both of their stares, taking a sip of his drink. Regrettably, the burn in the back of his throat as he swallowed wasn't strong enough to wash the taste of her away.

"This is going to be the worst night of my life," Peregrine said, throwing back his brandy.

Devyn pulled back, affronted. "Bit dramatic. You mean worse than when you thought I died."

"Yes," Calum and Peregrine said in unison.

Devyn looked between the two of them, obviously missing something. "Yeah? And why's that?"

"Clairville!" A voice called from behind Devyn. The voice sounded the same as a mortar shell, a dinner gong that day at her manor house, a death rattle. It was the sound it was all over before he wanted it to be.

All three men turned in the direction of a tall, bronze-skinned man with stupidly green eyes, immaculately dressed. Devyn recognized him from the theater. Of course he would look like a storybook prince with a deep tan.

"Your Grace," Peregrine said, standing to defer to the Duke.

Devyn didn't move. Calum didn't either, his eyes on Devyn. "*If you're knee deep in shit, guess we both got dirty boots, then,*" he'd said once.

"I don't believe you've met my brother, Captain Devyn Winter, and his comrade, Lieutenant Calum Sterling."

Devyn knew that Perry knew he wasn't a Captain anymore. Didn't know why he gave him a title he no longer held and demoted his best friend in the process, but fuck it. He'd never deign to contradict his older brother in Moria's Conquest's hearing.

"Your Grace," Devyn said, chin high, eyes cold. Devyn knew that he could intimidate men when he wanted to. There was a place he went in his mind when he was facing an opponent, and this man, this Duke, definitely was one.

The other man looked him over, both a little intimidated and a little unfazed at the same time. Other men always seemed to note Devyn's height, his shoulders, how large he was, how big his hands were. Some, itching for a fight and others desperate to avoid starting one. He'd love to put his fist through this toff's face. He'd been on strict orders from the physician now that he was making so much progress not to overexert himself. Already disregarded that bit of advice in the alcove, hadn't he?

Fuck it. He had nearly died in a rescue attempt of a comrade, a man with soft hands and floppy hair didn't scare him.

"Heard you were hit in Bajgah, terrible business," Moria's Pretty Duke said, sitting next to him.

Devyn stared over at him. "Did you?" Took a sip of his fresh drink, because *god damn it*, calling him *Moria's Duke* even in his head after making his fiancé moan his name? He should feel guilt, shame, maybe; but he didn't.

And that was the roughest part of it all. She'd been there too, she'd been willing, they'd both wanted it. God, he'd nearly died with her name on his lips. But having her fiancé sitting next to him an hour later was not where he'd thought this night was going to go.

Devyn looked at Perry, who mouthed: "Sorry," in his direction.

The Duke was talking. Several others in his party had wandered over. Apparently, he and Perry knew each other from Cambridge. Perry was the one who'd told His Grace, The Duke of Stolen Fiancés, that Devyn had gone down. For a second there, he'd thought Moria had mentioned it. He should have known better.

So now, here he was. An injured captain who'd given up the commission and leadership he'd trained and bled for, sitting next to the man who'd done what Devyn should have done. She deserved someone who'd choose her. That's what the Duke had done, not Devyn.

"Glad you made it out, Captain," The Duke said, clapping a hand on his shoulder.

Devyn raised a brow.

"Alright, you're... not a verbose man," the Duke said, looking over at Perry for some sort of commiseration.

Devyn's jaw clenched. Did this man misread *her* like he misread Devyn? Was he thick or just self-absorbed? Devyn felt anger spreading through his body like poison.

Someone called to him, the Duke held up a finger. "Clairville? You joining us for the stag party, or is your brother playing chaperone tonight?"

Perry met his eyes, chewed on his lip.

From behind the Duke's back, Devyn mouthed *Stag Party?* With incredulity.

It was Calum who spoke first. "Well, Yer Grace, ye won't believe it actually, but I got meself engaged as well. Captain," he said, giving Devyn a wink, "is takin' me out for me own stag party tonight so I'm sure ye won't mourn our absence."

His Disgrace looked at Devyn's best friend as though taking him in for the first time. "Oh, don't tell me you're the fellow Miss Dempsey is engaged to?"

The Duke called for a footman to bring another round of drinks.

Calum tried to put him off, but the Duke wouldn't hear of it. An empty display of power and generosity for an audience who could not have cared less, Devyn thought.

The Pompous Duke shook his head, "Lady Moria told me that her maid was leaving for…" he leaned closer to Devyn's best friend until he felt Devyn's glare and pulled back with a grimace. "You'll forgive my future wife, 'a redheaded Scottish soldier every bit as besotted as he is broad shouldered,' is the description she gave. And I'll tell you something," he paused to take a drink from a tray proffered between them, "People can say all kinds of things about her, but she's been more excited to plan Ella's wedding, and to see her happy. I'm sure your Ella is a most deserving young lady."

Devyn couldn't hear any more. He stood, walking away from the table and the assembly in his brother's club, without so much as a by-your-leave from the Duke.

"Peculiar though," the Duke's voice raised, stopping Devyn in his tracks. "She told me that Ella was marrying a Captain. Promoted after the former Captain was killed in action. But Clairville, you said your brother was the Captain, and this man is only a Lieutenant."

Fuck.

Devyn blew some air out of his mouth. He read the other man's face for signs of knowing, that look on a person's face when they've registered something and you've been caught out. Couldn't. His anger and loathing that they had come to this made it hard for him to be objective, the way a captain in Her Majesty's Army had to be. He wasn't one anymore. Guess that was for the best, then. He could get a dishonorable discharge or worse for what he was about to do.

Devyn threw his cane, Calum caught it in one quick hand.

"You want some fucking prize?" Devyn was standing so close to the Duke, his height and size making a natural buffer. A vein pulsed in Devyn's neck, his forehead.

The Duke shook his head, didn't back down or look away.

"Think I've already got it," he said, taking a sip of his drink as he kept his eyes locked on Devyn's.

If Devyn had been standing at a cliff, contemplating jumping, what he did next was the equivalent to throwing his arms wide and taking a leap. Because Moria was not a prize for some arrogant toff and he'd lay his body down right here in some overly decorated club to prove there was no price he wouldn't pay for her honor.

Devyn felt his muscles stretch and constrict as he reared back, planted his feet, and prepared to slam his cannon-sized fist into a Duke's face. He was already going to lose her, had probably already lost her, so whatever came next, he was prepared for.

Only, he was prepared to make the other man bleed.

He wasn't prepared for his best friend to wrap his own hand around Devyn's, and for Peregrine and some other man he couldn't see, to pull him back.

Lawrence Pembrooke tightened his hold on Devyn. "You and me, we're going to have a little chat. My brother's club. Tomorrow. Noon." And backed him outside to a waiting carriage.

Chapter Thirty-Nine

For days, the weight of both her Burn Book being publicly consumed, as well as her own secret reunion at the masked ball, held her down like it had strong hands pushing her under water.

Waves of regret and self-loathing filled her until she failed to see or breathe around it. She felt that it preceded her into a room making space for itself and that when people saw her, they saw her secrets, her shame, and her guilt too.

Except they didn't.

They mostly treated her with the same deference as they did before. Maybe even a little fear.

Even George. When he came to call, he prattled on about parliament again and she listened with rapt interest, asking animated questions like she could hide the lie with her equanimity.

George lounged across from her at her tea table with one bespoke boot across his other knee. "You're in a good mood today, practically buoyant."

Was he looking at her extra closely today or was that her guilt insisting that he was?

"Policy making is exhilarating." No, her voice was far too high; surely she gave herself away?

He chuckled, taking her hand. "If only I believed you." She thought she heard a note of condescension or knowing in his voice, but he looked up at her with hopeful eyes. "Dare I be so bold as to assume...that it's my presence you find exhilarating?"

She swallowed. *Tell him now*, the secret, given form and skin and teeth and claws, insisted.

"I don't think that's so bold, Your Grace."

"It's George, Moria," he said, grabbing one of her hands and pulling her closer.

They were interrupted by Lady Olivia entering the sitting room. "Good afternoon, Your Grace. My sister sent me in here to look for a book she left behind."

The words seemed to register between both George and Moria at the same time. "In other words, she sent you to spy..."

"I'll only be but a moment and then I'll leave you two to your.... discussion," Olivia said.

Except she didn't stay but a moment. The three of them turned at the open door as Noelle peaked her head in.

"This dratted bird of yours, Olivia. He won't go back in his cage. I need your help, please."

Olivia bit her bottom lip. "Should we leave the two of them unchaperoned with the way they are looking at each other?"

Noelle placed her hands on her hips. "Now, Olivia! Before I send your bird to work as a mine canary!"

"You wouldn't dare!" Olivia said, bolting from the room.

Moria laughed instantly. George covered his mouth, but his shoulders shook with mirth.

Once they were alone, he leaned forward, taking one hand of hers in both of his larger ones.

"Just how was I looking at you?" he asked.

Moria pursed her lips, searching for the right words. "Like you were quite hungry, and I was the last snack on the tray."

"You are. You are about to become my wife."

Moria bit her lip. That was actually a very cute metaphor, but didn't quite work with the pronouncement he'd made just a few days before. She edged closer, close enough to sweep the hair back from his eyes. "And would you...like to sample your last snack... before the shop closes?"

No! God, woman what are you thinking? Some part of her moth-eaten conscience railed at her.

His eyes were a familiar, soft green, the shade of grass beneath one's feet on a dewy morning. But there was a crease between his brows. "Sample? Why would I sample the last snack on the tray? And why is the shop closing?"

Moria's palm hit her forehead.

"Sorry, sorry," he said, realization dawning. "You were continuing the metaphor, I get it now."

He kissed her, but not solidly enough that she was thinking only of him.

"Olivia, what was that about?" Moria stepped into her sister's room, closing the door behind her.

"He's alive, isn't he?" Olivia said, not looking up from the scientific journal she was reading.

"What do you mean?" Moria questioned, hugging her arms close to her chest.

"Shall I go into detail?" Olivia looked up, narrowing her eyes at her. "I can go into heavy detail if that's what it takes."

Moria sighed.

Olivia threw her book down and stood with a triumphant: "I knew it!"

Moria placed a hand over her sister's mouth. "Keep your voice down."

"Don't worry, I haven't told anyone," Olivia muttered against her hand.

"Thank god you figured it out before anyone else in this family. No one can keep a secret."

"Why do you want it to be a secret?"

Noelle called from the doorway, "Why do you want *what* to be a secret.... Moria?"

Moria cursed audibly. Her sister and her lock picking. Why could no one in her family choose a normal hobby like she had, like the pianoforte and embroidery?

Olivia threw on a bright smile. "How...much in love...she is."

Noelle tilted her head to the side, disbelieving. "You'll have to put on a better performance than that, Libby."

Moria threw up her hands. "Devyn...is alive."

Noelle pushed off the door and came to sit on the bed with her sisters. Ran her hands through her hair, then stood again and paced. Noelle was unnerving when she was so quiet.

"Moria," Noelle said breathlessly, taking her by the shoulders, "Then you can't marry the duke."

"Why can't Moria marry the duke?" Lawrence questioned from the doorway with his hands at his hips in mock authority. Moria turned to her youngest sister and grunted in frustration.

"Oh, curse you, Olivia!"

Her younger sister held up her hands innocently.

Lawrence closed the door with his boot and came to stand at the edge of the bed with his younger sisters, he crossed his arms at his chest. "I knew something like this would happen. What is it now?"

Noelle hit him in the arm. "It's not what you think. Devyn is alive."

Lawrence swore and shook his head. "The nerve of that bastard for not dying when he was supposed to."

"I know, right?" Moria said.

"But you.... you're glad he's not dead, though, right?" Noelle bit her bottom lip.

Moria fell backwards on her sister's bed and looked up at the ceiling. "I've never been gladder of a damn thing in my life."

All three siblings whooped, laughing and jabbing each other in the elbows. Lawrence reached into his boot and drew out a flask. "We are all in so much trouble."

Kathleen knocked on the door and Noelle shushed everyone. "What are you all doing in there? And without me?"

Moria shook her head. Both sisters raised their brows. Olivia opened the door anyway.

"We're just...sharing in excitement with Moria..."

"About what?" Kathleen questioned.

"Can't tell you at the moment! It's a...surprise!" Olivia called. Kathleen let out a frustrated grunt, followed by the timely wail of an infant.

"I always hate your surprises, Libby! We will finish this conversation later, you four!"

Noelle, Olivia, and Lawrence turned to Moria. It was Noelle who spoke first. "You better tell us everything."

"Leave nothing out," Olivia said, both she and Noelle crowding around Moria on Olivia's bed.

Lawrence held up a finger. "No please, leave anything out that will offend my innocence."

Chapter Forty

THE LAST TIME DEVYN HAD BEEN AT THIS PARTICULAR club, he'd had her in his arms. They'd been interrupted by her former beau, who'd helped them sneak out, and they'd adjourned to his rooms. They'd played music together and shared some of themselves with each other. But the memory came unbidden now, partially unwelcome, as he sat in a leather chair at a table that was too small for his form, waiting for her brother.

"I'm not sorry to keep you waiting," Pembrooke said, looking like warmed-over hell as he sat across from Devyn. He looked like a man with so much privilege and very little purpose and Devyn might have been him once, before *her*.

"I'll make this short," Pembrooke said, holding up a finger to call over a waiter. "A full breakfast, all the trimmings," he said, refusing a menu. When they were alone again, he returned his attention to Devyn. "I have an offer for you."

Devyn leaned forward. "I'm listening."

"I want to open a club, a man with your connections and skills would be valuable."

Devyn gestured pointedly around them. "We are currently *in* a club, Pembrooke."

Lawrence shook his head. "A different kind of club. An athletic club. Exclusive, expensive, but a place in town for sport."

"And how do I factor into this?"

Lawrence leaned forward, matching Devyn. "Put up what you can spare in collateral. I have capital to invest as well, and a few interested parties. I have a particular design in mind. Somewhere for men to work on archery, rowing, boxing, fencing, swimming, the like. Help me plan it, train the men—"

Devyn gestured to the cane leaning against his chair. "Not sure if you heard, I was injured."

Lawrence scoffed. "Then maybe some of the toffs in this town might actually stand a chance going toe-to-toe with you."

Devyn turned over a cigar between his fingers. "What else?"

"We split the profits."

Devyn paused his movements. "That simple, huh?"

Lawrence nodded, tracing the rim of his glass. "It is. Because you and I, we have nothing to lose, and everything to prove. I think we could work well as business partners."

Devyn lifted his drink and tipped it in Lawrence's direction in mock salute in answer.

"I require something as collateral first."

Devyn snorted into his drink. "Of course you do."

"Moria's book," Devyn raised a brow at her brother's words. "It's an axe, hanging over her head currently somewhere in Mayfair. Help me get it back?"

Devyn sat down his drink, folded his hands. "Tell me what you want me to do."

Chapter Forty-One

~

SHE HAD TO SEE HIM AGAIN, FOR HERSELF. BEFORE SHE embarked entirely in the opposite direction, she had to know if it was real. If *he* was real.

And now she was in a cloak, in a moon-shrouded mews behind Clairville's London house, heartbeat racing two steps ahead of her horse's four hooves and her own common sense.

Devyn's firm hands settled like taut ropes about her waist as she slid down from her horse. She watched the flexing angles of his arms and shoulders, feeling her mouth go dry. She licked her lips to wet them before remembering to look away.

He had her now on firm footing and grabbed her, pulling her into his arms as he moved the horse out of their way. Devyn buried his head next to her hair as he pulled her in so tight she felt his skin, his sweat, mixing with her own.

He was supposed to be dead. She was supposed to marry another man. A Duke. A good man. They weren't supposed to be clinging to each other outside the mews of his brother's London house like time had stopped moving around them.

"My god, Moria," Devyn breathed as he pulled away. "Every damn time, it's like I just remembered how to breathe at the sight of you."

"Kiss me so I can breathe again, too."

He crushed her to him, marking her with a kiss that revived her and shattered her at once. She heard all the words he couldn't say, she was speaking them back with every lathe of her tongue against his. His hands tightened, flattening her against him.

"I should go," he broke the kiss to say, but he didn't move a solitary corpuscle. She was the first to move, keeping hold of his hand as she stepped toward a stone edifice.

"No, please come with me," she said, motioning toward the small cottage behind the mews.

For a moment, she thought he was going to deny her again; but finally, he relented. Nodding, he let her take his hand and followed a step behind her.

The dark, lively world of London at night during the season obscured the sound of her skirts over stones, two pairs of boots over pea gravel, one gold-tipped cane to steady his steps, as he followed her into the small cottage beside the stables. He'd followed her into a willow tree, a library, to her family's chapel, her bedchamber, an alcove at a masquerade.

"Devyn," she breathed, his name synonymous with prayer upon her lips as she closed the wooden door behind her. As soon as she latched the bolt, he was on her like a scent.

He was at her back, removing her hood with the most reverent touch despite his large hands, then trailing one of those large hands down her thick blonde plait, down her back. Over his shoulder, she took in the room around them. It was neat, there was at least a decent sized bed that looked clean and there were thick curtains pulled over the windows. There was no fire in the grate, but he'd make her one if she'd asked.

Hell, he doesn't need a fire to keep me warm.

His breath, heavy and full of heat at her back, was already warming her, from the space where his breath fell on her skin, to her insides. She stole his hands and wrapped them around her breasts. She instantly felt the answering sensation lower down, his shaft pressing against the folds of his buckskin breeches, against her back.

He was solid, not the preening and self-indulgent aristocrat she'd taken as a lover once; he was a beautiful specimen of a man who ached for her.

"What do you want from me, Moria?" His hands gripped her waist. He planted a kiss in the space where neck met shoulder. His lips traced over bare bits of skin, dropping kisses lush and soft as a man reacquainting himself with a lost idol.

She wheeled around to face him. "Devyn, I need you."

The words undid him. She could see the way they hit him, causing him to step backward, his gorgeously lashed eyelids a flutter, his lips without words.

"You're promised to someone else, Moria."

The scar along his face added credibility to the pain that lashed across his features.

Moria reached for him, the way she'd never been able to stop herself from doing.

"I lost you, and that very night, I had an impossible choice to make. Devyn, I chose myself that night. And I made a promise. I made my bed and now, I must lie in it."

He took another step back. "You torture me."

"I torture myself, Devyn!"

At the emotion in her words, he came to her. His hands gripped her by the hips and ground her against him. It was coarse and not full of any of the tenderness from before, but she leaned into it. She wanted his anger and his harsh, crude words. That she could bear, not knee-crumbling tenderness.

"You say my name while you intend to take that of another man. No, Moria. It is you who tortures all of us."

She stepped away from him then, drawing back her arm, and slapped him across one cheek. He was so much larger than her, he could easily have stopped her. And as her eyes fixed on the reddening mark across his cheek, she thought, *maybe he had.*

"Are you done, woman?" he asked, reaching for her.

She knew she was blowing hot and cold, but that didn't stop her from emphasizing each word.

"No, I most certainly am not done, Devyn." She advanced on him, punctuating her syllables with little jabs of her small finger at his chest.

"You left. After you properly courted me. You proposed to me. You made me promises that didn't seem to hold as much weight as your vows to your uniform. You led me to believe that no longer was I the girl that men loved in secret. That I was worth being loved out in the open." The tears streamed down her face and she let them fall for once without wiping them away.

Let him see.

"You did all the things I romanticized a beau doing for me. And then you committed the most unthinkable crime. You *died*. And I...I couldn't remember if I told you that I loved you. I was left with nothing but my pretty face and my reputation and my pride, for however long I could rely on them."

She turned from him, hugging herself to shore up her resolve. He was just standing there, taking her in, not making a move to quiet or comfort or touch her while she got the words out. She loved him more then for what he didn't do.

"And then he was attentive and he was generous. And he was a duke. I won't say I hated the attention that I received from everyone else, but it was his attention that won me. While you were...well, I knew what you were to me, but I had to mourn you in secret. Now you want to say that I am hurting *you*?"

She gave a small humorless laugh, feeling like she'd slowly become unhinged at having to relive this entire saga in front of him, at the spell that had been uncast as she said it aloud.

"Perhaps now you can begin to know what I have suffered."

He thundered his response, the muscles at his neck and temple alive with outrage. "You think I didn't want to give you all those things? That I wouldn't sell my soul to the devil if he showed up knocking right now to give them to you?"

She looked at him warily. He stepped closer, taking her face in his dwarfing hands.

"My girl, I have loved you quite desperately since the first time I saw you underneath that willow tree," His chest heaved against her own. "I've been desperate for you; to tell you how you haunted me, how you traveled down to hell and led me out each day, with the hope of seeing you again."

His fingertips brushed tenderly against her cheeks. "But I could never have given you the things for which you were born, the things you deserve. Now that you have found someone who can, and should, I'm so angry. And proud of you...and jealous too."

She had been staring at the wall of his chest as he spoke, not realizing he was backing her up. When her knees collided with the bed, she let out a little breath of surprise.

"So, Moria, if you want to punish me, then do it."

Her brows kissed in the middle, not understanding. Her eyes followed the movements of his hands as he pulled at the cravat at his throat revealing a tanned triangle of skin that weakened her knees, her resolve. Realization did not dawn until he placed the wadded piece of fabric in her hand.

All the air left her, left the room. Left England. Words lodged themselves in her throat, trapped against the frantic beating of her set-upon heart.

"Go ahead," he said, motioning to the wooden headboard with his jaw, extending to her his two wrists, firmly clasped together.

"Dear god," she breathed.

He stood still and expectant, his dark eyes trained on her with compelling force. She looked down at the strip of fabric he'd proffered into her hand.

"You're serious. You want me to-"

He stole the shock, the words, the air from her mouth with his own. In their place, into the parted seam of her lips, he gave her everything.

There was a world of pain between them, woven into their past, but they could create something wholly pleasurable together. He pulled her tighter into him, the bulge of muscles, less corded than once before but still stronger than most men, straining against her. Her core was suddenly alive with longing for this man.

She reveled in the feel of his large jaw muscles working against her own as his tongue slid deeper and deeper inside her mouth, gliding over her teeth, the silk of her bottom lip. She drank him in as well, her world closing in around only this man, only the touch of his body where it met hers, only his breath.

He reclined on the bed. She let him pull her down with him. She toppled onto him, a mass of tangled and needy limbs.

"I want you to do whatever you want to me. Use me. Love me. Let me love you in return."

"Devyn," She sighed his name on a feverish breath. "What about before—that you wanted to put a ring on my finger—" He stilled her words with a finger to her lips.

That finger softly padded over the rim of her bottom lip, promising exploration to other areas.

"I'm not done, woman. If you want me, you shall have me. All of me. My body, my family, my name. But the decision rests entirely with you, as most have never been. Until now."

His hands were in her hair, his breath was on her neck as his lips and his tongue teased every inch of her décolletage. "I want you to have everything you desire."

"Everything?" she asked, raising a brow, remembering the cravat in her hand.

"Everything," he breathed. He was absolutely carnal; raising his arms together unbound above his head, shirt half-open, hair tousled, one knee hitched up between them, chest heaving, eyes roving her form.

He was even more devastating than he'd been in the past, perhaps for how she'd nearly lost him. Was this how it worked? It just got better and better every time? She didn't want those hands tied up, she needed them on her.

"Undress me first."

"I don't need hands to undress you, my lady."

She ran a hand up his thigh. "I have envisioned all that you would do to me, and you will undress me, slowly and thoroughly."

He laughed darkly, making a great show of pushing up his sleeves as he knelt before her.

A bit of ink on his forearm caught her attention. Beautifully sinful that dark ink marking the tan skin of his muscular forearms. She caught it in her hand. A muscle ticked in his jaw. His pulse leapt under her touch. She had just asked him to undress her, and now she was unbuttoning his shirt. Tender caressing fingers at each of his shoulders pushed the garment onto the floor.

She brought the ink up to the light. Her stomach dropped through the floorboard. Her fingers traced the outline of a rose stenciled in dark ink on his forearm in delicate outlines.

Petals, thorns, stem, leaves. The depiction of her lost hope and secret pain.

"You..." her voice was thick as she traced it again. "You got a tattoo...of a rose? Why?"

His eyes held onto hers like a tether. "She's a piece of you I never got to hold in my arms. She'll always be there, where I'd have held her," he guided a strand of hair that had fallen in her eyes behind her ear, "And all the other little girls with your hair and your fire we might have had."

Her knees quivered, her heart buckling under the weight of his love for her.

"I love you, you know that?" she said the words so close to his mouth she could taste the whiskey on his breath, the dark stubble of his cheeks teasing her skin.

"Longer than you have," he said. Lips like fire and whiskey and rain consumed her. A kiss to end all her doubting, all her dithering.

No matter the past, they were here, with moonlight streaming through the curtains illuminating her secrets marked on his body.

"You still want me to undress you, Moria?"

She pulled back enough to speak the words into his mouth. "If you don't I might die."

"I've already gone and died enough for the both of us, no need to be dramatic." She could hear the laughter, the affection in his voice.

"Did I ever tell you that I like you in blue?" he said, removing her bodice and throwing it behind him.

"Then why are you throwing it on the ground like a madman?"

"Because I like you even more when you're fiery."

His lips teased her, she sucked his bottom lip into both of hers, biting it.

"Viper," he said, loosening her corset and letting it fall.

"Devil," she retorted, loosening his breeches.

"I thought I was the one undressing you," he ground out.

She lifted up her arms for him to remove her chemise, so her breasts were bared to him.

"Then get to work," she said, working him in her hands and

biting down on her lip as he palmed one of her breasts into his greedy grasp.

"Why the hell do you have to wear so many clothes?"

"Because valuables are kept hidden away."

Knee to knee with him on the bed in a cottage behind the mews that was rightfully his, he was working one of her breasts in his mouth, putting her hand in his close-cut dark hair and admonishing her to pull his hair.

"This is the valuable I've been dreaming of stealing for myself," he said, sliding underneath her and placing a lingering kiss at her sex.

Her eyelids fell closed, her eyelashes stuttered. His tongue slipped inside of her, her fingertips gripped his scalp harder. He inserted a finger to accompany the efforts of his wicked mouth, and just as before, she was helpless underneath his touch. Nothing had changed, nothing was sated between them. She still wanted him with the deepest level of want.

He sat up, kneeling on her bed before her in only his small clothes. She reached for him, but he almost pulled away from her touch. "Don't, just let me," he said.

"Is it your scar?"

He hung his head. "It's a horrible scar."

"You loved me, scars and all. Let me do the same."

When he was bared to her, she got on her knees. She kissed the taut ridges of his hips arrowing down to his manhood, she kissed the dark and prominent scar that hadn't had time to fade away. When she'd let him take her in that alcove, there hadn't been time, she hadn't been able to peruse his body for all his scars and marks. She was taking her time now.

"This scar," she said, kissing the ridged skin, noting how he closed his eyes at her touch. "It means you lived to see another day. It means you came back to me."

"This scar means that I was just a little too late," he said, over her head.

"Don't say that," she said, taking his erection in her hands.

He groaned. She took him into her mouth, not teasing or gentle, but hungry. All the time she'd waited and wanted him in every stroke of her mouth. She hollowed her cheeks, sucking him. Her hands gripped his backside, as his hands massaged her scalp. She kept giving him stroke after stroke, never averting her eyes from his.

Then his hand was clasping hers, pulling her to a sitting position on his lap. "Get off your knees, it's time for me to show you just how mine you still are."

He held his hands behind him on the headboard, gesturing for the cravat he'd given her earlier.

Moria was tying his hands when he asked, "Do you know how to tie a..." she looped the cravat into its final position, testing its hold, "A sailor's knot?" He cursed. "I don't know why I'm surprised; but somehow your expertise with knots has me even harder."

"That does it for you more than your cock in my mouth?"

Devyn laughed, nipping her playfully on her arm. Moria felt the pressure building at the base of her spine at the feel of teeth on her bare skin.

"I missed you. I missed your humor, just us...this."

"I have to tell you something," Moria said, straddling him.

He tilted his beautiful head to the side. "You waited till I was tied up to say that, you little deviant."

"Just listen," she let out a breath. "This doesn't have to stop. The Duke and I had a conversation—"

His eyes burned, hot and dark. "Do not speak his name, not to me, not here."

"He said that if he and I...didn't suit...if either of us wanted to... seek affection elsewhere...he wouldn't...he wouldn't be opposed."

"Untie me right now."

She shook her head and placed a hand at his chest. "You're staying here with me."

He held her eyes with his own. "You tie me up, and then tell me your husband won't care if you take a lover so long as he can do the same, is that what I'm hearing, Moria?"

"Devyn, we both get what we want this way," she ran her fingers in his hair, he pulled away.

"No, we don't. I don't get what I want, and neither do you. The Duke is the only one who does."

"You won't have to take Peregrine's title away," *and I won't have to risk Olivia's reputation with more scandals like a broken engagement or the rest of the Burn Book when, not if, Kate decides to share more of it,* she withheld. "Nothing has to change for us."

"I'm alive. *Everything* has changed for us."

"You said if I wanted, I would have you. Kiss me."

He did as she asked. She held onto his face, pouring all of her love into a kiss that she hoped he could feel, in every part of his being, like she did. His legs wrapped around her waist.

"Bring them closer," he said, gesturing with his silk-bound hand to her breasts. Moria pushed them close to his face. His tongue circled her nipples one at a time, suckling and tasting.

"Touch yourself," he commanded.

Moria brought a hand between her legs. "Lick your finger. Slip it inside."

One finger slipped between her folds. They both moaned. He kept suckling at her nipple while she touched herself.

When she started to grow wet, he said, "Let me taste," and she brought her finger to his mouth.

He sucked on her digit, drinking her in. "Fucking perfect. Now ride my face like your favorite steed."

"Jesus, you're commanding tonight."

"Just because my hands are tied doesn't mean I'm not running this show."

"That's exactly what it means."

His hips moved underneath her, providing friction that heated her throughout. "Ride. My. Face."

Moria stood on the bed so that her quim was level with his mouth. His tongue darted between her legs, and she held onto the headboard. Her thighs squeezed his face as he gave and took from her until she was dripping for him, and then he swallowed. It was the most erotic sight she'd ever seen.

"I'm ready for you to fuck me now," she ground out, sinking onto his erection.

"Holy fuck," he said as he slid into her. "God, you're so wet and so tight. You feel like a dream."

Moria placed her hands on either side of his face as she moved up and down his erection. He took her mouth in his and seared her, branded her with a kiss. His hips arched up into her, up and down, harder and harder.

He moved with her, his thrusts pulling back in time with hers. The sound of him slipping into her, against her thighs, mingling with their heavy breaths and sighs was all she could hear.

"That's it, angel," he groaned. "Take what you want," as he rammed into her. Her nails dug into his back and she felt the marks as she was leaving them.

"You're what I want," she ground out, pulling his head back by his hair as she leaned over him.

He let out a low laugh, tilting his hips. He took her in a circular motion. When she let out a whimper, he said, "Did I find the spot, angel?"

She nodded, her eyes glazed with lust and trained on the sight of him large and glistening and mounted beneath her.

"Say it."

"You found it, Devil."

"There's a good girl. What about these?" He took one of her breasts, so close to his lips, in his mouth. He released one with a loud, wet pop. "Can I fuck these too?"

"Take what you want, Devyn," she let out on a breathless voice.

She took his cock in one hand and slid it between her breasts, using her other hand to push them together. He slid himself up and down, watching her watching him. She tucked her lip between her teeth and clenched her thighs together. He grazed his cock against her nipple.

"So pretty. I like your wet quim better, bring her back to me."

Moria took his mouth in hers again, biting down on his bottom lip.

He pulled his head back on a curse. "Jesus, my lip's bleeding. What did I say?"

There was a note of laughter in his voice, free and unencumbered by the weight of their pasts.

"You say all the right things," she said, squeezing his erection. "You always do."

A slow smile spread across his scarred features. "You like it when I talk coarse to you? I told you I didn't need hands to make you wet." His beautiful rose tattoo caught her attention.

"I'd like your hands on me just the same."

"My hands would love nothing more than the feel of you."

And then when she untied the knot, he was gripping her hair, bringing her mouth to his. His lips claimed hers, his tongue snaking into her mouth.

He brought his cock to her entrance and buried it inside again.

"Fuck," he tilted his head back against the headboard. His other hand grasped her backside as he slid home again and again. "I think you're even wetter for me."

"I don't think you have seen the half of how wet I can be for you."

"Drown me."

Moria turned to face the headboard. He was on his knees behind her. He placed a cushion between her breasts and the headboard. With one hand squeezing her nipple, he used the other hand to arch her back.

"Spread your legs for me, Moria," His knees spread her legs wider, wider.

When he reseated himself inside of her, she had to bite down on his arm to keep from screaming.

She was holding onto the headboard, arching her back into him while he gripped at her hips. He slid in and out, slamming into the spot inside of her at an angle so deep she felt him everywhere. She felt both of them running rampant toward release when he cried out, "Where do you want me to come?"

She grasped at his arm, holding him. "I want to feel you come inside of me. I want to come together."

"Fuck, angel. I can't do that. You know I can't, even if I want to."

She curved her back and timed the thrust of her hips with his.

Devyn leaned to trail kisses down her spine. "Because god, you are the most beautiful sight I've ever seen."

With his dark hair against her brow, his lips against her skin, his fingers holding her against his onslaught, she said, "Yes. You are."

"You think I'm beautiful, Moria?" He said, shoved deep inside of her but she could still feel his eyes on her.

"Every inch."

"Every inch is yours."

When Moria's face fell, he stilled. "And you're mine," he grabbed her chin, turned her face to her quim. "You see that?"

His mouth overpowered hers, slipping his tongue deep inside her mouth from behind. It was an inartful kiss, but she was taken over by passion too. She pulled at his raven's wing hair, tore her nails hungrily down his curved back to leave a mark because he was hers too.

His cock slammed deeper into her. "You," timed with a thrust, "belong," another thrust, "to," thrust, "me!"

As he claimed her, Moria exploded. She shattered so brilliantly she felt the release roll over her in gasping waves. He bit her shoulder, screaming her name as he came inside of her on a deep, excruciatingly thrilling thrust.

She collapsed into the counterpane, and Devyn left the bed. She closed her eyes. And when she opened them, he was cleaning her up with a soft, damp cloth. Then he collapsed atop her in a tangle of limbs. This was what she'd wanted when she'd prayed for him back, a passionate frenzy in which she could no longer tell where he ended and she began.

"Think you can still walk?" He said, one hand pulling her against his chest, and the other playing with one of her freely flowing, blonde curls.

She hit him playfully in the arm. "Can you?"

He laughed, nipping at her shoulder. "Why would I want to walk? I have everything I need right here."

He brought her fingers to his lips to kiss each of them in turn.

"Devyn?"

"Hmm?" He said, settling into a pillow with one great arm behind his head. Moria pulled the coverlet and sheet over both of them.

"Will you tell me? What it was like? I want to know everything."

He arched a brow at her.

"Everything," she reiterated, kissing his broad, bare chest and resting her head on one of his tattoos. "I couldn't be there with you, you didn't allow me to be there for you when you got back, but I wanted to. Desperately."

"At first, I started my rehabilitation to spite you," he said, his hand drawing little circles on her bare shoulder. "But what was it all for, without this?" he said, taking her mouth in a slow, sweet, drugging kiss.

And then he told her, about all of it, as she lay warm and safe in his arms.

<h1 style="text-align: center">Chapter Forty-Two</h1>

MANY TIMES, MORIA WOKE IN A WARM BED WITH SOFT linen sheets in a small cottage, to the feel of Devyn's lips on her skin, his hands on her body and in her hair. They made love again, at some point. He kissed the top of her head and pulled her so close and told her to get some sleep. She had the same dream as many nights before, of shrouding green fronds blocking out the sun, Devyn's laugh, and the wind blowing her hair from her face. But this time, the man she'd dreamed about, dreamed to life, even, held her while she slept.

Now, she watched the sun alight on the sharp planes of his face, the slope of his shoulders and pectorals honed by battle with enemies both foreign and within sprinkled with golden light for the first time and likely the last. Even though Moria was curled in his arms, she felt like he was already slipping through her fingers yet again. They'd been pulled apart by circumstance so many times, maybe it was a sign. What they had was an aberration, it wasn't the kind of thing that was built to last.

She had been brought up with a singular goal: a nobleman's wife. But Devyn had been a rock in the current of her life, sending her wants rushing in a different direction. The more she wanted some-

313

thing, the more likely it was to be taken from her. Time had proven that.

Devyn stirred, his rose tattooed arm coming up to cradle his pillow.

Moria's eyes stung at the sight of his tattoo, a reminder that this wasn't an aberration. What he meant to her, what he *had* done for her, what he *would* do for her, was perfectly real.

Devyn opened one eye and looked at her. "Stop," he said.

Moria moved closer to him in the circle of his arms. "Stop what? You don't know what I was thinking."

"I do. I can hear your over-thinking from here. Stop complicating this."

If the world outside didn't exist, or if it could maybe just go on in her absence, she'd let her calling be to stay inside the protective encircling of both of Devyn Winter's massive arms. She'd let the tobacco and whiskey and parchment of his scent be the only thing she smelled. She'd wear those crumpled sheets as the only bespoke couture she needed. But several blocks from here, resided another man who'd made plans with her, who'd stood up for her, who'd been decent to her. Several blocks from here was her family, and a woman with a book filled with words she'd written that would make their lives more difficult.

Moria's panicked heart thudding reached her ears.

Devyn's breathing was steady, like he was. For a moment, she let the rhythm of his breaths temper her pulse and stampeding thoughts. His hands skimmed down her arms, falling on her abdomen, stroking over her hip, then lower, to her core.

Moria gave a strangled gasp. Her entire body responded at his touch, she knew enough of love and lust to understand that she had been starved for touch, craved affection and intimacy like this; and it wasn't something that could be replicated.

"What is it you want?" The smokey, wicked rasp of his voice curled inside her ear.

"You know exactly what I want," she turned in his arms to speak into his lips, the linen sheets clinging to her bare skin.

"Say it," his hands stilled, warm and powerful resting against her skin.

Moria wrapped her arms about his neck. "I want you to take me."

Devyn raised a brow. "And then?"

Moria traced a finger over the pointed slopes of his handsome face, committing him to memory. The wine in the bottle they'd been drinking had run dry, the sand in all their hour glasses had emptied. She'd been trying to outrun the goodbye for hours, days, now. But the time was nigh.

"And then, I dress, I return home, make my excuses, and prepare to say my vows in a church in a couple of days."

Devyn swore and sat up, the sheets covering him slipping to his waist. His exposed back bore the marks of all ten of her fingernails. Selfishly, she hoped the last signs of what they were to each other took days to fade. Moria swallowed the sourness rising in her throat. How was she so willing and free with her love for him in this room, and so reluctant to give him more?

"And I will be nothing more to you than some shameful secret," he said, eyes avoidant, hands steepled against his lips, voice thick.

Moria reached for him, but he pulled back. She felt a new kind of missing him when he held her off with a hand. "Let me," he said. "I have to say this."

He met her eyes, beyond her eyes, to all of her. "You are it for me."

At his words, she shook her head, dabbing at the tears that were already running free, but he kept going. "I didn't use the time that I had to stand before God and everyone we care about in a church, and I will not be able to make you a duchess, or even give you half the life you're accustomed to. But I have made plans, Moria."

He made her look at him; his soft grasp on her chin an affectionate tether, his other hand resting on her thigh.

"I have made plans with the skills and connections I have to provide a good life, albeit not a grand one. I have said all that there is to say by now, but I can love every part of you, every day that we have left."

Moria opened her mouth to speak, to acquiesce, to agree to whatever terms he'd just put on the table; but just as she'd known moments before, their time had already run out.

A banging sounded on the door of the caretaker's cottage.

"My lady, are you in there? Please, it's me, you have to come quick."

Moria and Devyn looked from the door some feet away, to each other, in recognition. It was Ella's voice.

Moria sank back against the pillows, defeat washed over her features. She dabbed at her eyes and cleared her throat. Devyn reached for her, she threw herself into his arms. She held onto him like she'd hold onto a cliff before flinging herself to the depths awaiting below. Maybe he'd feel the desperation in her trembling hands and pressing fingernails and know this was an impossibly hard choice.

"My lady?" Ella called again, sounding frantic.

"Yes, Ella, give me one moment."

"Don't," Devyn whispered, those arms she'd miss holding her against him, holding her together.

And when he removed them, silken inch by muscular inch, she crumpled. As she threw on her chemise, and he unbolted the door for Ella. She stood on shaky legs, searching through the haze of her tears for her stockings and her bodice.

"Let me, my lady," Ella said gently, turning her to loosely lace her into her corset.

"You said I needed to be quick. Has something happened?"

Moria saw Devyn out of the corner of her eye, the arch of his back as he pulled his shirt over his head. She'd miss that view. That nibbling voice in her head said *"you don't have to, he could be yours."*

But at what cost to everyone around them?

"It's Wednesday," Ella elaborated as she attempted to tame Moria's hair into something ladylike. "You're supposed to attend a luncheon in your honor in an hour."

Moria swallowed down her rising panic, focused on only her breaths as she pictured the faces who would be waiting for her. She could hear their greetings and their felicitations, she could smell the tea and all the sweet meats and cakes laid out on lace tablecloths. The luncheon was supposed to be for female friends and family of the bride only, but that number had been expanded to include so many faces she barely knew who only wanted to curry favor with a future duchess. Her holding court over preening nobles and elites alike who no longer held any past indiscretion over her. It's what she'd wanted.

"My honor," Moria said, the words weaker than she'd meant, "since that's worth so much."

She saw Devyn and Ella exchange worried glances. She looked down at the dress she was wearing. Ella had brought the dress they'd selected for the event. It was pink with pearl embellishments and two tiers of skirts. She hadn't even noticed Ella putting them on her. Matching gloves adorned her hands. It was beautiful and ornate, but it was all wrong.

A hiccup started in her throat and came out as a sob before she could chase it back down.

Devyn was pushing Ella aside to wrap her in his arms.

Yes, this was right. Holding him in her arms, the smell of him in her nose and the linen of his shirt against her cheek. He was stroking her hair and he wasn't telling her not to go, only that he loved her.

"Did you bring a carriage?" Devyn asked Ella, still holding Moria against his chest.

Moria didn't listen for her answer. It didn't matter if she rode in a carriage pulled by fine horses or walked several blocks, she had somewhere to be and she'd do what she'd been training for her whole life.

It would be so much easier if she could say something heart-breaking, deliver some blow that would let him see that she was just as awful as she'd warned him and he was better off without her. Only she couldn't think of anything terrible to deliver, the only aspersions she could hurl like stones, were at herself.

She looked up at him. "Tell me you won't miss me."

He shook his head. "I can't."

A single tear. "Lie."

She felt the great, bracing breath he dragged in. Hated it. Hated herself.

"I can't," he repeated.

"My lady, we really must make haste if we are to make that luncheon. And someone might spot the carriage if it sits too long at the Clairville mews."

She took his swarthy, beautiful face in her hands. "I wasn't good enough, or strong enough, or brave enough for you. But as God as my witness, I have loved you. It will never be enough. But I will keep on loving you. I promise you that. You are all there is for me too."

There was no Ella and there was no empty caretaker's cottage, and there was no luncheon or ladies to reign over for a moment. It stretched out and onto the shortest forever while he kissed her, force-fully and determinedly. If her last supper were Devyn's lips and sighs and the press of his body, she was Judas. This was the betraying kiss. She was a traitor and a sinner of the highest order and yet as her tongue clashed against his, she knew nothing would ever feel like this.

She was still holding him by the front of his shirt when he pulled away. He took one small hand in his dwarfing grasp, kissed it, and put it in Ella's. Ella's other hand came about her waist, and pulled her toward the door, but her eyes stayed on Devyn. She watched the bob of his Adam's Apple as he watched her leave. When she stepped over the threshold, he called her name, the sweetest sound in her world.

"Give 'em, hell, Moria."

Chapter Forty-Three

"Are you sure this is it, Dev?" Calum asked, eyeing the stylish townhouse they'd been knocking on for two minutes. It was the only question his friend had asked, not the elephant in the room of why Pembooke didn't retrieve it himself, why Devyn was still retrieving it when she hadn't chosen him.

"It's the address her brother and Miss Kelley sent me."

The door opened with an aging butler on the other side. "Gentlemen, do you have an appointment?"

"Miss Herring, does she live at this address?"

"Who's asking?" said a masculine voice from the foyer.

"Captain Calum Sterling," Calum answered.

"How do you know my daughter?"

"She's acquainted with my fiancé," Calum answered again.

"Katie!" The graying man bellowed, motioning for the two men to step inside. "You can wait in the parlor." The man led them to a room literally filled to bursting with books. There was barely room on the furniture, as it was also covered in books. A few moments passed in awkward silence and a redhead young woman appeared. Devyn recognized her from the opera, the Duke's box.

"The Pages, where are they?" Devyn demanded as soon as she entered.

Miss Herring shook her head, straightening her shoulders. "I don't know what you're talking about."

Devyn wasn't a man who'd hurt a female, so instead, he grasped her father by his lapels. The man dangled above the upholstered chair he'd been sitting in. His fleshy face started to take on a purple hue, Devyn cinched his grasp. "Your daughter is a snake, just like her father. And I'll wager what she did with that book, it was at your behest, wasn't it? You thought she could use it to ruin her and steal the Duke."

The man's eyes bulged, looking at his wife standing in the doorway. "Hector, you didn't," the woman breathed.

"A lesson, if I may," Devyn said, moving his face closer to the other man's. "Reverends *aren't* supposed to hand over their subjects to traders. And fathers are supposed to *protect* their children," he looked to Kate, "Not whore them out or ask them to betray their friends."

"She was no friend to me," Kate spat the words. Calum shook his head and grimaced.

Devyn tightened his hold on the man's smoking jacket. "Say that again, I dare you."

Kate rushed, "I'm sorry, I'll go and get the book, just *please* put him down. His lungs are still weak from travel."

Devyn released the man with a shove into the chair. "She's better than you deserve."

When Miss Herring returned, he snatched the pink and black book from her hands.

"And *you're* better than she deserves," Kate said as she slammed the door in his face.

Chapter Forty-Four

"I know your wedding rehearsal is in a few hours, but I thought I'd find you here."

Moria looked up to see a sun-limned wreath of gold curls, two altruistic dimples, and blue eyes.

Llewyn.

Moria finished snipping a few bulbs for propagation and placed them into a basket, smacking her hands together to shake off the dirt they'd accumulated. She'd needed a retreat, and sinking her ungloved hands into soil had been her first place of refuge.

"Don't know that I've ever been *findable*, actually."

Llewyn went "ha," and then tilted his head to the side, searching for her eyes. Moria returned his gaze, gave him a tired smile.

"I don't get a real smile?"

"There's no faking anything with you, is there?" she sighed. "Suppose you'll say it's something to do with God."

"Tell me," he said, pushing up his sleeves, crossing his arms at his chest. He leaned against a workbench, legs crossed in front of him like he had all day to set her to rights. Moria wished she could be like that, to have the kind of easy grace that she could offer to others that made things better instead of...imploding things. She didn't mean to do it. But that's what she did. She was always treading light-foot and somehow still messing the tidy, ordered rows of other people's lives, leaving boot tracks and crumpling the stalks of all their hopes.

"I am a walking disaster," she shrugged, turning to immerse herself in some mindless task. "You know this already."

"You're regretting your decision to marry the Duke?" No recrimination, barely any surprise, just an opening for her to divulge.

"I hope, or rather believe, God must be a little like...you, I guess. I have heard theologians and priests and vicars say that God judges our sins, and I know," she looked up at him and locked eyes for emphasis. "I have my share to atone for, but God sees all. And if God saw it all, then He surely saw the way..." she let out a breath for courage and rolled her shoulders. "My heart has gone through a series of fractures and breaks and mending over the years. And surely, He can also see that I'm trying. I'm a girl who's been planted into a pot that I outgrew a long time ago," Llewyn followed her gaze to the orchid she was pruning.

"And so, I replanted myself over and over but the conditions still weren't right. Not enough water, or too much water, or too much sunlight, or not enough. I think maybe it's me that simply can't just thrive in the space where I was planted and make the most of it. But I have seen glimmers, now and then, that He provided when I wasn't looking for it, giving you to me as a friend, for example. Bringing Devyn to me when I was lost, finding him when I was lost again. But now, this is it. I'm a hothouse flower that has to decide this is my lot and stop wilting and trying to make new roots."

She shook her head as if to clear it then winced. "I got very metaphorical on you, you seem to pull those out of me."

"I think you do yourself a disservice."

A noise came from Moria's throat. She could weather his sage advice and telling her to *'make the best of things', 'never complain', 'soldier on'*, all that nonsense. But if he complimented her in any way, she might lose it. And no, she was not going to ponder why that was.

Llewyn stood closer to her, taking the twine in her hands and propping up the orchid on the spindle to keep it from drooping.

"You are not a hothouse flower, none of this has to be your lot, and you have never wilted, even through the worst." Llewyn met her gaze.

"But you're a man of God, aren't you going to tell me that I need to honor my commitments and that anything less than that is a sin, and that-"

"As my most loyal friend, I must ask you, what commitments have you not honored?"

Moria leveled him with a glare. Must he make her say it? Was this to be a confessional, then?

"I see. Well. There's nothing for it then, the only way out is through."

Moria heaved the heaviest sigh of many a woman headed before the altar... or the executioner's block.

"You and God, you couldn't give me, perhaps, some clearer advice than that? Something along the lines of, *"don't marry a man you don't love just because you're* supposed *to do it,"* or...." her lips turned downward and she gave a noncommittal shrug. "Tell me the choice that would anger God the most? I don't know if I can deal with any more of his punishment, to tell you the truth."

Llewyn's face fell. "Is that what you think?"

Moria shrugged again. Words out of her reach.

"Look at me," he waited until he had her eyes. "God is just, but he is kind and loving. The trauma in your life is not because of you. What did you have to put yourself through to try and save Marcus' life? He gives beauty for ashes, that's what He does. All those people who followed your story and hung on your every word and read about you in the papers, it wasn't some fleeting beauty they were looking at. It was a girl who didn't let anything break her; in fact, it all made her stronger. And they didn't know what to make of that. And so," he heaved his own great sigh of a sage, gearing up for his final bit of wisdom. "You are promised to His Grace, the Duke; and Devyn is alive, that's a testament to His goodness. You saw none of this coming, but God is never surprised. And frankly, neither am I. So make a choice you must, and I think you know which choice that is."

Chapter Forty-Five

The guest list of the wedding of Lady M and the Duke of A was a more discerning list than the invites to Buckingham Palace. No one sent their regrets as this promises to be a spectacle. And the season has only just begun.

-Scandalous Lives of London

"It's filling up. How many people did you invite?" Olivia asked, sitting on a chaise lounge opposite her sisters in the bride's antechamber inside the cathedral.

Noelle inexpertly pinned a curl into Moria's coiffure with the help of Ella. Ella took the pins from her and shooed her out of the way.

Kathleen handed Moria a glass of champagne. "On my wedding day, mother gave me a brimming glass of champagne and said, 'though you've no reason to be nervous, I'm sure your nerves don't know that and showed up anyway unannounced. So, drink up.' And so I did. And so shall we."

"Slange var, mum," Olivia said, throwing back Lawrence's flask to her older sister's dismay.

Kathleen was the only one of Rosamunde's daughters who'd get to have her on her wedding day. But she had the same red hair, same green-grey blue eyes, same soft smile, sharing her words of encouragement.

"Except not sure we can say the same on this occasion," Moria said, tossing back half the champagne in one gulp.

"What reason have you to be nervous?" Olivia asked, eyes wide and worried. Then she broke into giggles and the inhabitants of the room all turned to look at her. "I'm only kidding."

Noelle suddenly gasped and Moria spilled her champagne. A million hands went to dabbing, and it turned out she'd soiled the bench beside her and not her dress.

"Mind telling me why you're gasping like that, sister; before you ruin everyone's formal wear?" Moria asked, scooting to the edge of the bench.

Noelle made an apologetic face. "Sorry, I just thought...it occurred to me..." She started pacing, and Kathleen was urging her to continue while Olivia was making an X with her hands to tell her to stop. Letitia was removing the cap from Lawrence's flask for a hearty nip of her own. Ella made a face at Moria in the mirror like she was trying to hide her laugh. Loving these women and being loved by them, god, what would she do without them?

Moria took Noelle's wrist, and her sister looked down at her and said, "What if he shows up here?"

Kathleen spit out her champagne. "I'm definitely missing something, aren't I?" She looked between her three younger sisters, sighed. "I'll do my best not to judge, just no more secrets and half-truths and lies by omission."

Moria was still holding onto Noelle, this time her hand around two of Noelle's fingers. "Devyn is alive."

Kathleen was wide-eyed, turning to look at the door. "Did you switch grooms on us on the day of your wedding, Moria Pembrooke?"

Moria shook her head.

Olivia laughed, seemingly at the absurdity. She interjected, "But...does she have to choose? Is there a possibility to pursue a relationship...of sorts...with both of them?"

Noelle's head was tilted to the side like she was trying to work out a complex math equation, Kathleen was rubbing her temples, Miss Kelley took a timely sip of her champagne as if to avoid speaking.

"Right, so what do you want, Moria?" Noelle asked gently.

No one had really ever asked her that, but Devyn had. Many times.

What is it you want?

How could it be that simple? It had never been simple, not a single day of her life. When she'd been born with the face that she had, the position and family she'd been born into? She wasn't whining or complaining about it. She knew she'd been hit with a much prettier fate than scores of women on earth at any given time in history. But what she wanted hadn't factored into things. There had been times when she had done what she wanted, and the consequences had chased her down and held her there.

Moria was still, the only sound and movement she made was her calculated breaths.

What she wanted was-

"It's almost time. Is she ready?" Jasper said from the doorway.

She was pretty certain her sisters were shooting daggers at him with their eyes and trying to clue him in that *no*, the bride was not, in fact, *ready.*

"Her veil isn't on yet," Kathleen said.

"Mo?" Jasper asked, and he kneeled down in front of her chair. His eyes were kind. They went a little more grey-blue when they were kind. When he was haughty and annoyed they were more jade.

"Do you not want to do this anymore?"

I will make you a duchess. You will have all that you want…You'll have no one's loyalty more than my own.

Moria shook her head. "No, I still want to."

"Are you sure?" Noelle asked, the others cut her a look.

"I made him a promise," she said as Kathleen finished pinning her veil in place. It had been made by their grandmother and worn by their mother.

"You made me a promise too." Jasper said, squeezing her hands.

"I did?"

"No more martyrdom, remember?"

"Hardly martyrdom marrying a Duke," Olivia said. "What? It's true! He has over twenty-thousand pounds a year without the hefty dowry he was given for taking her off our hands."

Moria looked to the collection of loyal supporters in front of her and nodded. "Olivia is right, the only way forward is through. Sometimes, you go far enough down a road, there's no turning around."

"It doesn't have to mean what you think it has to mean," Kathleen argued.

"I think it does," Moria said, standing and immediately almost toppling over from the sheer weight of the skirts, train, and lace veil nearly as long as the train. Jasper steadied her.

"If you're sure."

Moria tried to take in a full breath, felt the whale bone stays constricting the movement, and took in short breaths through her nose. "I'm not sure of anything, but this is what I have to do."

Ella fluffed her veil. Kathleen dabbed at her eyes, adding, "You're already the most beautiful bride to ever….bride."

Noelle placed a hand at Moria's back. "Not if she doesn't want to be one."

Olivia grimaced. "She does though? Just to a different man."

Don't think of him. Don't think of how his eyes go when you make him laugh, don't think of the way he smells or the way his body looks beneath you. Don't think of all the beautiful words he gave you from his beautiful soul.

She met her reflection in the mirror, straightening her shoulders.

Think of a different man. He's *the one you're marrying.*

"I love you, you know. All of you? I'm not good at it, saying how I feel. I think I'm a little bit broken that way. But thank you all sticking by me. You're all that's kept me getting up in the morning some days," Moria gave them each a small smile. "It was a long road to the altar, but you were the best travel companions a girl could want."

Chapter Forty-Six

DEVYN HEARD THE CLOCK TOLL. HE THOUGHT MAYBE HE'D drunk enough the night before that he'd slept past the wedding, but there it was.

One more hour and she'd belong to another man.

Legally.

But would her heart still bear his name?

He could smell her scent, like lemons and sugar in his room. Devyn jolted upright, looking around him. A bundle of letters sat atop his table.

D-

You're all there is for me too.

But when I was a different girl, I said a lot of awful things. I wrote them down. (Some of them were true, though). Someone stole that book, and shared my words. Without it, I was forced to make a choice to protect my *family from the shame of what I'd put on paper. And then you returned.*

You gave me so many better words.

I don't have enough good ones to give back to you. But these in our letters, all the ones I gave to you whispered in the dark, they were true. Those written in that book that so many people have read when I didn't want them to, they were from a different girl. You made me a better one. I'm changed for knowing you, for loving you.

Your Lady

DEVYN FINALLY REACHED THE CONCLUSION HER BROTHER had been leading him to with the book he'd asked his help in returning.

Devyn reached between his mattresses for the pink and black book he'd retrieved the evening before. He had time, he had to get to her. He rose from the bed, throwing on his clothes with a wince at the tightness in his hips and lower back from his still-recovering injuries.

Once dressed, he caught his reflection in the mirror, tying his cravat. This ensemble was something she'd picked out for him once. She probably knew the thread count and where the bloody silkworms who made the pants came from and he'd let her pick out all his damned clothes forever and wear them with a smile...if she'd just stop her foolishness. Call off this blasphemous wedding.

He looked again to the bundle of her letters. Ink and paper were a paltry substitute for a woman, especially a woman as earth-shattering as Moria.

He had told Calum the night before that he couldn't use the

Burn Book to win her back; he'd told her how he felt, she still hadn't chosen him.

But how was he meant to be inside her and hold her like they were the last two people on earth and then he was just supposed to let her be the property of another man forever? He read her letter back, then pocketed the parchment into his greatcoat pocket.

As he called for a carriage, Devyn decided he called *bullshit*.

Not over his dead body was he going to just give up. He had been dead before, but he wasn't now. Or more accurately, he had never been.

God, maybe he was still drunk. Didn't matter, he had a wedding to crash.

Chapter Forty-Seven

Moria would love to tell you about the march from her dressing room at the church to the altar where her groom waited, only she couldn't.

She'd just...walked?

Like it was any ordinary walk, she barely heard music or her brother's voice, or anyone in the church over how loudly her heart was roaring at her. She couldn't look at the guests, if she focused on what she had to do, she could almost pretend all these people weren't there. Or the flowers. Or the candles.

And somehow her feet carried her to him, to the man she loved waiting for her at the other end.

Wait, no that wasn't right.

This was the wrong church.

That was the wrong man.

He was taking her hand, pulling back her veil with hands that were all wrong.

But surely he wasn't? He was looking at her with something like love in his green eyes. Perhaps she was the one who was all wrong.

When they turned to face each other, he leaned in to whisper, "You alright? You're shaking."

She gave him a smile, hoped it was a good one, and nodded. He squeezed her hands back.

Get it together, woman. He wants you. You love him.

Someone was talking, she should be listening. The Vicar was her friend, she'd had to pull all kinds of rank to get this particular vicar to be the officiant and she should ingest his words. But in her chest, there was a familiar kind of ache that wouldn't quiet.

Jasper had given her away and sat back down, there was no going back now. Don't look over your shoulder at-

Bang.

The front door of the church barged open. Her heart ruptured on a tide of collective gasps and clearing throats and shuffling bodies. The sun fell behind *him*, rushing to gild his dark hair and scarred face. He didn't pause, walking up the aisle with determined grace, even with his cane.

"I have a very just cause as to why these two should not be married."

What was he doing?

"Who the hell are you to interrupt my wedding?" the Duke objected.

"Who am I?" Her soldier flicked up his brows. "Who am *I*?"

"If I may—" The Vicar stepped forward to interject, but when both men looked at him, he held up his hands and took a step backward with his Bible folded over his chest.

Devyn put a hand on his chest. "I'm the man that she was supposed to marry. But I died in battle. I'm the man who wrote her letters nearly every day for almost two years. I know she has a scar on her arm from where she fell off a horse when she was eleven," He was close enough now that his thumb traced a pattern on her forearm, and she couldn't help her eyes fluttering closed for the smallest second before remembering they were in God's house full of witnesses of the highest social caliber.

"Just there," he continued, a dark storm in his eyes. "She can tell you where all eight of my tattoos are, I can tell you with my eyes closed where all the freckles are on her face. And I know that she can play Mendelssohn with no music in front of her, but she prefers Elgar. She knows that I allegedly died in battle because I refused to leave a man behind, and she was angry, so very angry with me. I wasn't supposed to do anything stupid. I was supposed to come home," he turned to her. "To you," he said, bending lower, closer, to her.

"And so I did. Here I am," he gestured his arms wide, a broad and boyish smile cracking open on his handsomely scarred face. "A battle-scarred soldier. Marching under no banner but yours, my lady. Here to return your words back to you," Moria gasped at the familiar book he pulled from his jacket and wrapped her shaking hands around. "Promising you my own name, my family, my soul for the breaking. So you tell His Grace, and you tell me, what will it be, my lady?"

Moria looked down at the book she'd clutched to her chest. She meant what she'd said in the note she'd left. It didn't mean as much to her now; but she felt protective of her words, her book on full display for everyone to see. Her secret love on display for all to see.

The Duke stepped between them. "That was some speech," he turned to Moria, pointing a finger in her face. "I trusted you. We made plans, remember?" He said in a whisper that only she could hear somehow over the clamor of her heart and the collective chin wagging from the audience of their current melodrama.

The Duke placed a hand on his hip. "I can't believe that you would betray me like this. I could have made you a duchess, there's so much I could have given you, and you do this *here*?" He shook his head, confusion racing headfirst into ire, filling his eyes and his voice. "Today of all days you publicly stab me in my back like some common tavern wench with no loyalty, actually a tavern wench would know her place better than-"

"That is the last time you speak to her that way," Devyn wedged his body between them, his hands placing her behind him. "Or it is the last time you will draw breath."

"You would threaten a Duke over a cheating whore like her?"

"I would die for her!" Devyn roared in his face, still clutching the skirt of Moria's dress in one hand, placing his body in front of her like a shield. Moria could barely see for the tears in her eyes.

"This man needs to be arrested," the Duke called, looking for someone to support his claim.

What? No.

She was the criminal here.

If anyone deserved punishment it was the culprit. After his words, the effort he must have gone to to retrieve her words, the way he'd promised her his body and then so quickly demonstrated his claim wasn't for show by stepping between her and the Duke?

Her decision made, Moria grabbed onto Devyn's arm. She wasn't letting anyone take him away from her. Not ever again.

"Actually," Perry cut in, Tristan nodding in a silent show of encouragement. "Not to ruin such an impassioned speech, but I have to cut in here."

He made his way between the two men, placing himself in front of his brother the way his brother had done for him, repeatedly, in the past.

"Brother, what are you doing?" Devyn said in a lowered tone.

"What I should have done long ago," The Earl of Clairville adjusted himself to his full height to address the Duke. "You cannot have this man arrested. Technically speaking, he is an Earl. The true Earl of Clairville. And I'm sorry to say, Your Grace, he hasn't committed any crimes."

"Not yet, at least," Devyn sneered in the Duke's direction.

"Why don't we all discuss this in private?" The Vicar suggested.

Moria looked over her shoulder at the people assembled, her eyes falling on her family, her friends. The Vicar was right, he offered Moria his arm to lead her toward the sun-streaked transept. She took it. They could finish this conversation and she could say all that she needed to say without an audience leering.

"Moria, wait!" It was Olivia coming to catch up to her from her perch on the altar steps. She fixed the incredibly long train of Moria's gown, then took the book from Moria's hands, and kissed her cheek. "We are with you, whatever you decide. Don't let—"

"I think she's already made her decision, Olivia," the Duke cut her sister, her perfect baby sister, off with a mocking jeer. Moria had heard enough. She had her words back, she had her family's blessing, she'd seen the Duke's true colors. She had to move forward with her decision like she should have done in that cottage behind the mews. Before then.

With a grunt, she pulled the paste-stoned tiara from her head. Then, she flung back her veil in a bevy of lace and tulle. There was a collective gasp from the assembled crowd.

"You know what?" She turned to face the guests seated in pews, the weight of her lies and her masks pressing in when it was long past time to let them go. "He's yours," she took the crown in her hand and broke it into a third. It broke rather easily, actually.

She hurled a piece into the crowd. It landed near a guest with a thud, the crowd fell silent.

"Half the people in this room are mad at me over the book that was printed, and the other half think I don't deserve to be here. If you were hurt by the burn book, I'm sorry. I wasn't the only one who wrote in it, but I'm still sorry. I know many of you didn't come here because you were happy for me, you wanted to see what kind of duchess I would make. Apparently a bad one. I think everybody looks like royalty today, but you can try it on for size, see if the title fits as well as you'd imagine when he insults you," she found Devyn's eyes, "and the man you love, in front of you."

She hurled another piece of the paste crown, Gretchen caught it in one hand.

"Here, take it. Even *you* can be a duchess," a piece landed next to Kate Herring. Kate looked down at it like it was something toxic and life-giving both at once.

"And *you*? You could be a duchess." She heaved a piece of tiara in the direction of Letitia.

"Why not you? You are definitely duchess material." Another landed at the feet of Carina Smythe.

"Or you? Fancy being a duchess?"

Another piece of the crown. Moria threw two more.

The seam of one of the arms of her gown gave a little tear on her final throw. A couple of hairs slipped from her coiffure. She must look a fright, but Devyn smiled at her. She could only hazard a guess at all the reactions around her in that church, didn't bother to look too closely because his was the only one that seemed to matter. His smile, full of pride and awe, like she was both a madwoman and a heroine, suffused her with hope.

Moria felt so many pairs of eyes assessing and judging her, it didn't feel like a heavy weight she needed to carry anymore. At least not alone. "When you hold your future in your hands, it isn't all that you thought it would be. What if it's all fake? All for show? Do you still want it then?"

Silence.

She chanced a glance at her family, several had tears in their eyes; there was love, there was pride. Olivia and Noelle were holding hands.

"Because I don't." She turned to Devyn. "I'm tired of being the best liar in this town because I wanted to tell you all for a long time that my affections are no longer for sale. I made a promise to a man long before now and if he hadn't nearly died, I would have kept that promise. But then I thought maybe this was how it was supposed to be. It's what I thought I was destined for anyway," she clutched his hand tighter for support. "But clearly it wasn't, or you'd have died or my feelings would have changed. And they never have and they never will."

He was rushing her, pulling her into him with their enjoined hands, fusing his mouth to hers. She hadn't had the fortitude or the respect or whatever the hell one wanted to name it to care how *wrong* that was, in this place of all places, on today of all days. She was supposed to be kissing the man she'd come here to wed, having promised to love, honor, and obey him. But there was only one man she could make such a promise to, even the obey part, and he was kissing her in full view of society's highest inner circles.

A throat cleared in front of her, but Moria didn't let go of Devyn, only peeked one eye to see that it was Jasper.

"Oh god," she said, pulling her lips from Devyn's possession. "You're going to challenge him to a duel, aren't you?"

"Which he?" Jasper said, quirking one eyebrow. And then, he pulled the Duke by his lapel, and hit him with a stout right hook. The Duke was holding his bloodied nose in his hands.

"Westmoreland! What the fuck have *I* done?"

"No one talks to my sisters like that," Jasper said, his fists still balled. "Not even a Duke."

Lawrence scoffed, taking a step forward to back his brother up, but Fitz and Henry held him back.

Devyn looked to Moria, still holding her against him. "That was *wicked*," he said next to her. She had to bite her lip to stifle a giggle.

"If you're still here hanging around like a bad smell," Jasper turned to the guests seated in the pews, "then you might as well adjourn to Pembrooke House to dismantle the mounds of food and mountains of cake waiting for the luncheon for this farce of a wedding." He turned to the Duke with an accusatory finger, "Except for you, you slanderous villain."

"I'm going to love being part of your family," Devyn said, his mouth so close to her hair. Her eyes closed at his nearness.

"And I'm going to love surprising you every day and keeping your bed warm every night."

He hung his head against her shoulder. "I'm getting hard in a church, thanks for that."

Moria whispered in his ear, "Get us a carriage back to the house, and I'll get on my knees for you. I'll make you my church."

Devyn swore. But he didn't answer her, one hand gripping her waist, he called for Llewyn.

"Vicar! Do you perform hand fastings?"

Olivia gave a little squeal, squeezing Peregrine's hand. On the other side of Peregrine, Tristan gave Moria a wink. Kathleen said, "Moria, you did change your bridegroom on the day of your wedding, you little minx!"

Fitz and Noelle both collapsed into each other laughing. Lawrence lifted a flask in salute to Moria and her soon-to-be-bridegroom, then handed the flask to his cyprian, Sarah. Letitia had picked up the flowers Moria had dropped and handed them to her. Lady Gretchen and Carina both grasped Moria from behind in an obsequious embrace.

Moria looked over her shoulder, it was just those she cared for most in the church now, those who weren't invested in catching one lady of means as she fell from her pedestal, long vacated.

"This is by far the best wedding I've ever been to," Carina offered, squeezing Moria's waist.

"It's about to get even better," Devyn parried, kissing the top of Moria's head. "Everything only gets better with you, my lady."

And when their hands and lives were bound together with an altar cloth as London's diamond and the captain who stole her heart spoke ancient words in Latin and vows of their own making, Moria couldn't hold back her tears. Of all the tears she'd cried over loves won and lost, these were the happiest.

Epilogue

Moria trailed a languid, loving finger down the side of Devyn's face, the map of his pain written in scar tissue. Devyn untied the fastings of her dress.

"I wanted to ask you earlier, but...as you likely haven't forgotten, it was madness."

"Ask your question," she said, kissing the scar that ended at his jaw.

He ran a hand over the dress before laying it gently atop her trunk in the lord's quarters of Wintersea Manor. Their new home. They'd dismissed the servants for a few days of solitude and enjoyed their first interrupted days and nights together, making plans for the title Devyn had begrudgingly admitted he relished taking responsibility for now that he'd seen her, the woman he loved, in his ancestral home, as the lady of the manor he should have given her long before now.

"Were these willow fronds? On your dress? That you wore to marry the duke?"

Moria wrapped her arms about his bare torso. "I tried. I couldn't replace them. I couldn't wear a different dress."

"Oh, Moria," he said, dropping the dress and holding her against him, kissing her bare shoulder. "You really are a mess."

"And *you*! You stormed a church."

"I did," he grimaced.

"You stopped my wedding," she poked him in the chest.

"I told you. You are it for me, you very mean girl. I'd do it again."

"And I'd choose you in front of all of London again. I'm sorry I forced your hand."

He pulled her to sit atop his lap at the edge of his bed. "How sorry?"

One hand at his chest, she pushed him backward on their bed. "I promised I'd get on my knees for you."

SOME TIME LATER, WHEN THEY'D BOTH SATED THEIR LUST and expended all their energy christening what was to be the home they'd share and rebuild together, she lay on his chest in the portrait gallery.

"I wrote to you," she said, sharing his air, supplying it. He pulled the tapestry covering them up higher to shield them from a draft.

"I know, I wrote you back," he said. One hand squeezed her hip and bringing her closer.

"No," she said, eyes catching on his mouth. It was a testament to what a good mouth it was that with a face like that, it still caught your eyes. "I mean, when you were...gone...I still wrote you letters."

Devyn made a noise in the back of his throat. She'd drunk down all of his sounds like the sweetest wine, but this was the painful kind. Made her feel a little wobbly and not in a good way.

"You left them for me, but I didn't have time to read them. I was too busy stopping your wedding. What did you say? *'That was very unchivalrous of you to go and die when you explicitly told me that you wouldn't?'*"

Moria bit her lip to hold back a smile. He could always pull those out of her.

"No. Sometimes I felt a little angry, but mostly just...pain. Like... there was some shard of glass in my shoe and every step made me bleed but I couldn't not walk, and I couldn't take it out because to never think of you at all like you'd never been, it hurt worse." She sniffed and looked away.

Devyn pulled her close with both hands on her hips and swept her into a kiss. She'd imagined him kissing her like that, while she'd written to him and missed him and conjured the feeling of him on her body. Her imaginings hadn't been near potent enough.

"I love you," he whispered into the space between them, trailing her hair out of her face and behind her ears. "Can I read your letters, my lady?"

"I think I'll save them for special occasions."

"This isn't a special occasion enough for you? We are married, on our honeymoon, and you are a countess now."

Moria grimaced. "I was supposed to be a duchess though, but now I'll have to defer to my sisters."

Devyn reversed their position. In a single motion, he was on top of her. She let out a sound that was part laugh, part huff of breathy surprise.

"You minx," he said, holding her arms beside her head and grinding his manhood against her. "And in front of all my ancestors too," she gave him a hearty laugh, twining his fingers tighter with hers, "I'm going to enjoy making you take that back."

She tapped her chin with a finger, "Mmm, probably not as much as I will."

Devyn's fingers found her entrance, one of his long digits slipped inside. Moria bit down on a groan. His lips caressed her neck, hers trailed patterns down his back. Another finger slipped inside her, Moria felt the circular seal of his signet ring against her. She felt her walls clench around his patient strokes.

"I was right," she ground out, grasping him as he worked her. "Having a title looks good on you."

He curled his ringed finger inside her again, again, taking her bottom lip between his teeth.

"Let go, my lady."

"I'll go anywhere you go," she breathlessly replied, arching her back as he made her see stars above their joined bodies on the painted ceiling. "*My lord.*"

"Together," he said, holding her against his chest and placing a kiss at her temple, "Countess."

Moria could barely hold her thoughts together as she panted out, "I have one more place in mind before we sail for Italy."

"I can't believe you wanted to come to one of my salons before setting off on your honeymoon," Noelle said, greeting Moria with a kiss on each cheek. Moria stood back and gave her sister's demurely tailored dark blue dress with gold detailing an appreciative nod.

"The only thing worse than coming back here, would be not coming back," Moria said with a tight smile. Her husband's warm, gentle, dwarfing hand was at her back. The contact of his signet ring brushing against her back, curving to rest at her hip, braced Moria with courage for what she was about to do. He released her as she walked on to the orchestra platform of Pomfrey House's ballroom she'd commandeered as a stage, leaning back on his gold tipped cane.

The literary salon Viscountess Ludlowe hosted usually took up the massive billiards room at Pomfrey House in London; they'd had to move this evening's event to the ballroom to accommodate the number of guests.

A couple hundred chairs took up the room, filling up with

bodies dressed in Bond Street's finery looking for their name on a chair, and some standing along the back wall.

An evening with London's former diamond, currently married to her besotted, newly minted and mysterious Earl, had drawn out a crowd ready to witness whatever new spectacle the former society favorite had in mind to entertain them with.

"Ladies and gentlemen, if you will please take your seats," Viscount Ludlowe announced. The audience followed, wordlessly. Turning to his sister-in-law and guest, he asked, "Lady Moria, would you like to tell us what your entertainment for tonight's salon entails?"

Moria stood from her chair on the little stage. "Many years ago, there were quite a lot of you who, collectively, made one young lady feel inferior. Like she had something to prove," she paced, her husband nodding to her to keep going, "I know what you're thinking, "just *one* young lady?" Turns out, she wasn't the only one. She made friends with two other young ladies, and together they saw a lot of things, heard a lot of things, said a lot of things, in order to feel superior."

The Countess of Clairville placed her hands behind the back of her mauve gown, walking along the stage. "One day they decided to write them down, as insurance. Any piece of information was like pawns in a chess game to these ladies. Rarely, if ever, did they use it, and only when out of options. Then someone they trusted used that book in an effort to bring one particular lady down, to take from her what wasn't meant for either of them in the first place. What was in the book was never meant for anyone to see, and so, I've called you all here, to say that I have never been sorrier, and so that you can have it back."

There were a lot of questions and general comments from the gallery. Lady Moria cleared her voice, and the general melee came to a halt.

"You see, I'm trying this new thing where I don't talk about people behind their backs. I'm giving you your entry, you can do with it what you will. There were over 127 entries in total in that book, and so, if you sat at a chair with a card for your name, I'd like you to look beneath your seat."

Devyn's heart was in his eyes when she looked to stage left. She didn't know if she'd ever get used to seeing him look at her like that, if she ever wanted to get used to it. Her friends, a couple of her siblings flanked him, giving her smiles too; but her eyes focused on him. He'd found her a scarred girl. He'd never given up on her through it all, even when she'd almost resigned herself to a role she wasn't suited to play.

A storm of hands opened gold envelopes they'd found beneath their seat, some laughing, some ripping the contents to shreds, some raising their voices.

One lady jumped from her seat, marched up to a gentleman, and slapped him.

Another lady knocked another lady's hat clean off her head and onto the floor. When she shoved her, a third lady joined in; on whose side she was fighting, was unclear.

More than one gentleman got up wordlessly and stormed out, leaving the lady at his side behind.

More than one lady shoved a man somewhere in her general vicinity and hurled accusations.

At least several ladies, young and old were in heated arguments or an all-out brawl.

"Quick question," Noelle said, leaning down to her older sister's height. "Is this the scene you were picturing tonight?"

Moria grimaced and shook her head. "The ladies have gone... wild."

Noelle sighed, then nodded to her husband.

Fitzwilliam Pomfrey put two fingers in his mouth and let out a loud whistle.

Nothing.

He repeated the motion again, this time louder and shriller. The movement in the ballroom stopped. Moria had to stifle a laugh at the sight of Lady Althea, her sister's grandmother in law, holding a small potted fern over her head as if about to hurl it at another lady.

"As I shall remind you, you are all in fact, ladies, and gentlemen. I have never witnessed such behavior," Fitz said with a disapproving grimace.

Many of the occupants of the room took stock of their state of agitation, the dishabille of their wardrobe, or the toppled chairs or ferns around them.

The Countess of Clairville motioned with a hand to a large table on the other side of the ballroom.

"In an effort to try and fix the way all of us young ladies specifically relate to one another, lady to lady, I have erected a table, laden with cards and quills and pots of ink. I'd like you to write an apology to whomever you may have wronged, to set it right, as I'm trying to do with all of you."

When no one moved to follow her directive she kept going, suddenly the bravest that she'd been, no longer held back by her need to overcome, by the need to prove herself. She was fully loved, for who she was, all parts of her.

She began speaking, finding Kate Herring looking back at her as she swallowed a lump in her throat, and the words flowed out of Moria. "Everyone deserves the chance to be unencumbered by the weight of a secret, to move out of its shadow," Moria said, holding her friend Tristan's eyes from the second row. "Everyone deserves the chance to put things right, while you still can," she said to Lawrence, her eyes following the empty seat beside him that would have been Sarah's. "Everyone deserves the chance to say what they've been carrying in their heart and be heard," she said, looking to Bridget Kelley.

And the amends that were made, with some reluctance and not

without effort, became more of what the Countess of Clairville was known for, as well as the besotment in her eyes when her husband peppered her with kisses as she exited her little stage, rather than all of the scandals of her past.

Acknowledgments

To start, the first person I would like to thank is you, the reader for taking a chance on an indie author and a debut. There are so many books out there, and I'm glad you picked up this one. I hope that something in this story resonated with some part of you. If you find that your story or your traits mirror any of Moria's, then I hope she makes you brave like she did for me.

I began this story as the second in a series following six orphaned and very chaotic siblings, but Moria's story captivated early beta readers of that first book. That book died in the query trenches, but I learned a lot. Her voice, her character, her journey, and *by god-* her soldier!, is what captivated readers, and I knew I would need a strong hook to reel in hesitant readers to a historical. It was a fun game with readers to drop references and plot points from one of my favorite movies in my formative years into a Victorian Era backdrop, and adding my own flair to make it something unique. A lot of the historical detail for the time period is from my own addiction to period dramas, my English degree, and the historical romance books I love so much. I hope that you will stay tuned for more books from the other characters, as well as Devyn and Moria cameos, or even in a bigger picture sense, that you will pick up more historical romance.

I want to thank my parents, who were my first readers and who never stopped encouraging me to pursue the thing that gives me so much clarity and purpose: writing. I'd never have found the courage to pursue sharing this on my own without the industrial spirit you instilled in me, and demonstrated in your own professional and personal lives.

A huge thank you to my grandparents, who instilled in me a love for storytelling and books and took me on endless trips to the library, always taking an interest in what I was reading or writing in a way that made me feel like my creativity was valued. It was also my grandma, Bobbie, and her historical romance books that first brought these books to me. It feels like coming full circle now to share one of my own with the world. (If my grandma asks, yes, this is a sweet, clean romance!)

I'd like to thank my brother, for always leading by example and integrity, for being my biggest supporter (and sometimes, devil's advocate!) for all thirty-five years of my life. I wish the world could all have big brothers like Jasper, Lawrence, and Jake.

Next, I have to pay homage to my critique partner, Rebekkah Knight, for listening to me rant about my characters and reading drafts and critique paragraphs with honest and careful intention. A contemporary romance writer and a historical romance writer came together to make this the best it could be.

Megan, where would I be without you? We may be separated by miles but so much of you is a part of all of the female friendships in the books I write.

To some of my first readers and friends who helped this book to reach its full potential: Jessica S., Natalie, Lili, Rachael R, Ashlie, Leslie, Lindsey R., Lauren T., Autumn, Emily M, Savannah, Charlotte, Kristen, Chloe, Jordan, Kelsey K., Celine, Chelsey.- thank you! And a huge thank you to all who applied to ARC read or who ARC read my book or signed up to shout-out my book on their podcast with the help of Once Upon a Book Tour.

Dana, my editor, you are the real MVP for all of your developmental edits that helped really fine-tune the character arcs.

Rachel, my PR goddess, I have truly just enjoyed working alongside you to bring this book to readers. I am grateful for all of the joy and support you've brought to this journey.

Props to Melissa Smith editing for the incredibly insightful beta read feedback, Chapter by Chapter editing for the copy edits, Giovanna Capel for an outstanding cover, Kathryn Sheridan for formatting this manuscript into something pretty and professional, Emma Mitch! For signing on to bring this book to life in audio.

Lastly, this last shout-out is for my two little marvels, Blair and Owen. I wanted to lead by example so that one day, you boldly chase down every dream you have. And I will be cheering you on every step of the way.

<h1 style="text-align:center;font-style:italic;">About the Author</h1>

Carly Kaye is a Tennessee-based single mom and former English teacher. When not playing with her kids, Carly also works as a freelance copy-editor and spends her free time either volunteering in her community, hanging out with friends and family, or in other worlds (aka, reading). She was inspired to write a balance of humor, angst, spice, the different faces love wears, and yearning- a redemption arc for a beloved character, but of all women who've experienced being given a label. You can look her up on socials: @carlywritesandreads.